Y0-ABJ-271

A BURNING DESIRE

Gray's tenderness was agonizing. To be completely consumed by him was her one desire. Only he could quiet the tempest raging within her.

Then, granting her silent pleas, Gray attacked her lips with the fiery passion she longed for. His kiss was hard and demanding.

"So much time has been lost, so much time wasted, and all because of my foolishness," Gray whispered.

Ameran caressed his face. "There won't be any more wasted hours, Gray." She took his hand and led him to the cot. Her boldness surprised her, yet the longing inside her couldn't be denied any longer. She wanted him! Every part of her desired him with a yearning that could only be satisfied in one way.

JOLENE PREWIT-PARKER

SWEET STOLEN PASSION

ZEBRA BOOKS
KENSINGTON PUBLISHING CORP.

ZEBRA BOOKS are published by

Kensington Publishing Corp.
475 Park Avenue South
New York, NY 10016

First Printing: July, 1993

Printed in the United States of America

To Jake:
In Whose Hand a Stick Becomes a Sword

Chapter One

"Burn the house!"

"Burn the witch!"

"My brother would be alive today if it were not for her!"

"And my uncle!"

"And my sister's betrothed. They would all be alive!"

"Too late for her to escape!"

"Do not get too close lest she cast an evil eye on you!"

"Send her to hell where she belongs!"

Death to the witch . . . Send her to hell . . . Kill her . . . kill her . . . kill her . . .

Crazed, drunken laughter sounded over the roar of the channel's waves as the foaming whitecaps crashed into the rock cliffs and ledges behind.

Ameran Michol hid on bended knees among the tall willows in the tiny cove between the rocks and her house. She held her pose, motionless, hardly daring to breathe a sigh for fear the wind would carry the sound to her enemies.

There was no mistaking the angry voices of her neighbors whose wrath and suspicions she knew only too well: Raoul . . . Gaston . . . Louis Phillip . . . de Maurier . . . boys whose advances she had shunned, and men whose lusts had turned to hate when she denied their demands. One of those who clamored to burn the witch alive had apparently forgotten that it had been she who had saved his little daughter from a life of misery by blowing out the fire when the *petite jeune fille* had fallen face-first into a fire. How quickly Monsieur Leger's gratitude had turned to hatred. And the pious man who had demanded she be sent to hell—did he not realize she had been condemned there already by the circumstances of her birth, and that hell was the tiny fishing village where she lived with neighbors who were eager to shed her blood?

The loudest of the voices, the cruelest of the laughs could belong only to the evil Duke of Caron. The moon did not have to be full for her to see the twisted smile on his ugly, prickly red face. She had known she would live to regret not having plunged her dagger into his groin when he had tried to lay claim to her. And now he had come back to incite her neighbors to destroy her.

Ameran felt herself tremble, but it was not from the water chilling her bones. Only a little while earlier she had been lying upon her bed of straw, not daring to close her eyes, staring instead out into the darkness, when all of a sudden a feeling of doom and dread had overcome her. Even before the angry voices had been heard or she had seen the flaming torches coming across the drawbridge of the chalet perched atop the hill overlooking the sea, she had fled from her home.

The particular night they had selected for her execution by fire came as no surprise. The night before she had lain awake anticipating it. They held her responsible for the six of their own whose lives had been lost night before last when winds and waves and unending rains had sent the fishermen to their watery graves.

"A bag full of gold to anyone who will go into the shack and drag out the witch!" yelled the Duke.

The shouting ceased, and there was a long silence.

Ameran's heart ceased in midpulse. If they discovered she had already escaped, they would come after her, and her fate would be sealed. They would all have their turns with her before tying her up to the stake and turning their torches on her.

"There is not one brave man among you peasant fools? Cowards!" roared the drunken leader. "Cowards all of you!"

Ameran dared to breathe a little easier. For the moment she was safe, for not one of the men, fools they may be, would dare be so bold as to do the task the Duke would reward well.

"I shall give you a chance to save yourself, Ameran Michol!" called out the Duke from atop his white mount. "Come out of the house! Repent! Beg for salvation and forgiveness, and you shall live."

"Never!" she whispered to herself. "Never!"

She would rather take her chances with the channel's fury.

"Then burn in hell, witch!"

A lone torch was tossed onto the roof. Another

9

followed, then another until the thatch had erupted into a blaze of orange and gold.

The villagers' horrible laughter and curses, condemning her to hell everlasting, roared over the thunder of the waves and winds once again.

Ameran's coal black eyes gleamed with hatred. If only she were the witch of their accusations! What a pity she did not possess her mama's power to condemn them all to misery! Like her mother and grandmother she had been born with a caul covering her head, but she alone had made the choice not to follow the strange practices of her mother's family, and to let such dark and evil mysteries lie sleeping inside her.

Wading through waist-deep water, Ameran struggled to make her way across the cove as quickly as her legs would permit. She found great solace in the angry shouts behind her; as long as her tormentors thought she was being roasted alive, they would not be searching for her.

Her old tattered cloak gave little relief from the wind whipping her body, and the sharp, pointed rocks along the coast impaled the tender soles of her feet. Yet the blood oozing between her toes did not impede her progress. Though it was dark, she had traveled that path many times before. But while feeling her way through the blackness, her feet betrayed her, causing her to trip and fall every few steps. By this point her legs were bruised, her flesh torn, but still she kept battling the forces against her. There was not one place on her body that did not ache, but in that pain she found the strength she needed to continue on.

The cliffs she had played on as a child loomed ahead of her. If only she could make it to the ledges overlooking the sea, she would be safe. Sanctuary could be found there inside the caves, where no one would dare venture and disturb the restless souls of sailors lost at sea. The eerie darkness inside would be like an old friend, protecting her.

Ameran looked back only once, just as she was about to begin her climb up the treacherous summit. A ball of fire was all that was left of her home. The drunken laughter of her would-be murderers had been carried by the wind out to sea. They thought the witch was dead.

Warily, she made her way up the ledges and over-hangs. One false step would send her plummeting into the angry swirling abyss below.

She would live! She would spite them all! And she would make it to the safety of England's shores in the tiny fishing boat Papa had kept hidden in anticipation of this day.

Her limbs felt little pain, nor did they feel the sharp chill of the night wind as she felt her way along the precipices. There were many times she had proceeded along that same treacherous path to the tiny opening in the rocks that would lead her through dark crevices and craggy corridors barely wide enough to permit her passage.

Ameran felt her way to the chamber where she had played as a child, a place of refuge from her mama's rantings and neighbors' taunts.

The damp, musky air filled her with renewed courage. Let them come after her now! They would not dare; as much as they loathed witches, they feared

11

the spirit of the dead even more! And there she waited, huddled close to the cave's walls, waiting for the first light of day that would direct her to England . . . the haven of her dreams.

A little while later, wet and cold and weary of listening and waiting, Ameran let her mind drift back to the day two years ago when she had first set eyes on the man who she had thought would deliver her from her tormentors. It seemed a lifetime since she had reveled in the protective strength of his embrace.

Lord Grayson Carlisle was a man like none other. She would remember his every feature until the day she drew her last breath. And when her heart longed so desperately for him, she could conjure up that magnificent visage and fall asleep dreaming of the joys they had found in each other's arms.

As stern as his face was, with big, blond, eagle brows, it could also speak of a tenderness few men would dare show. A narrow scar received in a duel with a Dutch officer ran from the rise of his cheek to the corner of his mouth, but when he smiled, and he so often did, the severity of his countenance softened. *Mon Dieu,* but he was handsome! Those big, blue eyes the color of the channel's angriest waves would thaw even the most frigid of hearts.

Damn him! Why had he betrayed her? Why had he done what she had been so certain he would never do, and abandon her just as her mother said he would? And why did the memory of his face still linger in her mind even now — now when her very existence was in jeopardy? If only he had not forsaken his vow to take her and her mother to England! Why did she love him then — and still, always, forever? Her

12

last breath would be drawn with thoughts of him on her mind!

Her recollections made her smile in spite of the misery he had caused by his deceit, and Ameran remembered the very hour she had first encountered him. She had been sitting on a rock ledge that jutted far out into the channel. Her dress had been pulled up around her knees, and her bare legs were dangling into the cool water. Sea gulls had been swooping down all around her and plucking morsels of bread from her fingers. The birds' antics had so delighted her, and at first she gave little notice to the Sun King's pleasure palace when it floated by, for its appearance was not an uncommon one. Exquisitely gowned ladies and Versailles noblemen were always on board laughing and dancing and singing. Louis Quatorze himself was more often than not in their company. But something about that floating pleasure palace had caught her attention on that particular day, and once she set her gaze on it, she could not pull it away.

Standing on the bow was a solitary man who seemed lost in a reverie. He paid little heed to the merriment around him. His hands were locked behind his back, and his form stood tall and erect. He looked as royal as the King, as, lost in his reverie, he directed his gaze to the depths of the water. Big and blond, and with a powerful visage that demanded respect, he held the pose of a warring commander off to do battle. What made him suddenly look up to where she was sitting, she did not know, but when he did, his stare locked with hers and held it tight until the barge had disappeared around the next cliff. She could not have broken the spell had she tried. She no longer belonged only to herself. The strange force that had drawn her to him had taken charge of her every thought from that day forward. Every waking moment of the next seven days that followed were spent on her cliffside perch waiting and praying for just one more glimpse of him, but the purple, red, and gold satin sails of the Sun King did not billow past again. Then, just when she had given up all hope of ever seeing him, a ship had moored in the safe waters off the coast. This ship had flown the banners of their neighbors across the channel, and even as she had scrambled down the rocks to investigate, she had known in her heart who she would find waiting on the shores. And she had known intuitively of whom that valiant English commander had come in search.

Ameran rested her chin against the great, stone monolith. She remembered every word spoken, every glance exchanged, every touch that passed between them as though their meeting had occurred only yesterday. A hundred times a day and twice that many more at night she would relive in her memories those five magical days.

"I am Grayson Carlisle, commander of King Charles' royal Navy," he announced with quiet dignity. "I was sent on special assignment to the King of France."

Ameran curtsied and told him her name. She could not take her eyes from the imposing form only an arm's reach away. She did not fear him. She knew instantly he was not like other men she had encountered.

Those blond brows raised inquiringly. "That was you sitting on the cliffs feeding the gulls, was it not?"

Ameran noticed a subtle softening of his expression with the slightest of smiles. "And that was you on the King's floating palace, was it not?"

His eyes flickered. He seemed pleased by her recognition. "I had hoped to see you on the return voyage, but it was well after dark when next we sailed past, and I knew you would not be there." His arm raised, then returned to his side. "I was disappointed. I waited every day hoping for one more glimpse of you."

Ameran could feel herself being drawn closer and closer with each passing second. He was speaking the same exact words she, herself, longed to say.

He stared at her many long seconds before continuing. "I described you to everyone I met and asked if they knew you, but no one did. Up until this very moment, I feared you to have been a vision of loveliness conjured up by my imagination."

"I am here, monsieur. I am here." Coal dark lashes swept her cheeks. She wanted to tell him how long she had awaited his return and how in her heart she knew he would come, but she could not say the words she longed to say. It was difficult enough just steadying her legs under her.

Grayson's hand brushed her cheek. "You are even more beautiful in life than in my dreams."

Ameran met his eyes and smiled. So she had ventured into his dreams, just as he had hers.

"Your words are English, yet your accent is French. How is that so?" His eyes still caressed her face with a tenderness she longed to feel in his embrace.

"My mother was English. My father was French."

"I look forward to the opportunity to meet them."

"I am afraid that cannot be, monsieur."

His brows raised inquiringly once more.

"My father is dead," she explained. "My mother, she is not well."

The lines eased from his face. "I am sorry. Might I be of some help. I have a physician on board who . . ."

"No, no, no." Ameran tried to calm her words. How could she tell him that what her mother suffered from was not some sort of malady that could be treated by a physician? He could not possibly understand that Mama's troubles stemmed from an obsession in the black arts. "That is very kind of you to offer, monsieur, and I am most grateful, but it would do no good."

"I have made you sad. Forgive me."

The touch of his finger on her chin made her quiver. Nothing or no one had ever affected her so.

"There is nothing to forgive, monsieur. In truth I have never known such happiness." She wondered if such boldness would offend him. But when he smiled deep into her eyes she knew it had not.

"Please, call me Gray." His intense gaze took total possession of her soul once more. "Say my name. Let me hear my name from your lips."

"Gray . . . Gray," she said, her soft voice trembling.

His smile was one of satisfaction, hers of contentment.

It seemed only natural that they should stroll down

16

the pebbly beach, their arms touching, their hands brushing together. The day was the sabbath, and the beach was deserted. They were the only two beings who mattered in the whole world.

That evening, he did not want to take his leave from her, any more than she did from him. His good-byes were spoken with his fingertips upon her lips and the promise that they would come again at morning's first light.

She was waiting on the beach that next morning, and her heart soared as high as the gulls in flight when she caught that first glimpse of him rowing through the mist. Their reunion was one of old friends. He opened wide his arms, and she ran inside their embrace. They held tight to each other, his lips on her cheek, hers on his shoulder, neither one daring to speak or to move for fear of disturbing the paradise they had found.

Gray folded her into his arms and drew her still closer to his chest. "I could not sleep last night for thinking of you, and when my eyes grew so heavy they could not stay open, I dreamed of you. It seems I am completely under your spell."

His words were like thunderclaps to her ears, and she pulled back. There were those in the village who would warn him of falling victim to her evil ways. Would he still seek her companionship when he learned of her neighbors' accusations that she bewitched young sailors and lured them to their deaths, and that she cast horrible spells of death and destruction on all she encountered?

"What is wrong?" He lifted her chin so he could gaze deeper into her eyes. "You look so sad."

17

She shook her head. *"Au contraire.* I have never been happier."

Her smile was happy, yet her heart was sad. Too soon it would all be over, and they each would return to their own worlds.

In the middle distance, fishermen began pulling in their nets. Soon they would be venturing back to the village with their catch, and it would be better if she were not seen. If the catch was poor, she would certainly be found at fault. Yet she could not bear to make the necessary excuses and take her leave.

It was as though he could read her thoughts. "Return with me to my ship." His hand reached out for hers. "I want to show you the *Fair Winds,* and I want you to meet my good friend, Gideon Horne. I have told him about you, and he is eager to make your acquaintance."

Her refusal was immediate. "I cannot."

She could see the pain in his eyes. There was a slight blush to his cheeks. "No, of course not. How bold of me even to suggest it. I am sorry."

A few brief moments of bliss had ended in despair. She would have liked nothing better than to visit his ship, but she could not subject Gray to the consequences if her actions were observed. The fishermen might turn on him, and there would be appeasing her mother's wrath if *she* were to find out. At best, the *Fair Winds* would be subjected to a storm, and the worst . . . no she could not bear to think of the disasters which could befall the man who possessed her heart.

Her moment of grief ended quickly as she held out

18

her hand and beckoned to him. "Come with me. I know a place where we shall be safe from prying eyes."

Gray touched the sword at his side. "When you are with me, you will be safe."

She found great solace in his promise, and in the strong hand closing around her.

"I suppose there are those among your neighbors who do not like the English," he said as they began the walk which would take them to the caves. "I am not offended just as long as you do not share their contempt."

"I find the English most pleasant and charming." Her smile was shy. For the time being, she would let him think the possibility of offending her neighbors was the cause of her concern.

Her hand safe and secure in his, Ameran led him a short way down the beach to an opening in the rocks. "No one will follow us in here. These caves are said to be haunted with the ghosts of fishermen who perished at sea." She neglected to tell him of the rumors that she and her mother were rumored to dance naked here with the devil every full moon.

"You are not afraid of ghosts?" He held her arm protectively.

"Live men are far more dangerous than dead ones."

Gray stopped and turned her around to face him. He pushed back the dark curls from around her cheeks. "I hope you do not fear me."

"I could never fear you." She held her breath. "Never," she said, though her head was spinning and her legs felt as though they would give way beneath her.

Gray held tight to her shoulders. His eyes captured hers. "I cannot explain what I am feeling, Ameran, for I have never felt this way before."

"No, nor have I."

He lifted her hand to his lips and kissed it. "I had hoped as much." His sigh was relieved. "There is much I wish to tell you, much that I desire to learn about you."

Ameran felt certain she would burst from the happiness inside her.

Holding tight to his hand, she led him along the maze of dark passageways to a chamber deep within the caves. She had come upon the room as a little girl when she had gone exploring, and through the years it had become her secret refuge from Mama's tirades, as well as from taunts and jeers of the villagers. Papa had called it her treasure room, for there she had amassed a collection of maps, books, paintings of faraway places, rugs, ropes and nautical tools, pretty dishes and bits of pottery, anything that had been spit up from the channel.

Ameran placed a cushion onto the frayed rug atop the earthen floor and invited him to sit. Then she poured him a cool drink of water from a tall pitcher decorated with colorful bird and flower designs.

"If you are hungry, I have some bread," she told him when he had finished his drink. She was eager to please him.

His eyes did not stray from hers for one instant. "I lost the desire for food the moment my eyes beheld you."

Ameran sat down beside him. She knew that

feeling well. She hung on to his every word as he told her all there was to know about him.

"I wish this day would go on forever," he told her when it came time to leave.

She held his hand tight against her cheek. "I fear it has ended all too soon."

He had yet to kiss her. How she yearned for the feel of his lips pressing tight to hers. Mama had made her promise never to give herself to any man. Yet when she was with Gray she longed to do just that.

"It does not have to end," he said quietly.

She could not believe she had heard him speak those words, and when he said nothing further, she was certain the words had been spoken only in her imagination.

The next few days had been filled with more glory and splendor than most lifetimes possess. They were together from dawn until dusk. It did not matter where they were or what they were doing . . . rowing in and out of tiny coves in the skiff, talking in the caves, picnicking along the beach, swimming in secret inlets, feeding the gulls from high atop the rocks . . . it did not matter just as long as they were together.

On the fourth day, talk turned once more to his departure. Treaties had been signed and correspondence completed and delivered from King Louis to the commander of the *Fair Winds*. Soon, the *Fair Winds* would set a course for England. Soon he would be leaving her for good. And still his lips had not sought from hers the passion she longed to give. Still he had not asked for that which she would have been only too happy to give.

"Dare I hope that you feel for me the way I feel for you?" he asked her soon after they had retreated to the solace of the caves.

She was too thrilled to utter her reply.

"You do feel for me as I feel for you?" he asked hopefully.

"Oh, yes. Yes," she said over and over.

Gray held tight to her. "I love you, Ameran. I swear I do. Never have I before declared my love."

Tears of happiness streamed down her cheeks. "And I love you. I do. Oh, I do."

He stroked her cheek. "Our time together has been brief, and yet I feel as though I have known you all my life. And I want to spend the rest of my life loving you."

Never had she known such bliss. She had not dared expect such happiness.

"I intend to take you to England with me."

Her heart stopped. She would gladly follow him to the ends of the earth, but what about Mama? Poor Mama. She could not leave her.

It was as if he could read her thoughts. "We will take your mother with us, of course. There are physicians who can cure whatever ails her."

Ameran could not believe her ears. Mama would object, but she had no choice. She must consent to leaving France. Without Papa in Mer, there was no one to protect them from superstitious neighbors who held them accountable for every storm, every bad catch and every death or injury at sea.

"You would do all that for me?" she asked him.

"Aye, that and more, too." Gray's hold around her

tightened. "I want to make you my wife. I would be a good husband. I am a wealthy man. You would not want for anything." His smile melted her. "And I would love you more and more with each passing day, though I do not know how I could possibly love you any more than I do at this very moment."

Ameran lost herself in his eyes. Their blue calmed her apprehensions. "I am yours, my lord, to do with whatever you wish."

"Then you will return to England with me?" he asked excitedly.

"I would go wherever you commanded," she replied softly.

Gray pulled her still closer. "Such good fortune is more than I could ever hope for and far more than I deserve. I promise you will never regret your decision."

At last, his lips pressed hers. His kiss was tender, yet possessive. Its ardor hinted of a passion still to come.

More kisses followed, and still more, and she felt herself being consumed by him. She knew that she had been intended for no man save her English sea captain. A burning desire, an aching need for still another kiss and yet another claimed her senses.

Another kiss traced the soft fullness of her mouth.

"My dearest darling, I have yearned for this moment from the very first time I set eyes on you," Gray told her, his voice breathless.

Ameran felt herself sinking deeper and deeper into his possession. *"Moi, aussi, mon cher.* I, too, my dearest." She buried her face into his rugged chest. What she was feeling deep within dismayed her. Was this not the dreaded sin that her mother had warned her of time and again? Desperately she wanted to yield to the burning sweetness inside her. Gray was not like the men of her mother's cautionings. His promise of marriage was sincere, not just a cheap ploy to get her into his bed.

Without warning, Gray let her go.

Ameran reached for the wet stone overhang to steady her quaking body. What was the matter? What had she done?

The distress Gray was feeling covered his face. "I am sorry, my love. Can you ever forgive such deplorable behavior?"

"Forgive you?" Ameran knew at once the source of Gray's worry. She smiled and held open her arms and beckoned him inside. "There is no reason for apologies. You have done nothing wrong."

He smoothed her hair with his cheek. "You are certain?"

"I have never been more certain of anything in my life. I love you, and I want you just as much as you do me." Without any shame, she drew his head to hers and kissed his lips with a hunger that surprised her. She could feel his surrender to the urgency of her lips.

"Oh, my darling, my darling Ameran," he moaned over and over. "You are certain of how you feel?"

"Yes, yes, a thousand times yes," she assured him.

Gray quickly ripped off his shirt and laid it across the torn carpet.

Ameran gasped with awe. His shoulders were just as broad and as strong as she had imagined. His chest was finely chiseled. She exalted in his manly scent. How she longed to reach out and touch him, but she was afraid. How was she supposed to behave? How would she know what to do?

Timidly, she reached up and touched the gold cross around his neck. Diamonds, rubies, and emeralds were encrusted in it. "I found that many years ago when I was a wee lad," he explained. "I was diving in a lake and found it wedged under a stone." He kissed each of her fingers with great tenderness.

Her hand wandered across the shadow of the cross imprinted by the sun onto his bare flesh. "It's beautiful."

"Time was when I thought it the most beautiful piece of workmanship in the world." Ever so gently, he eased her back onto his shirt. "Then my eyes beheld you."

Her heart beat faster and faster.

"For years, this cross has brought me good luck. Yet my good fortune has never been greater than it is right now."

Tiny tremors shuddered over her as he slid the tattered crimson material down her shoulders. Soft, fleshy mounds sprang up to greet him.

Gray outlined the lightning-bolt birthmark with the tip of his finger. He smiled. "How unusual. My King possesses the same mark on his shoulder."

Ameran caressed his arm. "Mama used to tell me I was born with that mark because she had been frightened during a thunderstorm."

Gray kissed her mouth long and hard. His groan was tormented. "You are even more beautiful than I had imagined. If you do not desire me as much as I desire you, then please, you must let it be known now. One more moment and I might not be able to control my longings."

Ameran wove her arms around his neck and invited him still closer. His kisses roused the rosy tips of her breasts to crested peaks. Ameran cried out in joy.

The cave spun round and round. Her hands began an exploration all their own across his strong shoulders, over his massive chest, and down his back to the tautness within his trousers. She wanted desperately to feel his flesh on hers.

Gray slid her dress over her hips and down her legs. His eyes stopped on the black leather sheath fastened around her lower right leg. Gently, he unfastened the belt, took out the dagger inside the sheath, and placed it within her reach. "If you change your mind, and I do not honor your wishes, I beg you plunge this dagger into my back."

Ameran tossed the dagger away. "Your wishes are as mine."

Gray tugged his trousers down his legs.

Ameran tried to look away. She knew she must, but she could not. Her eyes feasted on his manliness. She knew instinctively that it would be the source of great pleasure.

Gray drank thirstily from her mouth while his hands roamed over her, fondling, caressing.

Strange, wonderful sensations fluttered inside her. She was certain that at any moment she would faint. Her arms tightened around him, her fingers digging into his flesh.

Gray lowered himself onto her at last. The agony

was sweetly excruciating, the pain sharp but brief. Ameran gasped, not from the pain but from the tremendous joy that filled her moments later.

Gray kissed her tenderly. "There will be no more hurt, my darling, only joy."

She sighed with exhilarated exhaustion. "It did not hurt much. *Vraiment*. Truly, it did not."

"I could never hurt you." His words whispered through her hair. "I could never hurt you. I want only to love you, my darling."

Ameran held on tight. "And I want only to love you. Please, you must teach me."

Gray gently pushed himself farther inside her.

Ameran kissed away the concern written across his brows. "Do not worry, my brave sea warrior. What I am feeling is not pain." She moved her hips to meet his in hopes of convincing him.

The long scar down his cheek relaxed. Gray pushed harder still.

Arms and legs entwined around him, Ameran held on with all her might. Her soft curves tucked themselves against his manly contours. His blood coursed within her. Her flesh melted into his. Strange gusts shook her. The heavens reached out for her. She soared to great heights, then gently floated back to earth atop billowy clouds.

Their moans of delight reverberated from off the cave walls. The girl inside had surrendered to the woman Gray had created. Never more content, Ameran lay in the haven of his love.

A little while later, Gray lifted his head from her shoulder and smiled. He brushed her lips with whispered words of love.

She felt as though her heart would burst with joy. "I love you. I love you," she told him over and over.

"Forever? From this day forward?"

Ameran left a trail of kisses across his chest. "Forever. From this day forward. I promise."

Ameran had tried desperately to will away the images of that their first encounter, but the memories stubbornly refused to be cast out. All that day had been spent discovering the glories of their newfound love. Then, all too soon, it was time for Gray to return to the command of his ship.

"I will be back as soon as the day breaks," he promised.

"I will be waiting."

Gray sealed his promise with still another kiss.

She knew he did not want to go any more than she wanted him to.

He started to leave, then turned back. "I want you to wear this." He took the cross and chain from around his neck and fastened it around hers. "A part of me will always be with you." With one more quick kiss, he headed back to the skiff and began rowing back out to his ship.

Ameran watched until he had disappeared into the fog. For a moment, she wondered if the day she had just spent had been a dream. If it had been, she prayed she would never awake.

"WHORE! HARLOT! HARLOT! WHORE!"

How Mama had ranted and raved upon her return to their humble cottage that evening!

Ameran's hand had gone immediately to her heart.

28

The gold cross tucked inside her dress and out of view of her mother's accusing eyes gave her the courage she needed.

"I know where you have been, and I know what you have been doing!" Her mother's blood-streaked eyes would not let her escape. "What a stupid girl you are! Have you not the good sense to realize he will use you and cast you off like some wharf whore?"

Ameran tried in vain to calm her mother. She knew Mama did not mean to inflict pain. She said horrible things when she was angered, but she was always quick to beg for forgiveness as soon as the fits ended.

"Shhhh, Mama, do not upset yourself."

Her mother grunted and moaned and gnashed her teeth.

Ameran began to cry, not for herself but for her mother. There was a time when her mother had been a beautiful woman. So beautiful she had bewitched a King, Papa had confided in her. Little by little, her mother had changed right before her eyes. Beautiful hair the same raven blue-black as her own had grayed and become coarse and brittle and knotted from neglect. Her once smooth, soft face had wrinkled, and big circles darker than soot masked her eyes. Her nights were not spent sleeping but in stomping the floors and damning anyone who had crossed her that day.

"You have become the whore of an Englishman!" she wailed over and over.

Ameran did not know how her mother knew, but she always knew. Her powers gave her the insight to see that which her eyes could not. "Please, Mama, shhh. Do not say things you will regret." She tried desperately to console her mother. "It is not wicked and shameful as you think. He is wonderful. He loves me. I love him. He is going to take us back to England. No one will harm us there. He will protect us."

Her mother fought her way out of Ameran's arms. "Curse England! Curse its wretched king! Damn them all to hell!" Her mother spat at the ground. "And damn your sea captain. He will die! Die! Do you hear me? Die!" She began to laugh. "Perhaps I will create a storm with high waves and ferocious winds that will capsize his ship, and he will drown at sea." Her laugh was crazed. "Or perhaps I will command sharks to eat away his skin bit by bit."

Ameran shivered. She knew her mother's power all too well. Many were the times her mother had wished some misfortune to befall someone, and a horrible tragedy had indeed occurred.

"You are not going to leave me, are you, *ma cherie?*" Her mother's voice became as pitiful as a child's. "I can see in your eyes you are going to go and leave me here to die. I will never see you again."

Ameran held her mother close. "I will never leave you, Mama. I will always be here for you."

Her mother began to sob like a babe.

"Shhhhh, everything is fine. I am here." Ameran smoothed the tangles from the knotted strands and kissed her forehead. Ever since she was a child, she had to comfort her mother when she had one of her uncontrollable spells. Not even Papa with all his love and kindness had been able to calm her.

30

"This captain, he will take us both back to England with him?" her mother asked calmly some time later.

"Yes, Mama, and he will look after us and protect us. He wants to make me his wife." Just the thought of marrying the love of her life brought tears to her eyes.

Her mother's face became twisted and contorted with anger and hate. "To England, to England, to England we shall go." She let out another nightmarish laugh. "More plagues, more fires, more assassins stalking. He does not yet know the meaning of the word *suffer*. But I shall show him. Revenge will at last be mine!"

Ameran held tight to her mother, praying that the fit would soon pass. How it frightened her when her mama went on like that! It chilled her down to her bones to think of what her mother could do.

Her mother's laughter turned to sobs and whispers. "I shall never see you again. I shall never see *ma belle bebe* again. Once he has taken you from me, you will be lost forever," she moaned over and over.

Tenderly, Ameran cradled her mama in her arms and kissed the tear streaked cheeks. "I will never leave you, Mama. I will take care of you. *Toujours*. Always. I swear."

Sybil Chandler held onto her daughter for dear life. *"Ma belle fille.* I do not deserve a child so wonderful as you. All will be fine. I shall make certain of it."

Affixed to her lips was a strange smile that would have inspired great fear and dread had Ameran seen it.

* * *

The next three days were as beautiful as those that had preceded them. Looking back, Ameran supposed that had she died then, her life could have been no more fulfilled than if she had lived to be a hundred. Each daybreak she would anxiously wait on the shore for the first glimpse of Gray rowing out of the mist. He would belong to her until night fell, then his ship laid claim to her commander once more. Each morning, Ameran would take him to her caves, for only there could they be safe from prying eyes. Locked in his embrace hour after hour, she came to know the joys of being a woman completely sated by the man she loves. Mama had made no more mention of the Englishman who was going to take them back to the land of her birth. If Mama suspected she was still going to him each morning, she said nothing. She had come to accept her daughter's solitary sojourns and did not interfere.

Ameran drew her cape tighter around her and huddled closer into the stone mass. How was she to have known such happiness would turn to grief and shame? How was she to have known the glorious joy she felt would soon be replaced with unending agony? She had been waiting on the beach at daybreak on the appointed morning, but it had not been Gray who had rowed out of the fog. From Gray's description of his oldest and dearest friend, she had recognized the stranger immediately as Gideon Horne. At a distance, the two men looked remarkably alike.

32

They could have been brothers, for both men had hair the color of sea oats, and each had the massive chest and shoulders of a warring seafarer. Like Gray, Gideon's commanding features were bronzed by wind and sun, but any trace of compassion or contentment was absent from his visage. The lines of Gideon's mouth were cruel and became crueler still when he smiled.

Ameran had known at once that something was very wrong. She ran out into the surf.

"Where is Gray? What has happened? Is he ill?" Thoughts of her mother's curses ran rampant inside her head. "Where is he?" she begged over and over.

Gideon's eyes stripped her. She disliked him instantly, even before he opened his mouth to speak, but because he was Gray's oldest and dearest friend, she held back her feelings.

"Where is Gray? Why did he not come? I beg you, tell me now, please."

There was no kindness in Gideon's chilling blue stare. "He is on board his ship where he belongs. He has sent me to attend to his business."

"You have been sent to escort my mama and me back to the *Fair Winds?*" she asked after considering the possibility that today was the sailing day and Gray was on board making ready for the departure.

Gideon chuckled without breaking a smile. "Is that what he told you? The sly devil! Just like him to send me out to mop up his mess."

Ameran could not move. Mop up his mess? That could not be.

"I am sorry to be the bearer of such bad tidings, *mademoiselle,* but my dear Lord and Commander

33

Grayson Carlisle has no intention of taking you back to England." Bold eyes traveled over her, omitting from scrutiny no part of her rounded body. "Oh, he may well have considered taking you home with him during one of the many pleasurable hours you gave him, and I certainly cannot fault him for it. Even a gentleman such as I may have been tempted to make promises which I have no intention of keeping if it meant winning your luscious favors, *mademoiselle*."

Ameran could not believe what she was hearing. It simply could not be true. Gray loved her. He had sworn love eternal over and over as she lay in his arms. Surely those declarations and promises had not merely been clever devices to bed her. Yet, where was he now? Why had he not come on his own? Why had he sent his second in command to deliver the shocking news? Was he too much of a coward to face her himself?

A multitude of thoughts scrambled inside her head. No, this man named Gideon was playing a cruel trick on her. If Gray were going to leave without her he would have come to tell her himself or else just weighed anchor and sailed away.

She reached for the cross around her neck in hope of finding the strength she needed.

Then she knew the answer to the dreaded question.

Gideon followed the path of her hand. "I have been instructed not to return to the ship without Gray's cross. I am sorry."

Ameran bit her lip and held back the tears. She refused to let Gideon Horne see her cry. He did not sound the least bit sorry. She had a strange feeling he actually enjoyed being the bearer of heartbreaking news. Head held high, she unfastened the clasp.

Gideon reached out for her. "Allow me, *mademoiselle*."

Ameran quickly stepped out of his reach. She did not want his hands to soil her flesh, even in a gesture of aid. When she lifted the cross from between her breasts, she felt as though she were ripping out her heart.

Gideon held out his hand and she dropped the cross onto his palm.

Gideon closed his fingers tight around the cross and chain. "It would not be wise for Lord Carlisle to return to Whitehall without this." He laughed. "The Duchess of Morrow would make his life a living hell."

The Duchess of Morrow? Ameran asked herself. Gray had made no mention of such a person. He had sworn that he had told her all about himself there was to know.

Gideon eyed her closely. "I assume Gray made no mention of Constance. Considering the circumstances, he would have been a fool to speak of his betrothed."

"His betrothed?"

"Constance and Gray are to be married as soon as we arrive home."

Ameran gave a resigned nod. So she had been nothing more to Gray than a passing fancy, a diversion to occupy his hours away from his true love. How could she have been such a fool? If only Gideon would leave so she could fling herself down onto the shore and cry until there were no more tears left inside her.

Gideon held up the cross and admired it.

"Constance gave this to Gray so that he would always have in his possession a reminder of their love no matter where he was," remarked Gideon.

Ameran could not wait to get home and scrub the spot between her breasts where that cursed cross had hung. It must be true. Gray had lied to her. He had felt no love for her, only lust, and she had been so willing to satisfy his needs! She wondered if he were laughing to himself the entire time he was making love to her. How convincing he had been! She had believed every word he uttered. Mama had been right all along. She really was no better than a wharf whore. As far as Gray was concerned, she was only one among many.

Gideon dangled the cross in front of her. "It is worth a great amount of money, as I am sure you have discovered." His eyes were cold and accusing.

Ameran's black eyes glared hate. "I did not steal that medallion, *Monsieur* Horne, if that is what you are suggesting. Gray gave it to me."

Gideon smiled and dropped the cross and chain into his pocket. "Perhaps he did. He has been known to do some very foolish things when he allows his heart to rule his good sense."

Ameran sighed. So she had not been the first taken in by his false promises and declarations. There was no satisfaction in that discovery.

"I apologize if I offended you, *mademoiselle*. I only know what I was told."

"Gray told you that I stole it from him?" she asked in angered disbelief.

Ameran felt naked underneath Gideon's thorough

36

scrutiny.

"It is not difficult to understand how a man could be led astray by a woman with your beauty. I, myself, might even be persuaded to venture inside those caves with you, given the opportunity and the invitation."

Her heart sank to her stomach. Gray had revealed the most intimate detail of their lovemaking.

Gideon's hand slid down her shoulder and over her breast.

Ameran slapped him away. "If you cherish that hand I would advise you to keep it to yourself."

Gideon's laugh was cold. "You are every bit as fiery as Gray said. He did indeed have his hands full with you." His voice softened, but it was no kinder. "I understand the grief you are experiencing. I have ways of soothing your agony." He grabbed hold of her and thrust her into his chest. His tongue jabbed kisses into her neck. "One hour with me, and I swear you will forget the name of the *Fair Winds'* commander. Perhaps you will even be able to convince me that a woman of your remarkable talents should accompany me back to Court."

In one swift sweep, Ameran lifted her skirt and jerked her dagger from its sheath. She held it up high, ready to plunge it into Gideon's heart if he did not let go.

The blade caught the early morning light; its sharp tip glistened.

"Step back, *Monsieur* Horne," she warned him. "I have used this before, and I will not hesitate using it again." Her fingers were tight around the ivory handle.

Gideon laughed, but he did as she commanded.

37

"Oh, *mademoiselle*, I wish I did have one hour to waste with you. I would enjoy bringing you to your knees. You would not be the first wildcat I had to tame, but I daresay you would be the most challenging. I would—"

Ameran brandished her knife in front of his face. "No man has ever made that boast without living to regret it."

Gideon looked at the knife, then at Ameran, then back at the knife again. "You stinking, filthy French. Whores, all of you. Even that pompous fop you have on the throne."

"If you find us French so distasteful, then why do you not leave?"

"With pleasure, *mademoiselle*. With pleasure." Gideon gave a mock salute and a mocking laugh. "I will give Lord Carlisle your love."

Ameran waited until Gideon was back in the skiff and rowing back toward the command ship before lowering her dagger. One would be a fool to turn one's back on Gideon Horne even for an instant.

Then the tears she had tried so hard to hold back flooded her eyes. Her heart could not hurt any more had it been carved from her breast.

Slowly, she put the dagger back into the sheath around her leg, but not without first giving it a long, hard look. How easy it would be to plunge it through her heart and end her misery on the very spot where her happiness had begun. Then she would not have to remember for the rest of her life how she had loved, only to be betrayed.

"No, you must not even think such thoughts," she told herself. With Ameran gone, who would look after Mama and protect her from herself? Life would go on. The days would end and begin all over again, and every waking moment would be filled with memories of the man she had loved. That would be her punishment. That would be her hell.

How well Ameran remembered that day. When she returned home, Mama had made no mention of Gray or of England. Nor had she mentioned it once during the long, agonizing days which followed. After all, she had known all along. It had been just as she had predicted.

Not one hour passed when she did not try to make herself hate Gray, to damn him to a horrible death. After all, she was the daughter of Sybil Chandler, and she had within her the power to curse and condemn — but she could not. Try as hard as she could to dwell on the pain he had inflicted, she could not rid her mind of the tenderness and the passion she had known in his embrace. How could she condemn to hell a man to whom she had given her heart and soul? She would as soon condemn herself to spend eternity there with him. But her hell was knowing that she could never possess him again. Again? He had never belonged to her at all.

Nearly every day after she had watched that majestic ship sail out of view, she had climbed up to the precipice where their hearts first touched, hoping she would see the *Fair Winds'* tall mast come into view once more. For days she had waited, for months, but that time had never come.

Finally, she had been forced to realize that he was

lost to her forever. By then he had most likely forgotten her name, and her face had become a blur in his memory.

Still, in those few clear days when the cliffs of Dover came into view, she liked to imagine him staring across the channel and yearning to reclaim their lost love. Oh, but she would have forgiven him and welcomed him back with open arms.

The bats soared closer, and she shooed them away. The sounds she was hearing were not echoes of waves battering the rocks, but of her own sobs. She had almost learned how to live with the torment of losing Gray, but the agony of having her *petite bébé* ripped from her womb would haunt her the rest of her days.

Mama had known even before she, herself, had suspected the cause for the powerful change in her body. Mama had known, but said nothing. Day after day, night after night, she had been plagued with a horrible sickness. Too late she had discovered the medicinal herbs her mother had brewed into a special tea to soothe the horrendous pain in her belly had torn it from her womb. Mama had thought she was doing her a great service. She did not understand that a child, Gray's child, would have filled the empty void in her heart. Mama had told her the pains she was experiencing and the bloody mass that had been expelled from her body were all atonements for her sins. Mama had not told her any differently until she lay dying from chills and fevers last winter. Her other deathbed confessions had been even more startling.

"Guido was your papa, but his blood did not flow in your veins," Mama had said as her fever raged higher. "The blood of the English king flows in you. You are of royal descent, *ma petite chou chou*. You are of royal blood."

Ameran bathed her mother's burning flesh with cool water. "Shhhh. Do not speak nonsense, Mama. Just rest."

Her mother tried to raise herself out of bed. "You must believe me. Heed what I say." She began an uncontrollable cough. "The King of England is your father."

Ameran cradled her mother's head in her arms and tried to get her to drink some tea. Her mother would not make it through the night. The best she could do was make her last few hours on earth as peaceful as possible. "Here, drink this."

Her mother pushed the cup away. "Listen to me, *ma cherie*. Listen to what I say. You must find a way to get to England. With me dead, the villagers will come for you. Without the powers you chose to abandon, you will not be able to defend yourself against the likes of the Duke of Caron and his filthy swine followers." She began another fit of coughing. "Go to Whitehall. Tell the King that you are Sybil Chandler's daughter. Show him the lightning bolt on your shoulder. He, too, has one in the same exact spot."

The hand holding the tea cup began to quiver. Gray had made mention of that coincidence himself. Could it be true? Could she really be an offspring of King Charles?

Her mother held tight to Ameran's arm. "It is true. What I say is true. You are who I say. Listen to me. If you have never listened before, listen now. I would

41

not lie to you on my deathbed."

Ameran knew in her heart that what her mother was professing was true. "Did Papa know the truth?"

Sybil gave a sad nod. "Guido was a good man. I could not deceive him. He loved me so very much, much more than I deserved. He adored you, *ma petite*. He worshipped you. No father could ever love his daughter more." She was tired, but she forced herself to speak. "You have heard many times the story of how I was tried and convicted of witchcraft when I was no older than you, and how Cromwell sentenced me to hang, but I was able to bribe a guard and escape the Tower on the eve of my execution."

Ameran nodded. She held out the tea cup. "Please, Mama, drink this. It will make you well. It will make you strong again."

Sybil laughed. "I am dying, *ma cherie*. You and I both know that in a few hours more I shall be dead. Please, let me tell you those things I should have told you long ago." She took another deep breath and continued. "I fled to France where my *tante* Louisa was dressmaker for Maria Mazarine. I was allowed to live with her in the court of King Louis Quatorze." Her dark eyes began to haze. "Tantie and I had been invited to attend a grand ball. The queen was especially pleased with the new gown Tantie had created for her." Her voice grew softer still. "The *grande fête* was given in honor of an Englishman who was the rightful heir to the throne of England but had been forced into exile by Cromwell. Our mutual hate of Cromwell and his Puritan fanatics drew us together. Charles was a wonderful dancer. All the ladies of court were quite taken by him, but that evening he had eyes for only me. I must confess, I, myself, fell victim to his charm." Her voice was soft with remembrances. "During the festivities, his wig caught on fire when he danced too close to a lighted torch. Most of his face was burned. He begged for someone to help him. I laid my hands across his face and repeated the words I had been taught by my mother, and almost at once, his pain began to ease. The wounds healed overnight, and there were no scars. I swore Charles to secrecy. He promised to tell no one. Had anyone suspected the reason for his miraculous recovery, I would have burned at the stake, and Tantie would have been expelled from court. Charles was quite in awe of me. I became his mistress. He swore to take me to England and make me his queen, but he forgot the promises he had made when he was restored to the throne." Sybil struggled to lift her hand and touch Ameran's cheek. "When Tantie found out I was with child, she arranged a marriage between myself and Guido. I was so miserable at having been betrayed and abandoned, I did not care what happened to me. Guido was both father and mother to you. When Tantie died, my secret died with her. It was not until years later did I learn that Guido had known all along. Poor man! I should have been more of a wife to him. He deserved better."

Ameran held her mother close. Her body trembled. She knew her mother was afraid to die. "Shall I get the priest, Mama?"

"He will not come, *ma cherie*." Sybil pulled her daughter closer. "Go to England. Go to the King. Tell him you are the daughter of Sybil Chandler, and show him the lightning bolt mark you bear on your shoulder. He will know you are who you say. Remind him of the Great Fire and the Great Plague," she instructed Ameran, her gnarled fingers gripping her shoulders. "Warn him of assassins. Tell him there are those among his most trusted who are plotting his death. Warn him of the twenty-ninth day of May. Warn him that his day of joy might well be his day of doom unless he gives you the refuge you seek." She began to choke on her words. "Tell him you possess the power to rid him of the curses Sybil Chandler called down upon him. Tell him . . . tell him you are his daughter."

Soon afterwards, her mother had drifted off into a deep slumber and did not awaken. Ameran had sent for the priest, but he refused to come. She had to bury her mama alone, for no one wanted to risk being condemned to hell by touching the flesh of a witch.

Her mother was dead, and her only protection against the villagers was in pretending to be that which she had for years denied. Her neighbors had left her alone until the Duke of Caron placed a price on her head. Now she had no alternative but to flee to England. Once there, she would seek an audience with the King and beg for his help. She would be granted asylum by the man who had borne her mother's love as well as her hate.

The crossing would be treacherous, but she would endure. Would Gray be at court with his beloved Constance? Part of her hoped he was. The other part prayed he would be a thousand miles away.

Chapter Two

"Am-er-an . . . Am-er-an . . . Am-er-an Michol . . ."

Smiling, Ameran pulled her worn cloak tighter around her shoulders. Sometimes her dreams about Gray were so real she could almost hear him beckoning her. He might be absent during her waking hours, but when her eyes closed, he would return to her side where he belonged. In those sleep-filled hours before dawn, he was there to caress her, to kiss her, to love her, and to thrill her.

"Am-eran . . . Am-er-an Michol. Are you in here?"

The echoes of her name resounded off the walls of the caves.

Ameran came awake with a start. That was no voice from her dreams. That voice was real. And so was the faint light coming toward her.

Mon Dieu! Someone was coming in after her, but who among the villagers would be brave enough to venture into the pitch-black abyss? Whoever was there knew just where to search! The footsteps and the light got closer and closer.

Ameran huddled deeper into her crevice. She was trapped like a helpless animal. There was no escape. The cave would be her tomb after all.

Ameran tried to calm her fears. She would not

whimper like a spineless coward. She would not give her tormentors that satisfaction. If she were to die, she would not die alone!

Twisting her body ever so slowly for fear the slightest twitch could be detected by her would-be executioners, Ameran lifted her skirt and took the dagger from its sheath. If there was to be blood shed, it would not be hers alone.

The flickering light came closer. A few more steps and she would be able to distinguish who among the fishermen possessed the courage to enter the domain of ghosts and demons. She hoped it would be the Duke of Caron. Now she could finish the task she should have completed earlier.

Her fingers held tight to the blade. The sound of another person's breathing got louder and louder. Then, a gasp muffled in her throat. Surely, she must still be asleep and dreaming. He could not be real! The figure approaching her had to be a creation of her exhausted mind, a cruel trick played on her by her memories. The face onto which the flame's shadow was cast looked rugged and tired. Pale, winged brows joined in an agonizing frown. Even though she couldn't see them, she knew the eyes peering through the darkness for her would be a deep, dark blue, the color of the channel on a stormy day. He *was* real! He was there in the flesh! He was no sweet imagining! He had returned at last! After all that time he had finally come back to her.

Ameran stepped out from between the rocks.

Gray stood in front of her, torch held high. His eyes closed for a moment, then opened again. He didn't utter a word. He reached out too her, but drew back his arm before she could take hold.

Ameran whispered his name over and over. "Gray, oh Gray! I cannot believe it really is you." She slipped the dagger back into the sheath, then slowly lifted her hand to his face and lovingly traced the scar down his cheek. "I have dreamed of this moment for so long."

"You're alive." His voice was heavy with sighs.

Ameran threw her arms around him and held onto her savior. "Dearest, darling Gray. You have come back. How I prayed you would."

Ameran waited for him to take her in his arms. She longed for him to hold her so tight against his powerful chest that her breath would be forced from her lungs, but he did not. He remained as stiff and as unyielding as the stones on the floor of the cave.

"Gray? What's wrong?"

His eyes did not meet hers as he untangled her arms from around his neck. "We must hurry." His words were solemn. Gone from his voice was the tenderness it had possessed only moments before.

She tried to look into his eyes and search for any clue that would tell her why he was behaving so distantly, but he would not meet her querying gaze.

Her confusion lasted but a moment. Then her smile was quick to return. Why he had suddenly gone rigid to her touch was a mystery no longer. Of course he had already gone to her house in search of her and upon finding it ablaze had hastened to the one place he knew she would seek refuge if she had not been consumed by the flames. There would be time later for their sweet reunion. For the present, their only thoughts must be those of escape.

Gray stepped aside so she could pass him.

Her cape slid down around her shoulders. Torn ruffles did little to conceal the bare fullness rising beneath the faded silk.

Gray's eyes settled on the bare flesh. His stare was long and hard.

Ameran reached up and caressed his cheek. She knew all too well the thoughts running rampant inside his head. She quivered under his scrutiny.

"Cover yourself!" Gray brushed her hand from his face and stepped out of her reach.

Ameran gathered the cloak tight around her shoulders. Her face hot with shame, she looked away.

If he truly did not love her and never had, then why had he come back?

"Gray?" she whispered.

"Yes, what is it?" he asked impatiently. He took great care to keep his distance and make certain their eyes did not meet.

"Your words are so hard and cold," she began softly. "And you look at me as though you despise me. Why did you come back if you hate me so?" She all but choked on her words. He did not even bother to pretend he loved her. She had a feeling he did not even like her. Why had he come?

Gray refused to face her, concentrating on the rock pillars to the left of him. "I have been instructed by His Majesty King Charles to escort you safely to England."

Ameran's heart stopped beating. He did not even deny hating her! At least now she knew the truth. Gray had not come on his own accord. He had been ordered to France by his King.

She bit her lip so hard she could taste her own blood. She would not cry. She gathered her cape tighter around her. What a fool she had been to think love had brought him back, when he had never loved

her. She had been nothing more than a means of satisfying his lust. He had never shared any of the feelings
she had felt for him. An obligation to the King! He
cared nothing for the woman he had betrayed and
abandoned. That morning as he sailed away from
France, he had given no thought at all to whether she
lived or died!

Ameran fought harder to be strong. Why should
she care why he had returned? He would take her to
England. That was all that mattered. He would serve
her purpose just as she had served his.

"I am ready." She summoned all the dignity she
possessed.

Gray offered her his hand.

She ignored it and brushed past him. He was her
way to freedom. Nothing more. At one time she
might have loved him, but now he was only a regret.
He would never know how much his hatefulness
pained her.

Head held high, hands clenched angrily inside her
cape, Ameran paused outside the cave a short time
later. Dawn was at that moment breaking across a sky
shadowed with clouds of smoke. All that remained of
her home was a thick, gray haze. The air was calm
and deathly quiet. By now the villagers were wallow-
ing in a drunken stupor. What tales they would create
of the evil spells she had worked on them when their
search for her bones ended in failure.

She walked on without looking behind her again.
She hated France. It may have been the country of her
birth, but it had never been her home. In her heart,
she had always known that the country across the
channel was where she belonged, even though she had
never set foot on its soil. Thank God the King had

found it in his heart to take pity on her. If only he had sent someone else to fetch her. Still, the voyage would be swift, and as soon as she arrived at Court and had her audience with the King, there would be no need to have any further dealings with the high and mighty Lord Commander Grayson Carlisle.

They walked on in silence.

Ameran was grateful for the tiny rocks which jabbed through the worn soles of her shoes as they hurried down the beach, the discomfort of their pricking kept her thoughts from Gray. Occasionally in a moment of weakness she would steal a quick glimpse of him in the corner of her eye, while pretending to be looking over her shoulder for unwelcome followers. Around his neck he still wore his gold cross. Its stones reflected the early light of day in magnificent splendor. Had he thought of her once during their separation, or were his sweet rememberings only for the Duchess of Morrow? She wondered if he had married that Constance of whom Gideon had spoken. Not that it mattered one way or another. Any love she still harbored for him had died in the caves the instant he looked at her with disgust.

Looking behind her once again, Ameran gave him another quick inspection. How he had changed! So unlike the man she had known and loved. His resemblance to Gideon was even more pronounced now. His face was hard as stone, just like his heart. His look was hostile. Gone was the kindness once expressed there.

He had left behind a naive, lovestruck girl who hung onto his every word, but he had returned to a woman who could be just as cold as he. Lord Grayson Carlisle had broken her heart, but her spirit remained strong. Wealth and power did not give him the license to hurt and humiliate, and she was going to tell him that just as soon as she could do so without stumbling over her tongue. No one was ever going to make a fool of her again!

Tears swelled in her eyes, and she quickened her pace, lest he see them fall. She was nearly there. If only she could hold on but a little while longer. Damn him!

Moored in the deep waters of the channel was the *Fair Winds*. Its sails were unfurled and ready to set sail at a moment's notice, and its hull was gently listing in the water, just as it was every time it sailed into her dreams to take her to safety.

A skiff was drifting back to the mother ship. Gray pointed a little way up the beach to a rope and anchor lying in the sand.

Someone had deliberately cut the line, but Ameran said nothing. She looked all around. If someone were watching them, they remained well hidden.

"We shall have to swim out to the skiff." Gray's voice was no kinder than it had been when he had ordered her to cover herself.

Ameran kicked off her shoes, then shed her cape and let it drop onto the pebbles. Gray could object until he was blue in the face, but the less she wore the better her chances of reaching the tiny skiff that was drifting farther away. She almost smiled in spite of her misery. How surprised her enemies would be when they discovered her shoes and cape. What stories they would spread about her escape!

Gray called out her name, but she ignored him as she waded on out into the channel. She could hear her teeth chattering. The water was raw and biting. Winter's chill was not yet gone. When she could no longer touch bottom, she stretched out and began to swim. Her limbs were soon numb.

It had been late spring when Gray was there before, and the water had been warm and refreshing. As she reached out and pulled the water toward her, she could not help but remember how they had swum naked in the little cove outside the caves. What a fool she had been to think their joy would last forever. Could he, too, be remembering their romantic moonlight swims? No, he was probably eagerly anticipating the hour when his obligation to the King was concluded and he would be free of her once and for all.

Attacking the water with an even fiercer vigor, Ameran shot out ahead of him. She would not relive the past. Not now, not ever! Those few days were lost forever, lost and destroyed just like the baby her mother had ripped from her womb.

She lifted her head up to see how far she had yet to go. She was close, so close, yet the struggle was all but gone from her limbs. The current was against her, and she was growing weary of fighting it. If her strength gave out, the tide would push her back to the shore she was fleeing. Cramps plagued her arms and legs. She was not sure if she was still swimming or just merely floating. She had long since ceased to feel her arms and legs. Hold on, she told herself over and over. Only a little way to go. She would survive this ordeal if for no other reason than to spite Gray.

With all that was left of her strength, Ameran reached for the skiff and held on to the side. She was about to summon the last bit of strength she possessed to pull herself over the side when a pair of strong hands suddenly reached around her waist and lifted her up. Ice-cold flesh thawed at his touch. The fingers burning through her wet gown stole what little breath she had left inside her.

Gray swung himself over the side and without a word began rowing toward the *Fair Winds*.

One last glance was directed to the shore. She was safe now. Never again would she set foot on French soil. Never again would she be at the mercy of the likes of the Duke of Caron and his bloodthirsty madmen! If she really did possess the dark evil magic of their accusations, then let the mighty Caron and his dogs burn in hell!

Her eyes turned once more to the *Fair Winds*. She could feel Gray's stare burning holes into her body, but she could not chance her gaze colliding with his, for if it did, he would surely see in her eyes that she had never ceased loving him.

Gray rowed in silence. She could feel his heart calling out to hers, just as hers was pleading with him, but she dared not utter one sound.

Finally, it was Gray who broke the icy silence.

"You must be cold."

His words were almost gentle.

Ameran shook her head and huddled closer to the bow. Her flesh had all but turned purple, and she had no feeling in her fingers or toes. There was not a place on her that was not shivering, but he would be the last to know. What did he care anyway whether she was cold or not?

He motioned to a dark blue bundle between them. "Put on my cloak."

"I don't need it."

His icy glare chilled her even more. "Put it on, I said. You board my ship looking like that, and I shall have a mutiny on my hands. Now do as I command. Don't make my task any more difficult than it already is."

Ameran was furious. Her eyes flared smoke, but her look of contempt went unnoticed. It was all she could do to keep her tongue to herself. She was the one being forced to suffer, not he. She would rather swim to England than be subjected to his hatefulness one more moment. He had no reason to despise her. Why did he view her with such abhorrence? Why was he playing the victim when it was she who had been wronged? He and Gideon made a fine pair after all!

Gray tossed her the cloak. "You'll be more comfortable with this on."

Only when she glanced down at where his gaze had settled did she realize what he was talking about. The wet silk clung to her body like paint and outlined its every curve. She could have shown no more of herself had she been wearing nothing at all.

In her own time, she slipped the cloak around her. Lingering on it was the salty, sweaty smell of a man of the sea. She tried hard to ignore it, but its heady scent was overpowering. It made her dizzy just as Gray had made her dizzy when he had encompassed her in his wonderful embrace. Having his cloak around her was like being in his strong arms once again. Even now, she could sense that he was staring at her with the same intense longing of times past, and she could tell as well that he thought his looks were going undetected. Could it be that he, too, was plagued with memories of happier times between them? It almost made her wish the channel between their hearts would narrow, but as the feeling slowly began to creep back into her exhausted limbs, so did her good sense. What had once been could never be again, and yearning for it could only result in more heartbreak. She blinked away the tears. It was over. The joy they had once shared together could never be relived or revived.

Chapter Three

Gray rowed up alongside his ship and tossed the skiff's line up to a sailor leaning over the rail. Ignoring his offer of assistance, which sounded more like another of his commands, Ameran began to scale the rope ladder that had been thrown over the side. Halfway up, her legs became entangled in the hemp rungs. She turned, tripped, and very nearly lost her balance. Gray reached out and steadied her. His hands were strong and powerful against her thighs. She very nearly let herself melt into his hold, but quickly pulled herself away.

"Do not be afraid. I won't let you fall."

His words were kind and reassuring. *Don't be afraid,* he had told her their last day together. *You will never have cause to fear again. I will protect you with my life. On that you have my word.*

She could almost hear him saying those very things again.

No! No! It would be best not to remember.

Ameran climbed faster, trying to get out of his reach. The cliffs she had been scrambling up all her life were ten times higher and ten times more frightening. Oh, why did she let him affect her so!

Strong hands held her once again in spite of her si-

56

lent protests. Her legs were even more unsteady than before.

Finally, at last, she was over the rail, and before he could lend any more assistance, she swung herself down onto the deck of the *Fair Winds*.

The ship's crew was lined up at attention. Dour faces and frowning eyes bore deep into her.

Why did they view her with such open hostility, she wondered. Perhaps they could sense their captain's aversion to the task set him.

Ameran quickly scanned the crowd of men for Gideon, then breathed a sigh of relief upon discovering he was not among them. She would rather do battle with the entire lot of them than to look upon the face of the man who had taken such obvious delight in tormenting her.

Ameran was determined not to be intimidated by the sailors' rude gawks and whispered laughter as she walked among them. She held her head high, and when she did look at them, she did so with eyes just as viperish as their own.

A huge cheer erupted when Gray jumped over the side and onto the deck. The smile on his face was quick to fade when he saw her watching him. Once more, his look became sullen and distant. The command to weigh anchor given, he motioned for her to follow him.

Hugging her cloak tight around her, Ameran walked several steps behind him. She slowed her pace even more to make certain she kept her distance from him. The crew of the *Fair Winds* made her feel uncomfortable, but none more so than the man she had once loved with her whole heart and soul. She dared not look anywhere but straight ahead as she walked past

Gray's men. Bold and suggestive stares were cast in her direction. Lips smacked hungrily. A few snickered, and one sailor murmured something about the King's private store.

With that remark, Gray turned angrily around to face his men. His stare was even more cutting than those he had directed at her. The men disbanded and went on about their duties.

Gray then lifted the hatch in the center of his ship and motioned her to follow him down the narrow, ladderlike stairs. He offered his hand to assist her, but Ameran ignored it.

"You will stay in my quarters." His tone left no room for challenges.

"I don't want to be a burden," she said with mock concern.

"You won't be. I assure you," he said, making no attempt to hide the bitterness in his voice. "I often sleep topside in a hammock like my men."

Ameran refused to look at him. How easily he had rid himself of her when she no longer amused him. What a fool she had been not to have seen through him all along.

Gray opened a door at the end of the corridor below deck. The furnishings were sparse: a bed built out from one wall and a desk from the other. Atop the desk were a big red leather bound volume and a collection of brass nautical instruments similar to those in her own collection. Taking up the center of the room was a huge black trunk with gold latches and locks. The lid was open. Ameran sneaked a curious peek inside. Satins and silks in a rainbow of colors were stuffed inside.

Gray turned his back on her and made an entry in

his logbook. "I am sure you will find something to your liking," he mumbled under his breath.

Ameran pretended not to have heard him and knelt down beside the trunk. She was almost afraid to touch such splendid gowns. Timidly, she reached into the pile and took out a silk gown that was the green of tiny spring apples and caressed it longingly. She brushed her cheek with the silk.

Something made her look up. She caught Gray's eyes carefully watching her. He was smiling. His fierce countenance once again bore the face of the man she had once loved.

The words choked in her throat. "I have never seen such elegance. The King sent these to me?"

His jaw set hard again, Gray gave a stiff nod.

"How kind," said Ameran softly. "How very kind and thoughtful." She dug down farther, brought up a pale blue gown of finest satin and gasped in awe. "How beautiful!" Chuckling, she glanced down at the shreds of clothes she was wearing. "I don't suppose I could be presented to the King of England wearing such rags as these."

Gray slammed the red volume shut with a loud grunt. He took a pair of angry strides in her direction, his hands clenched by his side, and fixed to his face was a glower that scorched her flesh. His heart beat furiously in his throat.

For a moment, Ameran was certain he was going to raise his hand against her. She stood proud in defiance. He would not have the satisfaction of seeing her cower in his presence.

Gray gave the trunk a mighty kick. The lid fell shut with a bang. Then he yanked the pale blue gown from her hands and ripped it in two.

Startled, Ameran jumped back. Her eyes dared him to strike her. It was all she could do to keep from giving him the kick he deserved. How dare he be so hateful! She had done nothing to hurt him. After all, he was the one who made promises he had no intention of ever keeping.

"Stay here. Under no circumstances are you to show your face on the deck," he commanded as soon as he had regained his statuelike calm. "Have I made myself clear?" he asked, teeth gritted.

"Perfectly." She watched as he made his way to the door. Finally, she could keep quiet no longer. "Why do you despise me? I've done nothing to make you hate me. I don't deserve to be treated like a criminal."

Slowly, he turned back around. There was a strange look on his face, but he said nothing.

Ameran instantly regretted having blurted out her question. No doubt her outburst would give him the satisfaction of knowing the overpowering effect he still had on her. She found the confusion and dismay on his face completely baffling.

Ameran took a deep breath. She had come too far to retreat. The time had come at last for explanations and answers no matter how deeply they might cut into her heart.

"Despise you?" Gray's voice was whisper soft. "I could not despise you if I tried, and God knows I tried. I loved you."

Ameran reached for the desk to steady herself. That admission was not the one she had prepared for or anticipated. He had loved her! He *had* loved her! What had she done to cause him to abandon her? He had to tell her now, before she lost what dignity and control she still possessed.

Gray offered no explanation as his sea blue eyes searched her soul. That look was one she knew well, for when he had asked her to return to England with him, his gaze had been just as imploring.

Their stares bolted together in blue-black lightning. Try as hard as she might, the spell was not to be broken, and she was held captive by his eyes once again as so many times before.

Hot, wet tears streamed down her face and stung her cheeks. There was nothing that could be done to restrain them. One moment more and all reason would be lost. She had to ask him. She had to! Otherwise she would never know the truth. It was all she could manage to keep her words steady when her legs were about to buckle.

"If you did indeed love me as you say you once did, then why did you betray me? Why did you abandon me?"

"Betray you? Abandon you?" Gray took a step toward her, then reached back for the wall as if to brace himself. "But it was *you* who betrayed *me*. *You* were the one who left me."

They stared at each other in stunned silence, each trying to comprehend the other's accusation.

"You were the one who told Gideon that you never had any intention of returning to England with me," announced Gray after what seemed hours of painful silence. "You told him that I had meant nothing to you. I had been just a passing fancy, nothing more than an escape from the boredom of village life."

"Mon Dieu!" Ameran's legs gave way and she dropped down onto the lid of the trunk. "Gideon told you that? How could you have believed him? How

61

could you have left without hearing those words from my lips yourself?"

"I never considered the possibility that Gideon would tell me anything but the truth." His words were puzzled, as puzzled as the shadows crossing over his face.

Gray stared out the porthole as if the answers he sought could be found at sea. "Why? Why would he have lied to me? He knew how much I treasured you. All else ceased to be important the day I found you. My titles, my lands, my wealth, they meant nothing. That which had one time seemed so crucial to my existence became insignificant when compared to you."

Tears of joy streamed down her cheeks. Gray had not left her of his own accord after all. They had been victims of a trust and friendship betrayed. No longer did she fear the shame and humiliation of baring her heart to him.

"After you left, I didn't want to live. I prayed to die so that the memories of our time together would cease tormenting me every hour of the day. I haven't lived since you left." Her smile was weak, but happy. "Only at night when you filled my dreams was I truly at peace. At dawn, my hell began all over again. Each day without you became an eternity."

Gray stroked her shoulders with a tenderness she remembered all too well. "On the day we were to sail home, I couldn't come for you as I had promised. Fevers and chills and pains like those which had never before assailed me prevented me from rising from that very cot. I begged Gideon to go for you and your mother, and he promised to bring you to me. I fell into a deep sleep, and when I awakened, I was home. Gideon told me I had been made a fool. He said you had confessed to him that you had never loved me, and he laughed at my wanting to share my life with you." Deep, winged brows creased in heartfelt agony. "Gideon told me you had invited him into the caves and promised to show him the joys you had shown to me."

"He's a liar!" Ameran exclaimed. "Oh, if I ever get my hands around his neck, I shall choke his life right out of him." Then, she grew frightened. "You didn't believe him, did you, Gray?"

He shook his head. "I was too weak to challenge him. If only I had not been attacked by that mysterious ailment, then none of this would have ever happened, and we could have spent these last three years together."

Ameran bowed her head. His breath was so warm on her cheek. How could she tell him the excruciating pain that had befallen him stemmed from a curse her mother had placed on him? He would never believe her. Oh, there was so much she had to tell him . . . about Mama . . . about the baby . . . but no, not now. There would be time enough later.

Gray knelt down in front of her. He took her tiny hands in his large ones and studied each finger intently before speaking. "Tell me all you remember about that cursed day when we lost each other."

Ameran sighed. She remembered it all. She had forgotten nothing. Three years had passed, yet she remembered each and every detail of her meeting with Gideon just as vividly as if it had happened only yesterday.

"The moment I saw Gideon, I knew something was wrong," she began, holding tight to Gray's hand. "I feared you were ill, and I wanted desperately to come to you, but Gideon only laughed and told me that you lacked the courage to come yourself and had sent him to mop up your mess."

"Mop up my mess?" Gray blared. "Is that what he said? I'll kill him for that."

Ameran tried to calm him. "Shhh, darling. It's over now. We've found one another again."

Gray kissed her cheek. "Yes, we have found one another again, but had it not been for the man who I considered my brother, we would have never been separated from each other." He took a deep breath. "Please, continue, and I shall refrain from outbursts."

Ameran's words were sad with remembrances. "Gideon told me you had a change of heart. He told me you didn't love me, and you had no intention of keeping any promises made to me in moments of passion."

Gray pounded his fist into his hand. "I'll make him answer to both of us!"

Her eyes lingered on the cross she had once worn around her neck. "Gideon said I was to return the cross that I had stolen from you."

"Stolen from me?" Gray shook his head in disbelief. "But he knew I had given it to you. He knew how much I loved you and how much I wanted to take you and your mother back to England with me. He knew it all! I told him! I made him promise he would bring you to me, and he swore he would." Gray's sigh was long and labored. "Merciful God. I cannot believe that of Gideon. Gideon, of all people, the one man I trusted above all others. He was my friend. He was my brother. How could he have put a wedge between us?"

For the longest while, Gray remained lost in his thoughts.

Ameran said nothing. She could sense the struggle inside him.

Gray's voice softened. "Yet I know that you would not lie to me." Frown fading, Gray pulled her to her feet. Rough fingers stroked her cheeks with the wonderful gentleness in which she had once reveled. "My poor, poor darling. Of course you thought I had betrayed you. After all those lies, what else were you to think? I would not blame you had you wished me dead."

"Oh, no, no, never! No matter what happened to separate us, I could never have stopped loving you. Oh, I tried, I tried. I'll admit that. The pain Gideon inflicted was excruciating, but I still loved you. I still wanted you and needed you every hour of the day." Arms clasped tight around his neck, Ameran burrowed her head deep into his shoulder. "I loved you then, and I love you now, Gray. I do. I love you." She held on tight. She would never let go of him again. "We can't right the wrongs or recapture the days we've lost, but we must put the past behind us. All that matters is that we have found each other in spite of all the obstacles placed between us. What do three years matter in a lifetime of years to come?"

Gray held her close, their hearts pounding in unison. "You've been my first thought upon waking and the last before sleep finally calmed my tortured soul at night. These past three years have been a living hell, and I have only myself to blame for both our misery. What a fool I was not to question Gideon. I should have returned to France myself when I had recovered, but no, I was too proud. I believed Gideon, I am ashamed to admit. I believed him without question. What untold anguish I brought upon us both because of my stupidity!"

"No, no, dearest." Her lips brushed his. "You had no reason to suspect Gideon would deceive you. He had been your most trusted companion for years."

"Yes, but in my heart, I had known you forever. So much wasted time." His cheek nuzzled hers. "So much wasted time, but now that I have again found you, my darling Ameran, I swear that no one, not even the King himself, will come between us ever again."

"Oh, Gray! Dearest, dearest Gray, I do love you so!"

"And I love you." Gently, slowly, savoring each taste, he kissed her.

His tenderness was agonizing. To be completely consumed by him was her one desire. Only he could quiet the tempest raging within her.

Granting her silent pleas, Gray attacked her lips with the fiery passion she longed for. His kiss was hard and demanding.

"I can't count the nights I've lain awake reliving over and over in my memories our brief moments of love," he whispered between kisses.

"And I, as well."

"So much time has been lost, so much time wasted, and all because of my foolishness."

Ameran caressed his face. Every detail of his strong visage had been committed to memory three years ago, and not one had been forgotten. Gone was the tense fierceness of earlier. What remained was the loving, caring countenance of the man who had pledged to her love eternal.

"There'll be no more wasted hours." She took his hand and led him to the cot. Her boldness surprised her. Yet the longing inside could be denied not a moment longer. She wanted him! Every part of her desired him with a yearning that could only be quieted when they were as one once again.

Ameran knew that Gray's thoughts were the same as hers.

Arms and legs entangled, they fell back laughing onto the bed, their hands working furiously to rid the other of the layers of cloth separating them. Vows of love unending were whispered over and over.

Gray flung her cape across the room and tenderly eased her gown down her waist. "What a fool I was! I'll never forgive myself," he murmured as his mouth found its way to soft, blushing summits that became hard as pebbles on the beach when he took them between his teeth.

Quick, nimble fingers loosened the ties holding his shirt. Her hands dived inside to the smooth muscles bunched beneath, and stroked and kneaded and caressed just as she had done in her dreams the past three years. His flesh was hard as stone, yet it seemed to tremble at her touch.

"You can't be faulted. You mustn't hold yourself at fault." Her words were as rasped as her breath. "You were . . . betrayed by a man . . . whose companionship and trust . . . you had shared . . . for many, many . . ."

Ameran bit her lip to contain the pleasure mounting within his every touch. Gray clawed at her gown. Silken shreds fell in swirls around her legs.

How many nights she had dreamed of such a reunion! She could feel him growing harder and harder against her, so hard she wanted to rip his breeches from his limbs. Surely no ecstasy had ever been sweeter!

"Oh, Gray, darling, darling, Gray, this is too wonderful to be real." He was hers, hers forever! "I'm not dreaming, am I, darling Gray? Please, tell me this is no trick of my imagination."

He ran his tongue down her chest. His fingers trailed playfully behind. "If we are dreaming, my love, then I pray that we never awaken."

He kicked his breeches across the room, then ripped off his shirt and flung it behind him.

They could have found each other no more easily had they never been parted. The years of unfulfilled longing raging strong inside her, Ameran threw her arms around him and pulled him down on top of her. He eased himself inside. It was as though he was taking possession for the first time, but the pain was short, and oh, how wonderfully sweet!

Moaning, she urged him to take her with even more force, and he rammed himself harder and deeper in answer to her pleas. She rose to meet his movements with thrusts as hard and forceful as his own. Fingers digging into his back, she held on for dear life. She was drowning in a sea of tumultuous desire, and he alone had the power to save her. She bit into his shoulder lest her cries of joy ring across the decks, but her delight was not to be contained. She had waited so long for the hour of complete bliss to once again overtake and overpower her! Now that that hour was upon her, and she could wait no longer.

"Oh, Gray, Gray, darling Gray," she moaned over and over. Her body was no longer her own. All control was lost. With a hoarse gasp, Gray gave a final thrust, and then exploding his might inside her, relaxed, all energy drained from his body.

Hours passed before either stirred from their slumber.

Ameran traced the scar on his cheek with tiny kisses. "I was afraid to open my eyes for fear you would have disappeared."

"Never again, my love, will you be rid of me," he replied, his words thick with fatigue.

She sank back into the bed with a contented smile. How wonderful it felt having Gray locked in her embrace. If only he could remain there forever!

A while later, when he made a weak effort to lift himself off her, she pulled him back down. "Don't move, my love. You're where you belong for always."

Gray rested his head on her shoulder. He said nothing, yet his breath was labored and deliberate. The hard set of his jaw had returned, and once again, he stared across the room, deep in his own reverie.

Ameran waited, hesitant to speak, but when his brow's frown did not relax, she could stay silent no longer. "What is troubling you, my love?"

"Oh, my darling Ameran. What a wicked trick fate has played on us. Never have I known her to be so cruel."

Ameran turned her head so he would not see the tears. Thick lashes blinked quickly. That which she had tried so hard to banish from her thoughts had returned to haunt her happiness. Just because time had stood still for her during their long separation didn't mean the same could be said of Gray. She believed him with her whole heart when he said he had never stopped loving her, but he was a man, and his desires and needs were much stronger than her own. No doubt Constance was the reason for his quick depression. Constance, Duchess of Morrow . . . And what of her? The guilt Gray was experiencing for betraying the wife he had taken during their time apart had to be

69

blamed for the stubborn creases of worry etched upon his face. How could she endure what he was going to soon tell her? Surely, it would have been easier going to her grave without this blissful reconciliation than to know once more the joys found in his embrace could never be hers alone.

"If he so much as lays one finger on you, I swear I shall kill him with my bare hands."

Her eyes came open at once. Were her ears playing tricks on her? What was he talking about? Who was he going to kill with his bare hands?

"I don't care if he is the King of England, I will kill him if he tries to bed you."

Ameran quickly raised herself up. Her look was one of astonishment. Had she heard what she thought she had heard? Surely not.

"Gray, what are you talking about?"

He repeated his vow. "I will kill him!"

"The King bed me?" she asked, completely confused. "A bastard I might be, but I am still his daughter nonetheless."

Gray's mouth dropped open. He rolled the rest of the way off her and looked up at her in stunned disbelief. "His daughter?" asked Gray.

"He didn't tell you?"

Gray ran both hands through his hair. "He told me that he was entrusting me with a very important assignment. My instructions were to go to the village of Mer on the coast of France in search of the new French mistress King Louis was giving to him. King Charles told me her name was Ameran Michol. I begged him to send Gideon or one of his other commanders. I couldn't bear the thought of doing the task myself, knowing of the hours we had shared together, but the King would not send anyone else in my place."

"I? His mistress? I don't understand. Why would the King tell you such an utterly ridiculous story? His mistress indeed!"

Then, slowly, the reason why the King would conceal her real identity began to make more sense, but she made no mention of it to Gray. Later. There would be time later to tell him of her mother's strange practices, which King Charles had himself witnessed and experienced. Undoubtedly by spreading the rumor that he was sending to France for a new mistress, the King was taking precautions against those at Court who might have remembered the evil vixen, Sybil Chandler, and would object to the presence of her daughter among them.

"Why did you not tell me three years ago that you were the King's daughter?"

"I only learned of it myself this past winter," she answered. "As Mama lay dying, she told me of her love affair with Charles when he was exiled in France. When he was restored to the throne, he left her with the promise to send for her and make her his queen, but he never did." Ameran showed him the lightning bolt birthmark on her right shoulder. "You made mention of this yourself and remarked that your King had a similar one in the same place. It is no coincidence that we share this mark of birth."

Gray nodded. "I remember."

"Mama said I was to go to England and show this to the King and he would know I was telling the truth. Since winter, I have been writing to the King, pleading with him to give me sanctuary in England. Then when you said he had sent you to fetch me, I knew he believed what I had written to him in my letters."

71

"Why didn't he tell me himself?" asked Gray solemnly. "He's placed me in his trust many, many times before, and I have never betrayed him."

Ameran shrugged her shoulders. "Perhaps he felt it best if no one knew of his love affair with an accused witch who had been sentenced to burn at the stake. I made no mention of her identity in the letters, for fear his advisors would intercept them. I only described to him the circumstances of my birth."

"Your mother was accused of witchcraft?"

Ameran gave a sad nod. "Cromwell was determined that she and all like her, be they evil or good, burn at the stake. Mama managed to escape the eve of her execution, and she fled to the Court of King Louis where her aunt was a dressmaker for the Queen."

She then recounted to Gray what she knew of her mother's love affair with the exiled King of England and how she had saved his face and his life when his wig had caught on fire.

"When rumors that Mama had blown the fire from Charles's face spread through the court, everyone feared her. They were afraid that she would work some kind of evil magic on them and so she was expelled from court. She had nowhere to go. A poor, kind fisherman took pity on her and protected her from superstitious neighbors who held her responsible for every misfortune that befell the village. So Mama married him."

Muscular arms tightly enfolded her as Gray kissed away the sadness of her memories. "What a hellish existence you have had to endure, my sweetest darling. And I am lower than a gutter rat for abandoning you when you needed me most. When I think that had it not been for the King, I might never have . . ."

Ameran silenced him with kisses. It was too agonizing to dwell on. "Shhhh, dearest. Don't think of the past. We shall have the rest of our days together." Thoughts of the Duchess of Morrow once again faded her smile. "Time has not lessened your desire for me, has it?"

"How can you even think so?" he mumbled into her ear.

"But what of Constance?" The truth must be known no matter how much it might hurt, she told herself over and over while awaiting his reply.

Gray threw back his head and roared with laughter. "Constance? Why, that woman was a thorn in my side when her husband was alive and an even more prickly one now that the Duke's dead. Constance? She poses no threat to us, dearest Ameran. Only in death could the poor Duke have the last word."

"Then Gideon . . ."

"Ah, yes, Gideon again. Of course. How else would you have known Constance's name?" Anger pulsed in his temples.

"Gideon told me you were in love with her and were going to marry her. That was why you couldn't take me back to England with you."

"Gideon is a liar, and I shall deal with him as soon as we are back in England." His dark blue eyes raged. "Betraying one's friend is inexcusable no matter the reasons, but betraying one's commander can never be forgiven or forgotten." Once again, Gray gathered her close and smothered her with kisses. "Don't let thoughts of Gideon or of Constance plague our happiness. If either of them utters a word that upsets you, they will have me to answer to, and I can assure you, I will show no mercy."

73

Ameran snuggled down into the crook of his arm. Finally she was where she belonged. It was almost as though the separation had never occurred. Gray was right. Nothing would ever part them again. How could she have ever stopped believing he would come to her? She had the King to thank for much more than aiding her escape from France. He had given Gray back to her.

For a while, Ameran watched as Gray lay sleeping. Fate had been kind to them. They'd endured the agony of separation and were rewarded with a love even stronger than before.

Once more, she felt desire stirring inside her, and she pressed herself closer to him. A movement against her bare thigh assured her that even in his slumber, Gray longed for her with the same urgency as she for him.

Wicked thoughts danced inside her head, making her giggle. Dare she be so bold? Less than an hour had passed since their reunion, yet she hungered once more for his touch.

Quietly, careful not to awaken him, she eased one leg over his well-muscled hip and waited. When he showed no sign of opening his eyes, she lowered her head to his chest.

At first her lips trembled as they nipped at the rock-hard contours, but the shyness was quick to fade as they glided down his stomach. She knew what she wanted and felt no shame about exploring all those wonderful places which gave her untold pleasures.

Anxious fingers, eager to please, began their daring quest. Taut muscles rippled at her touch. His own need pulsed against hers. He had yet to lay a hand on her, yet her insides were on fire.

Glancing up, she realized he was no longer sleeping. He looked mesmerized by her caresses. The rise and fall of his chest had quickened, and his heart pounded violently.

Not a sound was uttered. Words were not necessary. Desire-glazed eyes relayed their hearts' yearnings.

A caldron of fire boiled within. The torment, though sweet, was mounting. She could wait no longer for him to stoke the fire within her.

Feeling only the uncontrollable urgency of her desire, Ameran led him inside her. Expert hands, digging into her buttocks, guided her to complete enjoyment, and together the two of them satisfied the demands of their long separation, each becoming totally and completely satiated by the other.

Chapter Four

"Tell me about the King," requested Ameran when they had stirred from their sleep sometime later.

Gray let out a loud laugh. "Have you no mercy, woman? You drive me to the brink of death, then expect me to converse as well as to love?"

With renewed zest, she began tickling him. "You'll have no rest until you satisfy my curiosity."

"I must satisfy that as well?"

Ameran dug her fingers deeper into his ribs.

Gray gave up, laughing. "I surrender. I surrender. What is it you wish to know?" He sank back onto the bed, his naked form powerful and sleek with sweat.

"Everything. Tell me all there is to tell about the man my mother loved. What kind of a ruler is he?" she asked, content once more to snuggle in the crook of his arm. "Is he kind or uncaring, evil or good? Tell me all you know."

Gray gave careful consideration before proceeding. "It has been said of King Charles that he has never said a foolish thing or done a wise one."

Ameran shook her head. "I don't understand."

Gray kissed the birthmark on her shoulder. "Then I shall explain. The King never says anything foolish; however, he never does anything that is wise. The King counters his critics with the reply that while his deeds were those of his ministers, his words are his alone. As a man, he is most likeable, but as a regent he is less than perfect."

Ameran sidled closer. How she loved that smooth, massive chest. How she loved his feel, his smell, especially after they had just devoured each other.

"His worst fault is that he relies too heavily on his advisors. Those in whose judgements he places the most trust are the very ones who are out to undermine him for their own gain." Gray propped himself up onto one elbow while his free hand busied itself with following the path of soft curves beside him. "Damn, woman, can I never get enough of you?"

Ameran playfully pushed him away. "The King, sire."

Gray sank back down onto the bed and crossed his hands over his chest. "Ah, yes, the King. Very well." He expelled a loud, exasperated sigh. "In spite of his shortcomings, which are far too many to detail, he does possess some rather admirable traits."

Ameran listened attentively. The smile stayed on her lips.

"Granted, the King is selfish and pigheaded at times," Gray continued. "But he does have a good nature and the charm of his manners. Charles is a scholar, an avid reader, and a patron of drama, painting, and architecture. His keen interest in science has led to the founding of the Royal Society of which he is president."

Ameran pushed away the hand that had begun a deliciously slow exploration of her curves. "Please, continue, Lord Carlisle."

Gray shook his head. "You are extremely cruel for

one so exquisitely beautiful. But if you insist you would rather converse than . . ."

"I would," she giggled. "Do go on."

"The King is basically a good man, not at all the immoral rake his enemies portray." Gray laughed. "Although he does keep the Court ablaze with one scandal after another."

"He sounds most interesting."

Gray grew serious. "He is, and he's a fine King, though I fear neither destiny nor history will reflect kindly on him."

"No sovereign's rule is without problems," she observed thoughtfully.

Gray agreed. "But King Charles seems more so plagued than most. It's no secret he cannot tolerate his national assemblies, nor they him. For all the world to see he is ruler of a nation not only separated by geography, but by politics as well." Gray shook his head. "And the entire world knows as well, unfortunately so, that England is in no position to fight a foreign war even if necessity demands it."

Ameran resisted the temptation to once again give her fingers free reign over his body. "And what of his close alliance with France? It's common knowledge that your people don't approve of King Charles's dependence on King Louis."

"They're your people as well, my darling." Gray kissed her lips tenderly. "There are those who believe his alliance with Louis will eventually lead to his downfall, for it is no secret that Charles yearns to achieve an absolute monarchy like his French mentor." His lips were warm on her neck. "Charles's misdirected ambition has caused him to restore Catholicism, to raise a standing army, and to put himself into debt by accepting extravagant gifts and enormous sums of money from France. It is rumored that the King will never again find it necessary to call on Parliament or rely on his ministers' mercies for financial strength because of the Sun King's immense generosity."

"The mighty Louis Quatorze does nothing without expecting much in return," Ameran told him.

Gray caressed her cheek. "I am very fortunate indeed to have such a clever beauty in my company."

His touch sent her senses reeling. "My father was but a poor fisherman, yet he had a keen mind for political affairs," she explained. "Surely your King realizes that such a voracious lust for power might in all likelihood lead to his demise."

"I don't believe King Charles possesses such great insight," said Gray solemnly. "He's ruled for twenty years, and during that time, the King has willingly admitted to following a crooked path of bribery and flattery and corruption whenever the need arose. He swears he has not his own best interest at heart, but that of Britain, and I am inclined to believe him. His enemies are many, but they can rest assured he will reign until his death." Gray's frown deepened. "A death which I fear might well prove somewhat untimely."

"His future does appear somewhat grim, doesn't it?" she commented as Gray solemnly considered their discussion. "What about Charles the man? Is he as interesting as Charles the King?"

Finally, Gray smiled. "Considerably more so, I daresay. He takes great pleasure in saying of himself that he is the only sane man in a society of lunatics. He refuses to be bullied by anyone, especially by a Parliament that dangles money at him like bait in a trap. He could so easily charm his ministers, yet it seems as if he does everything in his power to torment them with his obstinacy."

"What else can you tell me of Charles the man?" She was curious. She wanted to know everything there was to know about the man who was her father.

"Charles has three great passions in his life," Gray began with a sly grin. "Horses, women, and whatever else can be mounted. He prides himself on being an admitted adversary of virginity and chastity. If it were not for the gossip of his latest scandals and conquests, Whitehall would be rather dull. No woman, be she serving wench or nobleman's wife, is safe from his amorous advances. Those who he finds especially pleasing are made ladies-in-waiting so they can be at his beck and call at any hour of the day or night."

Ameran frowned. "How dreadful for the Queen."

"The Queen is rather dreadful herself," laughed Gray. Muscles flexing, he enjoyed a long, catlike stretch. "That woman can give a tongue lashing that will make the devil himself cower. Little wonder Charles shies from her bed."

"Little wonder he has gained the reputation as the Merry Monarch," Ameran remarked.

"A name no doubt given him by those who still adhere to the teachings of Cromwell and his Puritans," said Gray.

Ameran's smile was quick to fade. Her teeth clamped tight together. Cromwell . . . Puritans . . . She hated both with the same passion. Their lack of tolerance for anyone different from themselves was all the justification they needed for cold, brutal murder. Charles Stuart at his absolute worst could never possibly be as horrible as those madmen. It had been a great blessing for England when the "great protector" died!

Gray took hold of her arm. "What's wrong? You've suddenly gone quite pale."

"I'm fine. I just got lost in my thoughts for a moment."

Ameran braved a smile. Perhaps it would be best to tell him the whole story of her mother now rather than waiting until they reached England's shore. He would understand. He would trust her when she said she would not invoke evil powers to do her bidding. There mustn't ever be secrets between them.

"Gray, have you any recollection of the Great Plague?" she asked slowly, praying that she had made the right decision.

If Gray thought her inquiry strange, he made no mention of it.

"Aye, I remember it well." His countenance was dismal. "I was but a lad on the verge of manhood. I was sailing on the *Glorious* then. Against my parents' wishes, I had signed on as navigator's apprentice." He sadly shook his head as he remembered. "We were about to sail up the river, having completed our voyage to Tangiers, when the dockmaster rowed out to meet us and cautioned us to stay aboard." His voice softened. "My mother, my father, and my three sisters had all fallen victim to that scourge." Frowning, he rubbed his head as if to erase from inside the terrible recollections etched there. "Victims of the plague were piled twelve and fourteen high, carted out of town in the dark of the night, and thrown into one mammoth pit. Nightmares of the dead being carted out of town and thrown in a common grave sometimes still haunt my sleep."

Ameran pressed close to him. Knowing what she

81

knew about her mother's curses, she feared her beloved would turn against her.

Gray folded her tight in his arms. "Over seventy thousand lives were taken during that four-month period from May to September. Seventy thousand lives! It's hard to conceive so many dead. And all because of rats and filth and such abominable living conditions where no man nor beast could survive."

Tears streamed down her cheeks.

Gray wrapped his arms more snugly around her. "I didn't mean to make you sad." He kissed away her tears as quickly as they fell.

Ameran tried to smile. Dare she tell him the truth? Would he still love her if he knew that rats and filth were not the only culprits of that horrendous occurrence?

"Thank God for the Great Fire the following year," he said as he pulled her still closer. "Nothing short of another great catastrophe could bring an end to the stinking alleyways and disease-breeding hovels." His chin rested atop her head. "The greater part of London went up in smoke. More lives were lost and a great deal of property destroyed. Luckily, the remnants of the Plague went up in flames as well, and thanks to that inferno, London and her people once again began to thrive."

Ameran shivered in spite of the warm hands around her. Up until that very moment, she'd only dared to imagine the magnitude of her mother's evil doings. The damage was far greater than she'd ever thought possible. Seventy thousand lives . . . seventy thousand men, women, and children . . . little babies . . . all destroyed.

"It's truly remarkable that the King ever survived

those early years of his reign," Gray remarked as he settled them both beneath the covers. "The Plague, the fire, and there was always the constant threat of war from France, Spain, and Holland."

Ameran quivered in her lover's arms. Seventy thousand dead, and all because of her mother. Had it not been for her mother, Gray's own family might well still be alive.

Ameran began to cry. Gray kissed her tears before more could fall. "Let's not talk about this anymore."

Ameran reveled in his caresses a little longer before finally pulling away. Dark-lashed lids hid her emerald gaze from his eyes. She couldn't bear to look into those dark blue depths for fear of the revulsion she might find there at her story's end.

"Gray, there is something I can't keep from you any longer. I have to tell you, even though it may risk my losing you forever."

Gray tried to pull her back to him. "Nothing you could ever say would make me turn away from you."

She held him at arm's distance, her eyes dwelling on the wall behind him. She took a deep breath and began. And when her story had ended, she dared a quick look at him. The smile was gone from his lips, but his eyes bore no hate.

"I don't doubt the truth of what you say, or the sincerity of what you believe. It troubles me greatly that your heart is so burdened, but wicked though you may believe your mother to have been, she could not have possibly been responsible for such great disasters of nature."

He reached for her again, and again, she pulled away.

"All of my life, I have heard her rantings and ravings

of how she had called down every curse imaginable and inflicted it upon the man who had betrayed her. She loved him. He promised to make her his queen when he was restored to the throne, but he abandoned her, and he turned her love to hate."

This time, Gray would not let her escape his arms.

She could not relax in his embrace. "When word arrived that the King of England had taken the daughter of the King of Portugal as his bride and queen, Mama cursed the union and declared the Queen would be forever barren. And the King has no legitimate heirs to this day."

Gray's nod was solemn. "That's true, but it's no secret that the King spends more time bed-hopping between his mistresses' beds than he does in his wife's."

"It is no coincidence that the King has no heirs to succeed him," she said with firm conviction. "Mama willed it so."

His smile was kind and understanding. "I see I cannot convince you otherwise."

Ameran's sigh was hard and sad. She couldn't make him see the truth. "I just want you to know everything. I don't want to keep anything from you. I don't want anything to come between us ever again."

"Nothing will, I swear." He tenderly kissed her cheek.

"Mama swore that his reign would be plagued with problems and calamities which had no end." Her eyes searched his. "There've been assassination attempts on his life. Haven't there?"

"No more than any other ruler."

"There've been those of his blood who've plotted his death. Haven't there?" she asked quietly.

Gray's pose was pensive. "There have been rumors, but . . ."

"One of the curses Mama placed on your King was that a plot to assassinate him would be masterminded by his own son." She looked to him for an answer, and when Gray hesitated, she knew of the truth in the statement she had just made.

"Mama said that he would die on the twenty-ninth night of the month of May. He would die the same day he was born."

"Of what year?" he asked.

"That she didn't say, but I fear . . . I fear it will be soon." Finally, she allowed her body to relax into his. "She hated him, and she condemned him to miseries untold. Her heart was so filled with vengeance that there was no room for love, not even for her own child. But she was my mama. Her life gave me life, and as much as I've tried to despise her for her dark, evil ways, I can't."

"Your mother's gone now," Gray said kindly. "You have to put all the unhappiness of the past behind you."

"I can't. I just can't," she said softly. "A part of her will live on in me." Her body began to stiffen once again. "Like Mama, and her mother, and hers before her for centuries past, I was born with a caul, a thin shroud of skin covering my face, and like all those before me, I possess the power to soothe fire from burning flesh." She reminded him of how this strange power had for a while won her mother the gratitude of a man who would sit on England's throne. "I made use of that strange power only once, and the child who I saved ran from me in fear."

Gray bundled her closer still. "You're kind and

good. There's no evil lurking inside you, and I'll defend you to anyone who says differently." He sealed his pledge with a kiss. "You mustn't bear the shame of your mother's evil secrets and practices."

"My mother feared that you would take me away from her. That's why you were struck with that peculiar ailment on the day the *Fair Winds* set sail from France's shore. You recovered only when you reached England and no longer posed a threat to her."

Even though he didn't ask, there was something else she had to tell him before she looked beyond the past. "I don't follow my mother's practices of witchery and sorcery. I used to cover my ears when she tried to explain her evil secrets to me."

His lips brushed hers. "You're good, Ameran. You don't have one drop of evil in your blood. Please, I beg of you. Let the past stay in the past, and let's concentrate only on our future together."

Their future! Ameran threw her arms around him. Her flesh pressed tight to his. They would be together always! Nothing, no one, past or present, would ever divide them again. Not Mama, not the Duke of Caron, not Gideon, not Constance. Theirs was a love that would withstand all obstacles and defeat all foes.

Words that Gideon had once spoken in cruelty made the smile fade from her lips.

"You don't believe that I've bewitched you, do you?"

His strong body melted deeper into hers. "My beautiful, beautiful vixen. If I have indeed been bewitched by you, I pray I never escape the sweet spell you've woven."

"There's no escape," she whispered as her lips rained kisses down his chest. "You'll be mine forever."

"And you mine. Now that I've found you again,

you'll never be rid of me. That I promise!" After one last, hungry kiss Gray swung himself over her and out of bed. "Now, you get your rest while I go topside to insure I'm still in command of my ship."

Gray dressed quickly as Ameran's gaze lingered longingly on every part of his body.

"I'll send the cook down directly with some food. You must be famished after your ordeal." He smiled. "We have to keep you strong."

Gray started out the door, then two quick strides later he was kneeling beside her. Smiling, he brushed the hair from her cheek. "When I return later, there'll be no time for sleep. I daresay before dawn's first light you'll be pleading for mercy."

Smiling contentedly, Ameran languished back onto the bed. She reached for his hand and lay it upon her breast. "We shall see who pleads first for mercy, Lord Carlisle."

Chapter Five

Ameran sat up in bed with a pillow tucked between her back and the wall. Long, silken legs dangled over the edge of the wooden frame. The thick woolen blanket covering her slipped lower and lower onto full, luscious breasts.

Gray leaned over and kissed the rose-tipped nipples.

Ameran pulled his head to hers and kissed him. With a long, contented sigh, she fell back onto the pillows.

She couldn't stop smiling. It was all just too deliciously wonderful to be real. Finally, at long last, she was back in Gray's arms, back where she belonged. All misunderstandings that had kept them apart the past three years had been resolved. Gray was hers. She was his, and she couldn't be happier. It didn't matter how the King reacted to her presence, nor did it matter how she was received at Court by Constance or Gideon. All that mattered was that Gray loved her, and about that she had no doubts.

"I can't remember ever having eaten so much at one time," she said as she pushed away the platter of roasted lamb and potatoes and carrots that the *Fair Winds'* cook had prepared for their supper, this their second day of drifting upon the waters of the Channel separating France and England. She couldn't help but think of all the nights she had gone to bed hungry, or of the mornings she had awakened to the same need for food that had gone unfulfilled day after day. While Guido was alive, there had always been fresh fish on the table, but after his death, meals such as the one she had just indulged were scarce. But all of that had been left far behind her along with the torn rags she had left on the beach. From now on, her life would be filled with love and happiness.

She heard herself laughing out loud.

"What is it you find so amusing?" Gray asked as he dove beneath the covers and nibbled a piece of potato that had dropped onto her belly.

"I, a king's mistress. I've never heard anything so absurd," she answered, giggling as he nipped at her flesh.

Gray's expression sobered very quickly. "I didn't find it so very amusing."

"No, nor did I," she said, suddenly quite solemn. "Is that why your men viewed me with such contempt?"

"They feared any gift given King Charles by Louis. The English have grown weary of the French influence in their King's bed. Louis's last gift, Louise de Keroualle, possessed far more power over the King's actions than any minister of his Privy Council."

Gray's kisses were soft and tender. "I've had words with my crew, and I assure you that from now on they'll treat you with the courtesy and respect deserving a lady who is to wed their commander."

Ameran could hardly contain her joy. She was going to become his wife. At last! Just as he had promised three years before.

"Oh, Gray, I love you so very much," she said, throwing her arms around him. "You don't know how much."

"Aye, my darling. I think perhaps I do." He cupped her chin between his hands and gazed deep into the emerald depths of her eyes.

Ameran wrapped her legs tight around Gray's waist. "The love I see in your eyes is a reflection of the love I have for you. How you must have hated me when the King commanded you to come for me," she said softly, pulling him closer.

Gray shook his head. "I never hated you. Not for one moment. Oh, there were plenty of times when I wanted to. I prayed to, but the harder I tried, the more I remembered how beautiful you were, how much I loved you, and how much I longed to be with you." His sigh was heavy. "And then when I found your home still smoldering from the fires set by the villagers, I hated myself, for I knew that I alone was responsible for every second of suffering you had been forced to endure. Had you been consumed by those flames, I never would have forgiven myself. If I hadn't found you in the caves, there would have been no reason to go on living. I couldn't have lived with the knowledge that I had set those flames myself."

His muscles tensed and the flesh beneath his cheek's scar was drawn tighter.

Her hands kneaded the tension from his shoulders while her soft, willing lips soothed the worries from his brow.

"Shhh, my darling," she whispered. "We're together now. And we'll never be parted again."

His arms were tight around her. "No one will dare

try to separate us ever again. No one, I swear. If anyone is brave enough to try, then they'll live only long enough to regret their hateful deed."

"Never again will our hearts know the excruciating agony of the past three years," she vowed, tightening her limbs around him.

Gray ran his hand up the silken expanse of her leg. "I have a feeling that if we continue this joyous reunion of the past few days, there may soon be three of us this time next year."

Ameran felt herself pale. Her smile began to wilt, and she was powerless to make it stay.

Gray laughed. "Don't look so distraught, my love. It's but a fact of nature."

She suddenly felt very ill.

"Ameran, you look as though you have seen a ghost."

She tried to compose herself. "There's no ghost, but there is something in my past that will haunt me until the day I die." Her words were shaky. She had to tell him.

Gray held her hands to his face. "Tell me. Share your sorrow with me."

Tears streamed down her cheeks. "You mustn't hate me. I swear I wasn't to blame for what happened."

He kissed away her tears. "Blame you? Never. Hate you? I'd rather fall upon my sword and end my life."

Ameran tried to hold back the flow of tears. There was no way to deliver the news. She had agonized many long hours over the *petite bébé* whose cries she would never console. As her mama lay dying, she had finally found it in her heart to confess to the horrible deed.

"Your child—our child—once grew inside my

womb," she began suddenly. "But a deadly potion prepared by my mama ended the life of our little one before it had a chance to begin." She buried her face in the smoothness of his chest and began to sob. "I didn't know what I was drinking. Mama tricked me. Had I known . . ."

"Shhh, shhh." Gray comforted her with soft words and tender kisses. "My poor, poor darling."

"Mama is not to be hated. She's to be pitied," said Ameran between sobs. "Her mind was so twisted and tormented by hate and revenge. She would even destroy those who loved her the most."

She felt something warm and wet trickling down her cheek. Her tears had already been shed. Gray's were just beginning.

"We'll have many babies, my darling," she told him. "Many sons and daughters."

Gray tightened his hold on her. "The hell you had to endure was because of me. Can you ever forgive me?"

Smiling, Ameran wiped the tears from both their eyes. "Forgive you? There's nothing to forgive."

She pushed the table away from the bed.

"Your hunger's been satisfied?" asked Gray, a gleam in his stormy sea gaze.

"My need for nourishment has been fulfilled," she said as she traced the length of his jagged scar with the tip of her tongue. "My hunger for you will never be satisfied."

Laughing, Gray rolled her over and stretched out on top of her. "Then it is my duty, my lady, to see to it that you're deprived of nothing."

"How fortunate I am to be at the mercy of so gallant a gentleman."

His kisses ignited the flames smoldering inside her.

" 'Tis I who am the fortunate one," Gray said, smothering her with kisses hotter still.

Ameran pulled him deeper into her. "We're both fortunate, indeed."

Her breaths were short and deep. She pulled him closer. Having found him again, she could never face a life without him.

Early morning light streamed in through the tiny window above Gray's desk. Ameran awakened consumed with a horrible dread that the joys she had known the nights before had all been sleep-filled fantasies.

Her fears were short-lived. What had happened was real indeed. She was no longer hovering on the edge of death in the caves. She was safe aboard the *Fair Winds,* safe under the protection of her beloved. No one could harm her now or ever again.

Lovingly, she caressed the spot where her Gray had lain. Just the feel of the place where his flesh had been made her tingle. It was almost too good to believe that they were really together again after three years of yearning and despair.

Just when she was beginning to miss him and long once more for his tender embraces, Gray returned carrying a basket of hot, tiny bread loaves. Just the sight of him weakened her limbs. How handsome he looked in his uniform of dark blue, and gold buttons and braids.

"Good morning, my Lord Carlisle."

Gray put down the basket of bread and pulled her to her feet. "Good morning, my soon-to-be Lady Carlisle."

"You still have intentions of wedding me, sire?" she asked, a devilish gleam lighting up her emerald eyes. "After last night, and the night before that I . . ."

Gray silenced her with more kisses. "It was brought to my attention in the early hours of dawn, my beloved, that the sooner I wed you, the less likely you will be to escape my grip."

"I have no desire to escape." His kisses made her breathless. "I shall be your most willing prisoner, my lord."

"Nay, my love, 'tis I who am your prisoner." Gray picked her up and laid her back onto the bed. His eyes did a slow, intense study of the naked beauty before him. He knelt down beside her, his knees resting on the plank flooring. One hand held her head tight against his chest while the other explored the luscious curves before him. "Truly there is no man alive who is luckier than I."

Ameran began to loosen the ties of his shirt. "Let me show you just how lucky you truly are."

Laughing, Gray pinned her arms over her head and held her tight. "There'll be time for that later. For now, there's much to do in preparation for our arrival at London Harbor."

She knew her eyes betrayed her disappointment.

Gray sat down on the edge of the narrow bed. "Believe me when I say there is nothing I'd like more than to drift over the channel for another few days, but there's nothing we can do here that we can't do at Whitehall, and I assure you the surroundings are far more luxurious and befitting."

"I don't need luxury, Gray. I need you."

"You have me." Gray released her hands. "Just as I have you. That's the way it will be from this time forward." He kissed each finger, then held her hand to his cheek. "There are important matters at Court which I'm quite anxious to resolve."

Ameran knew Gray was eager for a confrontation with his friend. Gideon Horne! If she never set eyes on him again, it would be too soon. The Gideon Horne she had encountered three years before was cruel and conniving. She'd seen a side of him that she was certain he had kept well concealed from Gray, and the reason for Gideon's deception troubled her greatly.

"Forget about Gideon," she begged, holding him tight. "All that matters is that we've found each other in spite of the obstacles and adversities placed in our way. Forget about Gideon, please."

"I can't dismiss his betrayal, Ameran. Nor can I forgive him. Past years of friendship demand I permit him the opportunity to defend himself when confronted with his vile act."

She could barely speak. "But I'm afraid for your life. The Gideon Horne you know may be loyal and devoted, but the one I met is dangerous."

"Don't worry, Ameran. We'll have no further problems from my second in command."

Ameran dropped her gaze. She knew it would do no good to argue with him. Gideon *was* dangerous.

Gray shook his head sadly. "There've been many things about Gideon that have come to light as of late, things which I don't like. I prayed that my misgivings were unfounded, but now, with what you have told me, I've begun to wonder if perhaps . . ."

His sigh was heavy into her hair. "No, it can't be. There must be a cause, a good one, for this misunderstanding."

Not even Gray's arms around her could quell the

fear in the pit of her stomach. What could she say that would convince him that friends turned foes made for the most despicable of enemies? How could she tell him that which she knew only too well to be true?

Gray's lips sought hers and she gave way to the sweet kiss as the flames of passion were fired once more.

A little later, Gray laughed and pulled back. "Enough, my lovely vixen!" Playfully, he gave her leg a slap. "We'll be arriving soon and I want you standing on the bow of the *Fair Winds* alongside me when we sail up the river into London Harbor."

Ameran beckoned him closer once again, and once again he could not refuse her anything.

When the time came for Ameran to stand on the bow beside Gray, she could sense his pride at having her there at his side. She'd known from the very moment he had walked into his quarters and found her attired in one of the gowns from the trunk that he was in awe of what he saw before him. She had chosen for their arrival a delicate muslin gown and shawl a spectacular shade of emerald green. The gown was cut low on her shoulders with a collar of embroidered lace delicately covering the rise of her breasts. She had brushed her hair over and over with the ivory-handled brush that she had also found packed in the trunk. Her long, dark curls fell almost to her waist and were pushed back from her face with a band of braided brocade woven with all the colors of the rainbow.

Ameran held tight to Gray's arm. Every few minutes, she glanced up and saw his handsome face smiling down at her. He had told her that she was a treasure more precious than any he could ever hope to find. His men looked at her differently now. Their stares were not bold or hateful. Their eyes now held respect. Heads bowed in reverence when she passed by. Those who did dare to lift their eyes had acknowledged her presence with quiet smiles.

Ameran looked down into the blue-black waters churning beneath them. The waves seemed to part as the ship plowed through them under the power of its full sails and the wind behind them. She still couldn't believe this was all happening. Still she feared that any moment, she would awaken and find herself deep in the bowels of the caves, or at the mercies of the evil Duke of Caron and those whose murdering hatred he had incited.

She felt herself shiver at the thought of what might have been her fate at the hands of the bloodthirsty mob had she not escaped.

Gray put his arms around her. "If you're cold, my love, I could send below for another wrap."

"No, I'm not cold." She held tight to his arms. "I've never been happier. That's why I'm trembling."

Gray squeezed her tighter. His eyes centered on the gentle slope of her breasts. "Something's not quite right."

Her heart sank. She had so wanted to please him. Her disappointment lasted but a moment.

Gray slipped his gold chain from around his neck and onto hers. The jeweled cross fell between her breasts.

"There. Now all is perfect," he said with satisfaction.

Ameran caressed the cross. A tear formed in her eye. She remembered the day Gray had given it to her three years before, and she remembered just as vividly how Gideon had so cruelly snatched it away.

Gray kissed the tear before it could fall. It was as though he knew her thoughts. "Gideon will pay. I promise. He'll pay for the grief he's caused us."

Ameran didn't trust herself to speak for fear she would burst into tears. She didn't want revenge or restitution. All she wanted was for Gideon never to cross her path again.

The heavy clouds of fog surrounding the *Fair Winds* began to lift.

Gray pointed ahead to the coast line that was coming into view through the haze. "We're almost home."

"Home," she softly echoed. "Home." France had been the country of her birth, yet she had been a stranger there. Many were the times when she had looked to England for her future. It didn't matter whether or not the King showed her any kindness. Home was the place she would spend the rest of her days with Gray.

Gray patted the hand clinging tight to his arm. "Have no fear, my love. I intend to do all in my power to insure your comfort and happiness forevermore."

Ameran threw her arms around him. "You're too kind to me."

"Nay, my darling, I haven't begun to show the magnitude of my love for you," he said solemnly.

Smiling, Ameran looked on ahead to the outline of trees and buildings in their path. Then her smile began to fade and she squinted into the haze. A small boat with a sail unfurled was coming out to meet them.

Gray saw it coming the same time as she. "Mr. Rogers," he called out to his navigator. "There's a boat coming out to meet us."

"Aye, Captain. I have it in my sight already," came the loud reply from behind them.

Ameran stood motionless as she watched the boat

move closer and closer. There were two men rowing and a third standing between them waving to the *Fair Winds*. She could see by the strong set of Gray's jaw that he knew the identity of the welcoming party.

Even before she would see the face of the man standing, she knew that her worst fears were about to come true. In a few moments, she could once again come face to face with Gideon Horne, and she feared no man the way she feared him. No enemy could pose a greater threat than one who came in the guise of friendship.

She only hoped Gray would not let the loyalty of past days blind him.

Chapter Six

Ameran watched with dread as Gideon scaled the rope ladder up the starboard side of the ship.

"Don't worry, my love," Gray told her, his hand holding hers tightly. "You have nothing to fear from anyone, not ever again."

Ameran gave a weak smile. Gray didn't give his friend the credit due him.

Gideon jumped down onto the deck and strode quickly toward Gray. "Hello, Gray," he called out in a friendly voice. "I'm most anxious to see this latest gift from France. I would have been happy to have accompanied you on this mission if you'd asked."

Ameran refused to cower behind Gray a moment longer. She met Gideon's hateful glower head on and didn't flinch from his cold, cruel eyes.

Gideon looked as if he had just come face to face with a ghost. "Is she the gift from the King of France? Surely there's been some mistake."

"Yes, a mistake that will soon be corrected." Gray didn't return his old friend's perplexed smile. He turned to one of his officers behind him. "Mr. Forrester, see to it that we're not disturbed. Lower the sails and drop anchor. It's not time yet to sail up the river home."

Mr. Forrester, a tall, lanky man who wore a patch over his right eye, saluted. "Aye, sir."

Gideon's smile was not a comfortable one.

As he motioned Gideon on ahead and down to the captain's quarters below, Gray's face still bore the same, solemn expression.

Ameran cut her eyes to Gideon only once during the walk down the long corridor to Gray's room. There was no mistaking the hate burning in his blue, conniving glare.

"I know why you're angry and you're well justified for such wrath; however, you have to permit me the opportunity to defend myself." Gideon's eyes settled once again on the jewel encrusted cross around Ameran's neck.

As Gray closed the door behind them, Gideon slumped into the closest chair. Meanwhile, Ameran slipped into the shadows to escape Gideon's venomous scrutiny.

"I don't want any lies," Gray told him simply.

Ameran had no doubt Gideon was going to lie, even before he offered his defense. He might have given the appearance of a man defeated, a man who would break down and tell the truth now that he was cornered, but Ameran knew his humble demeanor was only a ploy.

The scar along Gray's cheek deepened. "You lied to me three years ago. Why did you betray my trust in you? Before you say one word, let me caution you against explaining your actions with any more untruths."

Gideon gave a resigned nod. "You're right. I did lie, but I didn't do so without good cause."

Gray stood over him. "What good cause was that?"

"I had heard rumors in the village that she . . ."

"Her name is Ameran, Ameran Michol," interrupted Gray, his jaw still clenched.

Gideon began again with a meek nod. "I'd heard rumors in the village that Ameran was a witch, and that she and her mother had been responsible for many sailors' deaths." Gideon rubbed both sides of his forehead. His look was the submissive look of one who had been caught in his wrongdoing. "I didn't want you to fall victim to their dark, evil trap. I didn't want you to be lured to your death."

Ameran studied Gray's expression. It remained unchanged.

"You lied to me, Gideon. You deliberately lied to me. There's no excuse for deception." Gray's solemn countenance remained unchanged.

Gideon bowed his head. "I did lie to you. I did. I won't try to convince you otherwise. And for those lies I'm truly ashamed." He lifted his head slowly and his gaze sought Gray's.

Ameran could hear his words even before he spoke them.

"But before you condemn me for my actions, you first have to understand my motives." He stood to face his accuser. "I love you like a brother. I didn't want to deceive you, but it was the only way to guarantee that you depart Mer alive." He looked to Gray for some response, and when he saw none, he continued. "I had heard tales of how Ameran and her mother would conjure up mammoth waves that would suck an entire ship's crew into their watery graves." His stare didn't waver from Gray's. "I had an obligation to you, and I also had a responsibility to the *Fair Winds*. I couldn't take the risk of having my ship or its commander put in jeopardy, and if I was wrong, then so be it." He bowed his head once more. "I'll gladly take any punishment you choose to administer to me, for in my heart, I know that what I did was right, and if I had it all to do over again, I would repeat my actions."

Ameran couldn't bear to hear another lie. She stepped out from the shadows beside the bed. "You told me Gray didn't love me. You told me he was betrothed to another," she said as she closed the gap between them with three short strides. "You told me he never wanted to set his eyes on my face ever again. Is this what one would say to a witch? A witch who has the power to destroy a ship full of men?" She shook her head. "I don't think so, Gideon Horne."

Gideon reached out for her, but Ameran shrank from his touch.

"I was a desperate man," he told her. "I would have said anything to protect the man to whom I had sworn loyalty and brotherhood. I see now that I have needlessly hurt you both, and I beg your forgiveness."

Ameran turned away from his lying eyes. She could only hope that Gray saw Gideon for what he really was — a threat to them both.

Gideon turned to Gray once more. His words were as humble as his downcast expression. "It's as I said. I swear. I did what I did not out of malice, but out of love."

Ameran could sense Gray was about to weaken, but there was nothing she could do.

"You don't realize how serious your lies were. The fact that they were told with good intentions does nothing to lessen their blow."

Gideon's smile was one of submission. "Do what you have to do."

Gray let out a long, troubled sigh. He paced back and forth across the room debating what had to be done and trying to resolve the conflict within himself.

Ameran studied one man, then the other. Gideon was even more dangerous than she'd thought. Had she not been victim to his cruelty, she, herself, might have been swayed by his skillful lies. She looked to Gray. The hard set of his jaw was starting to relax, and his eyes bore no anger, only fatigue from the ordeal of confronting his old friend. He'd been taken in by Gideon's false declarations of loyalty and devotion. It was just as she had feared. Gideon had won.

Then Gideon reached for the dagger on top of Gray's desk.

Ameran gasped. Surely he wasn't going to kill Gray. Then she realized her fear was unfounded. Gideon was perhaps even more clever than she thought.

Gideon held the knife in both hands, the blade resting on his right, the ivory handle on his left palm, offering to Gray with much solemnity, as if they were participants in some grand ceremony. "If you believe my intentions less than honorable, then I beg you. Put an end to my suffering here and now. I can't bear to have you look upon me with shame and distrust."

Gray took the knife and put it back where it had been. "I couldn't plunge that knife into you any more than you could plunge it into me," he said.

A few moments later, Gray looked to Ameran.

She nodded and smiled. He could have done nothing else. Gideon had escaped his day of reckoning this time, but she knew Gray would never forget. He might forgive, but he would not forget. As for herself, she would not do either.

"You won't lie to me again." Gray didn't ask a question; he stated a fact.

Gideon clasped Gray's arm. "I'll never incur your wrath again. I swear." Then he turned to Ameran and dropped down onto one knee in front of her. "You have every right to hate me. I've greatly wronged you. I don't dare ask for your forgiveness, but I do ask that you permit me the opportunity to redeem myself in your eyes."

She knew he could see the distrust in her eyes, just as she could see the lies in his.

"Let me earn your trust," he entreated.

Ameran stood proud, eyes unblinking. Never had there been a more formidable foe than Gideon as a friend. "As you wish," she said softly.

Gideon kissed her hand. "You won't regret showing me kindness that I don't deserve. I'm not the horrible ogre you met on the shore that cold morning three years ago." He rose slowly, then took both their arms in his hands. "I'll prove myself worthy of you if it takes me the rest of my days," he told them.

Gray's face bore a relieved smile.

Ameran dropped her gaze, knowing in her heart that at that very moment, behind his friendly face, Gideon was plotting and scheming—contriving a plan that would only cause destruction and despair. If only Gray had seen the Gideon she had seen, he wouldn't be so quick to forgive.

"What of the happenings at Whitehall?" asked Gray as he poured three glasses of port. "Is everything the same since I left?"

"The King's taken ill again," Gideon said between

gulps. "He still fancies himself a young man and spent the morning before last playing tennis, hawking in the afternoon, then later in the day dove into the Thames. One of the guards had to drag him from the water. He became very unsettled and fevered, and then collapsed."

"The physicians are certain his malady was brought on by fatigue?"

Ameran detected a note of suspicion in Gray's tone.

Gideon laughed. "The King is determined to live up to his reputation."

Gray's expression was distraught.

"Don't look so grave, my friend," said Gideon jovially. "A few days rest, and the King will once again be climbing the wall at Saint James for yet another assignation with a nobleman's wife or daughter."

Ameran sat down in Gray's desk chair, the glass of port she held to her lips. But she did not sip from it. She was uncomfortably aware of Gideon's searing glances every time Gray's back was turned, and she couldn't help but wonder, and fear, the evil thoughts lurking inside his cruel mind.

"I trust your sailing to Wales was an uneventful one," said Gray to Gideon.

Gideon stretched out his legs and rested his black-booted feet atop the trunkful of clothes the King had sent to Ameran. "The Duke of Monmouth didn't go without objections. The King attempted to placate him by sending the Duke of York to Scotland, but everyone knows that was just a ploy. He'll recall his brother back to England in a short time and no doubt leave poor Jemmy to rot in Wales." Gideon shrugged his shoulders. "Of course, it's to your advantage the

Duke of York remain in Scotland. As long as he's there, your post as Royal Commander of the Navy is secure."

"It's not a post of my choosing, Gideon. You know that as well as I."

Gideon lifted his glass to Gray. "Aye, my friend, but you know as well as I that you're far more compatible than he to that assignment." Gideon swung his legs back down onto the floor. "So tell me, where's the *mademoiselle* Louis has sent to sway Charles against the Dutch?" He gave a long wink. "I should like to see for myself if she's worth another war."

Gray didn't share in his humor. "There is no gift."

Ameran kept silent. She wanted no exchange of pleasantries with Gideon. It was difficult enough being in the same room as he.

Gideon's eyes narrowed into slits. "No gift? Then why were you sent to France? Or is that another secret shared by you and our King?"

Ameran could not mistake the bitterness in his tone. She wondered if Gray had detected it as well. He had. She could tell after only a glance in his direction. But he said nothing.

Gideon looked from Gray to Ameran, then back to Gray again and laughed. "Your post might not be as secure as you think, Lord Admiral, if your intentions are to keep the royal peace offering to yourself."

"There is no royal peace offering," said Gray, his words firm and deliberate.

Gideon's pale brows knotted together in deep meditation. "The King sent you for Ameran. Of course, that's it. Your meeting after three years wasn't chance. The King sent you to fetch her. But why?"

"It's not my place to question commands." His face

softened when he cast his eyes on Ameran. "Just be grateful whatever the reasons."

Ameran's cold reserve melted under Gray's loving gaze. She could tell Gideon wasn't satisfied with the answers given him. She had a feeling there hadn't been much Gray had kept secret from his old friend.

Gideon stood up quickly. "No matter the reason. Fate has decreed that the two of you find each other again, and that's all that matters."

Gray took Ameran's hand firmly. "Indeed, that's all that matters, and woe to anyone who ever tries to come between us."

Ameran watched Gideon closely. If he thought the warning was directed to him, he gave no indication.

"No one will dare try. I promise you that," Gideon said as he walked over to Ameran. "I don't expect to be forgiven for the anguish and misery I've caused you. You hate me now, and with good cause, but one day you'll look upon me as a trustworthy friend. I would lay down my life for Gray, and I would do no less for you, my lady. I shall pray for such an opportunity." He gave a low bow, then reached for her hand and brought it to his lips. "I shall depart the *Fair Winds* now and make preparations for your arrival at Court. A carriage will be waiting at the harbor," he told Gray. "I'll see you at Whitehall before dusk."

Ameran wiped her hand across the hem of her gown. Did Gideon take her for a fool? Didn't he realize that she could see straight through his theatrics? How glibly he spoke of honor, trust, and loyalty, those virtues which she was certain he lacked. She prayed Gray hadn't been duped by his fine speeches.

Gray leaned down and kissed her cheek. "No reasons for the furrows of your brow. We have nothing to

108

fear from Gideon. He doesn't dare cross me. The consequences would be far too great if he did."

"You didn't believe him when he said he was protecting you from a witch's curse, did you?"

When Gray didn't answer her question at once, she knew her most dreaded fear had been realized. "Gray, you didn't believe him, did you?" she asked again.

"What he says is possible, I suppose," answered Gray thoughtfully. "If his intentions weren't as he professes, then I'll learn the truth soon enough."

"I don't trust him. Promise me you'll be wary of him. He's not the man he presents to you."

Gray tried to soothe her fears with kisses and caresses. "If I thought for an instant he intended any harm to you, he would never have left this ship alive."

Gray's warm embrace did little to soothe the shivering beneath her flesh. Gideon's words flowed like honey from his mouth, but his tongue was that of a viper. Like a viper, his bite would be deadly, she thought, still troubled.

Gray squeezed her closer. "You'll see, Ameran. Gideon won't cause us any grief. I'll bet one day you will find him quite charming."

Ameran shook her head. "Such a time will never come."

His eyes met hers. "His actions were wrong. I won't argue with that; however, it is possible that like any good sailor, he may well have had the best interests of his crew and commander at heart."

"So he says," she mumbled.

"He'll pay if I discover otherwise," Gray assured her.

Ameran said nothing. Gray was wrong. Gideon was a dangerous liar.

For the moment, Gideon left her thoughts, and she wondered how the King would receive her. Would he see Sybil Chandler in her? Would he see a witch intent on damning and tormenting him? Why had he answered her pleas for help? Thank God he had. She might have gone to the grave without ever knowing the real reason why Gray had abandoned her.

Ameran strained to see through the haze. "There's so much fog settled on the water."

"Most of it isn't mist, but soot," Gray explained. "Soap boilers, dyers, brewers, they all use coal from Newcastle in their industries," said Gray sadly. "The government can't discourage the use of coal because of the enormous revenues they receive from its importation."

The *Fair Winds* seemed to part the haze, and more of the port came into view. The shape of the city along the Thames rose out of the thick clouds. With its towers and spires piercing the sky, London looked like a romantic, fairy-tale town.

Ameran smiled. At last she was coming home, home to a country on whose soil she had never before set foot.

Boats and barges, some large, some small, passed alongside them, their passengers waving and yelling to the crew of the *Fair Winds,* the sovereign of the seas. Its commander was greeted as a returning hero.

Gray pointed ahead to the huge timbered bridge under whose turrets and crowning cupolas they would soon pass. "The top of the bridge gate used to be decorated with heads of traitors stuck on poles as a warning to any plotter daring to enter the city."

"I can't think of a better deterrent to anyone foolish enough to entertain thoughts of treason," she said, peering closer up at it as the ship glided under the bridge.

"This is the only bridge in all of the city," Gray told her. "Years back, another was proposed to connect Westminister and Lambeth, but the King opposed it."

"Why would he do that?"

Gray laughed. "Because the City Council bribed him with one hundred thousand pounds. You see, London has prospered because of the Thames and the good councilors didn't want to share that prosperity. More than a third of England's trade tonnage enters through this port."

"If that's the case, then I'd say the Council's money was well spent."

"Indeed," agreed Gray. He pointed to a monument surrounded by scaffolding on which a dozen men stood chiseling into the stone. "That statue is in honor of King Charles as founder of the new city, the city after the plague and fire. The King is holding out his hands as though he's protecting the city from further calamities and catastrophes."

Ameran said nothing. No matter how hard Gray tried to convince her otherwise, she knew her mother was to blame for the tragedies of nature suffered upon the city.

Ameran suddenly wrinkled her nose as foul smells assaulted them from all directions.

"The river isn't just the gateway to the city," said Gray wryly. "It's also the main dumping ground for trash and refuse from every ship tied up along the dock as well as every house and business place in the city."

Ameran cringed. More filth. More pestilence. More diseases. She wondered if her mother's thirst for revenge had yet been quenched, or would she perhaps reach out from beyond and contrive still more disasters?

Several ships nearly the size of the *Fair Winds* were tied along the wharves. Their crews were busy unloading cargos, which Gray pointed out, would be stored in the many warehouses bordering both sides of the harbor.

Gray bent over and kissed her cheek. "Is it as you imagined?"

"Far grander." Tears of joy dotted her cheeks, tears that Gray brushed away with the cuff of his sleeve.

"I still can't believe this has all come to pass," she said.

"I assure you that what's happening to you at this moment is very, very real. Your nights of seeking refuge from murderers in a cold, damp cave are over. You'll never again have to endure the likes of the Duke of Caron and his evil men."

Ameran pressed her cheek to his chest. "I wasn't thinking how fortunate I am to have escaped life as I knew it." She let out a long sigh of contentment. "My good fortune is that I've found you. Promise me you'll always love me just as much as you do now."

Gray shook his head. "I can't promise you that," he said with a sly smile. "You see, yesterday I thought I loved you as much as my heart would allow, and yet I awakened this morning to find I love you even more. So you see, I can't make such a promise knowing it will be broken." He sealed the pledge with a sweet kiss. "Come, Ameran Michol, daughter of the King of England. Your country awaits you."

After the *Fair Winds* had dropped anchor and docked, and its commander had given orders to be carried out in his absence, Ameran and Gray strolled along the wharf hand in hand.

At first, she was timid. What if someone saw the striking resemblance she bore to the Sybil Chandler of over twenty years before, and called out for the witch to be hanged?

But no one made such accusations, and soon she began to relax and enjoy the sights and sounds of the riverfront.

Ameran took in a deep breath of the salty air. She loved the smell of the sea even if it was laced with a few other pungent aromas as well. Nothing could mar her happiness, not even the odor of spoiled fish and rotting vegetables or the garbage floating atop the water. The air smelled sweetly of freedom, her freedom, and there was no smell more pleasantly fragrant to one who had been held captive by cruelty and hatred for so long. Thanks to the man who had betrayed and abandoned her mother long ago, she had been given the hope for a new life, an existence without fear. But most of all, she was grateful to England's monarch for giving back to her the man she loved.

Street peddlers hawked their wares in loud, sing-song voices. Toothless old women poked trays of smoked herring in front of them. Fishermen stood at their nets pointing out the choice prizes of their day's catch. Vendors in stalls along the riverfront displayed silks from the Orient, teas from Ceylon, and sugar-cane from the Jamaican islands. Children, barefoot and ragged, ran in and out of the crowd begging for coins.

A carriage was waiting for them just as Gideon had promised. Ameran was relieved when the driver told them that Captain Horne had gone on ahead. Soon the two of them were in the plush, velvet cushions, and the hooves of the four black steeds were clopping rhythmically on the cobblestones.

"We'll go to Whitehall," Gray told her as he squeezed her close to him. "I'll take you on a grand tour of the city later. The King insisted you be brought to him immediately."

The smile lighting up her eyes began to dim. If the King did in fact live up to his reputation, then he was no doubt responsible for a great many offspring. Why should her fate be of any consequence to him, and why would he send the commander of his Royal Navy on a mission to bring her to him?

It wasn't until Gray's voice ceased in midsentence that she realized she was lost in her own reverie.

"I'm sorry," she said. "I'm just so overwhelmed by it all. It's as though my thoughts are all jumbled inside my head."

Gray laughed. "Just as long as I'm not boring you."

"Never, my love. Never."

Ameran snuggled down close beside him and listened as he pointed out the sights along the route to Whitehall.

Most of the city was a maze of narrow streets and alleys where barrows, carriages, carts, and sedan chairs squeezed past each other. Along the way, there was a jumble of timber and stone houses and an occasion bell tower of the parish churches.

Never had she seen so many people. Atop the roofs, out on narrow balconies, hanging from the windows, milling through the streets. Seven hundred thousand inhabitants in the city alone, according to Gray. How easy it must have been for the plague to have swept through an entire city with so many people living together in such crowded surroundings. The buildings were so close they looked to be one on top of the other. It was hard to tell where one ended and another began. And the Great Fire! Little wonder it had spread its devastation and ruin so quickly.

Gray pointed out newer buildings that had been constructed of stone and brick, that raging inferno would never be repeated.

The streets slowly began to open up into wider passageways. Gray directed her attention to the river where barges and ferries packed with passengers, horses, and carts were floating upriver.

Ameran lay her head down on Gray's shoulder and closed her eyes. The click-click-clicking across the cobblestones lulled her into a peaceful repose.

When she opened her eyes a while later, the Royal Palace of Whitehall, with its spires and arches and balconies, was in front of her.

Gray pointed out the Banqueting Hall in the background and told her how it was a supreme masterpiece of architectural design conceived by a man named Indigo Jones. Its main facades bore row after row of tall windows, carved decorations, and pilasters in classical styles.

"It was built to glorify the House of Stuart," explained Gray. "The great Flemish painter, Rubens, painted magnificent murals on the ceiling for the present King's father."

Standing sentry in front of Whitehall was a regiment of guards boasting defensive armor with cuirasses and iron headpieces. Swords hung from their sides, and short carbines and pistols were slung over their shoulders. A second regiment of guards patrolled the grounds atop prancing white steeds with braided manes and tails.

The two guards standing at the entranceway of the grand palace saluted, parted, and ushered them through a maze of white pilasters.

The double oaken door to the castle swung open to reveal a hallway with floors of white marble and inlaid gold designs. Tapestries of richly woven colors, bearing the Stuart family's coat of arms, curtained the walls to their right.

Inside, ladies in full skirts (caught back to show exquisitely embroidered petticoats underneath) strolled through the great foyer on the arms of gentlemen in full breeches and wide cloaks.

Ameran was aware of the subtle glances cast her way, but told herself such looks stemmed not from recognition but curiosity.

Gray pointed out the various rooms, the throne room, the meeting rooms, the dining hall and the library and map rooms, as well as the residences of the lesser nobles. "The royal residences and those of the King's close advisors and councilors occupy the upper floors." He held out his arm. "And now, allow me to escort you to His Majesty."

Her knees were weak. She looked with dread upon the meeting with the grand man who had sired her. No matter what his reason for giving her refuge, she owed the King a tremendous debt of gratitude.

Two guards, also with iron headpieces and cuirasses, stood tall and erect on every sixth step of the ornately carved staircase.

"That is the first Charles Stuart," remarked Gray as they came face to face with a portrait of a man in a purple plumed hat standing beside a golden steed with a long flowing mane and tail braided with red ribbons.

Ameran paused for a closer look at the man whose ancestors she shared. The first Charles Stuart was curiously handsome, with a short, pointed beard and dark moustache. His hair fell in waves and ringlets around his shoulders. His eyes were weak, and his countenance lacked the strength of a powerful sovereign.

When Gray told her the life of the present King's father had come to an abrupt end on the scaffold, Ameran reached for her own neck, for such might well have been her own fate had she not escaped France.

"From all accounts, Charles the First met his fate with far more dignity and decorum than he ever displayed in life. So striking was his countenance as he stood patiently atop the scaffold that it inspired the poet Andrew Marvell to write: 'He nothing common did, or men upon that memorable scene, but bowed his stately head down as upon a bed.' " Gray moved slowly on. "Even his enemies viewed him with respect on that fateful morn."

They walked along in silence viewing more of the royal faces whose portraits lined the corridor's walls.

"The King's chambers are just ahead," Gray told her.

Her steps grew slower and smaller. More and more courage had to be summoned with each one taken. It was of little consequence she was about to come face to face with the man who sired her. What was most frightening was that she was about to stand in the presence of a King. That King had rescued her from death. For what reason she could only guess.

It was as though Gray could sense her apprehen-

117

sion. "The King is no loathsome creature," he said, his voice quiet and soothing. "You'll find him most agreeable. England may well have had shrewder regents, but she's never had one quite so charming."

Ameran tried to dwell on the stories Gray was recounting to her about the rest of the dour-faced monarchs and plump ladies with shy smiles and weighty jewels, but her thoughts did not waver long from the man whom she was about to meet. Perhaps he had at last grown weary of her mother's damnations and had called her there to put a final end to it all.

A pair of guards stood with swords crossed in front of a massive door engraved with laurel leaves. Their swords parted, and one of them opened the door to reveal yet another dozen guards standing at attention.

"Ready?" Gray asked.

Ameran's nod was reluctant. She collected her bearing and summoned her courage. She owed the King her gratitude. When that debt had been paid she could go on with her life, a life filled with love and hope, to be shared with Gray.

Chapter Seven

Ameran was certain her legs would buckle beneath her at any moment. Her feet were numb. They wouldn't willingly step one in front of the other.

Gray looked down at her and smiled. "Don't worry. I'm by your side."

His words gave her the courage to press on. As long as he was at her side, she had no cause to fear any man.

In the center of the room was a big, upholstered bed with oak cornices and elaborate valances. Velvet drapes secured with gold braids hung down from the canopy. Atop the bed were more dogs than she could count. All were of different shapes and sizes, but all possessed the same black and white coloring and long, silken ears. Some of the dogs were asleep, some whelping their young, and still others were playing and running across the bed, nipping and yelping at whatever hand or pillow got in their way.

Hovering around the bed were white robed men who were shaking their solemn heads and muttering in hushed voices.

A loud, boisterous voice blared through the somberness. "Od's fish!"

Ameran jumped.

Gray patted her arm and urged her on with a smile and a gentle nudge.

"Be gone with you. All of you! Out, I say! Out!"

There was a loud cough which followed and more hushed mutterings.

The dogs leapt from the bed. A soft word from their master brought them back.

"I've had my fill of your poking and your abominable prodding. I am a king! What I am not is a bull to be baited. I'm sick to death of your foultasting elixers and blistering agents that would kill a healthy man. There'll be no more emetics! There'll be no more clysters of purgatives. No more spirits distilled from human skulls. I won't tolerate anymore hot irons to my head. Do you hear me?" he roared.

There was dead silence.

"Od's fish! Your maddening behavior convinces me I'm truly the only sane man in a society of lunatics! Well, have you nothing to say for yourselves?"

"But Your Majesty," one spoke up timidly.

The King's look was fiercely challenging. "And if you try to bleed me one more time, I will slit each and every one of your throats."

The King began to cough again.

"You're not well, sire," came another shy voice. "You must trust us to know what is best for you."

"What is best for me?" came another roar. "Ha! That is for me to decide! Od's fish! My would-be

120

assassins have not caused me so much agony and pain." He waved his arms at them all. "Out! Now! Before I have you all locked in the Tower. Out!" he yelled. "Out! Out! Out!"

The bevy of physicians dispersed quickly.

"England is in no danger of losing her ruler to this bout of the fevers," chuckled Gray.

Ameran could not help but form a slight smile. The man sitting up in bed looked little like a King, with his headful of dark, disheveled curls and a night dress that bore stains of the previous evening's supper. Even so, he wasn't unpleasant to look at, with his swarthy complexion and bold chin.

It was then that Ameran noticed the woman sitting in a tall, velvet chair in the shadows of a large armoire. Her hair was pulled back from her face, making her plump features even more severe. In one hand she held a Bible, and in the other a string of rosary beads.

Ameran was wondering who the woman was when the King directed his wrath to her.

"You, too, Catherine," bellowed the king. "I've had enough of your tears and prayers for one day. I'm not on my deathbed in spite of my enemies' wishes."

"That is the Queen?" Ameran whispered.

Gray nodded. "Formidable as ever." He bowed politely as the Queen waddled past.

The Queen spoke not a word, but her steel cold eyes cut right through Ameran.

"Lord Carlisle, come closer. Cheer me up," called out the King, beckoning them closer with a wave of his hand.

Ameran lagged a few steps behind as they approached the bed.

"I daresay the mourners at my funeral will be more cheerful than those who tend to my health." He struggled to sit up in bed. His smile weakened. "I knew I could depend on you to carry out my orders with success."

Gray gave a solemn nod as the King turned his attention to Ameran.

She gave a bow, her eyes meeting his with a stare just as curious.

"What's her name?" he asked Gray, his eyes still intent on her.

"Ameran Michol, sire."

The King sucked in his breath. He shook his head as if he could not believe what he was seeing. "There is no doubt," he said, after the longest while. "She is most certainly the daughter of Sybil Chandler. Hair as black as a raven's and eyes that would bring a king to his knees."

Ameran's dark lashes fanned her cheeks beneath his close scrutiny. Had he seen her mother in her later years, his memories of Sybil Chandler would not be so flattering.

"Where did you find her?" the King asked Gray.

"In a cave, Your Majesty." Gray took a step forward. "The villagers had tried to burn her alive by setting her home on fire."

The King's sigh was heavy as he slumped back down onto the pillows. "So she practices her mother's evil, does she?"

Ameran could stand it no longer. She refused to be conversed about as if she weren't there.

"No, Your Majesty, I most certainly do not follow in the evil ways of my mother." She stepped closer. She would cower to no man.

"She's not a witch, Your Majesty." Gray took hold of her arm. "Her soul is pure. Her heart bears no ill will. I'll attest to that."

A slight smile crossed the King's lips. "You speak as if you know her well."

"I do, sire. We first met three years ago when I was in France. Then, for reasons not of our own making, we were separated." His arms closed protectively around her shoulders. "Had it not been for your command, she would have been lost to me forever."

"So you know she is not a gift from the King of France?" He lay back down onto the mountain of satin behind him.

Gray nodded. "I know, sire, and I am most relieved."

The King centered his gaze on the jeweled cross hanging from Ameran's neck. "I doubt the good Duchess of Morrow will rejoice in your good fortune."

Gray did not share in the King's humor.

"One of Louis's spies at Court is enough," announced the King with a frown. "I don't think I could manage another in my bed."

From earlier discussions with Gray, Ameran knew the King was referring to a Frenchwoman named Louise de Kerouelle who had been the closest confidante of his favorite sister, Minette. Minette had been the favorite of all Louis' paramours, and when she died a rather untimely death which many thought had been brought about by her jealous husband, Louis sent Louise to England to console Charles. According to Gray, Louise's task was to keep the Sun King informed of Charles's affairs of state in return for a substantial allowance. What Louise did not know, however, was that Charles was using her to pass Louis only that information he wanted him to have.

The King's stare was piercing and direct. "You have the sanctuary which you requested."

Ameran bowed. "I am most grateful, Your Majesty."

"What is it you want from me?" asked the King, his stare still pointed.

"Nothing, sire."

The King laughed. "Nonsense! Everyone wants something from the King. That's what I am here for. To fulfill all wishes and desires." He eyed her suspiciously. "I would venture a guess that you feel you are deserving of a title or a house in the country or a monthly pension. Perhaps all three. Well, what will it be? What do you as my long lost daughter want from me?"

Gray started to protest, but Ameran stepped in front of him.

"I'm desirous of nothing, Your Majesty. Nothing at all."

The King folded his arms across his chest. "Good. Then you won't be disappointed." His scowl was slow to disappear. "I hope you haven't entertained the silly notion that I intend to acknowledge you as my daughter. I'm already accused of siring every bastard child in the country and am expected to support them as well."

Gray's jaw set hard. Once again, Ameran did not permit him to defend her before the King.

"I asked only for asylum, sire. Nothing else."

"Then asylum is all you shall have." His words were flat. Then, his expression began to mellow. "However, if you possess some proof that I did indeed sire you, then I might perhaps . . ."

Ameran did not let him continue. "I have no proof I am who I say, Your Majesty." She could feel Gray's eyes on her right shoulder. "Permit me one question, Your Majesty, if I might be so bold as to ask it."

"Speak."

She began slowly, choosing her words carefully.

"You've given me the refuge I sought, and for that you will have my eternal gratitude, however . . ."

Did she dare ask such a question?

Ameran began again, this time her voice calmer and more in control.

"However, Your Majesty, is it customary for a king to send his finest warship and his Commander of the Royal Navy to rescue a poor mademoiselle in distress?" Resplendent green eyes did not waver from the King's dark gaze. "What is the real reason you had Lord Carlisle bring me to you?"

For a moment, the King looked furious at her impertinence. Then he laughed. "You have your hands full with this one, my Lord Carlisle. Beautiful and impudent. A volatile combination, I daresay."

Gray smiled. "I am indeed fortunate, sire."

The King's laughter faded to only the slightest twinge of a smile. He beckoned them both to the side of his bed. "You are correct, Ameran Michol. My reason for arranging your safe passage to England stemmed not from the kindness of my heart. True, I was sympathetic to your plight. Your letters were most convincing, but you must understand, a man with my duties and obligations can't afford to take pity on any one person and make her wishes come true. I'm ashamed to say that throughout the years my heart has perhaps grown cold. But I can't do all things for all people."

"I ask for nothing," she repeated. She wasn't sure if she liked him or not. He reminded her more of a pompous ass than a monarch. "I begged for you to grant me sanctuary. I admit to that, and I'm most grateful; however, I give you my word I'll never make another request of you ever again."

His dark eyes were piercing. He raised up in bed, holding onto one of the curtains for support.

"Do I also have your word that you'll rid me of any curses your mother inflicted upon me after our parting?"

Her gaze did not waver from his. So that was the real reason he had granted her asylum. She wasn't surprised. She had thought as much all along.

She tried not to judge him too harshly. After all, he was the King, and he did have a duty to protect his people. And she had to remember that whatever the reason, he had made her escape from France possible.

She supposed she could lie to him, to make the promises he longed to have her say, but she couldn't. "I'm afraid your kind deed was in vain, Your Majesty, for I have neither my mother's power to cast curses or her powers to lift them."

The King's sigh was long and labored. Then he

shrugged his shoulders. "Oh, well. I suppose I'm no better off than before."

Ameran's lips bore the tiniest of smiles. "Neither are you any worse for my being here, sire."

The King chuckled. "I don't know how my present state could be much worse." He eyed her closely. "So I'm your father?"

"That's what I was told, sire."

Charles let out another heavy sigh and sank back down onto his pillows. "Your mother was a magnificent woman. Her beauty was as none I had ever before seen. The first time I saw her, I knew she would become mine, and then when she saved my life . . . She told you about that, did she not?"

When Ameran nodded, he went on. "My face would have been that of some hideous creature had she not worked her magic on me. Had I remained in exile I would have kept her with me."

Ameran listened closely. There was no reason for him to lie to her now. Neither of them had anything to gain by more deceptions.

"But as it turned out, a new Parliament convened, and it was decided the Stuart line would be restored. I was recalled to take my rightful place on the throne of my father. Never has a returning king been greeted with so much love and adoration."

"You promised Mama you would send for her," Ameran softly reminded him.

He didn't say otherwise. "I couldn't. Sybil knew that I couldn't wed a commoner or have as my mistress one who was convicted of witchcraft." He poured himself a goblet of port from the silver pitcher atop the table beside him. "The day I said good-bye to her she was like a madwoman. She

127

threatened to unleash all demons from hell upon me, and she did. She made no mention of being with child, though I must confess I would have proceeded no differently."

The King took another long swallow from his goblet, then another still before he spoke again.

"Soon after that, her letters began arriving at Court. They were filled with curses and threats which would make the bravest of men tremble. And then there was the Great Plague, just as Sybil had said would come to pass." His words were heavy with guilt. "It began in May, and by September seventy thousand of my people had died. Pestilence and filth were blamed for the catastrophe. I refused to believe that someone other than myself could be directing my fate and that of England."

Ameran said nothing. The feel of Gray's shoulder on her was a great comfort.

"Then the next year, London had to suffer through the Great Fire," he said with tears in his eyes. "I took little solace in the fact that the flames would purge the city of its Black Death. Nor did I find any comfort in the claims made by religious fanatics that the fire was God's revenge on a city of wickedness." He turned up his goblet again. "And let's not forget the wars, just as Sybil had promised. There've been two. She predicted three. I feel the third won't be long in coming. The first was fought against Belgium; the second, against the Dutch, lasted for six years."

Anger reddened his face and his chin protruded. He reached for his goblet still again. "No doubt the third will be with that arrogant paragon of extortion across the way."

Ameran sought for the right explanation to console him. "Haven't there been other outbreaks of diseases in England's long history?" She offered him the same explanations Gideon had offered her.

"Yes, but . . ."

"And surely the London fire was not the only fire that had the ability to ravage a city," she suggested.

"That's true; however . . ."

Ameran didn't give him a chance to voice his objection. "As for wars, isn't it natural for one country to engage another in battle as a means of settling disputes?"

"Of course, but . . ."

"Then surely you can't in good conscience hold my mother liable for all disasters of nature and every armed confrontation," she told him patiently.

The King frowned, but it wasn't a frown of rage. "How can I hold anyone responsible for anything when I can't say anything in my defense?" His scowl began to fade and he was almost on the verge of a smile.

A sigh of relief escaped Gray's lips.

Ameran began to breathe again. The King had every right to be furious with her for overstepping her bounds, but he wasn't. If anything, he seemed quite amused by her impudence.

"The fire and the plague would have occurred without my mother's curses," Ameran said calmly.

One of the puppies nibbled at her shoe. She couldn't resist picking it up and cradling it to her breast.

"My mother was vindictive when provoked, but

not even she could control the course of nature or the direction of destiny."

Ameran was trying to convince herself of that fact as much as she was trying to convince the King. Otherwise, she couldn't bear the guilt for those who had lost their lives.

"All I know is that whatever the reason, each of Sybil Chandler's predictions has come to pass," said the King. There was no anger in his look or in his softly spoken words, only the faintest trace of sadness. "I have no legitimate heirs. Sybil Chandler cursed me with a barren queen just as she swore she would. I have no son to rightfully succeed me. I have enough bastards to raise an army, but bastards do not become Kings. It's just as Sybil foretold."

The King drank more port and stroked a pup that had curled up on his lap. "I'm not to rule a unified nation, just as your mother decreed. There has been one assassination attempt after another, just as she promised. My own flesh and blood have plotted against me. My own flesh and blood would rather I be dead. You still call this coincidence? You still believe my misfortunes are all natural progressions of history? Answer me, daughter of Sybil Chandler. What have you to say?"

Fits of coughing overcame him once again.

Gray put his hand on Ameran's shoulder. "We should leave now. Your Majesty must have your rest."

Still coughing, the King shook his head. "Stay. Speak to me, Ameran Michol. Speak to me those words which will ease my soul."

Ameran ventured a step closer. The King was a

troubled man. He wasn't at all the ogre she had envisioned him to be. She held no illusions as to his
reasons for summoning her to his side, and he had
no pretensions about convincing her otherwise. If
only there was something she could say that would
ease his worries.

His coughing stopped. His eyes searched hers.
"Have you come to Court to deliver the final blow?
Are you here to be your mother's final messenger
of revenge?"

She almost felt sorry for him.

"No, no Your Majesty, that is not why I've
come. I swear I come with no malice or ill intent."
Her own words were soft with compassion. "My
mama is dead, sire. Her hatred died with her. It
does not live on in me."

"But how could you not hate me? I could find
no fault with that which would seem most logical."

Ameran returned the puppy to its mother lying
at the King's slippered feet.

"How could I hate you, Your Majesty, when you
have given life to one who was so close to death?"
She shivered at the thought of death at the hands
of the evil Duke and his men, and pulled her shawl
closer around her shoulders. "Rest assured, sire,
you have nothing to fear from me. It is not my
wish to create any more chaos and confusion for
you. I want nothing from you. You have my sincere wishes for a speedy recovery."

She turned to leave, but the King held out his
hand and beckoned her to stay.

The King smiled a peculiar smile. "You are most
unusual, indeed. You remind me a little of my
dear sis—"

131

Whatever comparison he was about to make was drowned by the sound of his coughing.

"There is no need for you to be in any hurry to leave Whitehall," he said upon recovering from his hoarseness. "Your presence here will be a most refreshing change from the fishwives impersonating the Queen's ladies-in-waiting." He winked at Gray. "Any objections, Lord Commander?"

Gray laughed. "Nay, Your Majesty." He wrapped his arm around her waist.

Ameran slipped deeper into his soothing embrace. Surely no luckier woman could exist anywhere.

Lips pursed in meditation, the King nodded. "Good. I shall have the necessary arrangements made to have you installed in a palace apartment. If anyone asks, and I am quite certain they will, simply tell them you chose to leave France and return to the home of your ancestors." His mood sobered. "Make no mention of your mother. I've caused enough discontent within the Church as of late."

Ameran agreed. "I'm most grateful for your kindness." She bowed and turned to go.

Once again, the King called her back with a motion of his hand. "You—you say you have no proof that you are who you say?"

"You yourself made mention that I was a mirror image of my mother." She was aware once again of Gray's gaze on her shoulder.

"Coyness does not become one so bold," the King scolded. "What proof do you have that I'm your father?" he asked, filling his goblet once more.

"My father was a poor fisherman by the name of Guido Michol," she answered, her stare not faltering from the King's darker one. "Mama was near death when she revealed the details of her love affair with you. She had no reason to lie to me. I'm of your blood. My ancestors are yours, and nothing either of us can do will change that fact. Rest assured, however, a poor fisherman is the only father I will ever claim."

Ameran was starting to become annoyed. She had no intention of announcing to the court of Whitehall that King Charles was her father, but even if she did, why would the King be so concerned? After all, by his own admission, he had sired many bastards. She kept her ire to herself. She did owe the King a tremendous debt, and she would abide by his wishes.

"So a poor fisherman is your father? So be it." The King began another fit of coughing. The goblet didn't go far from his mouth. "I suppose you'll be residing at Court as well, Lord Carlisle?"

"I shall, sire."

The King laughed. "I can count on one hand the number of times you have stayed at Court since I gifted you with royal quarters . . ."

The King called out for his guard. The door opened. One came in hurriedly and saluted and bowed.

"See to it the apartment next to Lord Carlisle's is readied at once."

"Yes, Your Majesty."

One of the spaniels jumped onto the pillows and began licking its master's face. Laughing, the King scratched its floppy ears. Then, the ruler's mood became somber once more, and he again directed his penetrating stare at Ameran.

"Those damnable curses your mother cast on me, I don't reckon you have the power to lift them?" he asked hopefully.

"If I could, Your Majesty, I would. Truly I would." Her smile was sincere. "Any power my mother may have possessed died with her. You must believe that, just as I do. She can't reach out from the grave, sire. If that were the case, the *Fair Winds* and her commander would have never succeeded on their mission."

The King let out a tired sigh. "Since war with somebody, be it France, Holland, or Spain is inevitable, then all that is left is my death." He laughed, but his laugh was not one of good humor. "I don't know who presents me with the greatest cause for fear, my physicians or my assassins. We'll speak again soon." He yawned and settled back down his head upon his pillow. "My darling sister, Minette, also possessed hair as black as Newcastle's coal, and she, too, had those exact eyes of emerald fire, just like you . . . just like your mother."

Ameran started to question his remark, but she didn't, for his own eyes had closed in sleep. His mouth bore the tiniest hint of a smile.

She bowed to the sleeping monarch, as did Gray, then took her beloved's hand and tiptoed out of the room.

The third floor apartment in the east wing of the grand castle far surpassed her expectations. The room wasn't large, but its furnishings were exquisitely beautiful. There was a large looking glass inlaid with gold and a rose marble-topped toilet, a mahogany armoire, and a pair of dainty, high-backed chairs with embroidered rosebuds on the cushions. And the bed! Never had she seen anything quite so magnificent. For eighteen years, her bed had been a pallet of straw on a cold earthen floor. This bed wasn't a bed for mere mortals, but for gods. Drapes of silver and crimson velvet fell from the canopy to the floor.

Ameran ran her fingers along the colorful plumed peacock sewn onto the center of the bed. "I've never seen anything quite so beautiful. I'll be afraid to sleep in it for fear of rumpling it."

Gray closed his arms around her and pulled her tight against his chest. His chin rested atop her head. "Life without you has been a nightmare. Thank God those days are behind me forever."

"Behind us." She turned and drew his head to hers. "And we have many glorious nights yet to come."

Gray picked her up and swung her around to the bed. "Nowhere is it written that such glory can be experienced only after night falls."

Laughing, Ameran pulled him down onto the bed with her.

Gray slipped the soft brocade the rest of the way down her shoulder and kissed the lightning-bolt birthmark. "Why did you not show this to the King as proof that you are who you say?"

Ameran shook her head. "I've nothing to prove to the King. There's nothing he has that I want." Her arms tightly enfolded him. "He didn't answer my pleas for asylum because he is a good and caring King. The guilt that plagues him comes not from remorse at having deceived and abandoned

135

my mama, but from the pain he feels he's inflicted on his people, and from the pain of knowing that his own end is inevitable."

Her smile was faint. "He knows I am who I say."

"He must know that you're his daughter. Otherwise he wouldn't have extended the invitation for you to stay at Court," Gray said, his words soft in her hair.

"The King feels my presence here will keep him out of harm's way a while longer," she said, her cheek pressed to his.

Gray's kisses lingered down her neck. "If it's to your liking, I'll request an audience with the King and make a formal plea for your hand in marriage."

"If it's to my liking? How can you even think it wouldn't be?" She kissed him long and hard. "Nothing or no one will ever separate us again. Promise me that, Gray. Promise me."

Moaning, Gray buried his head between her breasts. "I was a fool once. That error will never be repeated."

Hurried footsteps could be heard coming down the stone corridor.

"Gray, oh Gray. Lord Carlisle," a female voice called out.

Gray moaned again. This time his groan was not one of joy. "Damnation! Must that woman continue to plague me?"

Ameran giggled. She had never before heard that melodious voice, yet there was no mistaking who it belonged to. "Should I be jealous? After all, I've been told that she's the most beautiful woman in all of Britain."

"And throughout all of Europe and the New World. Just ask her. She'll be only too happy to tell you." Gray pointed to the reflection in the looking glass opposite the bed. "There is the most beautiful woman in all the world and she belongs to me alone."

Ameran pulled his face to hers. "We belong to each other."

"Grayson! Grayson!" the voice called out.

Laughing softly, they heard the door across the way open, then a moment later slam shut.

"Aren't you going to introduce me to my rival for your affections?" teased Ameran.

Gray's mood grew serious. "I assure you, my darling, you have no rival for my love. Even if there were no Ameran Michol in my life, I wouldn't woo the affections of the great Duchess. Her kiss has proven deadly to more than one poor, unsuspecting soul."

"Having you spurn her probably makes her love you all the more." Ameran slipped her gown the rest of the way off her shoulder to reveal plump, full breasts that catapulted into Gray's hands. "I know I would be devastated if you were ever to reject me."

"Never."

Kisses stifled their laughter, and they fell back onto the many-colored peacock, groping, caressing and tugging to rid themselves of the bulky bindings entrapping their eager bodies.

Their voices blended in a harmony of soft moans and whispers of love as their bodies melted together, arms and legs entangling, until they found the sweet source of their joy.

137

* * *

Ameran was roused from her sleep a little later
by a tapping on her door. Her arms reached out
for Gray, but found only the wrinkles where he had
lain. With a disappointed sigh, she remembered he
had returned to the harbor for a final inspection of
the *Fair Winds* before dark. He had departed with
the assurances he would return to sup with her and
to warm her bed.

Certain it was Gray returning, Ameran jumped
from the bed, wrapping herself in one of the soft
bed covers, running to fling open the door.

The smile on her face all but turned to stone.

Introductions were not necessary. The stunning,
pale-haired woman glaring at her could only be the
one Gray so often called the thorn in his side. Her
eyes were a soft gray, yet as cold and dreadful as
the cruel smile on her lips. She and Gideon would
make the perfect match.

Ameran collected herself quickly as she pulled
the bed covering tighter around her shoulders. The
Duchess of Morrow was every bit as striking as she
had been told. She was tall and willowy, and a
massive mane of wheat gold hair was piled high
atop her head. Jewels adorned her neck, her ears,
her arms and her fingers. She possessed a look of
elegance, of refinement, and of a determination to
take what she wanted, with no regard for anyone.

Constance's stare darted from Ameran to the
rumpled bed, then back to Ameran. "I wish to see
Lord Carlisle."

"As you can see, he's not here." Ameran remained undaunted. Very little frightened her, and

yet she knew that Constance would be as formidable a foe as Gideon.

Constance stared rudely at Ameran's body. "You are indeed just as lovely as Gideon said." Her eyes flamed hatred. "But I give you fair warning, Gray belongs to me, and I won't let anyone spoil the plans I've made for us. I hope you understand."

Ameran didn't back down from the hateful glower burning her flesh. She'd faced even more formidable opponents than Constance.

"I believe that's a matter best discussed with Lord Carlisle."

"You've taken him from me, and I demand him back."

Constance's look was not at all unlike that of Sybil when she ranted and raved.

"Gray is not a possession," she told the Duchess calmly. "He has the power to choose for himself."

Constance's smile was ice cold as she pointed a long, red-jeweled finger in Ameran's face. "Leave Whitehall tomorrow, or I'll destroy you."

Ameran didn't blink. "Many have tried to destroy me and failed. I don't believe you'll be any more successful than they."

Constance spat at her, just as her mother used to do in one of her frenzies. "Stay out of my way, whore. Witch! Cross my path and I'll see you burn at the stake."

Her accusations caught Ameran off guard. Witch? How might Constance have known? Only the King and Gray . . . and Gideon! Gideon, of course!

"If you think me a witch, then proceed with caution," Ameran told Constance, her words slow and

139

deliberate. "Or I'll cast a spell on you. Now please leave. I've grown tired of our conversation." She deliberately cut her eyes to the bed. "Gray will be returning soon and I want to be well rested when I greet him."

Constance stormed out of the room but not before throwing Ameran a hostile glare.

Ameran slammed the door shut behind her, then sank back against it. Her knees were shaking and her heart still pounding from her unexpected encounter with the woman who had declared war on her. The Duchess of Morrow was far more dangerous than perhaps Gray could even imagine, and if Constance and Gideon were allies and not the bitter enemies they professed to be, then she and Gray were in far more trouble than he suspected.

Chapter Eight

Ameran strolled through the gardens with three playful spaniels nipping at her heels. The sun was warm, and the sky a cloudless blue, except for sprinklings of gray from the city's smokestacks.

Ameran let out a sigh of contentment. The past week had been the most wonderful of her life. Her days were lonely without Gray, but their separation during the day only made their nighttime reunions sweeter. Louis Quatorze was once again making threats against England as punishment to King Charles for negotiating with the Dutch. England's King responded by strengthening his military and naval power, and with the Duke of York still in exile in Scotland, outfitting more ships for service fell on Gray's shoulders. She hoped there would not be war. She couldn't bear the thought of another separation from Gray. If need be, she would go into battle at his side.

Ameran sat down atop the rocks bordering the fish pond and watched the fat goldfish swimming in and out of the underwater tunnels and trestles. The spaniels played at her feet. She took turns taking each in her lap and stroking their silken coats.

Across the way, sitting on a stone bench beside a

fountain where water spouted from the mouths of cupids, was the Queen and her constant companion, the Duchess of Morrow. Ameran found herself wondering what scheme the two of them were plotting to get rid of her. She had heard from Maggie, one of the upstairs waiting maids, that the Queen had ordered her husband to banish the devil's vixen not only from Whitehall but from London as well. Gray had assured her that if there was one thing the King never did, it was to bow to the demands of his wife.

After that first dreadful meeting, Ameran had not come face to face with Constance again. She had only caught a fleeting glimpse of her from her apartment window at sundown late one afternoon when she had been waiting for Gray. Constance had been sitting on a bench outside the garden maze of hedges that had been trimmed in the shapes of animals. Gideon had appeared in the garden at the same time, and the two had disappeared inside the labyrinth of low hanging trees and shrubs. When she mentioned to Gray of the peculiarity of such a meeting for two who professed dislike for each other, Gray shrugged it off and assured her she could have only been mistaken, for Gideon and Constance never exchanged a civil word.

But Ameran knew better. How else would Constance have known she had been accused of witchcraft, if not from Gideon? She didn't know how she was going to do it, but somehow she had to make Gray realize that an enemy who pretended to be a friend was the most dangerous foe of all.

A ball came rolling through the grass and stopped at Ameran's feet. The puppies fought for possession of it.

Two boys who had been playing nearby came running up to her. Ameran called out cheerfully to them, then picked up the ball and tossed it to the smallest of the two, a little fellow with a headful of dark curls and big, wide eyes the same color. The older one thanked her while the younger one hid behind him. Then, the boys threw down the ball and dove laughing onto the grass with the puppies.

Ameran watched them, smiling. She and Gray often spoke of one day having a family. She touched her stomach. Perhaps, even now . . .

"Charles . . . Jamie," a cheery voice called out.

A woman appeared from around the pink budded bush in between the pond and the garden wall. She had the same rosy cheeks as the little boy. She was plump, but pleasantly so, and her head was a mop of chestnut waves and curls that had escaped the ribbons and combs.

"There you are, my darlings," she said, arms opened wide.

The boys rushed to give her hugs.

"Nearly lost yer old mum, ye did, with that tricky game of hide and seek."

Laughing and fanning herself with a lace handkerchief, she sat down on the bench beside Ameran.

"Hope me laddies didn't trouble ye none," she said, a little out of breath. Her words had the same sparkle and merriment as her hazel eyes.

"Oh, no, not at all," Ameran quickly assured her. "I adore children, especially little boys with dimples," she said, tweaking one's nose and tousling the curls of the other. "I was getting rather lonely with my own company."

The woman smiled. Her dimples danced just as her sons. "Tell the lady yer names, lads."

"I am Charles, Earl of Burford," said the older, more solemn one. He made that announcement with much pride. "And my brother's name is . . ."

"I know my name. Mummy, tell Charlie to let me tell the lady my name."

"Of course," said the woman, pulling them both onto her knees.

"I am James. Charlie's the eldest. He was named for our father. Our papa is the King of all England. Do you know that? I was named for my papa's brother." He crawled from his mother's lap to Ameran's. "I am the little Earl of Beauclerk," he said, his tiny chest sticking out proudly. "But Mummy calls me Jamie, and you can, too, if you would like." He examined the gold cross Ameran wore, carefully turning it over in his hands. "That's pretty. You are, too." He kissed her cheek, then jumped down giggling.

Ameran laughed. "Your son is quite a charmer."

"Just like his father, he is."

Ameran studied the little boys. They did indeed bear a striking resemblance to the King.

"I'm Nell Gwyn." She held out a plump hand with fingers adorned in jewels. "Actress and royal entertainer extraordinaire." Her laugh was husky. "No doubt ye've heard about me already."

Ameran shook her head.

"Ye will soon enough." She looked across the way at the Queen and Constance, and threw back her head. "Od's fish! Them two don't look like such high and mighty ladies to me. Do they to you?"

Ameran looked at them again. "I'm not quite sure what to make of either of them." Then she held out her hand to Nell. "My name is Ameran Michol."

Nell laughed. "Oh, I know who ye are all right,

dearie. Why, all of London knows who ye are. Your reputation is as muddy as me own." She shooed her boys away. "Run along and play, laddies. Missus Turner'll be coming to fetch ye soon for supper."

The boys gave their mum a peck on each cheek, then were off across the lawn with the spaniels scampering close behind.

"I hope I didn't offend ye," said Nell. "I meant no harm by it."

Ameran smiled. "I've had worse said about me, I assure you."

Nell twisted her head this way and that, her face all smiles. "Ye be far too pretty for a witch. Yer hair's not tangled, and I don't see a wart on yer nose."

"Is that what people are saying about me?" asked Ameran, her smile starting to fade.

Nell looked across the way and gave her head another haughty toss. "'Twas that Duchess of Morrow who started it, but everybody reckons her gossiping's out of spite and jealousy seeing how 'twas ye who won the heart of Lord Carlisle. She's been barking after him for years." Her face wrinkled into a grimace. "She's not much older than ye, and already she's been through three husbands. They all die mysteriously," said Nell knowingly. "Poison, I suspect, but nobody dares confront her because of the Queen." Nell gave Ameran a comforting pat on the back. "Ye don't need to worry about getting banished from Court on her account. The King has strongly advised she keep her thoughts to herself."

Ameran was pleased. "The King really told her that?"

Nell nodded. "He did, indeed." She eyed her with good humored suspicion. "Do I have cause to be jealous of ye, too?"

"Jealous of me?"

"Mmmmm. Seems like the King has found favor with ye." Nell's perusal was one of curiosity, not ill will. "Are ye really a gift from that scoundrel Louis?"

Ameran shook her head. "Had I stayed in France, I wouldn't be alive today. I came not as a mistress to the King, but as a victim seeking refuge from those who tried to harm me."

"Good!" Her plump face shook when she laughed. "I don't like to share me Charlie with anyone, be she a serving wench or a grand lady."

"You'll have no trouble from me," Ameran assured her.

Nell gave a knowing nod. "I figured all that talk about a new French mistress was nothing but gossip. Charlie's already got one, and she's been nothing but trouble." Nell craned her neck. "Speak of the devil, here she comes now. Out for her afternoon ride, I'd wager. Old sow."

A small gilded carriage with red spokes turned up the lane to the fish pond.

Ameran was relieved. She could tell just by talking to her for those few minutes that she had nothing to fear from Nell; however, she had made the promise to the King to keep quiet the circumstances of her being there, and she did not want to compromise that vow.

Nell got up and waved for the driver to stop.

A dark-haired woman with porcelain skin and a scowl on her freckled face leaned out the window. Many strands of pearls dangled out the window, as did breasts which were just as freckled.

Nell threw Ameran a sly wink over her shoulder.

146

"Lovely day for a ride around the gardens, isn't it, madame?" called out Nell.

"Is that why you stopped my carriage, Mistress Gwyn?" came the impatient retort.

Nell's smile was sugarcoated. "Oh, no, no, no, dear lady. I stopped yer carriage because I know how concerned ye must have been as of late about the King's health, and I just wanted to assure ye that His Majesty is exceedingly well." She patted her hair and preened like a young girl. "As a matter of fact, I've never known him to be in better form than he was last night." Her voice grew still louder. "Mind ye, he was indeed hot from fevers last night, but those fevers were of a different sort."

Ameran tried to keep from laughing out loud.

The lady in the carriage forced her scowl into a smile. "Your report on the King's health is much welcomed, madame. It makes me look forward to this evening with even more anticipation. Drive on," she commanded her driver without as much as a second glance behind her.

Hands on her hips and grinning from ear to ear, Nell watched the carriage proceed.

"Catholic whore!" Nell spat after the carriage. "What a fit she's causing me Charlie. Why, she's telling everyone he married her in some kind of a Popish farce, and now she's trying to convince him to legitimize her bastard, the Duke of Richmond, so that puny halfwit could be named heir to the throne. I ask ye, have ye ever heard of anything so preposterous?"

The laugh Ameran was trying hard to keep contained burst out. "I beg your forgiveness, madame. I don't mean to be rude."

Nell joined in the laughter with her. "Ye do not have

147

to beg my forgiveness, dear girl. I feel it all quite amusing meself."

Head to head, the two women giggled like school-girls as Nell told Ameran about her revenge on Louise not so long ago when the Frenchwoman boasted that the King was going to pay her a visit later on. Nell had made sweetmeats and gave them to Louise as a peace offering. Unknown to Louise, Nell had added jaleps, which had a laxative effect, to the ingredients, and when Louise had to repeatedly excuse herself from their little tryst, Charles had sought Nell's company instead.

"Little does that French trollop know that with her high and mighty ways and intelligent chatter, she can't keep me Charlie content. He's already tired of her. Told me that himself. Nell, my girl, he said, women come and women go, but there'll never be another Nell Gwyn in my bed." Nell sat tall, her chest thrust out. "Od's fish, little Charlie and Jamie have as much claim to the throne as her bastards. Why, at Jamie's birth, me beloved master insisted he be given the sur-name 'Beauclerk.' Do you know who Beauclerk was?"

Ameran shook her head. She was still laughing. Nell was the only woman she'd ever engaged in con-versation, save for her mama, who ranted and raved more than she talked. Nell was so charming and so very delightful.

There was no mistaking the pride in Nell's voice. "Beauclerk was the surname of King Henry the first." Head held high, she smoothed back her chestnut locks. "And me darling King insisted me boys be given titles. I didn't have to ask him. He made Charlie the Earl of Burford, and he just named a ship in his honor. And little Jamie is Lord Beauclerk. He's a wonderful man, me Charlie," said Nell with a long, adoring sigh. "And I'll wring anybody's neck who says differently."

Jamie came running up to his mother. "Mummy, Mummy, hide me. Charlie always knows where to look for me."

Nell pulled up her crimson skirt. "In here, quick. He won't think to look for ye there."

Jamie laughed. "You're wonderful, Mummy. I knew you would help me," he said as he dove under her skirt.

Charlie came bounding across the lawn after her. "Where's Jamie?"

Nell shrugged her shoulders. "Oh, dear, surely we haven't lost the little angel?" She gasped. "Ye don't think he could have fallen in the fish pond, do ye?"

Charlie pointed to a little boot sticking out from beneath the ruffles of his mother's skirt. "All right, James Beauclerk, I surrender. You win."

Jamie jumped out, nearly upsetting Nell.

Nell grabbed hold of Ameran's arm to keep from toppling back into the fish pond.

"Here I am, Charlie. See. Was that not a grand place to hide?"

Charlie ruffled his brother's curls with affection. "It was a splendid hiding place. Splendid, Jamie." He sat down beside his mother. "Do you think Papa will come to tea today, Mother? I'm most anxious to read to him from my new book."

"And I want to give him the horse pictures I drew for him," chimed in Jamie.

Nell gave both her sons huge hugs. "I don't think he'll visit us today, my darlings. He has a very important visitor from France and has to spend the evening discussing politics and the like."

The boys gave resigned nods.

Ameran could sense their disappointment. No matter his faults, the King must be a good father to the boys, for they were obviously completely besotted by him.

"I have an idea." Nell pulled the lads closer. "I'll send word to the King that Missus Turner is baking her special mince pies for tea tomorrow, and you know how he loves her mince pies."

Jamie jumped up and down. Charles smiled and clapped his hands.

Ameran took great delight in watching Nell play with her sons. Her own unhappy childhood tore at her heart. Her mother had never laughed and frolicked with her. How lucky these little boys were, and what a refreshing change Nell had to be from the shrew who was the King's wife.

"It was a grand pleasure meeting ye, Ameran Michol," said Nell as they all prepared to part company a little later. "I've a feeling we're to become grand friends." She nodded across the way to the Queen and the Duchess who were still sitting on the bench and staring. "We've a lot in common since we've both provoked the wrath of the two most dreadful women at court."

Ameran smiled, but she saw little humor in having such connivers as enemies. Her look of dread must have provoked Nell's sympathies, for Nell opened both her arms wide and beckoned her inside just as she had done to her boys. "No need to worry about those two, lovey. They'll think twice before going against the King's wishes."

150

Ameran glanced up at the two, who made no attempt to hide from her the fact that they were plotting to rid themselves of her.

Nell tossed back her curls and laughed. "I suspect they're wondering what it is we're plotting. Perhaps they're thinking we've been comparing techniques and procedures for pleasing our lord and master. Od's fish, girl. I've made ye blush, haven't I?" Nell pinched her cheeks just as she had done her little one. "Between you and me, we might cause quite a stir at Whitehall." She took her boys by the hands. "Come along, my little men, Lord Burford, Lord Beauclerk. Let us go see what delicacies Missus Turner has prepared for our supper. We shall see you here tomorrow?" she asked Ameran.

Ameran nodded happily. Already, she was looking forward to their next visit. A friend at last! She couldn't wait to share her good news with Gray.

But when she told Gray about meeting Nell, he didn't meet her revelation with the enthusiasm she had expected. He sat her down on the bed in the middle of her dressing for a late supper gathering with the King.

"Nell is just as charming and as witty as you have observed, and she does indeed enjoy the notoriety of having outlasted all of Charles's other mistresses; however, I'm not certain it's in your best interest to be seen in her company," explained Gray gently. "Her reputation is considerably tarnished to say the least."

"Why I've never heard anything so absurd!" Ameran plopped back against the pillows with her arms crossed tight. "She's the first and only woman at court who's shown me any kindness whatsoever. All the fine ladies like your Constance and the Queen treat me as if I were a trollop found in the gutter."

"That's exactly the impression you'll convey if you persist in your association with Missus Gwyn." Gray sat down on the bed beside her and tried to pull her close, but she pulled away.

"I grant you, Nell Gwyn is most charming, and she poses no real threat to anyone at Court," Gray went on, his own arms crossed as hers. "However, there are times when she does overstep her position as Royal Mistress and tries to take on the responsibility as chief Councillor as well." His words were calm. "Missus Gwynn is quite opinionated, and I fear her outspokenness will cause her serious grief in days to come."

Ameran knew no good could come from arguing the matter further. Gray's mind was made up, just as her own mind was made up. She saw no harm whatsoever in continuing her afternoon chats with Nell in the gardens or anywhere else she had a mind to meet her.

Gray leaned over and kissed the tip of her nose. "Don't pout, my darling. It doesn't become you. Besides, this is a night for celebrating." He stood up and took off the jacket to his uniform and began next with his trousers. "It appears that our friend across the channel is somewhat bothered by the King's strengthening of the military and the navy and has sent an emissary bearing the one peace offering Charles will never turn down."

"Money?" she asked, starting to smile.

Gray nodded. "And a great deal of it."

Ameran was relieved. "So there'll be no war with France?"

Gray reached to kiss her. This time she didn't turn away.

"There'll be no war now that Charles has convinced

Louis that he's not a puppet who dances on command."

Ameran wrapped her arm tight around Gray's neck. Her tongue darted playfully in and out of his ear. "I'm your puppet and I'll dance upon your command."

Gray allowed her to pull him back down onto the bed. "There you are mistaken, sweet Ameran. You're the one who makes me dance."

She threw a leg over him and sat perched atop his chest. "If what you say is true, and I truly am in command," she said with a devilish twinkle in her eyes, "Then why do we not forgo the royal supper and dine in bed, just the two of us?" she suggested as the tip of her tongue traced the outline of his scar.

Gray rolled her over. "Mmmm, a delicious idea. However, one simply does not decline an invitation to dine with the King. An invitation is not merely a request at one's convenience. It's a royal command for which no excuses are accepted."

"Mmmm. What a pity." Ameran slowly slipped the velvet ruffles of her gown off her shoulder. "And I suppose it would be a crime punishable by imprisonment in the Tower if we were to be less than prompt for such an engagement." She fluttered her dark lashes teasingly.

With a loud moan, Gray untied the ties closing her bodice. Plump breasts, young and tender, sprang forth to greet him. "I'll gladly accept any punishment the King deems fit," he laughed as he burrowed his mouth into their softness.

Ameran wound her arms tight around his neck and pulled him to her with all her might. Life with Gray was even sweeter than in all her imaginings.

Gray pulled off her gown in one quick swish while

Ameran tore at his shirt as he kicked his legs free of his trousers.

Her legs wrapped tight around him, pulling him closer still, pressing him deeply into her flesh. He slipped inside her, and soon their bodies were moving in gentle rhythm.

"Will I never have my fill of you?" Gray groaned.

"Never, my darling. Never." Back arched, she met his thrusts with an urgency just as demanding. "If I have no other purpose in life, it is to see that you never grow weary of me."

Their sighs erupted into moans, and afterwards, they lay together, still pressed tight into the other, with smiles of contentment upon their lips.

Chapter Nine

All eyes were on them as they walked into the grand dining hall arm in arm amid hushed mumblings and stares.

Ameran had said nothing to Gray about her fears, yet it was though he could hear them aloud. "Don't be frightened. They're all staring at you simply because they're all in awe of so captivating a beauty. Don't be scared. I'm here with you."

"I'm not easily frightened," said Ameran, putting on a brave front.

She held her head high and proud. Even if someone did remember who Sybil Chandler was, there was little likelihood they would make any connection between her and her mother. Perhaps she should have worn something a bit more sedate, but her spirits had been so uplifted after their lovemaking that she had chosen the gayest of all the dresses given her by the King, a red velvet with a low cut bodice framed in soft white rabbit fur. She tried to ignore the rude glares and whisperings which she knew were directed at her, but every face she cast her eyes on was hostile.

Ameran stopped in her steps. "Witch's daughter," she had heard someone hiss. Her eyes sought Gray's, and the scar on his jaw tensed. Ameran hoped that perhaps now he would realize that Gideon was not the friend he professed to be. Quickly, she scanned the group of twenty or so who had assembled along a mahogany table that stretched across the center of the hall. Gideon was not there. Good. She would only have to deal with one adversary that evening.

The seat at the head of the table was vacant, as was the one to its right. Constance had taken her place to the right of where the Queen would be sitting.

Ameran's eyes met Constance's hateful stare and held firm. She wasn't afraid of the Duchess of Morrow, and she wanted that understood by all.

The King's secretary, a bespectacled little man who spoke with a lisp, ushered them to places a few seats down from Constance. Mr. Devoe seated Ameran between Gray and a tall, solemn-faced man whose silver goblet did not stray far from his lips. He scarcely gave her a glance when she sat down beside him.

Still aware of being the subject of the guests' mumblings and stares, Ameran was all the more determined to look each and every one of her silent accusers straight in the eye.

"I'm most relieved your friend Gideon isn't in attendance," she remarked.

She waited for Gray to come to his friend's defense, but he didn't. "Nor will he be among the King's intimate circle for some time to come."

"Oh, why so?" she asked, curious.

Gray took a long time before answering. "Gideon has fallen from the King's good graces. I fear it will be some time before he's welcomed back."

So she and the King had something else in common, she thought.

"What did Gideon do that offended the King?" she asked. She could tell from Gray's creased forehead it was not a subject he wished to discuss.

Finally, after a long sigh, he began. "Gideon was named in a plot to overtake the King and have the Duke of Monmouth put on the throne. The accusations didn't stand, and the charges were dropped. But the King chose not to listen to Gideon's defense."

"Was Gideon involved in such a plot?" she asked, quite certain that he was.

Gray shook his head. "I don't know. Before I left for France, I would have defended Gideon's innocence with my life, but of late I've seen a side to him that I didn't think existed."

Ameran was quick to change the subject. She didn't want Gray to be so burdened with Gideon's troubles.

"Who are all these people?" she asked. "I haven't seen more than a handful of them this entire week at Court."

Gray leaned close to her ear. "The gentleman to the left of the King's place is Monsieur Louis-Phillip Renault, secretary to the French foreign minister Barrillon. It's rumored that Louis has doubled his offer of two hundred thousand pounds if Charles promises to abandon his alliances with the Dutch and Spanish, cancel the new Parliament that is to be called, and relax the laws against the Catholics. Louis is also quite insistent that certain steps be taken now to insure that the King's brother, James, will be his successor."

Gray lowered his voice even more. "And then there is the matter of the King's own religion. Years ago, Charles promised Louis that he would convert to Catholicism in exchange for certain compensations. Charles has made no mention of his promise and continues to carry out his duty as defender of the Church of England. No one dares to question him about his religious inclinations."

Gray took a drink of wine and continued on as Ameran listened intently. "Beside Secretary Renault is Charles's French mistress, Louise de Keroualle. I've spoken about her before."

Ameran nodded, but made no mention of having seen Louise earlier in the park, or of witnessing the exchange between her and Nell.

Louise glanced her way, and the slightest flicker of recognition passed over her freckled face.

Gray directed her attention to a woman in a yellow fringed shawl who was sitting to the right of the man beside her.

"That's the King's most recent acquisition. Her name is Hortense, and she hails from Germany."

Upon seeing Ameran's hard-to-hide smile, Gray added, "His Majesty never ends his love affairs; he simply adds to his collection."

Ameran watched as the handsome, dark-skinned man seated across from Hortense blew her a kiss.

Gray leaned to her ear again. "It's been said those two are lovers. If they are, I hope they have the good sense to be discreet."

"The King certainly isn't," she remarked.

"He doesn't have to be. He's the King," Gray reminded her.

"I wonder where Nell is," she said without thinking.

Gray frowned. "Probably entertaining her Whig friends at Pall-Mall."

158

Ameran could tell by his tone that he wished no further mention of Nell Gwyn.

Gray scanned the rest of the dinner guests, pointing out those of interest. "England's Chief Minister, Lord Danby, is seated beside Constance. He looks rather well, considering he's spent the last few months in the Tower."

"Why? What did he do?" she inquired. The bald, scrawny man didn't look like he posed any sort of threat to the King or anyone else.

"King Charles felt he needed to be taught a lesson," answered Gray in a tone so somber that Ameran couldn't tell if he was in agreement or not with the King over sentencing so frail a man to the Tower.

"The man with the white moustache is Sir Leoline Jenkins. He's the King's Secretary of State. Beside him is Lord Halifax, one of the King's most trusted advisors, a position which I doubt he'll hold for long considering Halifax's insistence that the King rule in partnership with the Parliament."

Ameran nodded to an old man who was asleep in his chair. His hair was scraggly and uncombed, and his clothes were rumpled and seemed to swallow him whole. "And he?"

Gray's smile was sad. "His name is Macclesfield. In Charles' years before his exile, Macclesfield was his teacher. After his restoration to the throne, he became his Chief Councillor. It's my understanding the King has brought him to Whitehall to end the ambitions of those who aspire to have the Duke of Monmouth proclaimed legitimate heir."

"How can he do that?" she asked, very much interested in the old man.

"The Duke of Monmouth's mother was a woman

159

named Lucy Walters, who died when Jemmy was a lad. The Whigs seemed to have found proof that Charles had married her before she gave birth to Jemmy, thereby legitimizing his bastard. And Macclesfield is here to dispel such rumors by substantiating the King's claim that Lucy was never his wife, but a whore of many men."

"Do you feel the Duke of Monmouth's claim is a valid one?" she asked.

Gray didn't hesitate with his answer. "King Charles wants his brother to succeed him. I want what the King wants. The King says he has no legitimate heirs, and his claims should not be questioned."

Gray paused to drink from his goblet before continuing his review of the guests. "The man responsible for recreating a second city from the ashes of the first after the Great Fire is at the far end of the table. His name is Christopher Wren. At present, he has the monumental task of restoring Saint Paul's Cathedral to its long ago grandeur. We'll take a ride out there in the days ahead and see the progress for ourselves."

Ameran held tight to his hand. "I'd enjoy that very much."

"To the left of Mister Wren is Isaac Newton, esteemed scholar of the Royal Academy," continued Gray, an arm tight around her shoulders. "He and the King spend hours discussing and debating why the moon stays on the same path while it turns around the earth. I, myself, have never given much thought to such perplexing questions."

"Nor I," she laughed. "The earth is here; the moon is there. That's all that matters."

Gray kissed her ear. "And you're here, and I'm here, so that's what really matters."

She was uncomfortably aware of being the object of Constance's intense scrutiny, but met the hateful glowers with cool indifference.

Gray drew her hand to his lips and kissed it. "Do you remember how round and bright the moon was our very first night together?"

Ameran brushed a kiss across his cheek. "I've never seen a more spectacular moon than on that night."

"Now that the King's good health has returned, I plan to tell him of our intentions to wed," Gray whispered.

Ameran was thrilled. It was all she could do to keep from jumping from her chair and announcing the news.

Her eyes wandered back to Constance. The Duchess of Morrow had surely guessed what it was they were discussing, for her eyes were nearly smoking. Gray might not take Constance's threats seriously, but she certainly did. Constance would stop at nothing to destroy their love, and if she and Gideon were truly enemies, the common objective they shared — to cause as much anguish and discord as possible between her and Gray — would make them the best of friends.

Ameran forced her attention from Constance. "The man in the funny black hat. Who's he?"

"His name is William Penn," answered Gray. "He claims the King owes his family a great debt originating in the days when the first Charles borrowed money from his wealthier subjects to fight his wars, and has so requested the present King to grant him his own colony in America as repayment for such debt."

"His own colony? That's a most unusual request."

Gray nodded. "Penn is a member of a group of religious dissenters called the Quakers, who feel they're being persecuted by the Church of England. He wants the colony so he and his followers can go there to live and worship in peace."

Ameran sighed. "A place free of persecution? I didn't know such a place could exist. Will the King grant his request?"

"I believe that's his intention. The King has so often said that every man needs a place to live under his own vine and fig tree." He grinned. "And it would also be one less debt King Charles would have to repay." Gray scanned the remainder of guests seated at the table. "All the others are noblemen and noblewomen who for one reason or another have been favored by the King tonight."

Ameran stole another quick look at Constance. She might be wearing a gown of the whitest silk, but the air she possessed was not one of innocence and purity. Her eyes were as cold and as hard as the shield of diamonds and pearls clasped onto her flat chest.

The loud-spoken man on Gray's left engaged him in conversation about the fighting strength of His Majesty's Royal Navy, leaving Ameran to quietly sip her wine.

The man beside her finally acknowledged her presence. "I don't believe I've had the pleasure of an introduction. I'm Lord Craven." He put down his goblet only for a moment to kiss her hand, then reached for it again.

"I'm Ameran Michol."

"Do you reside at Court?"

She nodded. "And you?"

He motioned for the server to fill his goblet again. "I've only recently taken up residence again in Windsor. I've spent the past several years in the colony of

162

Charles Town in Carolina." He paused for a moment and seemed to be lost in his inner reflection. " 'Tis a lovely place, Carolina. 'Tis indeed. No other like it under the sun. Giant oaks draped with Spanish moss, pine trees that tower up to the sky, palm trees laden with the sweetest of coconuts, vast fields of marsh grass, and beautiful white-sanded beaches stretching as far as the eye can see." His sigh was sad. "How I shall miss that land."

"It sounds lovely," she said politely. She wondered what had ever prompted him to leave a place he so obviously loved. "Living there must have been quite an adventure," she said, making an effort to continue the conversation upon seeing how dejected he looked.

"Ahh, an adventure indeed. Every day there was a new adventure. Pirates, Indians, the French, the Spanish, they all made life extremely difficult." His smile was strange. "But even at its worst, Charles Town is closer to Paradise than any place on earth."

"It's a pity you had to leave, sir."

"A move I shall spend the rest of my life regretting." He turned up his goblet, then motioned for the server to fill it again. "But when I make my next fortune, I shall return to Carolina, and perhaps this time make wiser investments."

Ameran asked no more questions. She sensed he had said all he intended to say and desired nothing else but be left alone in his memories.

Just then the great oaken doors to the dining hall swung open and a hush fell over the room. The captain of the guards entered and announced the arrival of the King and Queen.

The guests stood and remained standing until the royal couple took their places.

163

Constance and the Queen were immediately head to head, directing their stares and whispers at Ameran.

King Charles gave a nod to the waiters standing at attention around the room, and almost at once, gold-rimmed plates with the Stuart crest appeared in front of each guest. Large silver trays piled high with roasted beef and pork, and platters of potatoes, turnips, and corn were passed from one diner to the next.

King Charles said very little throughout dinner. When he did converse, it was to do so with Monsieur Renault. Gray answered what questions asked him by Halifax and the other councillors present about the seaworthiness and battle readiness of his fleet, while Ameran moved her food from one side of the plate to another, still aware of the heated glances tossed her way by Constance and the Queen. She wondered what evil plot they were scheming to rid Whitehall of her presence. Occasionally, she would steal a look at the other guests. Louise was conversing in French with Renault. Hortense and the Monaco prince were still laughing and blowing kisses. Macclesfield had not yet awakened, and Danby and the man seated opposite him were involved in a seemingly bitter debate.

A few times, Ameran caught the King's eye, and he would give her a smile and a nod, then look away. It didn't matter if he thought her a liar. An accident of birth had made her his daughter. She wanted nothing from him, and she had a feeling the King had as much difficulty believing that as he did believing she was of his flesh and blood.

She was relieved when the King and Queen took their leave a while later, for their departure signaled permission for everyone else to retire.

Lord Craven slumped lower into his chair.

"I'll look forward to hearing more of this fine place called Carolina," she told him as she made ready to go.

"Ah, sweet, sweet Carolina!" he said as he nodded off with a smile upon his lips.

Constance brushed past Ameran and reached her arms around Gray's neck. "Darling, I've hardly had a chance to speak to you." She brushed her lips over his cheek. "If I didn't know better, I'd be certain you were ignoring me."

Gray untangled her arms from around him and reached for Ameran. "I believe you've already made Ameran's acquaintance."

Constance didn't give her a second look. "Visit me soon, Gray," she said, her words barely louder than a whisper. "There's so much between us that needs to be settled soon." Her breasts pressed against his chest. "Don't disappoint me and I shall never disappoint you." She waved to someone across the room and flitted off on her cloud of white silk to join them.

Ameran could sense his discomfort as he gathered her closer.

"Constance will try to come between us, but we mustn't let her," he said, hugging her close.

"We'll guard against anyone who tries to part us." She lay her head on his shoulder. "Anyone."

"Let's retire to your apartment and rekindle this evening's fire, shall we?" he asked as he kissed the top of her head.

Ameran gave him a playful wink. "Those embers are ready to blaze again, my lord."

They kissed a long, impassioned kiss, and when

Ameran opened her eyes, she opened them to a hate-filled stare of Constance's that made her shiver.

As they were on their way out of the dining hall one of the waiters handed Gray a note.

Ameran hoped there would be no delay. The sooner she was away from those prying eyes, the better she would feel.

Gray frowned.

"Bad news?" She desperately hoped he wouldn't have to return to the *Fair Winds*.

He shook his head. "No, at least, I don't think so. It's from Gideon. He says that it's imperative we meet at once to discuss matters of the utmost urgency."

"What matters are those?"

"He didn't say." Gray's hold tightened on her arm as they wove their way in and out of the dinner guests. "Gideon said he'll be waiting in my room. I promise not to take long." His hands began a playful quest across her body once more as they began the long climb up the stairs. "Don't fall asleep without me."

Ameran laughed and threw both arms around him. "It won't matter if I do, for I suspect you have ways of arousing the soundest sleeper."

Gray's smile was quick to fade. "I intend to find the origin of these rumors about you as well. Gideon knows certain information that no one else is privy to. I'll put a quick end to these rumors," he promised her.

Ameran let out a long sigh. "It's unfortunate I'm not a witch. There are those who I should very much like to make disappear."

She had no doubt that Gideon would deny any and all charges. He'd most likely place the blame on someone else, a crew member perhaps who had heard the rumors in Mer. When would Gray grow weary of Gideon's lies and excuses? When would he realize that Gideon is a master of deception?

"I won't be long, my darling," Gray told her as he walked her inside her apartment.

"No late night visits with the Duchess?" she teased.

Gray laughed. "The good Duchess wishes she could be so lucky."

"You really are much too modest, my lord." Her lips sought his; his tongue probed playfully inside her mouth. Then she ended the kiss abruptly. "You'll be careful, won't you, Gray? Promise me you'll be careful." Fear seized at her throat. Gray was in danger. She could feel it.

Gray lovingly pushed back the dark tendrils that had swept across her cheek. "There's no reason for you to worry for my safety. Gideon intends me no harm. Most likely he wants nothing more than to boast about his latest conquest in love. I'll return before you've had a chance to miss me."

"I miss you already." She tried to sound cheerful. "Now, go; out with you."

After Ameran closed the door behind Gray, she whirled around suddenly, then laughed at herself when there was nothing there to confront her. There was no one in the room save her. Maggie had already been in and turned down the bed and lit the candles.

Ameran changed quickly into a dressing gown with embroidered rosebuds lying against her breasts, and let her hair loose from the pearl combs holding it atop her head.

More shivers ran down her back, giving her the strangest feeling that someone was looking at her.

Once again, she rebuked herself for such childish fears. It was the note from Gideon that had her so upset, that and Constance's evil stares and the hisses of "witch's daughter" that resounded over and over inside her head. Thinking of Gideon Horne only made her angrier.

The floor behind her creaked.

Ameran whirled around. Her heart pounded so hard she feared it would burst from her chest. "Who are you? What do you want?"

It was then that she realized someone had indeed been watching her. Standing in the shadows of the armoire was a hooded figure in a black cape.

Her eyes flitted for one brief moment to the dressing screen beside the armoire, and she knew how he had kept his presence concealed.

The light from the candles danced on the sharp blade he was holding in his hand. The intruder lunged at her and the scream Ameran wished to release stuck in her throat. Kicking and biting and clawing at the face beneath the hood, she tried to free herself from his clutches.

Her assailant laughed harder. "I like a whore that fights." One arm clamped around her throat, nearly choking her, while the other ran the knife down her breasts, cutting at the rosebud fasteners.

"It's a pity I don't have the time to let you bargain for your life."

Even though his face was hidden from view, she could sense his cruel smile.

The knife's blade glistened threateningly as it began its plunge to her chest.

Ameran dug her teeth into his arm.

Cursing, the intruder released his hold around her

neck. "You little bitch! I'll teach you a lesson or two."

He lunged at her again.

Ameran planted her knee as hard as she could between his legs, causing the knife he held to fall to the floor. He dropped down onto one knee, still cursing and writhing in pain. Ameran kicked the knife under the bed out of his reach and ran screaming into the corridor.

At that moment Gideon and Gray rushed out into the hall.

"What is it? What is wrong?"

Ameran struggled to cover her breasts with the shreds of cotton that had once been a dressing gown. "A man, in a hood, in my room . . . tried to kill me."

Gideon charged on ahead as Gray charged after him.

"Wait, Captain Horne, what are you do—"

Then there was silence.

Ameran rushed across the threshold. The man who had attacked her was lying in a pool of blood with a dagger sticking in his heart.

Ameran ran sobbing into Gray's outstretched arms. Many were the times she had been near death, but never had it been but a beat of her heart away.

"Who was he?" Gray asked.

Gideon pulled back the hood. "I don't know. There's nothing familiar about him."

Ameran forced herself to look at her would-be murderer. He had hair redder than a cock's comb and a coarse beard the same color. His face bore a look of complete surprise.

"I've never set eyes on him before. Why would he want to kill me?"

By this time, a group had begun to gather in the

hall and one of the life guards who had just arrived kept them at bay.

Gray took hold of her again. "I don't know why he would want to harm you, but I swear to you, I'll find out."

Gideon took out the knife from the dead man's chest, wiped the blood onto the hood, then slipped the knife into his belt.

"It's all my fault, dear lady. I'm to blame," he told Ameran, his words more gentle than she'd ever heard him speak. "Had I not been so insistent about meeting with Gray, you wouldn't have had to face this horrible ordeal alone."

Ameran forced a smile. She wondered if Gray could sense the insincerity of his words.

Gray stared down at the body. "Would that I were the one who stabbed his heart." He took hold of Gideon's arm. "Thank you, my friend. Thank you. I'll always be in your debt."

"You owe me nothing. As I remember, you saved my life a time or two." He bowed to Ameran. "I gladly embrace any and all opportunities to keep the soon-to-be Lady Carlisle out of harm's way."

Ameran frowned. Something wasn't quite right.

She caught a glimpse of the dead man's knife at the foot of the bed. She remembered having kicked it out of her way when she ran from the room.

Her mind rushed back to the events of a few minutes before. There had been no sounds of struggle, only the sounds of a few words spoken in recognition by the dead man.

Gideon's eyes were intent on her. There was a smile on his face, a smile that was cold and hard.

Ameran tried not to betray her thoughts. "You're

injured. There's blood on your arm."

He waved aside her concern. "No need to worry. Just a flesh wound. I was able to wrestle away his knife before he could do me serious harm."

Gray embraced his old friend. "There are no words to . . ."

Gideon hugged him tight. "You'd have done no less for me."

Ameran's gaze settled back onto the dead man. It was all just a little too convenient, especially in light of Gideon's remarks that day aboard the *Fair Winds* when he told her he would pray for the chance to lay down his life for her.

He had gotten that chance, and in so doing, had gotten Gray's gratitude as well. Whatever differences there might have been between the two had been quickly mended by the death of the man who tried to kill her.

Heavy footsteps pounded down the hall.

The King rushed into her apartment. "What's all this commotion?" He saw the body in the blood. "Od's fish. What happened to this unlucky chap?"

Gideon was quick to tell the King what happened and to reveal the events of the assailant's death.

"Are you all right?" the King asked Ameran, his tone possessing the gentleness he usually reserved for his dogs, not people.

Ameran tried to smile. "As soon as my heart stops racing, I will be."

The King's eyes rested on her shoulder.

Ameran drew the rags that had once been her dressing gown tighter around her arms. When she dared another look into his face, she knew he had spotted the lightning-bolt birthmark.

171

The King turned to one of the guards who had followed him inside the apartment. "Who is this man?"

"I don't know, Your Majesty."

"Then I very strongly suggest that you find out within the hour," bellowed the King.

The guard saluted, then with a click of his heels left the room.

"You're certain you weren't injured," he asked Ameran, his voice taking on that uncommon gentleness again.

"I'm unharmed, Your Majesty," she assured him.

The King clasped Gideon's shoulder. "Such bravery will not go unrewarded."

Gideon fell down onto one knee. "I desire no rewards, sire, just the chance to redeem myself in your eyes."

The King didn't answer at once. "You'll have that opportunity, Gideon Horne."

"Thank you, Your Majesty." Gideon rose slowly, his eyes still downcast. "I won't disappoint you again."

"We'll see." The King turned to another of his guards. "Get the dead bastard out of here, and clean up the blood. Post one of your men outside the door all day and all night until I instruct you otherwise."

The King glanced back down at Ameran's shoulder, then forced her eyes to his. "I shall send for you in the morning. There's much we need to discuss."

Ameran bowed her head. "As you wish, sire."

The King left the room without further address, closely flanked by his guards. The largest of the guards remaining in the room slung the dead man over his shoulder with little effort.

The smell of blood and death enveloped the apart-

172

ment. A steady stream of red liquid followed the guard out of the room and down the hall.

Both arms around her, Gray led Ameran out into the hall.

Gideon walked to the right of her. He reached out for her only once, and she pulled out of his reach.

"I won't rest until I learn the truth about the assault on your life," Gideon assured Ameran.

She nodded. She didn't trust herself to look at him for fear her suspicions would be revealed.

Gray's smile was one of heart felt gratitude. "You truly are like a brother to me."

Gideon shook his head. "I know there've been differences between us as of late but . . ."

Gray motioned for him to be quiet. "There's no need for apologies or explanations. We don't have to share the same beliefs so long as we're united in friendship."

"As you say, my friend." Gideon gave Ameran another of his smiles. "Sleep well, dear lady. There won't be any more attacks. That I promise."

She wondered what was really behind his smile and his assurances.

Later, as she and Gray lay tightly enveloped in each other's arms, she could keep silent no longer. "Don't you think it strange my attacker called out to Gideon by name?"

Gray loosened his hold. "What?"

She repeated herself. "When Gideon rushed into my room, the man who attacked me called him by name. 'Wait, Captain Horne.' That's what the man said."

"Perhaps he knew Gideon." Gray gave her lips a

soothing kiss. "I know what you're thinking, but Gideon is rather well known. Because someone knows him doesn't necessarily mean he knows them." He gathered her close again. "You're tired, my darling. You've been through a nightmare. Sleep. I'm here."

Ameran couldn't sleep and she refused to keep her thoughts inside her all night. "Gideon is to blame for what almost happened to me. I know he is. I just know it!"

"I know you don't think kindly of Gideon, and I'd be the last to fault you for such feelings; however . . ."

"He *is* to blame, Gray. He is!" she exclaimed.

"You're upset," he said gently. "Tonight's events will seem much clearer in the morning."

Ameran rolled out of his arms. "Yes, I'm upset. Someone tried to kill me, and I'm certain Gideon was behind it." She sat up in bed, her arms hugging tight to knees drawn close to her chest. "Gideon's arm wasn't cut. The blood was that of the attacker. My assailant was unarmed. I'm certain of that because I kicked his knife under the bed."

Ameran jumped out of the bed and hurriedly tied her dressing gown around her.

Gray lit a candle on the bedside table. "Where are you going?"

She threw him his shirt and breeches. "We are going to get that knife. I intend to prove to you that what I say is true."

Gray let out a loud sigh. "I suppose I have no choice but to humor you if I intend to have a moment's peace tonight."

Ameran ignored his complaining and dragged him down the corridor.

The floors had been scrubbed, but the room still smelled of death.

Ameran pointed under the bed. "Look for yourself."

Gray let out another loud sigh, then dropped to his knees and peered under the wooden frame. A moment later, he came out empty handed. "Nothing there but dust."

Ameran pushed him out of the way and dove down for a look herself. There was no knife there. It was just as Gray said.

She stood back up and brushed the dust from her hands. "It's not there."

"That's most apparent."

Ameran frowned. "But it *was* there. There could only be one explanation for its absence now . . . Gideon."

"Of course, he knew the knife was there, and he sneaked back into the room to retrieve it."

There was no mistaking the sarcasm in his tone.

Ameran pushed him away and stormed out of the room. She returned to the bed in his suite in silence.

Gray's words were gentler when he reached for her a little later. "Ameran, whether you choose to believe it or not, Gideon saved your life."

Ameran pulled as far away from him as she could get. She hung to the edge of the bed, her back to him. "He didn't save my life. He did, however, make sure no one would know the truth about the motives of the intruder."

She didn't have to see his face to know that her announcement had fallen onto deaf ears.

"What did Gideon have to discuss with you that

was so urgent it couldn't wait until morning? Tell me," she begged.

Gray yawned. "He was concerned over our friendship. He wanted us to put our differences behind us before our relationship was put in further jeopardy."

"And such heartfelt discussions could not have waited until daylight?"

She could sense his hesitation once more.

"As far as I'm concerned, the discussion could have waited until tomorrow, but Gideon has been greatly troubled by our parting of ways and was most anxious to make amends."

"And make amends he did, didn't he?" She could tell she was getting nowhere.

Gray reached out to her. "Ameran, it's late. You're overwrought. Please, can't we . . ."

Ameran refused to be comforted. "Hear me out, Gray. I can't sleep with such a heavy heart."

Gray slumped back onto the pillow and stared up at the overhead beams. "Very well," he said gently. "I'm listening."

"You're listening, but you're not hearing." She turned to him, her eyes pleading. "Gideon planned the attack. I don't know if he intended for me to die, or if he wanted to scare me. Whatever, he's the cause of that man waiting in my room after you had so conveniently been summoned away."

"What could Gideon possibly hope to gain by such ill deeds?"

"Everything, Gray. He had everything to gain, and it appears he's succeeded." She laid her head down onto his chest. She didn't want to anger him. She wanted only for him to realize how dangerous Gideon really was. "By his actions, he's gotten back into your good graces, as well as the King's." She rolled over onto her stomach, her chin still settled atop his chest. "I believe Gideon, and probably Constance as well, hired someone to kill me, or at least make me think I was in death's way. Unfortunately for my attacker, he didn't know that part of the plan was for him to lose his life so Gideon could play the valiant hero."

"Please, Ameran, you don't know any such thing. You're only upsetting yourself by . . ."

"What I say is true!" she said, fighting to control her anger. "It's true."

"But you don't know that as fact."

Angry eyes pierced the dark stillness shrouding the room. "It's true, for I know it's true. You forget that my mother's blood flows in my veins as well. I'm privy to feelings and intuitions others can't understand."

Gray punched at his pillow. "Oh, Ameran, next you'll be telling me you intended to concoct some potion to render Gideon helpless."

"Would that I could. I'd do it without hesitation." Her words were as cold as the air between them.

"Bah!"

Ameran sat up in bed. "What did you say?"

"I said *bah!* All this talk of witches and spells and potions is as ridiculous as accusing Gideon of plotting to kill you."

Her words were calm, but laced with a chill. "You're a brave man to make such remarks when your life is also in danger."

"You're certain without one doubt that it was Gideon you saw in the gardens with Constance?" asked Gray after the longest while. His words were kinder, softer.

177

"I have no doubts." She said a silent prayer of thanks. "I would stake my life on it. I almost had to."

Gray stroked her hair in silence. It seemed an eternity had passed before he spoke again.

"I pray you're wrong."

"I pray I'm wrong, too, for your sake as well as my own." She brushed her lips across his. "But in my heart, I know that I've never been more right about anything."

With a soft moan, she rolled over onto her beloved. Daybreak would come soon enough, and there would be time then to worry and plan. At that moment, more than anything else in the world, she wanted to be as close to him as she could get, and for the time being, all else was forgotten.

Chapter Ten

"Why didn't you show me your birthmark when Gray first brought you to me?"

The King's question didn't surprise Ameran. After last night, she had expected as much. During the past hour as they walked along the Thames, making polite talk about the sailboats gliding over the water, she had wondered when that matter would arise. What she had not anticipated was the urgency in his voice when he demanded an answer.

"You didn't ask to see any such mark," she replied as she leaned down to pat one of the spaniels following close on their heels. "I told you the truth in my letters. I didn't see the need to prove to you or anyone else why I am who I say."

Hands locked behind his back, the King slowed his strides. "I suspected as much. You have your mother's eyes to be certain, but your dark coloring is more like mine." He smiled to himself. "When I was born, so dark was my complexion that my dear mother dubbed me her little black boy. Perhaps it was the Italian blood in my lineage." He studied her closely. "My dear sister Minette had a delicate little nose that turned up ever so slightly just as yours."

She felt herself blush under his close perusal.

The King's sigh was heavy, his countenance sad. "My poor darling Minette. She should have been a Queen, not a King's mistress to be poisoned by a spiteful husband." He laid his hand upon her shoulder. "Forgive my ramblings, dear Ameran. The older I grow, the more entranced in my memories I become."

They sat down on a bench at the water's edge. The guards accompanying them kept their distance. The puppies yelped and chased one another and tried to jump up into their laps. Ameran took pity on the tiniest, the butt of the others' sharp teeth, and put him up onto her knees, wrapping him up in her skirt.

"That little fellow is going to make a fine hunting dog," the King remarked.

"How do you know?"

"Because he knows he has much to prove to his master and to the other dogs."

Ameran smiled. She had a feeling there was a much deeper meaning to his words.

"I suppose Sybil Chandler's last breath was drawn cursing me," he said, turning his attention to the river.

"I won't lie to you and tell you she didn't hate you."

The King shrugged his lofty shoulders. "She had reason. I made promises I never intended to keep." His smile was weak. "A King is no more or no less than a man." He took hold of her arm, then, as if embarrassed by his gesture, let go. "I'm sorry an innocent child had to suffer for my foolishness."

"It's circumstance, not another's foolish acts, that determine one's fate," she mused aloud.

"Wise words for one so young." His mood brightened. "Is it true you're in love with Lord Carlisle?"

That was the one question she hadn't anticipated. "I am, Your Majesty."

"Anyone can see the man is completely besotted by you." He pulled at his thick, black moustache. "What I don't understand is why you didn't return to England with him when you first met?"

Ameran recounted the story of their separation, including Gideon's role in their parting. She was surprised at the ease with which she could converse with the King, and just as surprised with his interest in the plight of a pair of seemingly doomed lovers.

"So you hold Gideon Horne responsible for this cruel misunderstanding."

She nodded. "I do, Your Majesty." And so much more that, which she decided was best left unsaid.

"What does Gray have to say about Gideon's deceit?"

Ameran cuddled another of the puppies that had jumped into her lap. "He is, of course, most grateful to Gideon for saving my life last night."

"Gratitude has been known to be blinding. Shall we walk on?"

It was apparent to her the King had no intention of further discussions about Gideon, but Ameran sensed she was not the only one suspicious of Gideon's motives of the previous evening.

They stopped by the canal and watched the ducks for a while. The King took bread crusts from his pocket and tossed them among the flutter of wings. "Come, I'll show you my physic garden," he said when there were no more crumbs.

He then led her through a series of little gardens beyond the parade field, occasionally stopping to bend down and pat one of his dogs.

"Every time my ships visit new ports, the captains know to bring back to me exotic herbs and spices for my plantings. I don't understand why my learned physicians don't look to nature to cure man's ailments," he told her as they surveyed mound after mound of tiny leafed greenery. He pointed out different plants and explained what malady each would cure. "Unfortunately, it seems that those esteemed men of medicine would rather torture and butcher those who suffer than cure them."

They walked on past more fountains and gardens with flowering plants and low hanging vines. Once back inside the courtyard, there were horse soldiers on parade and foot soldiers on patrol. Noble gentlemen and gentlewomen were strolling about their grounds. The men bowed, the ladies curtsied to the King, and Ameran was uncomfortably aware of the sidelong glances cast her way.

The King seemed quite unconcerned about their quiet mumblings and inquiring stares.

"Would you have told me about your birthmark if I hadn't seen it for myself?" he asked, once they were inside the front corridor of Whitehall Castle.

"I don't think so, Your Majesty." She was grateful for the dim light inside the hallway, for the longer the King looked at her, the redder the blush on her cheeks.

"But why?" He did not seem to understand. "Why wouldn't you have showed it to me at once? Didn't your mother tell you that I, too, bear one on my right shoulder?"

"She told me. Yes." Ameran sought for the right words to make him understand that she demanded nothing of him, nor would she ever use the accident of her birth to accomplish anything she couldn't do for herself.

"That which I desired most, sire, my freedom, you gave to me. Without your intervention, I would surely be dead by now, if not by the swords of those who demanded my life, then by the violent waves of the channel."

The King looked shocked. "A Stuart never takes his own life. Others may take it from him, but he never gives it willingly."

Her own shock was apparent. "I had no intention of flinging myself into the channel in despair, Your Majesty," she hastily assured him. "I was going to cross it in a fishing boat."

The King's laugh was hearty. "Spoken like a true Stuart."

Ameran caught herself just as she was about to touch the sleeve of his coat. "I'm most grateful to you, sire."

The King didn't hide his pleasure. "I think I'll make you a countess . . . of Southwicke, perhaps. I'm certain there will be no objection if Lord Carlisle were to wed the Countess of Southwicke."

Ameran could think of no words to express her heart's feelings.

"That is, if being a countess is to your liking," said the King with a twinkle in his dark eyes.

"I don't know how to respond, Your Majesty."

The King clasped both her hands in his. " Perhaps one day we'll truly feel the affections of a father and his daughter, but until that time comes, I hope we'll be friends."

Ameran bowed her head. "Yes, Your Majesty. I'd like that very much."

"Tell me, Ameran Michol, am I as you imagined?" he asked just as they were about to go in separate directions.

"I didn't expect such kindness." Her words were soft, as was the look in her eyes. "And you're far grander than in my imaginings."

He seemed pleased by her answers. "I truly regret any sorrow the circumstances of your birth may have caused you," he told her, his voice soft and sincere.

"My life hasn't been entirely unpleasant, sire," she said, remembering the wonderful days spent with Guido listening to his stories and learning all those things he would have taught a son. And there had been times, though rare, when her mother laughed and played and sang songs to her. "There are those who have suffered more than I."

The King did not speak at once. "You're truly remarkable, Ameran Michol."

Ameran lifted up the tiniest of the puppies and gave him a kiss. He licked her nose, and she giggled out loud.

The King kissed her cheek. "I'll look forward to our next early morning stroll through the gardens."

"As will I, sire." She gave a little bow, then turned and ran up the stairs.

Something made her look back behind her. The King was following her with his eyes. There was a peculiar smile on his face. She was certain when he looked at her he didn't see the witch who had condemned his life and his reign to eternal damnation, but saw instead his little sister Minette.

Her good mood vanished the moment she opened the door to her apartment and found Constance seated in one of the rose-cushioned chairs in front of the gray stone fireplace. No doubt she had charmed the guard positioned outside the door to permit her entry.

Even though the room was just as she had left it that morning, Ameran knew that the Duchess of Morrow had been rummaging through her belongings, perhaps in search of potents and spells and thick, black volumes of devil's doings.

"If I'd known I had a visitor, I wouldn't have lingered in the gardens so long." Ameran made herself stay calm. Nothing would give the Duchess more pleasure than to see her upset. "If you've come to see Gray, he left before sunrise. I don't expect him back until this evening."

The room no longer smelled of death, and the blood had been scrubbed from the floors.

There was no trace of kindness or concern in Constance's smile. "It's you I came to see. I understand someone tried to kill you last night."

Ameran sat down in the chair opposite the Duchess, her hands folded in her lap. "I'm most grateful for your concern, but as you can see, I escaped without injury."

"Yes, I can see that," she said with a sigh. "I heard your attacker is a thief of wide renown. I'm sure he came to Whitehall to see what he could steal."

"He may well have been a thief, but that wasn't his purpose when he attacked me."

She had a feeling she wasn't telling Constance anything she didn't already know.

"Surely my health is not the reason for your visit?" she asked Constance, her stare one of accusation.

Constance stared at her long and hard. "Are you truly a witch?"

"There are those who say I am."

Constance appeared undaunted. "I thought so. After all, that could be the only possible explanation as to why Gray chose you over me. You cast a spell on him, didn't you?"

Ameran laughed. "He accuses me of that every evening as we're making love." She knew that would wipe the spiteful grin from Constance's face. "My spells have nothing to do with the devil's arts."

Constance smoothed the pink ruffles at her neck. "I hear rumors that you claim to be the King's daughter. Are they true?"

Ameran held her smile. "I suggest you ask the King." She could tell from Constance's fidgeting that she was starting to lose her patience.

"Your mother was condemned to die by hanging for being a witch," said Constance, not asking a question, but stating the information as fact.

"My mother is dead."

"Yes, so I've heard. Do you intend to stay long at Whitehall?"

"That's not a decision I'll make alone."

"Oh?"

Ameran relaxed in the chair. She could almost enjoy the intrusion into her privacy. "That's a decision to be made by my future husband."

Constance's laugh was without humor. "Gray will never marry you."

"We shall see."

Constance rose from her chair. "If I were you, I'd be wary. You might not be as lucky as you were last night."

Ameran couldn't resist sticking out her foot when Constance glided past in all her glory. As a result, the

Duchess of Morrow was sent sprawling across the floor face down.

Only the tiniest of smiles greeted the grand Duchess when she finally managed to recapture her cool composure. "Your luck might well be running out as well," Ameran reminded her as she opened the door and pointed the way out.

Only after Ameran slammed the door behind the Duchess did her limbs begin to quiver. Constance had all but admitted to scheming to have her killed. She might prove to be just as dangerous and as deadly as Gideon.

As soon as her heart had settled, Ameran decided to seek out the company of Nell Gwyn. Gray hadn't expressly forbidden her to see the King's favorite mistress; he had merely suggested it, and at that moment, she had to talk with someone who would listen. If anyone knew of the goings on at Court, it would be Nell!

Nell wasted no time letting her own feelings be known to Ameran when she learned of the happenings of the previous night and the confrontation with Constance less than an hour before.

"Gideon and Constance have always been up to no good, if you ask me," said Nell as she poured tea from a silver pot in the sitting room of her home at Pall Mall. "They pretend to be the most bitter of enemies, but on the sly, those two are closer than two peas in a pod."

"Gray is convinced they despise each other," said Ameran as she sipped her tea.

"They've succeeded in pulling the wool over most everybody's eyes." Nell offered Ameran a plate of sugar-sprinkled scones still hot from the oven. "That hussy's been through three husbands. They all died under mysterious circumstances." Nell winked. "If ye know what I mean. Poisoned I would wager. That seems to be the popular method, for it is hard to trace."

Ameran was aware of the dainty china tea cup shaking ever so slightly in her hand. She wondered if poison would be the method Constance and Gideon tried next.

Nell licked the sugar from her fingers and reached for another scone. "We had a bad scare at Court a few years back with one mysterious death after another. Even the Queen was suspected as being an accomplice in one such instance. Of course, poor Charlie had to hush those rumors in a hurry." Nell gave her a tight hug. "Poor darling. Ye must have had quite a fright last night. I'm surprised ye be up and about at all."

Ameran remembered her restlessness of the night before. "I can't sleep until I find out who's responsible for my brush with death."

Nell squeezed her arm. "Ye have Gray, darling. No need for ye to worry."

Ameran didn't smile. "Gray refuses to believe that Gideon is responsible for what happened." She then told Nell about the knife that had disappeared from under the bed. "Now, thanks to Constance, I have no proof to substantiate my claim."

"Ah, she be a shrewd one, that bitch. Mark my word, of the pair of them, she's every bit as low-down and conniving as Gideon. I've known women like her, I have, and they be more dangerous than wild dogs foaming at the mouth."

188

Ameran held the scone to her mouth but took no bites. "Constance wants Gray for herself. That's reason enough for her to want me dead, but what about Gideon? I pose no threat to him. He has nothing to gain from having me killed."

"I don't trust Captain Horne," Nell remarked between bites.

"I'm afraid one day he'll turn on Gray."

"That may well happen," Nell agreed. "Gray is everything Gideon wants to be and never can be."

"Gray told me Gideon once saved his life." Ameran frowned. "I'm sure Gideon will never allow him to forget it."

Nell chuckled. "Gideon does nothing unless it's to his advantage. Gray will be repaying that debt the rest of his life."

Ameran's face remained creased with worry. "If only I could convince Gray just how dangerous Gideon is." She then told her friend about her first encounter with Gideon and how his lies had separated her and Gray. "I don't know why Gray refuses to believe Gideon capable of any wrongdoing."

Nell took hold of her hand. "Gideon could talk his way out of anything."

"I'm afraid he'll cause us much more trouble," said Ameran sadly.

"If Gray doesn't keep an eye on him, then you must," Nell suggested.

"I know."

Nell offered her another scone. "I don't understand this friendship between Gideon and Gray. Gray and the King are very close, and Charles despises Gideon. Several months back, a plot was discovered to assassinate the King, and Gideon was suspected of being

189

one of the instigators, but he had covered his tracks so well that nothing could be proven against him, not when the three other instigators were all murdered in their sleep. Quite convenient for Gideon, wouldn't you say?"

Ameran agreed it was.

"With those dead, no one dared to accuse Gideon of any misdeed for fear they might be next."

Her face troubled, Ameran told Nell about the parting exchange between Gideon and the King the night before.

Nell's nose wrinkled. "That scoundrel. If the truth be known, he staged it all just so he could be some grand hero and have Gray and the King both in his debt." Her face softened. "Has the King spoken to you alone yet?"

Smiling, Ameran nodded. "We had a most enjoyable stroll through the gardens this morning."

Nell seemed pleased. "You're his daughter, aren't you?"

Ameran nodded. She knew Nell could be trusted.

Nell's smile was one of satisfaction. "I can see a lot of you in him, you know. Of course, there'll be those at court who'll swear you've bewitched him. The Queen, for one; Constance, for another."

Ameran was surprised at just how much Nell knew, information which could have only come from the King himself.

Ameran absently pushed her long hair back from her shoulder. She caught Nell looking at the bare flesh just revealed and knew what was on her mind.

Nell quickly looked away.

"Is this what you're looking for?" Smiling, Ameran

slid down the apple green ribbons fastening the sleeve of her dress.

"The King wondered if you bore the mark of the Stuarts," Nell commented. The tip of her tiny finger traced the marking. "He wanted so much to believe that you were his daughter, and yet he's been tricked so many times before. In spite of all else, he has a good soul. You must show it to him. Promise me you will. He'll be so pleased."

"He saw it last night," Ameran said, sliding the ribbons back up her arm. "My dressing gown was torn in the attack."

Nell took her hand. "With all his faults, and believe me, they be many, the King is a kind and wonderful man. He'll do all that's right by you." She squealed with delight. "That makes you Charlie and Jamie's sister. Why, me and you be practically related." She gave Ameran another tight squeeze. "What a fit that old prune-faced Queen will have when she finds out that news."

"For the moment, I don't want any one else to know of my relationship to the King," Ameran said solemnly. She knew her secret was safe with Nell.

"I won't breathe a word of it. I swear."

Ameran felt she owed Nell some explanation. "I don't want my presence at Whitehall to cause the King any trouble. You've heard talk of my being a witch, haven't you?"

Nell nodded. "Rumors Constance has started out of vengeance."

Ameran thought long and hard about what she was about to say, then revealed to Nell the darker side of her mother's nature.

"But that doesn't mean you're a witch," Nell was

quick to point out.

"I don't practice evil sorcery, and yet there are times when I feel if I did, I wouldn't be constantly plagued by troubles." She couldn't help but break into a smile. "For I would make all my troubles and those causing them disappear in a puff of smoke."

They laughed and helped themselves to more scones.

"Where are the boys?" Ameran asked Nell a little later.

"They be at Whitehall for their fencing lesson. Charlie's determined to make them expert swordsmen. He holds those laddies very dear, he does." Nell frowned. "He thought the world of Jemmy, too. I did as well. I adored that boy, but what a rascal he turned out to be. Ever since he was a little boy, he had dreams of one day being King, and any affection he ever showed his dear father was on that account. He's even making some wild claims that Charles and his mother were married. Od's fish! That Lucy Walters was nothing more than a tavern wench with a pretty face. She'd hop on the table with any gent who had a shilling to spare."

Nell sighed. "Oh, well, all the hopes the Duke of Monmouth might have entertained about succeeding his father will soon be nipped in the bud. Up until now, Charles has wanted to save his son from public humiliation, but now that it has gone this far, Charles has no choice but denounce such claims."

"Is it true that he's going to publish in the *Gazette* for all of London to see that any rumors regarding his marriage to anyone but the Queen are all vicious lies?" queried Ameran.

Nell nodded. "Sad to say, but there's no other way."

She shook her head. "I could claw out the eyes of anybody who ever caused my Charlie one moment of heartache," she said fiercely.

"You truly do love the King, don't you?"

"With all my heart and soul," replied Nell. Her eyes took on a faraway gaze. "I loved him the first time I laid eyes on him. I was only ten years old when the King came home to take his rightful place on the throne. I remember like it was yesterday. Me and me sissy, Rosie, climbed up to the highest roof top to see the procession. Ah, the world has never seen a more handsome and a more gallant gent than me Charlie Stuart." She placed her hand across her breast. "Me heart took to fluttering when I saw him, and I knew then and there he was the one." She let out a long sigh. "He was wearing a grand military uniform with silver chains around his neck, and a purple velvet cloak around his shoulders, and shiny black boots up to his knees. Atop his head was a beaver hat with a long purple plume curling out behind him. Those beautiful black locks fell onto his shoulders. Throughout the street was the smell of roasted rumps and hot pies, and there were bonfires all the way from Saint Paul's to the Stock Market."

Nell laughed as she reached for another scone. "I knew the moment I saw him that he was destined for me. Why, the King looked right up at me, straight up at me, and smiled. I swear he did. I swear it. I decided then and there I was going to save myself for him in spite of my ma's urgings that I find me a rich gentleman to support me."

Ameran listened attentively. She said very little as Nell told her about her childhood. Nell was warm and funny, and she liked being in the woman's company no matter what Gray said.

"Me ma, you see, owned a bawdy house where fine gentlemen could go and be served whatever they liked, ale, brandy, wine or one of the girls who tended them. Ma got Rosie started in the business early on, but not me. I wanted no man unless I loved him." She giggled like a young girl. "Why, I used to squint and scowl and make myself look ugly so they wouldn't put their filthy hands on me. They'd try to touch me, and I'd squeal like a stuck hog. I used to pretend I was having fits so the men'd think I was crazy and leave me alone."

Ameran couldn't stop laughing. "No wonder you were the finest actress ever to grace Drury Lane."

"Did Lord Carlisle tell you that?"

Ameran nodded.

"I'm surprised. I am. He don't like me very much." Nell poked her in the side. "I'd wager if the Lord knew you be coming to me house for tea, he'd be in an uproar."

"Oh, no," Ameran said quickly. "I told him all about our chat in the gardens."

Nell eyed her with suspicion. "And what did he say about that?"

She dropped her gaze. "He told me he was glad I had made a friend."

"Do ye have any aspirations for the stage, girlie?"

Ameran shook her head.

Nell laughed. "Good, cause you be a terrible liar."

"I should very much like to see you perform," Ameran told her.

Nell rolled back her eyes. "Alas, me dear, I am retired from the stage. Charlie didn't think it was a fitting profession for the mother of his sons, so he

194

bought me this fine house, and cut a hole in the gate at his gardens and can be here in less than five minutes when the mood strikes him."

"Do you miss the stage?"

"Terribly," she answered, a little sadly. "And there are times when I threaten to return, but all in all, I'm content with my life."

Nell poured them more tea. "When I was a girl at me ma's bawdy house, I knew 'twould be but a short time until Ma peddled me off to one of the flesh merchants in the street, so I got meself a job with Orange Moll selling oranges in front of the King's Theatre. And do ye know what happened? The finest actor of all times took a fancy to me. His name was Charlie Hart, my first Charles so to speak."

Nell smiled with fond remembrances. "He taught me to read and to act, among other things, of course, but I never forgot about Charles the King. Oh, no, I used to be green with envy whenever his mistress, Lady Castlemain, came to the theatre flaunting her fine gifts from the King. Charles Hart would get me bit roles in his plays, and the first time I was ever on stage, I looked right up into the King's box and he smiled right down upon me just like he remembered me from that day he seen me on the roof top. I cried for days when I learned he'd sent for Moll Davies that night to entertain him in private, and I all but pulled her knotted hair out I did when she come back showing off a ruby ring he'd given her."

Nell lounged back on the settee. "I didn't know it then, but me day was acoming. Charles Hart had me play a lovesick girl who follows her lover disguised as his page. I had to wear the tightest green breeches." She lifted her skirt and stretched out her short but shapely legs. "All of London, the King included, was smitten with this pair." She winked. "And that night it was me and not Moll the King sent for."

She let out another long sigh. "Are ye sure I'm not a boring ye, dearie?"

"Boring! No! Why, your stories are anything but," Ameran quickly assured her. "Please, do go on."

"If ye insist."

"Oh, I do. I do."

Nell settled back down. "I was escorted to his chambers where a few of his closest friends had gathered." She closed her eyes as if she was recalling all in great detail inside her mind. "There was Rochester and his wife, the old sow, Lord Buckingham and his lady, and Lords Buckley, Etherege and Mulgrave. I sang for them and danced and recited poetry Charles Hart had taught me."

Nell languished in her sweet reminiscences. "And then we were alone. Just he and I. I thought for certain my heart would stop dead! The only time in me life I've ever been at a loss for words."

Ameran clapped her hands in delight. "It must have been a dream come true for you."

"Oh, it was. It was indeed." Nell fanned herself with her handkerchief. "I shall go to me grave with such sweet recollections of how he wooed me." She fanned herself faster. " 'Tonight I am a man, an ordinary man by the name of Charles Stuart,' he said, 'and you are a beautiful woman, Nell of Old Drury,' and then he recited a poem to me. Me Charlie is a fine poet. 'I think there is no hell like love, like loving too well.' " Her dimples danced merrily. "And what a night that was. I knew I was in love. I was carried back to my lodgings in a fine sedan chair. All the girls asked to see what trinket he'd given me, but I knew what I had was far more dear than any bauble."

"How wonderfully romantic." Ameran felt herself growing more and more comfortable with her new-found friend. She only wished Gray was a little more understanding.

"Our next meeting was anything but romantic." Nell doubled over with laughter. "No sooner had we gotten settled in the royal bed when the Queen arrived unannounced, and I jumped behind a wall hanging to hide myself. The Queen thought Charlie was sick, so she brung him a posset. And then one of those damnable dogs of his came out from under the bed with one of me slippers and dropped it at her royal foot."

Ameran laughed so hard her sides ached. "What happened next?"

"Needless to say, the good Catherine took her posset and left." Nell laughed with her. "We've had some grand times, me and me Charlie Stuart. Oh, he's had other women—he has a reputation to uphold. Though I like to believe I be the one he always comes to in times of trouble or when he needs a tender ear." Nell winked. "Many are the afternoons he climbs over the wall and into my bedroom window."

Ameran thought Nell's acceptance of the King's in-fidelity was odd, but she said nothing. She, herself, couldn't imagine being so tolerant of a man she loved with all her heart.

Nell slapped her on the knee. "Here I've spent all afternoon talking about me, and we've done nothing to solve yer problems with Gideon and Constance."

"But you did get my thoughts off those two for a while, and I'm most grateful for that," Ameran assured her.

Nell squeezed her hand. "Watch out for them, both of them. Those two are up to no good. Don't let anybody convince you otherwise. Gray will find out for himself sooner or later."

"I hope it is sooner," Ameran remarked solemnly. "I have a feeling whatever game they're playing might well have a deadly ending."

Nell's concern was evident. "Take care, dearie. Keep one eye behind ye, and Gray, too." She patted her hand. "Ye know where I be if ye need me."

Ameran couldn't resist giving Nell a hug. "You're wonderful. Truly, you are."

"Ye be quite wonderful yourself, dearie." Nell tossed back her chestnut curls. "Fitting, don't ye think? After all, we nearly be relatives."

Ameran laughed with her. Somehow, she didn't expect Gray to see the situation in quite the same light.

Chapter Eleven

Ameran cuddled closer to Gray and watched the gentle rise and fall of his chest while he slept. She loved to watch him when he wasn't aware of her eyes on him. His face was so handsome, so strong. She couldn't wait to have sons that looked exactly like him.

She leaned over and brushed her lips across his cheek. The jagged scar cut deep into the flesh was not a mark of harshness, but one of dignity. She was so proud of Gray. Surely there had never been a more courageous sea warrior. He had earned the devotion of his crew and the respect of the King of England. If only he were not so blind in matters concerning Gideon!

Gideon. Just the thought of him made her cringe. Oh, he was a shrewd one. The way he bowed and scraped to Gray, and to herself, was sickening. But there had been times when she had caught him looking at her behind Gray's back, looks that made her feel cheap and dirty. He was up to no good, she was certain, but what exactly did he have planned? And why did she have such a foreboding of doom?

Ameran lovingly brushed the pale strands back

from Gray's brow. Poor darling! He was so kind and good. He couldn't accept that one who professed eternal friendship and brotherly love would cause a moment's unrest to him or to a loved one.

Gray reached out in his sleep and pulled her closer. His eyes weren't open yet, but upon his lips was the sweetest of smiles. His sigh was one of peaceful contentment.

She ever so gently kissed his cheek.

The fierceness was quick to return to her lovely, dark features. Gideon was as sly as a fox. He had answers and explanations for every discrepancy she brought to Gray's attention. Even though Gray had not said as much, she had a feeling he had been persuaded by Gideon that she hadn't kicked the knife under the bed at all, but had merely imagined doing so in her frantic state. Next thing she knew, Gray would be suggesting that Constance had come to her apartment not to rummage through her belongings, but to offer her friendship. Even the information about her attacker had come from Gideon, and Gray had accepted without question what he had been told. The man's name was John Taylor, and he was a thief from Bastings who had come to Whitehall to ply his trade. That might well be true, but she would wager if the complete truth were known, Gideon and Constance had employed him for a crime far worse than theft. She supposed the truth would never be known until Gideon was found out. She could only pray no one would have to suffer until that day came.

She laid her head on Gray's chest and inhaled the wonderful scent of his manliness.

The past two weeks at Whitehall had not been entirely unpleasant. Nearly every morning she had joined the King for his walks in the gardens, and the more time she spent in his company, the more she liked him. Had he not found her company entertaining, he certainly wouldn't have sent a messenger to her room the night before with news where he could be found the next day. The King was a good friend, and she felt at ease with him. After their discussion about her birthmark that first day in the gardens, no further mention was ever made of her parentage. He didn't try to be a father and she didn't aspire to be acknowledged as his daughter. She asked only for his companionship, and Nell had told her that this endeared the King all the more to her.

Queen Catherine was a different matter entirely. She made it a point to avoid her, and every time they passed in the corridor, the Queen would lift her crucifix to shield herself from Ameran's eyes, and hiss.

Excitement beyond her wildest dreams had filled her days and nights—parties, the theater, Newmarket horse races, sailing down the Thames, horseback riding with the fox and hounds across the countryside. She'd never thought life could be filled with so many delightful diversions.

Her smile of satisfaction was quick to turn to a frown. Unfortunately there had been a few encounters with Constance. Rumors of witchcraft had spread throughout Whitehall, and there were those who looked at her with suspicion and loathing. There were those among Constance's intimate circle of friends, Queen Catherine included, who were certain Sybil Chandler had come back from the grave to destroy them all.

A loud rapping sounded at the door, then a panicked voice calling out her name and pleading for her assistance.

Gray flung back the covers and Ameran jumped from the bed, running to the door, covering herself with a blanket.

Mrs. Turner was standing outside the room. Her face was an ashen gray, and tears were streaming down her cheeks.

"Ye must come quick, lassie. There's been a fire. Little Jamie, he's . . ."

She began to sob uncontrollably.

Ameran grabbed a cloak from her armoire and swung it over her night dress.

"I'm coming with you," said Gray, hurrying to get into his shirt and trousers. He put on his boots as they were running down the hallway.

Mrs. Turner led them down the back stairs and through a dark cellar out into a cluster of trees in bloom with white and pink buds.

The King was sitting beside another of the many fish ponds, deep in meditation with his head in his hands.

At the sound of running feet, he looked up. His dark face blanched white. "Mrs. Turner! What is it? Nell? The boys?"

The housekeeper kept running. "It be Jamie, sire. He's got burned."

The King took several running strides and caught up with them.

Hidden among the vine overhanging on the stone wall was a hole wide enough for a large man to squeeze through. Mrs. Turner led them through it and down a path lined by rosebushes about to burst out in bloom.

Nell was sitting on the settee in her sleeping gown, crying and cradling her little son close to her breast.

"Father!" Charlie ran into his father's arms. "You won't let Jamie die, will you?"

The King held his son close. "Shhh, don't fret, lad. Your brother will be fine."

His look was not as confident as his words.

Ameran knelt down at Nell's feet. She didn't have to ask what happened. The little boy's curly locks were singed and big blisters had started festering on his cheeks.

The King dropped down onto one knee. His big hand reached out to soothe his little son's whimperings.

Ameran could see the agony on his face.

"It's as though history has repeated itself," he said, glancing up at Ameran with a look of complete helplessness.

"A candle . . . his bed went up in flames . . . would have been burned to death had Charlie not dragged him out." Nell's body was wracked with sobs. She looked piteously up at the King. "You'll make him well, won't you?"

"I wish to God that were in my power, Nell." He laid his head on Nell's knee and gently stroked his son's arm. "There, there Jamie. The worst is over with."

"What's been done for the lad?" Gray asked Mrs. Turner.

It was hard for her to sound the words between her deep heaves for breath. "Cold water . . . compresses . . . salves . . . that beautiful little face. Scarred for life."

Nell held tight to her little boy, rocking him slowly

and humming a lullaby as tears fell from her eyes.

"Go to my physik garden," the King instructed Mrs. Turner. "There is a plant with long, fleshy stems along the east wall. Cut a dozen of the stems and bring them quick."

Mrs. Turner was shaking so she could hardly get her feet to move one in front of the other.

"I'll go, sire," spoke up Gray as he bolted from the room.

The King held Nell and his sons close. "There, there, my brave little soldier. I shall make a potent that will take the fire from your face."

"Thank you, Papa," a little voice whimpered.

The King's eyes sought Ameran's. "Your mother . . . she could . . . can you . . . will you do for my son what your mama did for me?"

"I pray I can, sire," she replied without hesitation. "Turn his face to me, Nell," she said softly.

Nell sobbed harder. "Such a beautiful little face it was. Just like a little cherub."

"Get a hold on yourself, Nellie. For the boy's sake," the King entreated gently.

Nell sniffed. "Please, please Ameran, you must try."

Ameran eased Jamie's face from his mother's bosom. It was hard to keep her smile. "Jamie, darling, it is I, sweetheart . . . your friend, Ameran. I'm going to try to help you, but I need to put my hands on your face. All right, love? I'll try not to hurt you."

Jamie screamed when her fingers brushed lightly over his cheeks. "It hurts! Please, don't hurt me."

"Shhh, baby, shhh," Ameran tried to comfort him. "It'll hurt but only a little and only for a minute.

I promise. Try and be brave, darling."

The King let out a big laugh to cover his worry. "He'll be brave. Why, he's one of the most courageous warriors I have."

"Truly, Papa?" asked Jamie, trying his best to smile.

"Truly, my son." The King blinked quickly.

"The fencing master says Jamie is as fine a swordsman as he's ever seen," piped up Charlie, doing his best to smile.

Slowly, Jamie turned his face the rest of the way to her.

"Dear God." It was all Ameran could do to keep from crying herself. How unfair for a child to endure such pain. She remembered another cherubic face that had festering blisters and smoke burns.

She was aware of the servants outside the room peering in and pointing and whispering, but she had to keep those little cheeks plump and rosy even if it meant her own demise.

Tenderly, she spread her hands over Jamie's little cheeks, and whispering words so soft that only he could hear, Ameran blew her breath through opened fingers and onto the seared flesh.

Jamie stopped sobbing. He looked up at Ameran and grinned. "Am I better now?"

Ameran laughed. "Soon, my darling, soon."

Nell stopped crying. She looked from the King to Ameran. "What did you do?"

"Some things are best left unexplained," said the King softly. "Jamie will be fine, just as I was fine that day long ago."

Still sobbing, Nell clasped Ameran's hand. "I will live out me days repaying me debt to you. You have

205

saved me babe's life. All that I have is yours."

"You owe me nothing, Nell." Ameran looked up at the frightened faces of the servants. They cowered one behind the other. Had she merely imagined it, or had one really cautioned: don't let her look at you for you will be damned for sure.

The King dismissed them with a wave of his arm. "Not a word of this to anyone, or I shall have the whole lot of you whipped and dragged through town."

Charlie put his hand on his brother's forehead. "Feel, Mummy. The fire is gone."

Nell caressed her little boy's cheek with a mother's tenderness. "His face is cool indeed."

The King helped Ameran to her feet. Heartfelt gratitude shone in his eyes. "Thank you."

Ameran bowed her head as Gray ran back into the room carrying stems from the bush the King had specified.

The King squeezed the thick, white liquid from the stems and rubbed the moisture onto Jamie's face.

"I'm so very tired, Papa," Jamie said with a sigh.

The King kissed the boy's cheek. "Then close your eyes, my little fellow, and sleep."

"You'll be here when I awaken?" he asked hopefully.

"I won't leave your side," the King promised.

Jamie fell asleep with a smile on his face.

Ameran's eyes fell upon the King. In spite of his shortcomings as a monarch, Charles the Second was a loving father to his little boys. In many ways, a King and a fisherman were not so different after all.

She felt Gray's hand on her arm. Her eyes were drawn to his. The love she saw reflected within

206

warmed her soul.

Ameran gazed back to little Jamie. His eyes were still closed, and the tiny hint of a smile remained on his lips. Nell's head was resting upon the shoulder of her beloved and little Charlie was curled up at his father's feet. All was well at last.

"We'll take our leave now," Ameran said softly to Nell. "I'll come by later."

Nell smiled and nodded, as did the King.

Several days after the incident with Jamie, Ameran was aware of suspicious glances being cast her way by an upstairs maid named Maggie. Usually, the serving girl liked to chat at leisure, but on this particular morn, she seemed most anxious to finish her work.

"What is it, Maggie? What's troubling you so?" Ameran stopped brushing her hair and gazed at Maggie's plump, troubled reflection. "You're usually so chipper and full of tales. Are you ill?"

"Oh, no, mum, not ill at all," she replied as she hurried on with her chores.

"Come on, Maggie, I thought we were friends. If something is bothering you, tell me. I might be able to help." Ameran put down the brush and waited for a reply.

Maggie glanced up from her dusting and looked at her as if she wanted to tell her all, but then quickly changed her mind and returned her attention to the table she was dusting.

"Why such a long face on such a pretty girl?" Ameran rose from her chair and walked across the room to the spot where Maggie was standing, eyes downcast. She suspected she knew what was behind Maggie's troubled face. Maggie was young and pretty. No doubt one of the noblemen had been making demands and causing her undue worry.

Ameran reached out a hand to the girl, but Maggie drew back from her touch with a look of fright on her face.

Ameran's smile was sad. Now she understood. She supposed not even the fear of lashings from the King had ceased Nell's servants' tongues from wagging.

"I thought we were friends, Maggie."

"Ere ye really a witch, mum?" Maggie took one timid step closer.

Ameran shook her head. "I'm not."

Maggie breathed a loud sigh of relief. "I didn't think ye be one of Satan's kind. Ye be far too pretty and much too nice."

"Maggie, who told you I was a witch?"

"Why, mum, everybody's talking 'bout ye curing Missus Gwyn's wee un. They say ye laid yer hands on his lit'le face, and now the skin that twas all burned and blistered is as soft as a baby's rump." Her brown eyes grew wider with amazement. "Die ye really, mum? Did ye really blow out the fire like folks say?"

Maggie was staring at her as though she were some freak of nature. Ameran knew that look well.

Ameran went on about her dressing. "It was the King who cured Jamie. He has a wonderful plant in his physik garden that draws out fire from a burn."

"What kind of plant that be, mum?"

"It's called an aloe, and it grows on a faraway island," she replied.

"I didn't hear nothing 'bout no allee plant, mum." Maggie didn't shy from her glances. "Was yer mum

208

really burned at the stake?"

Ameran shook her head. "My mother died just a short time ago from the fevers. What else did you hear?"

Maggie ventured closer. "Me friend, Charlotte, she be the Duchess of Morrow's dressing maid . . . well, Charlotte told me she'd heerd yer mama and the King were lovers and that the King be yer father."

"My father was a fisherman," said Ameran with a conviction that didn't have to be feigned.

Maggie's smile was one of relief. "So ye be common folk jes like me."

Ameran smiled. "Oh, I don't think either of us are common, Maggie Dehone. As a matter of fact, I think we're both quite exceptional."

All suspicion was erased from the girl's face. "I think we be pretty exceptional, too, mum."

Ameran smoothed the wrinkles from a skirt she'd just taken down from the armoire. "Maggie, has Charlotte ever mentioned Captain Gideon Horne?"

Maggie chuckled. "Ah, he be a handsome devil, that one. Made his rounds with all the maids. Tried to cozy up to me in the cellar once, but what I put between his legs wasn't what he wanted to get put there."

Ameran laughed. She waited, hoping that Maggie would say more, but she could tell the girl was biting her tongue.

Maggie picked up a porcelain swan and dusted it for the third time.

"I thought I saw Captain Horne and the Duchess in the garden one afternoon," said Ameran, wanting to prompt more talk of Gideon and Constance. "But when I made mention of it to Lord Carlisle, he told me I couldn't have possibly seen them together because they despise each other."

Maggie frowned. Ameran tried not to watch her for a reaction.

"Promise me ye won't breathe a word to a soul, mum. I don't want me friend to get into any trouble on my account." Maggie's giggle was shrill. "Charlotte told me Captain Horne visits the Duchess every night after everybody else goes to sleep."

Ameran smiled. "Lord Carlisle is apparently mistaken."

"Oh, not really, mum. That's what they want everyone to think." She crinkled her face. "I wonder why."

"So do I."

Maggie felt the blush of her cheeks. "Charlotte says she's surprised Captain Horne's got any strength left in him at all come daylight." The girl looked scared. "Ye won't tell nobody, will you, mum? I don't want me friend, Charlotte, getting in no trouble on me account. The last time the Duchess took her riding crop to her backside, Charlotte couldn't sit down for a week."

Ameran shivered. It wasn't hard to imagine the Duchess in such a fit of rage. "No one need ever know of our chat."

"Thank ye, mum." Maggie went on about her cleaning.

Ameran finished dressing in the dark green skirt and horseman's coat the King had instructed his tailor to make for her. She was going for a ride with the King, and she didn't want to be late. The King had promised to let her ride his favorite mount, a black stallion named Rowley who danced and pranced and snorted fire.

"Did ye know, mum, that the Duchess has been married three times, and all of her men have died mysteriously?" Maggie queried as she helped Ameran get the feathered riding hat adjusted atop her curls. "They was all elderly gents and very, very wealthy. Me and Charlotte thinks she done them in fer their money."

"Has no one questioned their deaths?" asked Ameran.

Maggie got the new black riding boots off the trunk. "No one would dare ask any questions, mum. The Queen would have them banished if they did." Maggie stood with her hands on her hips. "If'n ye ask me, I'd say the Duchess poisoned them. Charlotte says she's got all kinds of foul-smelling potions tucked away in her room. Good thing ye come along when ye did, mum. The Duchess had all but sunk her claws into Lord Carlisle, and he be too nice a gentleman to get done in by the likes of her."

Ameran shivered at such a thought. She would never let that happen. Constance and Gideon would have to kill her first. If only Gray would believe . . . the attempt to do that had already been made.

There was a knock at the door.

Maggie opened it and exchanged pleasantries with a guard who had the shyly handsome face of a boy. "He's come to fetch ye, mum. The King be a waiting."

Ameran gave her boots one last tug, and with a smile and a wink to Maggie, was on her way.

"Ameran, I know you can't find it in your heart to forgive Gideon, but the man did save your life," Gray reminded her that evening after he had returned from the *Fair Winds*.

He sat down onto the bed beside her. "I would have killed him myself had Gideon not gotten to him first. I can't fault him for doing what I should have done."

"What can I do to convince you Gideon planned it all?"

Gray frowned. "Let's not quarrel. Not tonight." His words were gentle yet firm. "Gideon has his faults, but I do owe him my life. And now I owe him your life as well."

"And he wants you to spend the rest of your life indebted to him." She rose quickly. "What can I do to make you see the truth? To make you see Gideon for what he really is?"

"It's you who doesn't see the truth."

Ameran stomped both feet. "I'm not a child. Don't speak to me as one."

"But you're acting like one, a very spoiled one," he tenderly scolded her.

She was angry, but she refused to give up. Too much was at stake. "Gideon and Constance are plotting against you, against us. Why, I do not know."

"That's ridiculous! They hate each other."

"I saw them together," she reminded him.

"You thought you saw them together."

"I've heard rumors that he sneaks up to her apartment every night when everyone else is asleep."

Gray laughed. "And from whom did you hear such nonsense?"

"I can't say."

"Gossip, that's all it is. Believe me, if Gideon and Constance were anything more than what they seem, I would know," he told her as he patted the space beside him.

Ameran remained standing. "You wouldn't know. You're so blinded by Gideon's facade of brotherhood and friendship that you can't see what's obvious." She knew she'd gone too far.

Gray's face tensed into a scowl. His temples throbbed.

"I'm sorry, Gray." She took a step closer. "No, I'm not sorry. I can't stand the thought of them destroying you. I won't let them. I'll do whatever I have to, even if it means angering you." Her body started to tremble. Her words softened. "I won't let anyone destroy you."

"No one is going to destroy me, least of all Gideon." He kissed her head. "Now I don't wish to speak about this ever again. Time will prove you wrong."

Tears swelled in her eyes. "I hope time doesn't prove one of us dead."

Gray wrapped his arms tightly around her. "Don't speak of such things. Speak only of the happiness we'll share once we're wed."

Ameran held tight to Gray. She'd feared her nagging might cool his desire to marry her. "So you still want me as your wife?"

Gray laughed. "You didn't think you could escape me so easily, did you, my beautiful, bewitching vixen?"

Her smile faded. "I wish you wouldn't say that, not even in jest."

Gray reached his arms around her once more.

"Don't take those rumors seriously. Maids' gossip. Nothing more."

"Constance started them, and she's no maid," she reminded him. "And she would have had none of that information at all if it weren't for Gideon."

"So we're back to Constance and Gideon, are we?" he asked with a sigh and a smile.

Ameran started to speak, then changed her mind. If she didn't watch her tongue, she might drive Gray away for good.

Smiling, she brushed her lips to his. "I love you."

"And I love you." Gray playfully gave her backside a slap. "Hurry along, love. The party tonight should cheer you up."

Ameran nuzzled closer; her tongue danced across his neck. "Do ye need cheering up, sailor?" she teased while her hands enjoyed free reign over his body.

Gray pinned her hands tight at her side. "Nay, wench, not I, for I am about to wed in a fortnight, and if my lady, the soon-to-be Duchess of Carlisle, were to catch you, she might well claw out your eyes."

Ameran flung her arms and legs around him. "In a fortnight? We're really going to be wed in two weeks?"

Laughing, Gray swung her around. "I swear it is to be so."

"But the King said nothing to me about it this morning while we were out riding," she told him.

"He didn't want to spoil my fun in telling you." He swung her around again, then carried her to the bed, dropped her, and pounced down beside her.

"I wish we could be married right this minute,"

she said wistfully.

"As do I, but the two weeks will pass quickly enough," he assured her. "The King has given his permission, although he's insisted on making you a countess before the ceremony takes place."

Ameran hugged him close. A contented smile escaped from her lips. She'd asked nothing from the King, yet he had given her far more than she ever dreamed possible.

"All that remains is for the Church to give permission," Gray continued. "The bans have been posted and read, so it will all be a matter of course before long."

She said nothing, but she didn't share his confidence. She couldn't help but be troubled by the prospects of what might happen if the Church took accusations of her witchcraft to heart.

"You have that faraway look on your face again," Gray said.

Ameran forced a smile. "I was thinking of what a wonderful life we'll have together."

"And we will have the most wonderful of lives together, my beloved."

Her worries were quickly forgotten, and she reveled in the love she saw reflected in his eyes.

Smiling adoringly, Gray untied the fastenings holding her dressing gown together. He then trailed soft kisses down her throat and over her breasts, slowly nibbling on the soft flesh. He devoured the velvety skin and his eyes feasted on her luscious body. "You're the loveliest sight any man could ever hope to behold. Surely a luckier man could not be found anywhere."

"No, 'tis I who am the luckiest of all." She pulled

his head to hers and kissed his lips.

As Gray tore his shirt from his shoulders Ameran kissed the muscular mounds of his chest. With a great groan, he sunk between her breasts, his mouth burrowing in their fleshy softness.

Ameran expelled soft moans and sighs as Gray left no bit of her skin unkissed while hungry lips wandered over the slight rise of her belly and down the inside of her legs.

He paused only long enough to kick himself free of his trousers, then fell upon her once more, the strength of his being finding at last her tenderest spot. Ameran locked her legs around his back and held tight to her lover. They whispered words of love over and over as their beings became one.

Ameran stopped abruptly from her hurried dressing a short while later.

"What's wrong, darling? You look as though you've just seen a ghost," Gray remarked as he fastened on his sword.

There was a tightening across her chest, and the ivory handled hair brush fell from her grasp. "Today is the twenty-ninth of May."

Mama's ominous prediction came to haunt her mind once more. The twenty-ninth day of May, the day commemorating the birth of the King as well as the day the Stuart line was restored to the throne of England. May twenty-ninth would also be the date of the death of Charles the Second.

The next thing she knew Gray was beside her, his gentle hands stroking the blue ruffles draping her arms.

"You've gone quite pale, Ameran. Are you ill?"

Slowly, and with much effort, Ameran slid the

216

ruffles the rest of the way up her arm. For years she had wondered why Mama had condemned England's king to die on that particular day. It hadn't been until she lay on her deathbed that the truth had been revealed at last.

Ever so gently, Gray turned her around to face him. "What is it? Tell me what's wrong."

With a slow, deep breath, Ameran unburdened her heart to Gray. "I suppose Mama thought it only fitting the King who had forsaken her should die on the day given to celebration," she concluded, her head resting on Gray's shoulder.

"But did your mama specify the exact year of such an occurrence?" With much tenderness, he lifted her chin and searched her eyes. "Did she say that the year 1680 would be the year such ill fate would befall Charles the Second?"

Her answer was hesitant. "No, she didn't."

"Then for all we know, the year might well be 1699 if and when such a disaster occurs." Gray kissed her cheek. "And until such time occurs, if in fact it ever does, we mustn't permit the anticipation of doom to rule our lives."

Her smile was for him. She couldn't be so easily appeased herself. Mama had been right about so many things coming to pass . . . but had she truly been the cause of them? Ameran supposed she would never know for sure.

Gray's lips brushed hers in the sweetest of kisses. "By far you'll be the most beautiful of all the ladies at tonight's festivities."

"By far the strangest," she said with a not so happy smile.

Gray slipped the ruffles down her shoulders and

kissed the soft skin. "What you are is wonderful and enchanting and very, very desirable. So desirable, in fact, that I can't keep my hands off you." Once again, he began nibbling her neck.

Ameran smiled at last. Even if Mama were right in her prediction, the year might well not be at hand, not just yet.

A moment later, she could sense Gray's scowl.

"Are you angry with me?"

He shook his head. "Never."

Still, she could sense his uneasiness. "Then what is it?"

He thought long and hard. "I'll speak to the captain of the guards and increase the watch. There'll be many strangers at Court tonight, unfamiliar faces who will be performing for the King, and we mustn't allow our defenses to be down."

Ameran didn't dare breathe. Could it be that Gray found reason for concern in the damning words of her mama?

His eyes found hers, and she could tell he knew the thoughts dwelling inside her head. "Only a fool would think the King's enemies would not take advantage of such a joyous occasion." He folded her tight in his arms. "There'll be no cause for worry, I promise you." His fervor grew with each kiss. "Rest well during the celebration, because when it is over and done, and we return here, there'll be no rest for either of us for the rest of the night."

Only after the bells in the tower tolled twelve chimes could Ameran truly relax and enjoy the song and verse tribute the King's players were performing

218

for their benefactor. She sipped from the goblet of red wine and savored the protective embrace of the strong arms surrounding her. Her eyes met with Gray's, and her skin tingled with sweet anticipation.

Gray squeezed her hand. "Rest well, my love, for the night has just begun."

She placed her head down onto his shoulder. Her joy was bittersweet. The King had escaped her mother's curse for one more year. Would he be so lucky on that next twenty-ninth day of May, or would Mama's ominous prediction come true before the year was out? She wished she knew, for the King's sake as well as her own.

Chapter Twelve

Ameran's heart sank deeper with each word Gray spoke. All the joys shared with her beloved during the week after the King's birthday celebration slowly began to fade. Up until that moment, the day could not have been more perfect. They had drifted down the Thames on a tiny sailing yacht, picnicked in a secluded cove, and made love in the tall rushes that had hidden the boat from view. Afterward, they had toured the magnificent abbey at Westminster and strolled through the village. Now, as they were sailing home, Gray had lowered the sails so the boat could float aimlessly down the river . . . and so he would have the time to tell her the dreaded news.

"It cannot be," she kept saying over and over. "I won't let it be true." She held tight to his leg. It just couldn't be! He couldn't leave her. The time they had spent together would become but fading memories which she feared time would not permit to repeat.

Gray's attempts at comforting her were in vain. "But it is true, Ameran, and nothing either of us can do will change it. The choice is not mine to make. The decision has already been made. The *Fair Winds* has been commissioned to go to Charles Town with a new group of colonists. The King feels it's of the utmost urgency to have me go and investigate certain matters on his behalf."

Ameran clung to him in desperation. "What matters?"

When she saw his frown, she feared she had gone too far, for Gray was not in the habit of discussing his every move with a woman.

Ever so gently, he took her hand and held it between his. "The King is displeased with news from Carolina. He's concerned that all is not as represented by the Proprietors," he explained patiently. "Before he makes further financial commitment, he desires certain assurances that such investment will yield more profit than loss for England."

She gave little notice to what he had just told her. "You've known of this for some time, haven't you?" She fought to hold back the tears. "You should have told me."

"I didn't want to spoil our last days together."

She blinked quickly. Their parting would be just as difficult for him as for her. "How long will you be gone?"

"No longer than necessary." He drew in a heavy breath. "I don't want to part from you any more than you want me to, but I have no choice. I'm obligated to fulfill the wishes of my King."

Ameran nodded. She understood only too well. Gray prided himself on his allegiance to King and country, and she would never expect him to choose between her and his duty to the crown.

"There's no one else who can go in your place?" she ventured quietly.

"The King requested I go. I can't refuse."

She nodded. "Of course not." She felt as if her heart were going to break in two. How would she ever endure a separation from him? She could not stand to be away from him for one day, much less . . .

"How long will you be gone?" she asked him again.

He hesitated, then quietly replied. "Nearly two months."

Tears swelled in her eyes, but she was determined not to let them fall. She could see from Gray's gloomy countenance that he was overwrought with the same inner conflict as she.

Suddenly, she smiled. "I shall go with you to Charles Town," she announced.

Gray didn't share in her joy. "That's not possible."

Her mind was made up. "And why not?"

"The sea is no place for a woman."

"What a ridiculous notion! Won't there be women among the colonists traveling to Charles Town?" she pointed out.

"Yes, but . . ."

"And haven't women made such a voyage before?" she pressed on.

"Yes, of course. However . . ."

"I see no cause for 'howevers.' "

Gray's scowl cracked into a smile. "No, you wouldn't." His words grew serious once more. "Ameran, you can't accompany me every time I set sail," he gently reminded her.

"I don't see why not."

He gave her cheek a resounding kiss. "There are times when you do try my patience."

"And there are times when I make you very, very happy." She pressed closer to him, so close she could feel the fire of his flesh burning through his clothes and hers. "Is that not so?"

His body responded to the urgency of hers. "Of course, that is so. But . . ."

Ameran ran her hand up his leg. "I can't bear the thought of being separated from you for even one night."

"The nights . . . they will indeed be troublesome."

She flicked her tongue inside his ear. "I can think of no reason why we should subject ourselves to such cruelty."

Gray halted her hand from its sweet wanderings and held it tight. "There are far worse cruelties I could never subject you to. Seasickness . . ."

She laughed. "I've ridden out waves in many a storm, and not in a big sailing vessel like the *Fair Winds,* but in a tiny fishing boat."

"But you haven't encountered scurvy and tropical sicknesses and pirates."

"I don't take ill often. As for pirates, I'd rather take my chances with you than have you take yours without me. Besides, didn't you tell me the *Fair Winds* was the fastest, strongest fighting ship afloat?" She dropped down onto her knees and rested her chin on his knee. "Please, don't set sail without me. I'm begging you."

"Don't make it any harder for me than it already is," he said softly.

Her eyes entreated his. "I'll remain confined to your quarters for the duration of the voyage. Your crew won't ever need to know I'm on board."

He held firm. " 'Tis very tempting indeed, my love, but I wouldn't have a moment's peace for worrying about your well-being."

Head resting on his knees, Ameran stared up at him sadly. "You wouldn't worry about me if you left me behind?"

"You twist my words so well to suit yourself, my darling." He gave her a quick kiss, then helped her to her feet. "Please don't make it any more difficult for either of us."

"I miss you already," she said with soft sorrow. Suddenly, an idea began to form inside her head, an idea she knew Gray must not discover.

"The time will pass quickly," he assured her.

"For you, perhaps, but not for me." She couldn't give in, lest Gray suspect what she was plotting. "I'll be lost without you."

"And I, you." He forced a smile. "But you'll have your walks and your rides with the King. He's quite fond of you. And you can always visit Nell and her boys if you grow tired of Whitehall."

"Oh, I can, can I?" Her face wrinkled in mock horror. "So now when it suits you, you give your blessing for me to be friends with Nell, do you?"

"Perhaps I haven't been entirely fair with her," he admitted.

"And why, may I ask, did you change your mind?"

"The day we walked into her home and found her cradling poor little Jamie in her arms." His face mellowed. "Nell Gwyn may not be perfect, but a finer mother cannot be found in all of London."

Ameran smiled. Nell would be pleased to hear that. "The King and Nell will occupy my days, but

MORE PASSION AND ADVENTURE AWAIT... YOUR TRIP TO A BIG ADVENTUROUS WORLD BEGINS WHEN YOU ACCEPT YOUR FIRST 4 NOVELS ABSOLUTELY *FREE* (AN $18.00 VALUE)

Accept your Free gift and start to experience more of the passion and adventure you like in a historical romance novel. Each Zebra novel is filled with proud men, spirited women and tempestuous love that you'll remember long after you turn the last page.

Zebra Historical Romances are the finest novels of their kind. They are written by authors who really know how to weave tales of romance and adventure in the historical settings you love. You'll feel like you've actually gone back in time with the thrilling stories that each Zebra novel offers.

GET YOUR FREE GIFT WITH THE START OF YOUR HOME SUBSCRIPTION

Our readers tell us that these books sell out very fast in book stores and often they miss the newest titles. So Zebra has made arrangements for you to receive the four newest novels published each month.

You'll be guaranteed that you'll never miss a title, and home delivery is so convenient. And to show you just how easy it is to get Zebra Historical Romances, we'll send you your first 4 books absolutely FREE! Our gift to you just for trying our home subscription service.

BIG SAVINGS AND FREE HOME DELIVERY

Each month, you'll receive the four newest titles as soon as they are published. You'll probably receive them even before the bookstores do. What's more, you may preview these exciting novels free for 10 days. If you like them as much as we think you will, just pay the low preferred subscriber's price of just $3.75 each. *You'll save $3.00 each month off the publisher's price.* AND, your savings are even greater because there are never any shipping, handling or other hidden charges—FREE Home Delivery. Of course you can return any shipment within 10 days for full credit, no questions asked. There is no minimum number of books you must buy.

who, pray tell me, will occupy my nights?"

Ameran nibbled on his ear and sidled closer. Now that she had an answer to her dilemma, tantalizing him with her body's sweetness was all the more amusing.

"Surely there will be one handsome soul at Court eager to console a lonely woman who has been abandoned by her lover," she said.

"I'm certain you'll find a multitude of such willing souls, but I'll pass the word that if another man dares so much as to raise his eyes to you, I shall run him through with my sword."

The devilment left her eyes. "I'm only jesting, Gray. You know I desire no man but you."

Gray held her close as the sailboat glided gently over the water.

The spires of Whitehall loomed into view.

Gray held her closer. "This separation will be hellish, I know, and I wish I could promise that it will be our last, but I can't. I'm a man of the sea, and I can't resist her lure any more than I can yours."

"I would have you no other way," she remarked sadly. No matter how much it might trouble her, she couldn't insist he do differently. Gray had spent his life at sea, and he couldn't abandon the sea anymore than she could ask him to do it.

"We shall be wed tomorrow," he said tenderly.

She shook her head. "We can't. The Church has to give us permission."

"I don't know the reason for the delay," he said, his face puzzled.

Ameran said nothing. She knew well the reason why permission had yet to be granted. Constance and Gideon had succeeded in their accusations of witchcraft. The Church would never grant their desire to marry. The King made her Countess of Southwicke, but even with a title, she was still a witch as far as the nobles and the Church were concerned, and the only permission they wanted to give was for her to be hanged.

Ameran shivered. She knew her life was in danger. Not even the King could protect her if Constance succeeded in turning all at Whitehall against her.

"What's the matter, Ameran?"

"I'm just worried about you," she said. True, Gray was the main cause of her concern, but she didn't want him to suffer because of her mother's evil ways.

"I shall return to you, my beloved. I shall." Gray stared down at the dark blue ripples parted by the bow of the boat. "In all my years at sea, I never gave a second thought to not returning home. Thoughts of dying never crossed my mind. Yet now I find myself troubled over that which I have no control." His voice was filled with anguish. He pulled her to his chest. "You're my life, Ameran Michol. I exist because of you. I exist solely for you."

"And I you, my darling. And I, you."

She was more determined than ever to be aboard the *Fair Winds*. When the ship set sail for Carolina she would be on it, with or without Gray's permission. Whatever dangers lay before them posed no threat as long as they were together. And they would be together. Nothing or no one was ever going to separate them again!

Suddenly, Ameran had another distressing thought. "Will Gideon be accompanying you to Carolina?"

"You have no cause to worry about contending with Gideon, for I will be setting sail with him as my second in command."

His answer gave her still more cause for concern.

"Gideon has convinced the King to let him prove his allegiance to the Crown by accompanying me on my mission," he told her.

Ameran's face remained troubled. She could find no solace in the fact that Gideon was going to accompany Gray, and she was certain Gray had interceded with the King on his behalf. Gray was a man of profound wisdom, but she couldn't understand how he could be so stupid as to allow himself to be manipulated and maneuvered!

Gray kissed the scowl from her brow. "Gideon is as fine an officer as I, and I welcome his company as well as his nautical expertise."

She remained silent. Nothing she could ever say would convince him that Gideon was far more dangerous than pirates, hostile Indians and Spaniards, and all diseases and natural disasters combined. Why did Gideon really want to go on that voyage? she wondered. What could he possibly hope to gain? Gideon Horne served no man but himself.

"At least he won't be at Court to arouse your suspicions by his every move."

Ameran held her tongue. There was no escaping Gideon . . . for either of them . . . not as long as Gray remained blind to the truth staring him in the eyes.

Once at the wharf, Gray guided the little yacht

227

into a slip, throwing the line up to a sailor. He then lifted Ameran up onto the dock, his fingers tight around her waist.

In silence, they walked over to the carriage waiting beside the Custom House. He gave the driver some coins and instructed him as to the destination.

"You're not coming with me?" she asked him.

Gray shook his head. "I'll join you by nightfall. There are still some matters which need my attention."

"What sort of matters?"

"The King has instructed me to double my crew for the voyage."

She wondered why he was frowning and asked him.

He quickly assured her that nothing was wrong. "Gideon has volunteered for the task of enlisting more men for our cause."

She started to ask if she could accompany him back to the ship, but decided against it. After all, she could well make use of the time alone. There was much to do and many preparations had to be made to ready herself for her voyage.

She touched his cheek and brushed a kiss across his lips. "I'll be waiting for you, my lord."

"I intend to go with him," Ameran announced to Nell a little later after directing the driver to take her to the house at PallMall.

"Oh, my. Oh, my." Nell's hand fluttered at her heart. "I know I should try and talk you out of such foolishness, but the truth of the matter is if I were in your place, I'd do the exact same thing. Follow me Charlie to the ends of the earth, I would."

Ameran was relieved. She needed Nell's help if her plan had even a prayer of succeeding. Then again, she hadn't expected Nell to oppose her.

Jamie ran into the room. "Ameran, Ameran! Charlie, come see who's here," the little boy screamed with delight.

Charlie ran into the room behind his little brother. Jamie hopped up into her lap and held tight around her neck.

Charlie smiled and gave her a subdued kiss on the cheek.

Ameran could feel the softness on her breast of the little face buried deep into the folds of her dress. There were no ugly scars, no blisters or scabs, just baby-soft flesh that bore no mark of the near-disaster. She hugged Jamie tighter. She couldn't bear the thought of him turning from her in fear.

"Guess what, guess what!" shouted the little boy excitedly. "Guess what Papa got for Charlie and me?"

"I give up. Tell me."

Jamie looked at his brother. "You go first."

Charlie sat down at Ameran's feet. "You must guess."

"Will you give me any hints?" asked Ameran.

Nell winked at her.

"All right, my present has four legs, a long tail and mane, and goes clippidy-clop when he trots down the courtyard." Charlie told her, his hands waving in excitement. "Oh, and she's the most beautiful chestnut color you've ever seen. Almost the color of Mummy's curls."

Ameran clapped her hands in delight. "A horse!"

Charlie nodded proudly. "Papa had his groom bring her 'round this morning. I've named her Lady."

"Why, I think that's a fine name," Ameran told him.

"Mine's a pony," said Jamie. "He's black all over save for a tiny little star right here." He drew the outline of a star on Ameran's forehead. "Papa says I'll be jumping fences soon and can go on the fox hunts in the fall."

Nell shuddered out loud. "I believe me and yer papa might have a word about that."

"What did you name your pony?" asked Ameran.

"I call him Rowley after Papa's big horse," Jamie announced. "Papa said he thought that was a fine name."

"I do believe I'm in agreement with him."

"Run along and play, boys. Ameran and me have things to discuss," Nell told her sons.

Charlie took Jamie by the hand and helped him down. "Come on, Jamie. Let's go finish our drawings for Papa."

Nell's face shone with pride. "What a wonderful idea, Charlie. I 'spect the King will be round tonight after his meetings have concluded."

The boys ran out of the room laughing and cheering.

"You've fine sons," Ameran told Nell as she looked after the boys with a strange longing.

"It is a joy you will experience soon as well, my dear." She offered Ameran a chocolate from the silver tray on the table, and when Ameran declined, took two for herself. "Tell me more about this trip you're planning."

Ameran smiled. "I haven't done much planning, I confess."

"We'll work out all the details, lovey," Nell assured her as she popped another chocolate into her mouth. "You know, of course, the King is not going to be at all pleased with your decision to leave. He so enjoys yer company."

It made her feel good to know that he shared that happiness with her.

She took a deep breath. "I can't tell him my intentions."

Nell's plump face showed no surprise. "No, I don't suppose ye can, can ye?" She patted Ameran's knee. "He is so very fond of you. Your absence from court will grieve him immensely."

"I'll miss the King," Ameran said truthfully. "And I'll miss you, Nell Gwyn."

"Not as much as I'll miss you." She blinked quickly. "But enough of that sentimental nonsense. We have to figure out a way to get you on board the *Fair Winds* without you being found out."

Ameran shook her head sadly. "If only the Church would permit Gray and I to be wed."

Nell already knew óf her dilemma with the Church. "Don't ye worry on that account, dearie. Charlie'll set the Archbishop straight. He usually has his way with those high and mighty men of God."

"If only he could exert as much influence over Constance and the Queen."

"In good time, dearie. I'm sure he'll put them in their places, too."

"I don't understand why the King made no mention of sending Gray to Charles Town. I've been with him nearly every morning, and yet he hasn't said a word to me about his plans."

"I learned a long time ago, it's not my place to question the desires of the King," Nell told her gently. "He's the King and his desires are subject to approval from no one." She gave Ameran's arm a comforting pat. "Rest assured. If it were not a matter of utmost urgency, the King wouldn't make such a demand on Gray. He's been very troubled as of late by certain events in the colony. He was even forced to put one of the Lord Proprietors, the Earl of Shaftsbury, into the Tower. Luckily for the good Earl, the King is as quick to forgive as he is to enrage."

Ameran wanted to know more about what kind of troubles the King was experiencing in the colonies.

Nell's laughter was loud. "Why, the only kind of trouble the King ever has—money, of course!" She was eager to explain. "In the early years of his rule, the King was most anxious to compete with Spain and France in New World exploration, but he lacked sufficient funding and received no support from Parliament. So, he gave all lands from Carolina south into Spanish-held Florida and all land as far west as the south Seas to eight powerful Englishmen in hopes they would pay for settlements there. Me Charlie put up some of his own money for the expeditions, but did the Proprietors share their wealth from Carolina with him? I'm sorry to say they did not! They've made fortunes in exports to England and Barbados, yet hardly a farthing has made its way back to the King's pockets.

"That isn't the only reason for the King's concern," Nell went on. "Many of the settlers are unhappy in their new home. They say the Good and Absolute Lord Proprietors of Carolina aren't protecting them against the Spanish and the savages, and besides, there's rarely a Proprietor present in the colony at all. As subjects of the crown, they've presented their grievances with the King, who is obliged to help them. Your Lord Carlisle is one of the few men the King can still trust to be fair and honest in his dealings with him."

Ameran nodded. "Gray is above reproach."

"Charlie's said many a time he wishes he could put Gray on the throne. At least that way, England would be assured a competent ruler when he's gone. May such a day be long in coming," Nell added with a quick glance up. "It'll break his heart to lose you and Gray both on the same day."

"You sound as if we're never coming back, and we are. We are," she said, trying to dispel her own fears. "You'll explain the circumstances to the King, won't you Nell? King Charles has been so kind to me, and I have no wish to cause him any distress. But I cannot bear another separation from Gray! And I . . ."

She hesitated. She didn't want to cause Nell any undue worry.

"Yes, what is it?"

Ameran reached for Nell's hand. "I fear for Gray's safety, Nell. I've had dreams, horrible dreams, of Gray's dying by Gideon's hand. I don't like Gideon's insisting on accompanying Gray on this mission."

"Don't worry. Gray is a smart man. One day he'll see Gideon for the rascal he is." Her fingers closed tight about Ameran's. "It's for your safety that I worry. Consider your decision wisely, Ameran. The sea is no place for a woman."

"I fear Gideon far more than I do any of the other devils prowling the seas," said Ameran as she tried to erase from her mind the terrible visions of Gray's bloody corpse. "One expects to be wary of one's enemies, but defenses are at their lowest among friends, and that is when one is most vulnerable."

"You're wise for one so young, and so beautiful."

"If I were wise, I could convince Gray that Gideon's heart is as black as the devil's." She met Nell's worrisome gaze with a look that was fierce with commitment. "I would rather die with Gray than live without him."

"No more of that talk. No more." Nell tried to be cheerful. "Tell me, how do you propose to stowaway on the *Fair Winds?* 'Tis a pity you cannot simply walk on board."

"That's exactly what I intend to do."

"Surely you can't be serious."

"Oh, but I am," she assured Nell. "The *Fair Winds* will be carrying more colonists to Carolina and I intend to be one of them."

"You be mad, lassie. Gray will recognize you for sure."

"No one will recognize me," she said with much certainty. Ameran leaned closer to her friend. "Not after you've finished with me."

It took a few moments for Nell to catch on to Ameran's plan, but when she did, she gave it her nod of approval.

" 'Twould be a shame to shrivel so beautiful a face, or to conceal that luscious body beneath a man's attire. When I have finished with you, not even I will be able to recognize ye!" she said proudly and confidently.

Ameran threw her arms around her friend. "I knew I could depend on you."

"Ye can, love, ye can. Ye saved my little babe, and there is nothing I would not do for ye." Her eyes glistened with tears as she tried to smile. "I can forsee but one problem."

"What might that be?"

"I shall miss ye terribly." Nell held tight to her hand. "Next to me babes and me Charlie, I feel closer to ye than any one else in the world."

The words began choking her throat. "It shan't be for long."

Nell shook her head. "Are ye sure ye know what ye be doing?"

"My place is with Gray," Ameran said softly. Her smile came slowly. "He might not think so, but it is."

"And just when do ye intend to make yer presence aboard the *Fair Winds* known to the good captain?" Nell asked as she dabbed her eye with the sleeve of her gown.

"When we're closer to Carolina's shore than to that of England," said Ameran with a wink and a laugh.

Nell studied Ameran's features carefully. "I could make ye up as an old lady. Gray would certainly not recognize ye, and the rest of the men on board wouldn't dare lay a hand on an old hag." Her frown was deep. "But that would take much time and skill on your part as well as many boxes of powders and cream to create such a look day after day, and in that hot sun . . ."

Nell turned Ameran's head to the right and then to the left. "We do not want ye to draw attention to yourself. I could disguise ye as a young man, an indentured servant perhaps, who has bound himself to an unknown master in Charles Town in exchange for ship's passage. Yer hair could be concealed with a woolen cap."

Nell studied her for a moment longer, then shook her head. "No, the moment ye spoke, ye'd give yerself away for certain."

"I could be a female indentured servant. That way I could converse with the others and not be found out," she suggested.

"What ye say is true, dearie, but ye must remember it is the nature of the man-beast to take that which he desires whether the woman be willing or not."

Ameran could feel her limbs tremble. She hadn't given any thought to such a happening, but it was indeed very likely.

Nell patted her knee. "I don't say this to scare you, lovey, only to make you aware of what it is you're up against. Ye will not have Gray to protect you at first, and ye will have to fend for yerself."

"I've spent my life doing just that." Her thoughts lingered for a moment on the Duke of Caron, and she prayed a silent prayer that she'd never again encounter the likes of him. "I can take care of myself." She then told Nell about the knife she used to keep strapped to her leg. "I've used it before, and I won't hesitate to use it again should the need arise."

"Perhaps it would be better you stay a woman.

Less explaining in the event of the other passengers catch onto your scheme."

Nell pondered the problem thoughtfully. "Of course, for your own safety, we'll have to make ye as ugly as we can. We can black out a few of yer teeth, paint on a wart or two, a pox mark here and there, and there won't be any men fighting to bed ye."

"You're brilliant, Nell. Absolutely brilliant."

"A lady doesn't get by in this world on looks alone, dearie." She pinched one of Ameran's rosy cheeks. "I shall even show you how to act a little crazy. Men'll usually leave a woman to herself if they think she's teched in the head. Ye wouldn't mind howling at the moon every now and then, would ye?"

"I'll do whatever it takes to stay by Gray's side," Ameran said with firm conviction. "Anything."

"I will not have a good night's sleep until ye return safe to England." Nell clasped Ameran's hands between her own. "And when ye do return I promise ye a celebration such that Whitehall has never seen."

Nell's laughter was far from gay. The two women held tight to each other, neither speaking, but both thinking of the untold dangers lying in wait for Ameran.

When Ameran arrived back at her apartment, she was met by a much distraught Maggie who was pacing the floor and wringing her hands.

"It be Charlotte, mum. The Duchess be accusing her."

Ameran tried to calm down the girl. "Accusing Charlotte of what?"

"Why, haven't ye heard, mum? Everybody's talking about it. The Duchess is carrying on like a madwoman."

Ameran couldn't help but laugh. "Isn't that her usual self?"

"She be worse than ever, mum. Why she even accused poor Charlotte of stealing that cursed brooch, and her and Charlotte practically grew up together. Besides, everyone knows Charlotte couldn't thief a thing. What would a serving girl do with diamonds and pearls? Ain't like she could wear it cleaning."

A pearl and diamond brooch. Constance had worn it the night before at a royal banquet, Ameran remembered.

"I'm certain the brooch will turn up. Perhaps the Duchess misplaced it."

Maggie couldn't be soothed. "She swears it was stolen, and mark me word, not one soul at Whitehall will be in peace until it be found." Maggie's smile was weak. "Anything I can do for ye, mum, before I get back to helping Charlotte tear apart the Duchess's suite?"

Ameran declined her offer, then tried to hurry her along as gently as she could. It was nearly nightfall and she had much to do before Gray's return.

Maggie was almost out the door when she turned back around. "Do ye recollect the day, mum, when ye made inquiries about Captain Horne and the Duchess?"

Ameran nodded.

"Well, Charlotte said they were together late last night in the Duchess's suite until the wee hours." Maggie lowered her voice to a whisper. "There was another man with them. Charlotte said she could have sworn he was one of the Spanish delegates sent here last week to see the King. Wonder what business he'd have with them two?"

Ameran shook her head. She was wondering the same thing herself. Just what were those two plotting now?

Maggie's finger tapped at her cheek. "I wonder if that Spaniard could have snitched the brooch. Them devils ain't to be trusted."

The Spaniard wasn't the only devil not to be trusted, Ameran thought to herself.

"If you find out anything else, Maggie, be sure to come tell me. All right?"

Maggie gave a little curtsy. "Yes, mum. I'll do just that."

Supper had grown cold, and Ameran was already in bed by the time Gray returned from the *Fair Winds*.

"Why do you suppose Gideon and Constance were holding court late last night in her suite with one of the delegates from Spain?" she asked before Gray had finished kissing her hello.

Gray let out a groan, then turned his attention to the tray beside the bed.

Ameran poured his wine and watched as he hungrily attacked the food she had Cook prepare for him. She could tell by his silence that he was reluctant to discuss the matter with her.

"Do you not think it peculiar that a representative of England's most formidable adversary be part of a late night tête-à-tête with Constance and Gideon?"

"I think you'd do well not to listen to scullery maids' idle gossip," he said, his words gentle but firm.

Emerald eyes blazed icy fire. It was all Ameran could do to keep from pouring the rest of the wine on top of his head.

Chuckling, Gray grabbed hold of her arm and set her down onto his lap.

"Forgive me, darling. I didn't mean to sound so unkind, but Gideon couldn't possibly have spent the night with Constance or a Spanish delegate or anyone at Whitehall for that matter. He slept aboard the *Fair Winds* last night."

"You don't know if that's true, for you were with me all night," she reminded him, her arms tight around his neck. "How can you be certain what you say is so?"

Gray brushed his lips over her cheek. "Because Gideon wouldn't disobey an order."

Ameran sadly laid her head down onto his shoulder. No matter what she said or what proof she offered, Gray would never be convinced of Gideon's ill intentions. He wouldn't allow himself to be. She didn't want to cause hard feelings between herself and her beloved, but she couldn't sit quietly by and watch as Gideon destroyed Gray as well as the love they shared.

"Constance wouldn't be so foolish as to jeopardize her friendship with the Queen or risk her good standing at court by fraternizing with the enemy," said Gray as he stroked Ameran's hair with one hand and ate his stew with the other.

"I didn't realize you were so staunch a defender of Constance's good name and reputation," she remarked coolly. "Perhaps it's because the two of you were more intimate than you care to admit?"

240

She tried to rise, but Gray held her firm. "As we've discussed before, I'm no stranger to affairs of the heart. I admit to having more than my share of willing lovers, but the Duchess of Morrow not once graced my bed, and I've refused countless invitations to visit hers. Needless to say, the woman hates me, and with good reason, don't you agree?"

Ameran kept the smile from her face. "Then why would she befriend Gideon, who's most outspoken about his love and loyalty to you?"

"You're trying my patience, woman. Have you nothing better to do but nag on this our next to the last night together?"

"If I nag, it's only because I love you. I can't bear the thought of anything happening to you." She could feel herself start to lose control. If she wasn't careful, Gray would be counting the hours in eager anticipation of their parting. "Can't you see that Gideon doesn't have your best interests at heart? He's betrayed you. He's lied to you. He's deceived you. He's plotted against your King. How can you defend him? As for Constance, you yourself said that she hates you. She's capable of murder. From the King's suspicions, you know Gideon is as well."

She pounded her fists into his chest. "I don't want you to die. I love you. I couldn't live without you." She collapsed, sobbing into his arms. "I can't live without you."

"Shhh, shhh, my darling. There's no cause for such distress. No one intends me harm. No one wants me dead, least of all Gideon."

Her sobs quieted. She raised her head and looked him in the eyes. In a surprisingly calm voice, she told him. "I've had dreams, Gray, dreams in which Gideon hurt you and took great delight in doing so. One day you'll realize what I say is true, but by then I fear it will be too late. Your eyes will be opened only when you feel the pain of Gideon's sword running through your heart."

Ameran ran to the bed and flung herself down upon it, crying until there were no more tears left to stream down her cheeks. She was afraid to lift her head for fear Gray would be gone. But when his hands caressed her back in a soothing massage, she rejoiced in the fact that she hadn't driven him away.

She rolled over, smiling with arms opened wide. "I love you so much. I lost you once. I couldn't bear losing you again. I'd kill anyone who ever tried to harm you."

Gray silenced her with still more kisses. "There's no cause for your anguish. If anyone's heart is to be pierced, it won't be mine. That I swear to you. I'll always keep one eye on Gideon, and if his intentions are no good, neither loyalty nor brotherhood will keep me from doing what I have to."

Ameran nodded. She was tired of arguing. She was tired of harsh words between them. She wanted him to love her and she had made her desires known. Slowly, her eyes not straying from his, she undid the ties which drew her dressing gown tight around her body, laying open the soft, pink satin so his eyes could behold the willing flesh underneath.

With a heady moan, Gray sank his head between her breasts and hungrily devoured their soft sweetness.

"It will be hell to endure even one night away from

you," he told her.

"Then take me with you." She desperately wanted his permission to go. She didn't relish the prospect of still more lies between them.

"I can't. I can't."

"We'll be together, my love," she said, drawing him still closer. "Our bodies might be separated, but our spirits will still be as one."

Gray's chin rested upon her chest. His eyes searched hers. "You do know if there was any way possible, I'd have you by my side when the *Fair Winds* sets sail."

She didn't trust herself to speak.

"You'll never be out of my thoughts or out of my heart, Ameran. You do understand why I can't take you with me, don't you?"

"You do what you have to do." She hoped her eyes didn't betray her by candlelight. "You do what you have to."

Just as I'll do what I have to do, her eyes silently told him.

"I'm a fool to leave you," he said as he stripped and threw his clothes across the room. "My heart's never been in such turmoil. Never before have I questioned my duty to the King, and now, and now I . . ."

"Shhh, don't speak of that which you can't change." She reached for the source of her great pleasure and lovingly caressed it; Gray's moans told of his own pleasure. Easing up, she gently rolled Gray over onto his back. Teasing fingers worked their magic until his hardness pulsated in her fingers. Her long locks falling across her cheeks and onto his

243

outstretched body, she began at his toes and teased and tantalized her way up his legs, over his knees and across his thighs, her tongue tracing circles on the fleshy insides of his thighs. She could feel the quiver of his muscles as she eased her lips upon his manliness, and when she was certain Gray couldn't take the sweet torment any longer, she eased her body to his. Slowly and deliberately pressing his flesh to hers, she lured him still closer with her kisses.

Legs straining tight against his hips, Ameran guided him inside her and rocked into him with a slow, steady motion that teased and tormented still more. She could tell by his moans and whimpers that he was happy to permit her a free rein. Finally, it was she who could stand it no longer. Her innermost being was wracked with tiny tremors, and a mammoth quake overpowered her. Limbs numbed and weakened, she fell across him, her heart racing, her blood surging into his.

Arms tight around her, legs locked around her back, Gray rolled her over and began stoking the embers that were quick to ignite into flames again.

Reds and gold splayed the midnight sky much too quickly.

Gray's eyes were heavy from want of sleep. Ameran didn't try to tempt him back to bed as she had done so many past mornings. She could sense his reluctance to leave her for the *Fair Winds*. Much as she longed to soothe the turmoil tearing at his heart, she didn't trust herself to speak for fear of giving away her plans.

He dressed quickly and kissed her good-bye with

the promise of an early return that evening, their last night together.

She didn't begin to cry again until she heard the door close behind him, and then the tears she had fought so hard to control began to fall.

Last night there had been more dreams, dreams which carried with them more feelings of impending doom. How she knew such things, she didn't know, but the day would soon come to pass when Gray would be torn from her side, and there was nothing she could do to keep that time from coming.

"You've been uncharacteristically quiet this morning," the King told Ameran as they stood in the stable yard watching the royal trainer school the big gray stallion that had been sent by the King of Prussia. "I would far rather endure a woman's rage than her silence."

"I have no cause for anger or rage, Your Majesty. I've only been lost in my thoughts, and for that I'm sorry." Her sigh was long and weary. "I'm afraid I haven't been very good company for you this morning."

The King smiled, but said nothing.

They watched as the magnificent stallion reared and walked backwards on its hind legs, its front hooves pawing at the sky.

"I suppose you're upset with me for sending Gray to Charles Town," he said, taking his eyes off the horse for a few moments.

"It's not my place to question Your Majesty's commands."

"Trust me when I tell you I had no choice." His dark eyes were sincere. "If I could delay the voyage until the Church gave you permission to wed, I would. I swear I would. But I can't. It is a matter of utmost urgency."

Ameran nodded. The King could not very well wait for the Church to give permission, for it was most unlikely permission would ever be given as long as Constance and the Queen continued their meddling. Still, there was no point adding another burden to the King's already trouble-laden shoulders.

"I'm aware of the crisis in Charles Town and of the urgency in resolving the problems between the settlers and the Lord Proprietors."

"Problems and troubles. That's all I ever hear from Carolina." The King massaged his temples. "Cursed headache. Will it never end?"

Ameran's smile was sympathetic.

"England seldom shares in the profits from the colony, yet when it faces problems which are seemingly insurmountable, it is I who am expected to provide immediate solutions." His brow furrowed even more. "When financial difficulties present themselves, the Proprietors think all they need do is change the name of the settlement from Oyster Point to Charles Town, and I will be so flattered that I turn over the treasury to them. Ba!" His expression was grim. "There is a far greater danger confronting the colony at this time. The Spanish have aligned themselves with the Indians, and in all likelihood will soon mount an attack on the settlement. The lives of English men, women and children are in grave jeopardy. I can't in good conscience permit their massacre, yet I can do nothing to aid them if such a blood-bath were to occur tomorrow or the next or the next. I only pray help will arrive soon enough." He took Ameran's hand between his. "Thus the reason for this urgency. I pray you don't think me heartless for separating you and Gray so soon after your reunion."

News of an impending battle paled her dark features. Gray wasn't merely going on a fact-finding mission. He was going to war. All the more reason for her to be aboard the *Fair Winds* when she set sail.

"Gray didn't tell you the real reason for his mission?"

"No, he didn't." She could barely speak. It was far more dangerous than she had even begun to imagine.

"You mustn't be angry with him, my dear," the King told her as he turned his attention once again to the stallion. "Only he and a few members of my council are aware of the severity of the task before him."

Ameran did her best to focus on the magnificent gray as it pranced and pirouetted on command from the trainer. Poor Gray! Little wonder he did not heed her warnings about Gideon. He had far greater things to occupy his mind. The *Fair Winds* wouldn't only be taking settlers to the colony. The ship would also be transporting cannons and guns and powder and additional manpower to aid in the settlers' defense. Gideon wasn't the only life threatening force confronting Gray.

She debated as to whether or not she should tell the King about the meeting Maggie had reported to her, then decided against it. Still, she couldn't help but wonder if Gideon had been privy to the details of the voyage. Whatever game of lies and deception Gideon and Constance were playing, they had no doubt covered their tracks well to allay any suspicion from the King or anyone else. It was best not to arouse the King's suspicion. If Gideon were divulging secrets of state to the Spanish, the King would find out for himself soon enough. For the time being, she couldn't risk having her own suspicions found out by Gideon and Constance without jeopardizing Gray's well-being as well.

Ameran was relieved when the trainer led the horse over to the King for a closer inspection so he would turn his thoughts to other matters.

The King patted the stallion appreciatively as it snorted and stomped. "Fine animal. I wager he'll be winning many a race for me at Newgate."

"I know three months may seem like an eternity for one so young," the King told her as the trainer walked the horse back into the stable, "but the time will pass quickly. I promise. Don't fret for your Lord Carlisle or for his safety. There's no finer a commander nor a warrior." He lifted an arm to her shoulders. "I wouldn't send him to do battle unless I was confident he would return victorious . . . and alive."

The King took her by the arm, and they began their stroll back through the gardens. "I've given Gray my word that I'll keep you royally entertained," he said with a hearty laugh. "We'll go to Windsor for a spell. There's no place lovelier this time of year. We can ride for hours on end across meadows covered in flowers. And there's always tennis and yachting, the theater, and let's not forget the horse races at Newgate."

His tone softened. "I truly am sorry to snatch him from you so soon after you found each other again, but I truly have no choice. Please, dear daughter, don't hold that against me."

Dear daughter? Had her ears heard right? Had the King actually acknowledged they shared the same blood?

He continued on as if nothing was unusual in his words of endearment. "I give you my word that by the time Gray returns there'll be no more talk of such nonsense as devil-worshiping and witchery, and if the Church does not give permission for your wedding, I shall appoint a new archbishop who will."

"Thank you, sire." If only she could tell him of her plans, but she couldn't, for he would surely try and stop her.

"And there's a lovely country estate, only a morning's ride from Windsor, which I intend to give you as your wedding present. Would you like that, my dear?" he asked.

She could tell from his tone that he was eager for her approval.

Ameran took hold of the King's hand. "I'm grateful for all that you've done for me, sire. Your gifts have been much appreciated, but it is the time we have spent alone together that I most cherish. I have no need of titles or estates. All that I needed, you generously gave to me, and for that I'll never cease to be grateful."

"You may not need titles and property and jewels,

but I need to give them to you," he said with quiet contemplation. "You suffered much because of me, and I intend to make amends. Oh, I don't mean to make amends so your mother will stop cursing me from the grave. My intentions are to make right all those wrongs my daughter had to suffer."

She could feel the tears start to form in her eyes. She searched his dark gaze, just as he was searching hers. She wished she could tell him the truth. She wished she could confide in him of her intention to set sail with the *Fair Winds* on that next morn, but she didn't dare. It grieved her greatly knowing she would leave without telling him farewell or without providing him with the explanation which he would be sure to seek, but she had no choice. She only hoped the King would understand that. She had to go, and she had to protect Gray, not from the Spanish or the Indians, but from Gideon Horne.

"What is it, dear? Why do you look so sad?"

Smiling, she stood upon tiptoes and kissed the King's plump cheek. "I'm not sad, Your Majesty. I was merely thinking how fortunate I am to have enjoyed the pleasure of your company on so fine a day."

The King kissed the top of her head, then tousled her hair the way she had seen him do to Charlie and Jamie.

"No, Ameran, 'tis who am the fortunate one."

She gave him one last smile and looked into his dark, intense stare a final time, then turned and ascended the stairs slowly, forcing her gaze straight ahead, for if she glanced behind her, she would surely give away her plan.

* * *

On the eve of Gray's departure, Ameran said very little throughout their supper for fear of breaking down and confessing all. Like herself, Gray only went through the motions of eating the elaborate feast the cook had prepared and delivered to their suite as the King had requested. The few words they exchanged might well have been spoken between strangers . . . remarks about the succulency of the lamb, the brightness of the day's sunshine, the anticipated rain on the morrow, the King's magnificent new steed.

Finally, with a loud sigh, Gray pushed back from the table and pulled Ameran onto his lap. He held her as tightly as he could without causing her discomfort. His handsome face was hidden among her long, dark waves and ringlets.

"What can I say that hasn't been said?" he asked softly.

Ameran kissed his head. "Indeed, it's all been said, and many times over as well."

"I'll miss you." The kiss he placed on her lips was almost chaste.

"My heart will yearn for you."

"As will my arms," he added with a smile.

Ameran started to speak, but chose instead to keep the words contained inside her.

"What is it?" Gray entreated. "Tell me what it is."

"If I asked you to do something for me, if I pleaded with you, would you do it?" she asked, forcing his gaze.

"If it were in my power, you know I would." Knowingly, he stroked her cheek. "But we both know

I have no choice but do as the King commanded."

Ameran stiffened in his arms. "But the King did not command that Gideon accompany you."

Gray slammed his fist onto the table. "Gideon! Always Gideon! For God's sake, woman, why can't you cast your thoughts from him even on our last night together?"

His right arm loosened around her, but she refused to give up. If their bodies parted at that moment, they might never be joined again.

Her stare held firm. "No, I can't, not when I know in my heart that if Gideon has his way, our time together will soon come to an abrupt end."

"Gideon is a fine officer. There is none I would rather have at my side," Gray said suddenly as he resumed eating with her still on his knees.

"Was it your idea, or was it Gideon's that he sail with the *Fair Winds* on the morrow?"

Gray's fork stopped halfway to his mouth. "I don't remember. What difference does it make?"

Ameran refused to give him any peace. "By your own admission, you said that Gideon wants to redeem himself in the eyes of the King, but has it occurred to you that he might want even more to manipulate you into such a position of weakness that he can gain the power over you which he desires to have?"

Gray laughed, but his humor was wry. "You, my love, not Gideon, are the one who attempts to wield the greatest power over me by your sly manipulation."

It was all Ameran could do to keep from dumping the plate of roasted lamb, potatoes, carrots, and onions over his stubborn head. "I only want to protect you."

"To protect me from what?" His eyes were alive with rage.

"From Gideon, but most of all from yourself!" Still, she refused to move from her seat. Arms crossed over her chest, she awaited his defense.

Gray's knees were restless."Would you please get up? Something is giving me indigestion, and I don't think it is this fine meal."

Ameran sat harder on his legs. "When will you stop being to pig-headed? When will you realize that Gideon has taken advantage of your loyalty and your devotion for his own gain? He's abused those very qualities which you admire, which you demand in all other men. How can you trust a man like Gideon?"

"I would trust Gideon Horne with my life," he said stubbornly.

Tears swelled in her eyes. She could feel her strength fade. "Don't do that. Please, I beg of you. Don't trust him with so great and dear a treasure."

Gray's temples throbbed.

At that moment, Ameran would have not been surprised had he hurled her across the room. When he didn't lift a hand against her, she was just as sure he would stomp out of their suite and out of her life.

Her breaths were quiet and fearful.

Their eyes met.

Gray's anger was quick to melt. The hardness of his countenance relaxed as he touched her cheek.

She reached for his hand.

"Gideon won't hurt me on this voyage or on any

other," he said gently. "You must have faith in my judgment."

"Please," she begged. "Create a reason why he cannot sail with you."

Gray shook his head. "You can't ask me to do that."

"I'm begging you."

"I can't, Ameran. I'm sorry."

Gray rose and deposited her feet onto the floor. "I'm tired. Tomorrow's light will come much too soon."

Ameran nodded. What more could she say? Gray could leave her behind, but not from Gideon.

Gray undressed, got into bed, and turned his back to her.

Ameran did the same. She was miserable. The bed had never seemed so big and cold and lonely. She didn't sleep, and she could tell from the thrashing limbs and heavy moans beside her that sleep wouldn't come to Gray either.

Gray finally reached for her a little before dawn. "I would do nothing to place my life in jeopardy. I would do nothing to keep me from coming home to you."

They held each other tight, their words of regret soft whispers in the other's ears.

Daylight came much too soon.

Ameran waited and watched in silence as Gray dressed in his blue uniform of gold buttons and braids.

"Nothing could ever keep me away from you," he said, returning to the bed once more. "Nothing and no one."

He gathered her in his arms.

"Make me a promise," she asked.

"Anything."

She sniffed the tears from her eyes. "Promise me that you won't turn your back on Gideon, not even for an instant. Promise me that you'll keep an eye on him at all times."

Gray offered no objection. He merely nodded.

The tears began to fall down her cheeks. "I love you so much."

"Shhhh, we'll be together soon."

Ameran held tight to him. He had no idea just how soon. She couldn't stop the tears from falling. "I'm so sorry . . ."

His lips touched hers. "Don't torture yourself, my darling."

She refused to be quieted, and she wiped the tears from her eyes. "What I am most sorry for is that my love couldn't convince you to leave Gideon behind."

His jaw tensed, but his arms remained tight around her. "All will be well, Ameran. You'll see. Trust me."

"Yours is not the sincerity I doubt."

Tenderly, he caressed her cheeks as if he were trying to commit to memory each detail. "Know that I will always love you, and that my every thought will be of you."

"I'll be with you during your mission." Her eyes sought his. He didn't have the slightest notion how much truth was in those words.

"And it will be your memory which will hasten my journey back home."

Ameran settled her cheek against his strong chest.

She could sense his reluctance to let her go.

Gray held her tighter, cursing repeatedly the duties of his command between excruciatingly sweet kisses.

As she gave her kisses with an ardor matching his own, she longed to tell him their separation would be far briefer than he might anticipate, but she dared not for fear he would foil her plans.

His eyes were misting, as well, when they finally pulled apart.

"At this moment, you must be my strength," he said after another kiss.

Lovingly, she brushed a blond strand from his brow. "Our hearts and our souls will keep a constant vigil until we can be reunited."

"Farewell, Ameran."

Gray kissed her hand, then gave a bow. He turned around at the door, touched his finger to his lips, and blew her a final kiss.

No sooner had his footsteps faded down the corridor than Ameran leapt from the bed and began to make ready for her own voyage. She had thrown a few old dresses Nell had gotten for her into a tattered brocade travel bag that had shown up at the bottom of her armoire among a clutter of shawls and scarves.

She quietly slipped out the palace and through the garden to the house at Pall Mall. Nell was waiting for her and went to work at once, transforming her into a servant girl with rotted teeth and a pox-scarred face. The change was astounding. When Ameran looked into the mirror, a stranger stared back at her. Nell had dubbed her Lilly Warwick after a character she had once played. All that remained of the girl she had been was the knife strapped in its leather sheath around her leg. Nell whisked her away in her carriage, and with tearful hugs and kisses deposited her in the alley beside the Customs House.

Chapter Thirteen

Ameran sat in the corner of the old brick Customs House and watched out the window as casks and barrels, crates and trunks were carried on board the *Fair Winds*. The quartermaster's voice boomed over the noise of the crowd as he called out a check of his inventory and his helpers cried out their replies.

"Fifteen kegs of beer."

"Aye, sir."

"Thirty gallons of brandy."

"Got it here, sir."

"Eighty-four bushels of flour."

"Check."

"Fourteen suits of armor."

"Accounted for, sir."

"One hundred and fifty beds and pillows."

"Present."

"One thousand four hundred grubbing hoes."

"Check."

"Eighteen barrels of four-penny nails."

"There be nineteen, sir."

"Nine hundred fifty-six fishing hooks."

"Aye."

"Two hundred and forty pounds of glass beads."

"Them Indians will be happy with these, sir."

"Two hundred and eighty-eight pairs of scissors."

"Accounted for, sir."

"Forty-two barrels of gardening seeds."

"Aye, aye."

"And one set of surgical instruments."

"In the captain's quarters, quartermaster, sir."

Finally Ameran saw Gray appear onto the dock alongside his quartermaster. Her heart sank and a rock-hard lump formed in her throat. Knowing she had deliberately deceived the man who had sworn to her devotion and love everlasting grieved her greatly. She felt as if her heart would break in two, and once more she reminded herself it was not too late to confess all and beg that he allow her the same privilege he had allowed Gideon. But in her heart she knew he would never permit her to board the ship if he knew the truth. No, the only way was to continue as Lilly Warwick. She would rather endure Gray's wrath and risk losing his love than be an unwilling accomplice in Gideon's evil schemes. She had the most horrible feeling that Gideon meant to rid himself entirely of the commander of the *Fair Winds*.

Ameran counted with dread each and every cannon that was rolled up the ramp onto the ship by bare-chested seamen. She was surprised at the number of sailors on the dock, many of them quite unsavory-looking. Gray had told her they had taken on twice as many hands as usually made up the crew, but he hadn't told her that the *Fair Winds* was sailing to Charles Town with a small army.

A frightened-looking girl clutching a babe in arms

sat down on the trunk opposite. The baby was sleeping, and the girl was sobbing quietly into its tattered blanket.

"I don't want to go. I don't want to go," she kept saying in a singsong voice as she rocked back and forth. "Don't make me go. Please, I'm a beggin' ye. We'll never see home again."

Ameran looked around. There was no one else around to whom the girl could be addressing her pleas, yet she was certain the words were not intended for her, for the girl was staring glassy-eyed at the pole beside her.

The girl began to wail uncontrollably.

"Annie. Annie, where ye be, girl?"

A big man wearing a broad-brimmed, felt hat and a neck cloth lumbered toward them. "Ye had me worried out of me wits, gal."

The baby began whimpering.

The girl grabbed hold of his arm and would not let go. "Please, John, let's go home now. Please, home."

Ameran tried not to stare.

"That's where we be heading, Annie girl. That's where we be heading."

The girl shook her head sadly. "We'll never set foot in Charles Town. We'll die afore we get there. Little Mary, too. I'm a beggin' ye, John, on all that you hold dear, please, let's turn back now while there is still time."

John swallowed his wife with his massive arms. "Those dreams you've been having mean nothing, Annie. We're going to the colony, and I swear I'm going to make a good life for you and l'il Mary in

Charles Town, a far better life than we can ever hope to have here."

Annie held her baby tight. "They'll kill us," she said in an eerily calm voice. "They'll kill us all. They'll show no mercy. Not even to a poor wee babe."

Ameran desperately wanted to comfort the girl, to tell her all would be fine, but she couldn't, not when she had similar dreams herself.

"Message for Lilly Warwick," cried out a man as he came through the crowd ringing a bell. "Lilly Warwick. Message for Lilly Warwick."

Her heart nearly leapt from her chest. She knew she'd been found out!

Holding tight to her travel bag, Ameran made her way through the crowd after the uniformed customs official who was waving the piece of paper above his head. She recognized a few of the sailors from the *Fair Winds* milling about with the passengers, and she prayed they could not see beyond her rotten teeth and scars.

"I am . . . I be Lilly Warwick," she said quietly, not wishing to draw any more attention to herself.

The note could only be from Nell, she decided as the man turned around smiling. Three hours had passed since they had said their farewells. Undoubtedly, Nelly had forgotten to tell her something or give her one last bit of advice about the boxes of paints and powders in her bag. Surely, she had not been caught.

It seemed hours had passed before the note was in her hand.

"Do ye want me to read it for you, girlie?" asked the official as he tipped his hat.

She shook her head and walked away from the archway where most of the passengers had gathered, reading the contents as they walked along.

She couldn't believe what she was reading. She didn't know whether to be relieved or furious. Constance had accused her of stealing the diamond and pearl brooch that had been missing several days earlier. And Constance had demanded her apartment be searched for it.

Ameran angrily crumbled the note and tossed it into a bin of ashes and soot. If the ship weren't set to sail at noon, she would march right back to Whitehall and wring the Duchess's skinny neck! The fact that she wanted her apartment searched could mean only one thing — Constance had hidden the brooch there with full expectations of proving her accusations.

"Prepare your papers for inspection," another customs official called out over the drone of the crowd.

The passengers began lining up under the archway.

Ameran's heart beat faster. There was no turning back, not even to clear her name. She would deal with Constance upon her return home.

The line moved unbearably slowly as each document was carefully inspected. One man was turned away, another cuffed and dragged away cursing.

It finally came Ameran's turn to produce her papers. The official smiled down at her, a sad smile, full of pity for her unsightly appearance.

"So you were a waiting girl for Mistress Gwyn, were you?" he asked, carefully examining her documents.

"Yes, sir, that's what I be."

"Says here you are traveling to Charles Town to live with Master Brock Plemmons."

"Yes, sir, he be my uncle. He and me auntie Jane ere going to take me in. I gots no one, ye see."

He folded her papers and handed them back to her.

"The stage suffered a loss when Mistress Gwyn retired," he said, friendly enough.

"She be a fine lady, sir."

She heard a few snickers behind her.

The official gave her another sad smile and rushed her along.

Ameran hurried out onto the dock. It was yet too soon to breathe a sigh of relief. She hurried up the ramp with the other passengers, trying to get lost in among them.

Then she saw Gray striding across the deck in her direction. She pulled her scarf tighter around her head. She didn't dare look at him, for though the face was unfamiliar, he would recognize the love which shone from within her.

Gray stopped only a few feet away. She could almost reach out and touch him, and how she longed to do just that!

She waited for him to call out her name, to reprimand and scold her, and have her escorted back to Whitehall. When he didn't, she stole a quick look in his direction.

Gray was looking at no one. He stood leaning over the railing and staring out over the dock.

Her heart cried out to him. She knew she was in

his thoughts, and she knew that such musings were causing him great pain. She could feel his torment, and it took all the strength she could summon to keep from reaching out to comfort him. Soon, very soon, just as soon as England was far behind them, she would.

Most of the men, women and children who boarded the *Fair Winds* bound to Charles Town hung over the rail shouting and waving to family and friends below. Ameran made certain she was concealed in among them, waving to no one in particular. She soon lost sight of her beloved. Not too far away, she could hear a baby's crying, and a woman still pleading with her husband to turn back.

Muskets fired, cannons thundered, and loud cheers went up as the anchor was weighed.

Ameran said a silent prayer. Her voyage had begun!

After three days at sea Ameran felt as though her heart would be ripped in pieces. The days were long, the nights even longer. Every time she caught sight of Gray, her heart cried out to him those words her lips could not utter. How agonizing it was to keep silent, knowing she was the cause of his downcast expression. The temptation to join him as he stared out over the dark, rolling waves was nearly too great to resist. Such pride she felt each time she saw him come striding across the deck, hands locked behind his back, and calling out instructions to his men.

Loneliness and the fear and uncertainty of what

lay ahead formed a close bond among the passengers after that first night when they had all bedded down below deck on thin pallets atop the cold floor. Mothers sang soft lullabies to their children while their men discussed the adventure awaiting them. The older girls gossiped and giggled while their brothers told stories and played games. The peaceful contentment of that first night after all had succumbed to sleep was broken by a woman's wails and her husband's soothing words.

They were thirty-two in all, all voyaging to the land of dreams and second chances, six free men and their wives along with eight children and eight servants, three of whom were young women about her own age. The remaining passengers were indentured men who were bound out to serve for five years their Charles Town masters who had paid for their passage to their promised land.

Whenever messages or instruction were sent from the captain of the *Fair Winds,* it was Gideon who delivered them. The passengers were permitted to take their meals after the crew, and were allowed morning, afternoon, and evening walks along the deck, weather permitting. Contact with the crew was expressly discouraged. Affra Harrelson, a servant girl with Master Henry Wadell's family, had taken up that first day with a mate named Jason Connarn and announced to her employer on the second day that they intended to be wed.

The first time Gideon had visited the passengers at night in their quarters, he had shone the lantern right on her face, and Ameran was certain he had seen right through her blackened teeth and pockmarks. But his eyes had quickly turned from her in disgust, and his gaze had set upon Jewel, the prettiest of the serving girls. When Jewel stole out of the quarters after everyone else had gone to sleep, Ameran was certain she knew where the girl had gone, and she pitied her, for she had no idea what she was getting into by becoming involved with Gideon. And the next night, Ameran felt still sadder for Jewel when it was her closest friend, Allison, who Gideon summoned. Poor Jewel had spent the night sobbing into her pallet.

Ameran kept mostly to herself during those early days of the trip. From her existence at Mer, she was used to her solitude and reverie. She was glad to watch over the younger children so their mothers could wander with their menfolk around the decks, and from time to time during the day, she would chat to Annie and coo soft words to little Mary. Even though Nell had woven an interesting life history around Lilly Warwick, she was reluctant to reveal too many details, knowing her deception would eventually catch up with her, even if it were the time of her choosing. All anyone knew of her was that she was a servant girl going to Charles Town to live with her family.

Much to her surprise, and most everyone else's as well, Master Martin Hereford, a free man of considerable means and not at all unpleasant to look at, sought out her company several times during the day. He was a hardy man with rosy cheeks and an outspoken tongue that was not without an opinion on any subject. He had spent the past few years in Charles Town and was anxious to return to his lumber business there after having spent the past few months in Devon settling family affairs, so he would never again have to return to England. He had confided in her of his beautiful wife, Fiona, who had run off to Barbados with a sugar planter, and how he would never again marry a woman whose face could lead men astray. She did her best to discourage his attentions, knowing he would find out the truth soon enough, but he mistook her reluctance for shyness and pursued her even more intensely.

Martin would tell them stories in the evening about Charles Town and ease the women's fears about Indians and pirates. It was true Charles Town was a favorite haunt for pirates, he admitted, but the settlers had all agreed that as long as the buccaneers confined their killing and looting to the sea, their silver was as good as anyone's when it came to keeping the local merchants in business. As for the Indians, Martin assured his eager listeners, their neighbors, the Estitoes, were merely curious, and that any Indian trouble the settlers ever had was caused by the Yemassees and the Westoes from further south, and had been stirred up by the Spanish who told them lies about the English.

"There is no reason for fright." Martin had assured all those who voiced fear for their lives. "Charles Town is situated on a high bluff that cannot be seen from the sea. It's a fortified city surrounded by a walled fortress with a moat and six bastions. There are lookouts and watch houses that are manned day and night. Two regiments of the militia are on constant watch. In my absence, I feel certain still more entrenchments have been dug and additional cannons mounted."

To those who expressed concern for leaving behind civilization, Martin assured them great plans had been made for the city, plans which had already begun to be implemented. The streets had already been laid out and named, and sites for the church, town house and artillery ground for militia exercises had been cleared. The settlement was not without rules and order, for John Locke himself had written the fundamental constitution of Carolina, and laws were strictly obeyed. The wives were all relieved upon hearing it was illegal not to attend Sunday Church services.

"More than twenty houses have been built," Martin told Ameran one afternoon as they tried to stroll the decks as the ship pitched and rolled atop rough seas.

Martin took hold of her arm to steady her as an enormous wave broke over the side, pelting their faces with salty sprays of sea water.

"I intend to build myself a fine house, finer than any you've ever seen, on the highest knoll there is. It will be three stories high with balconies that open up onto the sea." He took her hand in his. "I've over four thousand acres of fine land. I'll have a house fit for a king, and all that I lack is a wife to share it with me, a wife who will give me sons. I want you to be that wife."

Ameran didn't know what to say. She chose her words carefully. She couldn't meet his face. Instead, she directed her eyes to the dark clouds hovering above them. "I'm most flattered by your attention, but I couldn't possibly be your wife. You see, I . . ."

Martin touched her cheek. "Shhh, my dear. I know what it is you are about to say, and I want you to know outward beauty does not a good wife make. I know that all too well. It's not important that your face is scarred. What's important is that your heart is without blemish."

"I have to ask you to go below," came a loud voice behind them.

Ameran jumped. She didn't dare turn around. She knew that voice.

"There's a storm coming. You'll be safer in your quarters. You'll have to go now," Gray instructed, his words firm and commanding.

Martin took Ameran's arm. "Of course, Captain."

Ameran held her scarf tight around her cheeks. She dared not look into Gray's eyes.

She could almost hear the beat of his heart as she brushed past him, her head painfully turned the other way. How she longed to reach out and touch him, to brush her hand across his cheek, to feel his flesh on hers one more time, but she couldn't.

Ameran didn't breathe easier until they had rejoined the others, and even then she waited and listened for the sounds of Gray's heavy boots coming to fetch her, and his voice demanding an explanation.

Martin patted her hand before leaving her to join the men. "Consider what I have said, dear Lilly. We'd have a good life together."

She turned away. She couldn't look at him, for surely he would see the shame on her face.

The storm lasted for two days and two nights. Night knew no end, and day knew no beginning.

Winds lashed at the sails. The heavens convulsed. Rain pounded the decks in torrents.

For two days and nights the *Fair Winds* was tossed about mercilessly upon the raging seas. It seemed they would all be lost for sure. Most of the passengers felt the end of the world was upon them. Some raised their voices begging for God's help, others called out for death and their soul's salvation. Children could not be quieted, and their mothers' cries did not cease.

The big, open room where the settlers were confined smelled of vomit and fear and the hint of death. The room was swelteringly hot and the stench of bodily waste was stifling.

Ameran feared for Gray's life as much as her own. Not once did she regret her decision to join her beloved on his mission. Knowing how concerned he would be for her safety, she was glad she had not weakened and made her presence known to him. When news came that an officer had been struck by lightning, she fought the need to go topside and see for herself that Gray was still alive, and then when word arrived that the dead man was not an officer but a cabin boy, she felt guilty at her relief, as if one life had been sacrificed to spare another.

Then, the third day of the tempest, their seventh day afloat, the seas calmed and the sun broke through the clouds with a resplendent light. Praises to the Almighty were unending, but a nagging dread that still another storm might follow quietly accompanied their rejoicing. All were starved for fresh air and sunshine, and when the apprentice to the quartermaster came below to tell them they were free to go topside, children and adults alike raced to the upper deck laughing with relief.

Their supper that night of salt pork, turnips, and crusted bread was no less a royal feast of Thanksgiving.

That night, long after they had all bedded down on their pallets and the last babe had stopped whimpering, Gideon came below seeking Jewel.

"Bring Allison with you," he told Jewel, shining the light onto her face.

"She's still sick from the storm," Jewel told him. "Why do you need her?" she pouted. "Don't I give you the pleasure of two women?"

Gideon laughed. "You're indeed more than I can handle. I had other plans for Allison."

Jewel giggled softly.

Ameran listened, eyes closed tight as she pretended to be asleep on the next pallet.

"I want her for the captain," Gideon said, no laughter in his voice. "Who's left? Affra?"

"She's already snuck out to meet her Jason. They're to be married in Charles Town."

"Fools," hissed Gideon. "The captain is desperately in need of a diversion. He's overwrought with melancholy."

"I'd be happy to keep ye both company," whispered Jewel.

"I share nothing with him."

"Ohhh, ye be hurting me. I was only teasing, Gideon."

"As I recall, you're not adverse to a little pain." He cursed softly. "There's no other woman who will come with you?"

"Lilly is the only one left without a husband, but she's not at all fitting for your captain. Her teeth have rotted and her face is poxed."

Gideon chuckled. "It's not the teeth or the face that gives a man his greatest pleasure. Get her."

Jewel nudged Ameran in the sides. "Lilly—wake up—Lilly. Ye want to have a little fun?"

Ameran pretended to awaken slowly. "What is it?"

"Wake up, girl. The captain wants to see you."

"Why? I've done nothing wrong."

"Don't ask questions. Just be grateful he'd send for you."

Ameran hesitated. As much as she wanted to see Gray, she couldn't do so under the pretense of being someone else.

Jewel tugged at her arm. "Don't be a fool, girl. Have ye some fun afore Martin there gets the yoke on ye."

Ameran was in a quandary in which there were no answers. She was desperate to see Gray, if only for a moment, just to reach out and touch him. That was all she would do, and then she would run away before he had a chance to see her in the light.

"Hurry, girl. Ye won't be asked twice."

She had to see him! Now was as good a time as any to end the charade. The *Fair Winds* had come too far to turn back. She could withstand his anger far easier than she could withstand being parted from him another moment.

"Time's a wastin', girl. It'll be daylight afore we know it. Ere ye coming or nor?" asked Jewel impatiently.

"Yes, all right, I'll come with you." Ameran

272

smoothed back her hair while Jewel looked on piteously.

"What's your name, girl?" Gideon asked after the door to the passengers' quarters had closed behind them.

"Lilly, sir. Lilly Warwick," she answered in a voice barely above a whisper.

Jewel hung on to Gideon. "She be a shy one."

"The captain needs to get his mind off certain matters. See that you do that," he said abruptly. "And don't get near the light," he added, none too kindly. "You don't want to scare him to death."

Without warning, he grabbed a breast and gave it a squeeze. Then he let out a loud laugh. "Keep his mind on those, and you'll do just fine."

Jewel knocked his hand away. "For Godssake, Gideon. You'll have her scared out of her wits even before we get there."

Ameran was grateful Jewel stayed between her and Gideon the rest of the way through the long, dark corridor.

They stopped outside Gray's door. Gideon handed Jewel the lantern.

Cruel fingers danced along her cheeks. "Make him happy, Lilly." He pinned her back against the wall. "Make him happy, and I might just have something for you myself."

Ameran dared not to breathe, lest he recognize her.

Gideon pressed harder into her. "Serve him well, and you can do the same for me tomorrow night."

Ameran had escaped sickness during the storm, but now she felt a wave of nausea was about to wash

273

over her. His groin thrust painfully into her thigh; his teeth bit at her mouth.

Ameran fought him off. She tried to claw out his eyes, but he held her arms high above her head.

"Ugly bitch," he spat at her while his hand tore beneath her skirt. "I've never had me an ugly woman before. Maybe I'd better try you first just to make sure you're fitting for the great Lord."

Jewel pulled him off her. "Thought ye didn't want to share with yer friends."

Gideon laughed. He let go of her. "Oh, there is one woman I'd gladly share with him, but she's in England awaiting his return."

Ameran felt her knees weaken.

Jewel wrapped her arms around Gideon and moved his body into hers in a slow, rocking motion. "Come on, love. My arse longs for that whip of yers."

"All in good time, whore." He bit Ameran's ear before pushing her aside.

Gideon knocked on Gray's door. "Open up. I've brought you something to humor you."

As Gray opened the door, Ameran sank against the wall, noticing that he looked weary, tired, and pale by the lantern light.

Gideon shoved her into him. "She's not much to look at, but she's anxious and willing."

Gray gently pushed her aside.

"It's late, Gideon," he said with no humor. "I'll be taking watch soon."

"Oh, she'll keep you awake, Capt'n," piped up Jewel.

Gideon slapped Gray on his shoulders. "Send her

back if you don't want her. Let her stay, and I promise you won't be so miserable come sunrise."

Ameran could tell by the hard set of Gray's jaw that he wasn't amused.

"Return to your quarters," he told her after Gideon and Jewel had disappeared into a room a few doors down. "I have no need of companionship." His voice was kind. "I offer my sincerest apologies for any discomfort my friend may have caused you." He gave a curt bow. "Good night."

She didn't have to deliberate as to whether or not to follow him into the cabin she knew so very well.

"Please, go." He slumped down in his chair, his hands holding his head.

Ameran knelt at his feet. He wouldn't lift his eyes to hers. "Captain Horne said you were in need of a woman. He said you were melancholic as of late and that you needed a woman to make you forget your woes." She stalled for time. She had to tell him the truth, but how?

His eyes insistently avoided her gaze. The dim light from the lantern atop his desk shadowed the turmoil on his face.

"There is but one woman who can make me forget my woes, and she is in England." His words were as miserable as the look on his face. "Go, please. Allow me to be alone with my memories."

Ameran rose slowly. "Your memories have come to you."

Gray raised his head. "I must be dreaming."

Ameran kissed him. "You're not dreaming, Gray. I really am here."

"But it can't be you. Your face." He touched her

cheek in disbelief. "Your face." And he began to laugh.

Ameran scraped some black wax from her teeth. "All in an actor's bag of tricks."

Laughing, Gray began picking the pox from her face.

"I don't believe it," he kept saying over and over.

"Believe it," she laughed. "It's true." And she scraped more wax from her teeth to prove it.

Gray left her side only long enough to go to the basin and wet a cloth. Tenderly, he scrubbed her face clean with one hand while the other caressed the soft flesh marred by no scars. "I fear this is a dream, and when I awaken, my heart will ache all the more."

"It's no dream." She held tight to him. "I couldn't let you set sail without me. I couldn't bear three days without you, much less three months."

He clung to her in desperation, as if he feared he might blink and she would be gone.

Their lips met in a long and impassioned kiss.

"You're not angry?" she asked when their lips parted.

"How could I be angry when I've cursed myself a thousand times for leaving you behind?"

She flung her arms around him again. "I was so afraid you would turn back when you discovered I was on board."

He gathered her closer still. "If we were still in sight of England's shore, I wouldn't turn back. I couldn't."

His kisses grew more inflamed. His hands began an agonizingly slow search of her body. Gray rose slowly a little later, lifting her from the floor as well.

"Now to make sure you are really who you say and not an imposter in another clever disguise, I must make a thorough examination of you."

Smiling, Ameran held up her arms so he could pull the neck to heel coverall and petticoat over her head. "I'd be disappointed if you didn't."

He released a moan of delight as each undergarment was discarded. His lips leaving an invisible trail of kisses down her quivering flesh, he knelt down before her to unfasten the leather sheath from around her leg.

His laugh was soft. "I pity the man who tries to do as I've just done."

"His joy would be short-lived. I promise you that," she laughed with him.

He rolled down the gartered stockings, his lips kissing the shapely expanse just revealed. Placing her arms on his shoulders, he took off her shoes and slid the stockings the rest of the way down.

And when she stood before him, bare-fleshed except for the necklace of jewels in the shape of a cross, and unashamed, Gray began his delicious quest from her toes to her lips again. As soon as his mouth had settled onto hers again, he swooped her up into his arms and carried her over to the mound of covers where he slept.

Hair fanning the pillows, she watched as he rid himself of his uniform. She had known much happiness before in his arms, but never quite so much as that moment when she opened wide her embrace and he came into it.

Every part of her ached for the strength of his hands stroking, caressing, embracing, and enfolding the hills and valleys and hidden little places that became alert at his touch. Her lips could not devour him as much or as quickly as she desired, and her hands strove to traverse every contour of his rock-hard body at once. Moans of delight escaped her lips. She whispered his name over and over, as did he hers.

"I can't wait. I have to have you now," he groaned as his lips brushed her breasts. "I can't wait."

"Nor I, my love. Nor I." Legs locked around his hips, she lured him inside her. She could feel the quiver of his loins on hers.

"I was a fool, a fool," he mumbled into her neck. "A fool for ever thinking I could leave you behind."

"We're together now, and that's all that matters. Together, now, finally, at last," she moaned into his hair.

He lifted her face to his, his look almost fierce. "Never, never again will we be parted."

Trembling limbs clung to him in desperation. One sigh of pleasure after another fell from his mouth. Breaths quickened; insides fluttered like a thousand caged birds just released. One shudder after another passed through her, and she felt herself being hurled far beyond the point of any return.

Gray sank deeper and deeper into her until he, too, had been overcome by a long, awaited fulfillment. He gave her a soft kiss, then lifted his head, a boyish grin on his face.

"If we're both still here, then it can't be a dream, can it? You won't be fading away out of my arms at dawn's first light?"

Ameran laughed. The tip of her fingers danced

through his hair. "I'll remind you of this in the morning, when you chastise me for having undertaken so perilous a journey."

His smile vanished. She regretted at once the words she had just spoken.

"The perils at sea are many," he said sadly. "The storm was nothing compared to the dangers we may have yet to encounter: pirates, Spanish war ships, hurricanes . . ."

He laid his head between her breasts with a sigh. "I'm ashamed at the immense joy I feel at our reunion, for I would rather die alone than subject you to the unspeakable horrors which might well lie before us."

"Oh, feel no shame, Gray." She forced his eyes to hers and lovingly caressed his cheek. "Feel only the love that we share for one another, and the happiness for so sweet a reunion."

He clung to her in fierce determination. "Oh, how I pray I won't put you in harm's way."

"I can never be in harm's way so long as I'm with you."

At that moment, Ameran felt no fear of the unknown, only a joy above all other joys at lying in his arms again.

"The *Fair Winds* is the greatest of all ships, and she could have no finer commander than my Lord Carlisle."

Finally, Gray's face broke into a smile. "I pray I can live up to your expectations."

She snuggled against him, their arms and legs intertwined too tightly to ever let go. "You do, my darling. You've never failed me."

And their sweet reunion began all over again. Once more, she surrendered completely to him, as he did to her, and as the passion and tenderness rose to even greater heights, she knew, as did he, that no matter what hazard may await them, together they could conquer all.

The door to Gray's cabin opened just as the still darkness was about to be overtaken by the early morning haze.

Ameran hid under the covers as a faint light came toward the bed.

There was no mistaking that smirk of satisfaction.

Gray cursed at his second in command. "Out, Gideon. Out!"

Gideon laughed. "Ahhh, I'm pleased you were able to find a moment of peace from the lovesickness plaguing you since we left port."

"Out!" shouted Gray in a tone that demanded obedience.

Gideon gave a mock salute. "Aye, Captain. You can voice your appreciation later when you've had your fill of her."

Ameran could hear his sinister laughter all the way along the corridor. That man frightened her far more than any dreaded ordeal which might lie in wait for them upon the seas.

Gray pulled Ameran closer into his arms. "You're shivering, Ameran."

That eerie feeling encompassed her once more. "I don't trust him," she said, still shaking. "He makes my blood run cold."

Gray let out a heavy breath, but for once, he offered no defense in Gideon's behalf.

The next morning when Ameran came face to face with the man who professed to be Gray's most trusted and devoted comrade, she didn't flinch, but instead met his startled gaze head on.

"Good morning, Gideon." She stood before him dressed as the servant girl, Lilly, but her teeth bore no black stains and her face was free of the pox.

Gideon's amusement at having found his commander still with a woman froze on his face.

"I don't understand," he said, his words pleasant, but his glare stinging.

Gray didn't look up from the charts he was studying. "We've had many stowaways aboard the *Fair Winds*, but none so beautiful. Don't you agree, Captain Horne?"

"You don't look at all pleased to see me," she told Gideon, her voice laced with mockery.

Hate-filled glowers collided.

Gideon forced a smile, but it wasn't a glad smile. He sat down on top of the trunk. "I'm just surprised, that's all. You're the last person I expected to see."

Gray looked up from his maps. He wasn't smiling. "Thank you for bringing her to me last night. It grieves me to think I nearly denied myself of her charming company. Once again, I owe you a debt of gratitude."

Gideon looked as if he still couldn't believe what he was seeing before him was really real. "The scars? Your teeth?"

"All in an actor's bag of tricks," she replied as she walked over to Gray and rested her hand on his shoulder.

"Ahh, Nell Gwyn," Gideon said with disgust.

Gray reached for Ameran's hand. "I used to not like that woman, but I find my opinion of her greatly changed."

A strange look flickered in Gideon's eye, a look meant solely for her, a look that made her shiver far more than the coldest day of winter.

Gideon strode over to them, laughing. He slapped Gray on the back. "You're indeed a lucky man, my friend. I've never made such an impression on a woman that she would forsake all to follow me."

Gray's smile was meant only for Ameran. "For certain I am the luckiest man alive."

Gideon reached for their hands. When Ameran was reluctant to willingly give him hers, he took it.

"I'm truly happy for you both." Gideon gave a bow and a wink. "Continue with your reunion. I'll see to the demands of the ship."

As soon as he had gone, Gray slipped his strong arms around her waist. His chin nuzzled the softness of her dark curls.

Ameran was quiet. Gideon's arrival had spoiled the joys of awakening once again in Gray's arms.

Gray seemed to sense the cause for her silence. "I wish I could convince you that Gideon means neither of us any harm." His smile was patient. "What if he proves to be every bit as loyal and devoted as he professes?"

"That will never happen."

Gray held her tight. "Then, if you're right, I'll allow you to gloat in your victory."

She knew his words were said in jest, but they struck at her heart all the same. "I wouldn't gloat in my victory, for your downfall wouldn't give me any cause for celebration."

Still, Gray didn't let her go.

"I wish there was some way I could convince you that the accusations I make against Gideon aren't the rantings of a jealous woman conniving to sever brotherly bonds."

Gray brushed his lips across hers. "I'm convinced that you truly believe that which you've made yourself believe." His face softened into a smile. "And it's that fierce love that you have for me which makes me love you all the more."

Ameran buried her head in his chest. Their time together was quickly drawing to an end. They'd found each other only to become lost to one another again. And such knowledge had never been more apparent or more frightening than at that moment.

For the longest time, Gray kept her locked in his arms. "I have no choice but to tend to the duties of my ship," he said with a heavy heart. "And I suspect you have some explaining to do to your new friends . . . Lilly."

She didn't want to release him, but she knew she had to. He was the captain of the *Fair Winds* and his men awaited his instructions, not Gideon's.

"Tell me something," Gray entreated as he buckled his sword around his waist.

Her smile was slow to come. "Isn't it apparent by now that I can hide nothing from you?"

Devilish merriment danced in his eyes. "You're not tempted to become Mistress Hereford and reside in a magnificent house atop Charles Town's highest summit?"

For the moment, thoughts of Gideon were put behind them.

She gave him a playful kick. "You were eavesdropping."

"I confess."

Ameran laughed. "Poor Martin. I fear my appeal lay only in my scars and rotted teeth."

Chapter Fourteen

Ameran relaxed in a hammock strung between two posts at the stern of the ship and delighted in the warm, gentle breeze fanning her face as she swung back and forth.

England was far behind them. They were in tropical waters now, and the ship traveled at a slower speed to avoid coral reefs which rose threateningly close to the ocean's surface. Sometimes, sailors would strip to the waist and dive overboard to swim in the tepid waters. In the afternoon as she stood on the bow with the captain of the *Fair Winds,* Gray would tell her stories about the Bahama Islands which lay just over the horizon. He told her of long stretches of pink-sanded beaches and of shipwrecked slaves who made the little islands their homes. Together, they delighted in the antics of the dolphins as they frolicked and played along the white caps as if they were performing solely for them.

Gray had recounted many tales of how those gentle sea creatures would swim alongside the ships for great distances, and how more than one sailor had been saved from a shark attack by the dolphins who butted the feared sea demons to death.

And at night, when the moon was full and the stars

bright, she could see the frightening fins of sharks circling nearby as if they were patiently awaiting some horrible fate to befall the ship.

Sometimes at night as they stood arm in arm on the deck relishing their moment alone, and the moon, big and full, mirrored on the sea, Ameran would catch Gray in a pensive moment. His brows were knotted, and a brooding look cast over his face. Having been detected, he would good-naturedly scoff at her concern and tell her he'd never been happier, but she knew something was worrying him, and she suspected that something was Gideon. Gideon was still Gray's shadow for most of the day and evening, and still laughed and reminisced about their time together, but Gray had very little to say to his old friend. No doubt Gideon would blame her for coming between them, but she could tell the rift in their relationship was much deeper than one caused by a woman. She wished Gray would confide in her.

The gentle rocking of the ship as it plowed through waves hardly more than ripples had all but lulled her into a noontime slumber. She could hear the commotion of the crew going about their tasks under the loud instructions of the quartermaster, who oversaw the administration of the ship, and the sailing master, who directed the turning of the sails.

The colonists had already retired below for their noon meal of bread and salt pork, resigned to this meager fare by the anticipation of fresh fish for dinner if the sharks didn't tear through the nets trolling behind the ship.

The morning had been spent below sewing and chatting and humming lullabies. Though she had dreaded telling them the truth about herself, and it hadn't been at all easy admitting to the lies and deceit, they all seemed relieved by her unblemished skin and white teeth. The men found her tenacity amusing, and the women, especially Allison, Affra and Jewel, were quite taken by the romance and adventure. Martin assured her there would always be room atop his high bluff if she changed her mind about Gray.

Ameran closed her eyes with a sigh and a smile. She supposed in an odd sort of way she should be grateful to Gideon, even though his behavior was despicable. Had he not sought out a woman for his captain, she might not have had the courage to venture into Gray's room on her own for fear he would turn the ship around or send her home on the first England-bound vessel they encountered.

A little later, Ameran roused herself from her slumber, uncomfortably aware that someone was shading her face from the sun. Her pleasant reverie had been broken by a nightmare: Gideon was hovering above her, his glare scorching her face. Still, she was determined not to cower from him. Gideon delighted in others' weaknesses.

"What do you want?"

The corner of his lips turned up in the loathsome smile that never failed to chill her blood. "What do I want? A beautiful woman like yourself should never ask a man such a suggestive question."

He reached out to touch her cheek, but she pulled away.

"Perhaps you should tell me what it is that you want," he said, still smiling, "and mayhaps we can find a way of satisfying both our desires."

The man was disgusting!

"I assure you, Gideon, I desire nothing from you."

His laugh was low and sinister. "I don't know why you feel such dislike for me when I've shown nothing but kindness toward you."

Ameran said nothing. Perhaps if she ignored him, he would soon tire of his ridiculous games and leave her in peace.

"If you still feel harshly toward me because of that little misunderstanding in Mer . . ."

"It was no misunderstanding, and you're as aware of that fact as I am." The calmness with which she addressed her enemy surprised even herself.

"I've tried to make amends. It can't be said that Gideon Horne doesn't try to make things right." He let out a labored sigh. "Surely you can't fault me for trying to protect my captain from falling under the spell of one who was believed to be a vixen from hell?"

"I'm no witch, and you know that as well as I do."

Their eyes collided in anger.

"If I were a witch, you can be certain I would have already made you disappear from my sight forever."

"I like your spirit."

"You'd like to break it, and most probably my neck as well."

"Won't we ever become friends?" His words were as mocking as his smile.

"Never."

"You say that with such certainty."

"I say that with much conviction."

"It's a pity you feel that way, considering Gray and I have sworn brotherhood and allegiance to our deaths."

Cold shivers ran up her spine at the mention of Gray's death. Surely Gideon had sensed by now that

288

something was troubling Gray. Why else would Gray suddenly go quiet in his presence? If only she knew what it was!

"How quickly you forget 'twas I and not your lover who rescued you from the murderer," he reminded her.

"I've forgotten little of that night."

"And yet you feel no gratitude?"

"Only curiosity." She knew well the cat and mouse game they were playing was dangerous, but the temptation to continue was too great to resist.

"I'd already rendered my assailant weaponless when you so gallantly came to my rescue," she reminded him, blinking into the sun. "Were it not for your dagger, he could have named those who had instigated the attack on my life."

Gideon didn't flinch and his face bore no guilt. "My haste in ending the man's life can only be justified by my desire to avenge any grief he may have caused you. Upon reflection, however, I do regret not having questioned him before my dagger found its mark." There was little remorse in his words.

Ameran said nothing, even though she could feel he was waiting for her to reply.

"Gray was most appreciative, as was the King," Gideon told her, the smirk still on his mouth. "It's not your gratitude I seek, only your friendship."

Ameran still uttered no words. Gideon had planned it all. She was more certain of that than ever. What still puzzled her, however, had her assailant been instructed to murder or merely to frighten her almost to the point of death?

"Perhaps you'll look more kindly upon me when I share my good news with you."

She was certain Gideon would never be the bearer of any news other than disastrous, and her annoyed look relayed just that message.

"It suddenly occurred to me a little while ago that if you and Gray truly wish to wed, I could perform the service myself."

Ameran eyed him with a suspicion she didn't try to conceal. "Oh?"

"I know what thoughts must be going through that lovely head, but I assure you, it would be a matter of most simplicity, and the results would be the same had the Archbishop performed the service." His smile was most charming. "The captain of a ship has the power to marry a couple who desire it."

"Gray can't perform his own marriage ceremony," she said.

"No, but I can."

"You're not the captain of this ship," she reminded him coolly.

Gideon eased closer. "No, but Gray can delegate such duties to me, only until the ceremony has been completed, you understand."

Ameran didn't back down from his impaling stare. Nor did she shudder from his scrutiny. "I understand far more than you think." Gideon would like nothing more than to have command of the *Fair Winds,* and that was one power he wouldn't relinquish.

"I thought my solution to your dilemma would please you," Gideon said with an eerie calm in his tone.

"You were wrong," she said just as calmly.

"Then I'll take my leave, madame, for it's apparent you find neither my company nor my friendship to your liking."

That evening, Ameran and Gray had just settled down to their supper of potatoes and mutton stew when Gray relayed Gideon's offer.

Ameran pushed back from the table. "I don't want him to marry us."

Gray kept eating. "Don't act so childish, Ameran. What does it matter who hears the vows, just as long as they're said?"

Ameran could feel her body's temperature start to rise, but it was from anger, and not passion. "Gideon has made a mockery of your friendship. I refuse to let him do the same to our marriage."

Gray shook his head and continued his meal in silence.

"Doesn't it concern you that Gideon would have to be made captain of the *Fair Winds* in order to perform the service?"

Gray said nothing.

"And that as commander," she continued, "he would be free to issue any command against you he wishes, and your crew would have no choice but to obey him?"

"I don't wish to speak further of this matter."

Ameran very calmly pushed back from the table and left the room.

She waited under the stairs for Gray to come after her, and when he didn't, she lacked the courage to return.

Her quiet sobs ceased when she heard footsteps. She was about to rush out into the corridor when she realized the footsteps she heard weren't Gray's.

"Tell the men to be patient. All has been taken care of."

Ameran shrank farther back into the cranny beneath the stairs. She didn't have to see the face to know the voice belonged to Gideon.

"But they're ready now," came another voice, just as mean.

"I'll decide upon the time. Do you understand?"

Ameran couldn't make out the other man's reply as the boots tromped up the stairs.

As soon as she was certain she wouldn't be observed, she ran back into the captain's quarters and blurted out the conversation she had just heard.

Gray gave his head a sad shake. "He might well have been speaking of dropping anchor at one of the tiny islands we'll soon pass so the men might enjoy some rest and relaxation."

"But he wasn't!" she yelled. "He wasn't!"

"Then tell me what you think he was up to."

"I don't know."

Gray frowned. "I can hardly put a man in cuffs and chains because of your suspicions."

"Grayson Carlisle, you infuriate me!"

Gray began to laugh. "We haven't made our pledge before the reverend and already we're behaving as old marrieds."

Ameran picked up the first thing she saw, a marble bookend, and threw it at him.

Gray ducked. But when he came up slowly a moment later, he was holding his head, and Ameran rushed to his side with one apology after another.

When he grabbed hold of her with both arms, she saw his head hadn't been injured.

"Next time I won't miss," she said, trying to wriggle her way free of him.

Over her objections, Gray covered her mouth with

his, and consumed her lips until her fiery words were but gurgles in her throat.

Helpless to deny him even at a time when she'd never been angrier at him, Ameran felt her lips give way to the sweet domination of his.

"Don't expect me to be meek and mild and docile, Lord Carlisle, for such is not my nature."

"As I well know."

The harshness of her face began to relax. "There are times, however, when I can be most agreeable."

His hands began a delicious journey along her hips. "You'll hear no argument from me about that."

Her arms remained by her side and she refused to give his roaming fingers free passage. "But now is not the time." Her smile was teasing, as was her body arched tight into his.

Gray moaned. "What do I have to do to sweeten your disposition?"

Her smile faded. "Promise me you'll take no chances."

Gray let out an exasperated sigh and made no effort to pull her back into his arms when she pushed free of them. "I can find other quarters for the night if you wish it."

Her frown held. "I've never heard such an absurd suggestion!"

"No, nor have I."

"I love you," she said as she closed the distance between them.

"I love you, even at times when you're impossible."

"I can't keep silent about Gideon," she said softly.

"You can't keep silent about anything," he laughed.

"Do you forgive me?" she asked as she slipped her coverall over her head.

Gray kissed the softness beneath her arms. "I have no choice."

Her smile was most beguiling as she tossed aside her petticoat.

"Ah, woman, you will be my undoing," said Gray as he surveyed her luscious loveliness in hungry anticipation.

"Better that I, who love you, be your undoing, and not Gideon — who doesn't."

Gray started to speak, but whatever it was he had been about to say, he decided otherwise and lowered his lips to her neck instead.

"Do you think the King will have me stripped of my command, or will he have me thrown in the Tower?" queried Gray as he feasted on Ameran's beauty. "Absconding with the King's daughter might well be a crime punishable by death."

Her heart stopped. She knew he spoke in jest, but the thought of his life's ending was no trifling matter. God forbid anything ever happen to Gray, but if it ever did, she would as soon die herself.

She tightened her hold on him. Never, never would she ever let him go.

His lips brushed her cheek. "The King will be furious with us both."

Ameran remembered their last walk together. She hadn't confided in him of her plans to obtain under false pretense passage to America on the *Fair Winds*, and yet when they parted company, there was a suspecting glimmer in his wide, dark eyes that made her wonder if he knew her intentions. She had a feeling it had come as no great surprise when Nell disclosed the truth about her departure from Whitehall.

"His fury won't last long. Nell will see to that,"

Ameran told him as she wound little sprigs of his chest's hair around her fingers. "After all, he, too, was born at noon with Venus, the star of love, shining high over the horizon. If anyone understands matters of love, it's the King. He, himself, has said there is no price too great to pay for true love."

Gray rested his head on Ameran's breasts, his tongue flicking their rosy peaks that hardened at his touch. "There's no price too great for your love."

Her fingers drifted through the thickness of his pale hair. "When I think of how close we had come to losing each other forever . . ."

He silenced her with the touch of his fingertips across her lips. "Banish such thoughts from your head forever. We'd have found each other again. I'm confident of that. We would have searched and searched from one end of the earth to the other until we were rejoined. It's not our destiny to be apart." His kisses were slow and sweet. His gentle yet powerful hands moved across the swell of her hips, kneading and caressing the gentle curves beckoning to him.

She purred like a kitten at his touch. Never would she grow tired of the feel of his flesh on hers. The feel of his strength roaming across her body, and the feel of his warm breath fanning her face gave her a feeling of being wonderfully alive.

Their bodies were still naked and moist with sweat from their lovemaking only a few hours before, yet she wanted him again, as he did her, again and again and again.

Leisurely, she stretched out her legs, entangling his limbs in hers. Arms tight around his muscular forearms, she gently guided him to the sweet places she yearned for his hands to be. Back arched, hips rising, she reached up to him, silently pleading for more of his tender loving. Satiny flesh burned beneath his all knowing caresses. Her eyes clouded with a deep longing. The dark blue depths of his gaze bore his own need and reflected hers.

They came together slowly, lover to lover, both anxious to give and to receive complete pleasure and satisfaction from their joyous union. Sweet, whispered words of love were shared with each quickened breath. One kiss began where another had just ceased.

One hand tightened around her waist; the other teased and tormented those secret spots where no other man had ever ventured before, places reserved solely for Gray, places whose joy no other man would ever know.

A moan of ecstasy slipped past her lips, then another, and still another as she surrendered completely to Gray.

Body slightly arched, she flattened her hands against the cords of muscles bunching up across his chest and kissed the rock-hard contours.

Gray let out a moan and collapsed atop her.

Their bodies melted together again, limbs and lips locked. At first gently, and then with a mounting passion, Gray drove himself deeper and deeper inside her. Ameran clasped her legs tighter around him, her eager fingers clinching, clawing, begging for yet more. Never had she known such sweet agony, such delicious desperation. She could feel herself soaring higher and higher to an awesome, shuddering ecstasy. Her body began to vibrate with a liquid fire. Gray gave one last thrust, then a smile and a groan and sank deeper inside her. With a soft sigh of exhaustion, he rolled off her and face down atop the bed. Soon, he began to snore.

Ameran leaned down to kiss his shoulder.

For a long time she watched him sleep. The smile would not fade from her lips. Her hand went to her stomach, gently massaging the taut flesh. Something wonderful had just happened. She was certain that a few moments before, another life had begun to grow inside her, a tiny being that she and Gray had created in love. No love between a woman and a man could be more complete.

"Gray, there's something I must tell you," Ameran began several mornings later as they breakfasted in his quarters. Only moments ago she had been rummaging through her travel bag in search of a hair ribbon, and her finger had been pricked by the point of an object whose appearance she found most distressing.

Dark blue eyes opened wide in mock horror. "Surely you're not going to confess to having taken a lover?"

She couldn't help but smile.

His fingers danced beneath the bed covering draped as a robe around her. "What is it you feel compelled to unburden from your soul?"

Ameran hesitated, then took a deep breath and began by telling him of the message sent from Nell shortly before the ship set sail.

"Nonsense," said Gray as he wolfed down his breakfast. "You're no thief, and I'll fight to the death anyone who says you are."

His promise did nothing to console her. "In Constance's eyes, I am a thief of the lowest kind."

"Only because you stole my heart," he said as his boot ran up her leg. "Don't trouble yourself with worries about Constance, my love. As for the brooch, she no doubt misplaced it, and when she finds it, which I am certain she already has, she'll realize her accusations were unjust and unfounded."

"That will never happen." She went to fetch her travel bag, then reached inside and brought out the diamond and pearl brooch. "I swear I don't know how this came to be in my possession." She turned her bag wrong side out for him to inspect. "As you can see, someone went to a great deal of trouble to sew the brooch into the lining of my bag."

"There can be but one responsible, and that can only be the accuser herself." Gray turned the brooch over and over in his hands. "It must have pained the Duchess to no end to part with this little trinket. Without question it's worth a small fortune."

"It was no sacrifice. I'm sure she was confident she would get it back," said Ameran, returning to her place on the bed. "After all, she named the thief herself and made sure it would be found in the belongings of the accused."

The scar upon his jaw pulsed angrily, just as it always did when he was enraged. "I'll deliver it myself upon our return to Whitehall."

Ameran held her face in her hands. "The fact that I have disappeared casts still more suspicion on me. You don't think me a thief, do you?" she said in response to Gray's long silence.

"I know you're no thief." His jaw tensed again. "Would that I knew why Constance would set out to prove you are."

"Isn't it apparent? She wants me to fall from the

King's favor, but most importantly, from yours."

Gray nodded slowly. "How convenient she wait until I had set to sea to accuse you."

"She's most shrewd."

"Not nearly as shrewd as she thinks," Gray remarked as he poured himself more tea.

"How black a soul for one so beautiful," said Ameran as she poured a cup for herself.

Gray kissed her lips lovingly and tenderly. "Her beauty pales in comparison to yours, and that is what has her so enraged."

"Spoken like the wonderful husband you truly are." Her delight at his lips having found hers again lasted briefly. "First, I am a witch. Now I am a thief. Will Constance never leave me in peace?"

Even as she asked the question, she already knew the answer.

Gray patted her hand. "Nell will set her straight, and everyone else, I'm certain."

Ameran stretched back out beside him. "I've noticed you're not so critical of Nell as you once were."

Gray stopped eating. "I thought I knew Nell Gwyn for the kind of woman she was, but I was wrong. Unfortunately it took a near-tragedy to open my eyes to the real Mistress Gwyn." He stared out the porthole and directed his softspoken words out to sea. "My eyes are often slow to open to the truth."

Ameran could sense his pain. Was it too much to hope for that he was discovering the truth about Gideon?

She waited patiently for him to confide in her that which she had so longed to hear, and when he did, she felt no victory in his revelation.

"I have my doubts about Gideon's true nature. I

should have had them long before now. A true friend wouldn't bring a strange woman to another friend in hopes of having him forget about his true love," said Gray sadly. He hung his head. "And there are other things that have struck me odd as of late about his behavior. I sense he's dividing the crew against me."

Ameran tried to comfort him, but her arms lacked the power to give him the solace he yearned for.

"Perhaps I never knew Gideon at all. Perhaps I made him out to be greater than he could have hoped to be. I don't trust him. I don't trust the man he has shown himself to be." His breath was deep and troubled. "And it grieves and troubles me knowing I may have unwittingly played a role in his successful deception, for I was his staunchest defender."

Her hold on Gray became even more fierce, and she shuddered to think what might well be her lover's fate if he were to make known any accusations regarding his second in command.

"You mustn't confront Gideon now," she told him. "You must wait until we return home to make known your suspicions both publicly and privately."

His nod was grave. "I'm painfully aware of the truth in what you say, and as much as I long to demand explanations from him, I dare not, for the risks are much too great."

Gray stared out the porthole as if the answers he sought were written upon the whitecaps.

Ameran followed his gaze.

Daylight was about the break over the horizon. The sky was splayed with a haze of pinks and ambers. The sea was mirror calm, its surface a reflection of the heavens above.

She said nothing. She didn't have to. She could tell

by the furrow of his brow and the tightening across his chest the troublesome worry that had burdened his heart. If cornered, Gideon might well turn on Gray rather than face and admit the charges against him. A mutiny might well ensue if Gideon were pushed too hard and too far. It had been Gideon's task, a task which he insisted be entrusted to him, to take on extra hands, and the new seamen might well lack allegiance to the *Fair Winds* or its commander.

She could tell by Gray's grim expression that such horror was no stranger to his own thoughts.

"Whatever game Gideon may be playing, he won't risk his reputation with King Charles," Gray told her, reading her thoughts. "He wouldn't dare attempt to take command. The crew he selected may well side with him, but my own men, Quartermaster Phipps, Lieutenant Bainbridge, Marlan, Rogers, Pittman, Garrison, Forrester and all the others who have sailed with me, they would never allow it. Those men can't be bought or bribed or cajoled."

The troubled lines began slowly to fade, and the scar on his jaw relaxed. "No, my men would never permit it. I would pit them against the best Gideon has to offer."

Gray's sentiments echoed her own. "If there's a confrontation, your men will stand by their rightful commander."

Gray nodded. His dark eyes sparkled with fiery blue anger. "And if my loyal friend is so foolish as to attempt to take command of my ship, I'll show him no mercy. He'll hang from the yardarm with the rest of his infernal devils."

"Gideon wouldn't dare cross you." She lay her head

down onto his chest and said a prayer. "He wouldn't dare."

Gray stroked her hair comfortingly. "No, no, of course he wouldn't."

Arms wrapped tight around him, she hugged him with all her might. He didn't believe that any more than she did, and she prayed to God they both were wrong.

A moment later, Gray backed out of her hold. His pale brows knotted together in distress.

"What is it?" she asked.

He hurried to buckle his sword around his waist. "Listen."

She shook her head. "I don't hear anything."

"Neither do I."

Then he told her what she had only just come to realize. The fact that they heard no sounds was most peculiar for a ship and a crew the size of the *Fair Winds*.

Her heart took a downward plunge. The tales of pirates and enemy warships that had been recounted over and over during the voyage came back to haunt her.

Gray touched his fingers to her lips. "Don't leave the cabin until I come for you. Do you understand?"

She nodded.

Her heart cried out to him, but she had to remain calm for his sake. "Be careful," she whispered.

"Bolt the door behind me."

She desperately wanted to run to him, to grab hold of him and keep him safely with her, but she didn't dare. Lord Grayson Carlisle was the commander of the entire British fleet. He wouldn't betray his duty to the *Fair Winds,* nor would he betray his duty to his King and country.

Ameran stood for the longest while in the center of the cabin right where Gray had left her. She tried to convince herself that there was a logical explanation for the sounds they didn't hear, but in her heart, she knew such an explanation didn't exist. She knew as well that her worst nightmare was about to come to pass, and atrocities she could not as yet imagine were about to be committed. But until such time came, she could do little more than wait . . . wait and pray that she had never been more wrong about anything in her life.

Chapter Fifteen

Ameran sat huddled in the darkest corner atop Gray's trunk, her fingers tight around the handle of the dagger strapped to her leg. Perhaps it was nothing, she kept telling herself over and over long after Gray's kiss of farewell. Perhaps the men had fallen asleep at their posts, she reasoned in an attempt to soothe her worst fears. After all, had enemy intruders attempted to board the *Fair Winds,* there would most assuredly have been a violent commotion topside, and yet there had been no exchange of fire, no warning bells, and no loud voices or hurrying scuffles across the deck.

At any moment, she told herself, Gray was going to return and tell her there was no cause for alarm. All was well! Yes, all would be well.

She said a little prayer. Please, let it be so!

She tried to occupy her mind with more pleasant thoughts. Gray had told her of a Bahaman cay nearby, a little island where the sands were pink and the waters a hundred shades of blue. The island would be in sight by early afternoon, and the *Fair Winds* would moor in the deeper waters outside the reef. All those wishing to go ashore would be taken there in the long boats for a few hours of fishing and exploring, shell collecting, and relaxing on the beach.

Quite suddenly, into the stillness, she heard a rush of footsteps pounding down the stairs, then the sounds of angry voices and of fists banging on doors. She was certain the noises were coming from the colonists' quarters at the end of the corridor.

Ameran crouched closer to the wall. Her ears strained to hear over the commotion. She could make out the sounds of laughter, but they weren't of amusement or good humor. There was something wicked, almost unholy, about the wild cackling. And then there were voices, loud voices speaking in a strange tongue. Spanish! The ship had been boarded by the Spanish, but how had they done so without meeting a struggle from the *Fair Winds'* crew? Gray's crew would not have given up their ship without a fight.

A loud thud coming from above her head made her hug the wall closer. Then, there was a discharge of guns, and the faint sound of metal upon metal.

Ameran clutched at her throat. Gray! He was in danger. Her dreams had foretold it. She had to go to him. She had to stand by his side—to die by his side if that was what fate decreed.

She hesitated for only a moment. Gray would have far less cause to worry if she remained where he had told her to stay, but she couldn't sit by and wait to be made a victim herself.

Making sure the knife was tight around her leg, she took another, a pearl-handled dagger, from Gray's desk, and held it tight between her fingers. She could plunge the blade into a target as well as any man. If Gray were in danger, she would fight alongside him. If it were his destiny to perish . . . No, she mustn't think such thoughts!

Trembling fingers brushed across her stomach. Gray would not die! He wouldn't! She refused to let him!

Careful to make no sounds, she unbolted the door, peeped out the crack, then eased it open just wide enough to squeeze through. She closed the door, cringing at the sound made by the creaking hinges, then took a few steps and stopped dead in her tracks. She stifled the gasp that escaped her throat. Standing guard at the passengers' quarters were two men she had never seen before. They were barefoot, stripped to the waist, and attired in knee pants without stockings. Gold hoops dangled from their ears, and gold chains hung around their necks.

Ameran pressed closer to the wall, praying she hadn't been detected.

She tried to calm herself. There was no time to be afraid. She had grown up no stranger to danger.

Her heart pounded faster and faster. She could feel her blood rushing to her head. Sooner or later, her presence would be discovered, and it was far better to go in search of the enemy than have him come after her.

She eased a few steps closer to the stairs leading topside. Then she ducked behind the railing and waited for footsteps to seek her out. When none came, she chanced another look down the corridor where the two men had been standing guard. They were no longer there. Just when she had begun to breathe a little easier, she heard a woman's scream, then the sounds of fists pounding flesh, and other, more piercing screams.

Before she gave way to the terror gnawing at her insides, Ameran bolted up the steps, the wood creaking loudly beneath her feet. She could hear no sounds of battle, only the rumble of foreign tongues and the low, throaty laughter that chilled her blood.

Her fingers tightened around the grip of Gray's dagger, and with her free hand she pushed up on the hatch.

Her stomach heaved up to her throat. The stench of blood and death assailed her nostrils long before her eyes focused on the gruesome carnage lying before her.

It was all she could do to keep from spewing forth last night's supper. The first body she saw was that of Jason Connarn, the betrothed of servant girl, Affra Harrelson. He was lying face up in a puddle of blood. The look chiseled upon his waxen features was one of mute terror. His eyes were bulging open, and his throat was slit from ear to ear.

She could not pull her eyes from the horrible sight. She thought of poor Affra down below, poor Affra waiting for her handsome sailor to rescue her from the Spanish devils. At least Jason's suffering was over. No doubt Affra's was only beginning.

Ameran kept staring at the young man's body, unable to move, her feet frozen in fear. There were more young men's bodies scattered across the deck, their limbs twisted, their blood spilled, and upon their faces the same horrible grimace of death. The navigator, Mr. Rogers, had fallen, as had Mr. Forrester, whose eyepatch rested upon his chin.

Then, she looked beyond the railings of the *Fair Winds* and saw another ship, this one half the size of the great British vessel, moored alongside. A black

307

flag flew from its mast, and Ameran realized the *Fair Winds* was indeed under siege.

A pair of arms tightened around her. Rough hands groped at her breasts.

Ameran whirled around, her knife poised to meet its mark.

The man kicked the knife out of her hand. He laughed and mumbled words she did not understand, but the meaning she could well guess.

He pushed her down onto the stairs, then fell on top of her, tugging at her skirt and untying his trousers.

He smelled like a pig, and his laugh was that of a demon from hell. His pants fell to his hips, and he pulled at the limp fold of flesh between his legs, making horrible, hissing sounds.

Fighting to keep her fear from taking an even firmer grasp on her, Ameran pulled her leg up under her, then carefully eased the knife from the leather band strapped around her leg. And she waited . . .

With another laugh of Satan, the demon dove onto her. His laughter eased at once, and his throat spasmed with pitiful gurgles.

She could feel the heat of his blood dripping onto her thighs. It took all the strength she could summon to roll the fat mass from atop her. Quickly, she pulled the knife out of his gut. The flesh tore even more beneath the sharp blade. She then returned her knife to her leg strap and retrieved Gray's from the step where it lay.

Slowly, she walked across the deck, tiptoeing and ducking in and out and around furled sails, masts, poles, and beams, all the while stepping over one slaughtered seaman after another. Garrison, Pittman, Quartermaster Phipps, Warner, Jessup, Johnson, Bainbridge, Marlan, and countless others whose faces she knew but names did not—all fallen to the enemy.

Ameran couldn't believe the horror she was witnessing was real. It had to be a nightmare, and she prayed she would awaken, but she knew she wouldn't. It was real, unbelievably real, and there was no escaping.

Her senses were quick to dull. She could no longer smell the foul odor of blood and waste. Her ears were numb to the screams and laughter coming from below. She knew the knife was clasped between her fingers, for she could see the glimmer of its blade catching the early morning light, yet she couldn't feel her hand gripping the pearl handle.

There was something strangely peculiar about the dead men, and at first, she didn't recognize what it was, but after stepping over one body after another, it finally struck her what was so odd. Gray's men hadn't fallen in battle. They hadn't drawn their weapons in defense. Nor had they been taken by surprise. The crew had been slaughtered, butchered mercilessly by those of their own whose corpses did not lie alongside them.

Ameran hurriedly scanned each face she encountered for Gray's face. His body wasn't among them. Perhaps there was cause for hope!

She didn't know how long she'd been walking among the dead when she heard laughter, cold, brutal laughter, coming from the black-flagged ship. She crouched lower and moved closer to the sounds. Taking refuge behind an oaken cask, she listened. She could hear voices, Gideon's voice, and she could hear that of Gray. He was alive! He hadn't perished!

"You're a fool, Gideon," she heard Gray exclaim. "You'll never get away with so horrendous a crime."

Gideon's laugh was mean and taunting. "Nay, you're the fool, my good Lord Carlisle. You played right into my hands, and now you're a captain without a ship or a crew to command."

Ameran peered out from behind the keg. It was all she could do to keep from screaming out Gray's name. His shirt was covered in blood. His left arm hung limp at his side. She had to get to him; she had to save him, but how?

There was a third man standing with them, a skeleton-thin man with bronzed skin and a head that was slick save for a few strands of hair at the base of his neck. His men stood to one side of him, and those of the *Fair Winds* crew who had sworn allegiance to Gideon even before the ship had left port stood opposite them.

"When the King receives word of your treachery, he'll send the entire fleet after you," Gray told him in a calm voice that bore no fear, only anger.

Ameran could feel Gray's anguish and despair. It tore at her heart far worse than any knife. His pain was her pain. Even at his most vulnerable, Gray stood proud and erect, regal and dignified.

"The King!" Gideon spat at Gray. "What a noble monarch England has on her throne. The King is too busy whoring and placating the Papist bastard across the channel to come to your rescue. It's too late for you, Lord Carlisle, and soon, very soon, it will be too late for your King as well."

The slick-headed man beside Gideon finally spoke. His words were spoken in English, but his

310

accent was Spanish. "Kill him and be done with it. If you can't, I can. You promised women for my men and you promised me gold and cannons."

"All in good time, Captain Monquez. All in good time." Laughing, Gideon turned up the green bottle he was holding and took a long gulp. "I intend to uphold my end of our bargain, but I'll do so when I'm ready. Do you understand?"

Monquez jerked the bottle from his hand. "I told you we spotted that Welsh devil near Gorda Cay morning before last. I've no desire to cross swords with him. Not yet, not until my cannons are in place."

Gray managed a laugh. "You have good reason to fear Captain Billy Blitzen. He'll make short work of you and your cuthroats."

Monquez lunged at Gray, his knife ready to slit his throat.

Ameran's cry caught in her throat. Gray was about to die and she could do nothing to save him. Knife poised above her head, she was ready to climb onto the railing and jump to the ship on the other side when Gideon's sharp words rang out.

"No! I don't want him to die yet. I want him to suffer first."

Monquez was slow in dropping his arm. "What will you have me do, sir? Cut off his fingers one by one? Cut out that cursed tongue?" He laughed. The blade of his knife ran down the jacket of his uniform snipping off gold buttons one by one, and coming to a stop between his legs. "Or I can start here, heh?"

Gray didn't blink. When he spoke, his voice was void of fear. "Don't be a coward, Gideon. Don't let Captain Monquez fight your battles for you. Take up your sword. Fight me like the man you profess to be. Prove you're worthy to command the *Fair Winds*."

Gideon's smile faded. "You're in no position to make any demands of me. I don't have to prove myself worthy. The ship is mine."

Monquez looked to him, not for a command, but for an explanation.

"Your fate is sealed, my good friend. I regret that I can only kill you once," Gideon told him, his remark cold and cruel."

Still, Gray showed no fear. "If I'm to die, I won't go to my grave alone."

"A fine boast for a man with one good arm and no sword."

Gray lunged at him.

It took four of Monquez's men and three of Gideon's to pull him off. While they held him, Gideon planted his boot firmly in Gray's stomach and delivered a blow that sent him sprawling across the deck.

Gray rose slowly. He fought to show no pain. "You're a coward, Gideon. I thought you were more of a man than to let others do battle for you."

"I'm more of a man than you will ever be," Gideon told him spitefully. "I have no intention of matching swords with you, but it's not because I fear your skill greater than mine. I know I could easily run the blade through your heart, but I don't want you to fall in battle, for that is far too honorable an end for you. I want there to be no honor in your death."

Monquez's eyes skimmed the water in all directions. "Hurry up and be done with it," he told Gideon.

"Be patient, Monquez. Can't you see I am enjoying this?" Gideon offered the bottle to Gray.

Gray slapped it away.

Gideon laughed. "It's not my intention to kill you. I'll let the sharks do the work for me."

Ameran couldn't keep from trembling no matter how hard she tried to steady herself. Dreadful thoughts reeled round and round inside her head. It couldn't be happening, she kept telling herself, but it was. Her nightmare was about to become reality, and there was nothing she could do to change the course of that which was dangerously close to coming to pass. The sharks with their razor-sharp teeth and thirst for blood would tear Gray from limb to limb, cleaning the flesh from his bones.

Gray's visage remained undaunted. Defiantly, he stood at the mercy of his captor. "You can run your blade through my heart, or you can throw me to the sharks, whatever method you choose. But I promise you this, Gideon Horne, I won't die. And I swear I'll come after you, and you'll pay the price of your abominable treachery against your country."

Gideon clapped his hands. "For a man who is about to go to his grave, you're quite eloquent." His glower was filled with hate. "I've lived in your shadow long enough. From now on, mine will be the name spoken in reverence, not yours. Yours will be a name hated and scorned, a name associated with the greatest traitor England has ever known."

Ameran crouched lower behind the cask. She was slowly starting to understand. How wrong she and Gray had been to think Gideon posed the greatest threat at home! His accompanying Gray on the voyage to Charles Town was a well thought out and deliberate plan. Gideon had selected the worst of scoundrels, knowing their loyalties would lie with

313

one of their own, and Gideon had known from the very moment the *Fair Winds* set sail that the ship would rendezvous with Monquez and his men. It had all been arranged beforehand that night in Constance's suite with the delegate from Madrid. And Gideon had known as well that Gray would never again set foot on the land he so dearly loved.

No! It couldn't be happening!

Hot tears streamed down her cheeks. But it *was* happening, and Gideon had no intention of letting Gray live. Gideon was a murderer, a traitor. Yet he would return to England in a hero's glory.

Never! If it were the last act she ever committed, she wouldn't allow Gideon that satisfaction.

Gideon laughed like a madman. "When the *Fair Winds* sails back into the King's harbor, Gideon Horne will be at her helm. No doubt the King will make me Commander of the Royal Navy when I tell him how you joined forces with the Spanish to attack a helpless French ship. He'll be appalled at my tales of your butchering and your pillaging."

Gray's smile was mocking. "No matter how carefully conceived your plans, you'll never succeed. Surely you're not so vain that you cannot see the folly of such a plot."

"Perhaps I should have Monquez cut out your tongue. Your idle rambling tires me." Gideon paced back and forth in front of Gray. "For years, I've planned and plotted your destruction and your demise. Now at long last I have all but succeeded in my great achievement. I've created an end worthy of so great a foe as you."

Gray said nothing. His stare didn't leave Gideon's face.

"Surely there are questions you demand to have answered before you become shark bait?" Gideon stood nose to nose with him. "Questions you long to have answered? No? Have you wondered in the last hour why I didn't let that Dutch officer kill you? Why I saved your life only to take it now?"

Gray shrugged his shoulders. "That's no mystery, Mr. Horne. You wanted me to ascend to greatness and glory because the only way you could get there yourself was by hanging onto my coat tails. When it came to choosing friends, you chose well. You were no fool. You selected those whose attributes you desired but could never possess."

"You bastard!" Gideon lunged at Gray, his hands tightening around his throat.

Gray lifted his good arm in his defense.

This time it was Gideon who went sprawling across the deck.

A rumble went up from Monquez's crew. Their captain raised his hand to silence them.

Gideon got up slowly, clutching his stomach. "Enjoy your moment of victory, Lord Carlisle, for you'll have no other." He walked circles around Gray, this time keeping one eye on his right arm. "Since you won't be present to witness for yourself the sequence of events which will soon transpire, permit me to tell you of them, and you can thus judge for yourself how successful I'll be in ruining your good name."

Gideon was obviously very proud of himself.

"As you know, there is a French supply ship in the vicinity laden with provisions and settlers of their own bound for the northern part of America. There'll be a few able-bodied seamen to escape the massacre, just enough to sail their ship back to

315

France and condemn the great Englishman Lord Grayson Carlisle who attacked their ship. I'll return to Whitehall at about the same time and tell my woeful tale to King Charles, how our beloved Lord Carlisle took up arms against our most trusted ally and plundered and pillaged their ship, killing in cold blood anyone who dared oppose him. I, of course, couldn't stand by and watch my country be dishonored, so I had no choice but take command of the *Fair Winds,* and unfortunately in so doing, I was forced to take the life of my erstwhile companion." Evil lurked in his smile. "What do you think so far?"

"The King will never believe such a tale," Gray said with quiet confidence.

"No, not at first, I don't think he will. However, he doesn't have to take my word alone. He'll hear reports from the French, since Louis will undoubtedly send delegates to Whitehall to discuss the unfortunate incident in detail. And of course, Charlie will have eyewitness accounts delivered to him personally by the *Fair Winds* own crew, those who survived, of course." Gideon bowed low. "And your name and reputation will become blacker than the Newcastle coals."

Gray held firm. "No matter your lies, King Charles will see through them."

"You give our monarch far more credit than he is deserving of." Gideon let out an exaggerated sigh. "But you'll never know the outcome one way or another, will you?"

With her knife between her teeth, Ameran crawled along the deck, her body pressed tight against the rail of the *Fair Winds,* to the point where the bow of the English vessel was touching the stern of the pirate ship.

"Aren't you concerned as to the fate of your men?" asked Gideon with a cruel smirk affixed to his mouth.

"The fate of my men has already been sealed. It grieves me greatly knowing 'twas my folly that led to their deaths."

Even though Ameran was in no position to witness the sorrow upon his face, she could hear it in his tone, and for the first time during his conversation with Gideon, his words were shaky.

"The dead and the wounded will be fed to the sharks," Gideon declared without emotion. "And the colonists will be marooned on an island."

"Without food and water they'll die," said Gray solemnly.

"Yes," Gideon said simply.

Ameran could hear Gray draw a deep breath. "What of Ameran?"

Gideon laughed. "I'll take exceptional care of her. That I can assure you." He nudged Monquez. "And when I have had my fill of that whore from hell, I'll auction her off to the highest bidder. Shame you won't be around to make an offer on so luscious a piece of womanly flesh."

Gray closed the distance between them in one long stride, but the moment before his fist found its mark on Gideon's jaw, Monquez and two of his men grabbed hold of him and kept him restrained while Gideon flaunted his superior position.

"I wish I could stay and witness the shredding of your flesh, but I can't, for Captain Monquez and I have a rendezvous with our friends, the French."

317

Gideon gave an annoyed wave of his hand. "Get rid of him," he told Monquez. "He ceases to amuse me."

With his last strength remaining, Gray held himself tall. His smile held. "Aren't you enough of a man to hoist me over the side yourself?"

"Get rid of him. Now!" Gideon screamed.

"No! No!" Dagger poised for attack, Ameran threw herself onto the pirate ship. Her mark sighted, she ran to Gideon and plunged her knife into his stomach while the others looked on in shock.

Gideon turned just as the blade met his flesh. Blood spurted from his side, and he doubled over in pain.

"Over the edge!" yelled Gideon, still clutching his side.

Gray kicked himself free of his captors, then charged at Monquez and toppled him over backward into the flagpole.

Ameran ran crying into Gray's arms.

"I am so, so very sorry, my darling," he told her over and over. "It's all my fault. You tried to warn me, but I was too blind to see the truth. And now you and other innocent souls will have to pay for my mistakes."

"Shh, shh, you're not to blame." Ameran touched her fingers to his cheek. "I love you," she told him, knowing their time together would be brief. "I'll love you forever."

Tears filled his eyes. "Forgive me, my love, for all that you must endure because of me."

Ameran clung to his neck. "If you're to die, then I'll die with you. I couldn't face life without you."

Gray untangled her arms from around his neck.

"Listen to me. Listen. You have to live. Promise me you'll survive. Do what you must, but don't willingly give up your life. Promise me. It will make my own end more bearable."

"I can't promise that which I have no intention of keeping," she said, her words barely a whisper.

Monquez came towards them, his sword brandished.

Gideon held up his hand to stop him. "Let them be. I find their devotion amusing."

They paid their executioners no attention.

"I intend to fight death until I can fight it no longer. You must promise me that you'll do the same." Gray held her tight. "Live, my darling. Live." His hand brushed her stomach.

He knew! He knew!

And she knew she must do as he urged for all their sakes, and their unborn child's.

Gideon clutched at his side. "Ah, parting is indeed such sweet, sweet sorrow." His foul laughter made him wince in pain.

Gray held her close one last time. "Live, Ameran. I'll survive the sharks and the sea, and I'll come for you."

It took six of Monquez's men to pry her from his side, and twice that many to boost him onto their shoulders.

"I'll have my revenge, Gideon," Gray called down to him.

Gideon laughed. "Ah, but I'll have mine first." He dropped his hand.

Ameran collapsed in a heap. She heard a splash, then began to sob. It was over.

Monquez poured a bucket of small fish over

319

the side. "That should get the sharks interested."

Ameran covered her eyes. Soon those creatures of the deep would be closing in for the kill. She could hear the ripples in the water, then there were no more sounds coming from the black depths below.

She could feel the strength slowly seeping back into her limbs, and she could feel Gray's presence inside her. Yes, she would live! Gray would always live inside her and through their child. She would avenge his death. She would see to it that Gray remained a hero in the eyes of his people and his King, and she would make certain Gideon received his just due. The next time, she would not miss her mark!

She felt a hand around her shoulders.

Monquez jerked her necklace from around her neck. Her hand went to the spot where the jewel-encrusted cross had lain. The flesh felt naked without it.

Monquez dangled it in front of her, just out of her reach. The sun bearing down unrelentingly upon them caught the sparkles of the diamonds, emeralds and rubies.

She reached for it. "Give it to me. It's mine."

Monquez laughed and fastened the chain around his neck. "It didn't take the sharks long to catch the scent of blood."

Ameran chanced a quick look over the side, then turned away in sickened despair. Dozens of black fins were slicing through the bloodied waters.

Gideon held his side with one hand, and took hold of Ameran with the other. "You're mine now," he said tauntingly. "Please me, or you shall be fed to the sharks as well."

Hatred blazed in her eyes. "They'd make far more fitting companions than you."

Gideon laughed and jerked her closer to him, his fingers bruising her flesh. He turned to the meanest of his lot, a young man whose face was a crimson mask of pox scars.

Ameran was familiar with the name and the face belonging to it. Tommy Tremble! More than once he had frightened her with eyes that stalked her every move. Master Jarvis had said there had been a man of the same name in the village of Prosper, and that Tommy Tremble would as soon slice a throat as not.

"Bring up the women," Gideon told Tommy. "Divy them up however you wish." He turned to Monquez. "Just as I promised. Your men shall have their women, and you shall have your gold."

Monquez eyed him suspiciously through narrow, little slits. "What other services do you require of me?"

Gideon forced Ameran's back into his chest and locked his arm around her throat in a hold that nearly choked her. "After we have rid the *Fair Winds* of her passengers, we'll secure your ship in a secluded cove on a nearby cay, and then, my friend, we shall go in pursuit of the French trading ship."

"And that ship's stores?" asked Monquez, his smile widening.

"Yours. Weapons, provisions, all yours," Gideon assured him.

"And her crew?"

"Kill them," he said without any feeling.

Monquez slapped Gideon on the back. "You'd make a fine buccaneer. Join us? The sea would be ours to command."

Gideon brushed his hand from his shoulder. "I'll sail the *Fair Winds* home and be greeted by all the glory befitting a true hero."

Ameran tried to spit in his face. "You're no hero. Your people won't worship you. They'll condemn you to a death a thousand times more horrible than the ones you inflict on poor innocents."

Ameran struggled to free herself from her captor, but Gideon only tightened his hold. "Save your strength, my beautiful witch. You'll have need of it later."

Monquez ceased smiling. He took several steps back. "She's a witch?"

Gideon ran his tongue across her shoulder. "Only a term of endearment, Captain Monquez."

The Spanish pirate nodded but didn't venture any closer.

"Tell your men they have one hour to get their fill of English women." Gideon's face was without the slightest hint of regret. "We set sail within the hour."

Cheers erupted aboard the pirate ship, and soon Monquez's men were drawing lots to determine who would take the first turns.

Gideon's face contorted in pain as he pulled himself over the side of the pirate ship and onto the deck of the *Fair Winds*. He held onto Ameran's hair, making sure she followed him.

She tried not to look down into the churning red waters below for fear of what she might see, but she couldn't help but cast her eyes downward to the spot where Gray had been thrown. She let out a little gasp. Gray hadn't been mutilated or devoured. He was clinging to a board. His body was lifeless; his limbs showed no movement, yet he was hanging onto the board. He wasn't dead yet! He was still alive! And as long as he was alive, there was hope, hope for him, hope for her, and hope for all of them.

Gideon savagely pulled her to him, hurting her, crushing her with his hateful body. His mouth bruised hers . . . teeth biting, tongue probing deep down her throat.

His kisses gagged her and she bit at his lip. He spit out blood, then raised his hand to strike her. Her eyes met his in defiance, daring him to lay his palm across her cheek. His hand held its place, but it moved no closer to her face. "By the time I've finished with you, whore, you'll be begging me to keep you by my side."

"I wouldn't place any wagers on that." She walked on out in front of him, taking possession of her hair as she went. Somehow she must keep Gideon from looking down and seeing what she had just seen.

Gideon took hold of her once more with his right hand while his left held onto his side.

She knew her flesh would bear the marks of his fingers for a long time to come.

"I'll let you tend to my wounds first," he said rather pleasantly as if they were two acquaintances out for an afternoon stroll around the deck. "Later, you can tend to my other needs."

Ameran found much comfort in the knife strapped tight to her leg. She would tend to her own needs above all else. And she wouldn't sleep until Gideon lay dying in a puddle of his own blood.

Chapter Sixteen

Ameran lay in bed, the bed she had shared with Gray, and stared out into the darkness. She couldn't sleep. The chain clasped around her wrist and fastened onto an iron ring on the wall beside the bed was a grim reminder that sleep would never come again. Each time her eyes closed, she would relive over and over the horrors she had witnessed. Her body had grown numb, her feelings deadened by the vile abominations she had been forced to observe. She'd been completely powerless to help the victims of Monquez and his men and the renegade crew of the *Fair Winds*. She would forever be haunted by the screams of women who had been stripped of all dignity and tied limbs spread while the cutthroats took turns inflicting the worst suffering and degradation imaginable. And when the sea rogues had their fill, they had thrown the women naked and bleeding to their husbands and children imprisoned below. She would forever hear the murderous laughter of the pirates as the dead and wounded were rolled overboard to blood-hungry sharks which tore their flesh apart. Perhaps still worst of all, she had been forced to stand on the ship's bridge at Gideon's side and watch as the colonists were marooned on a cay with no fresh water. They knew as well as she that they would last no more than three or four days. Gideon, Monquez, and their devils only laughed at their desperate plight. And Gideon had made her a witness to it all: to all the misery, and humiliation, the death, the torment, and the ugliness, as if by making her watch he could make her an accomplice to the atrocities he had committed.

For days and nights on end she had waited for Gray to come and save her. Gray! Her true love who was her husband in her eyes, if not in God's! There was no way he could have survived the monsters of the deep. He was dead, and no wishing or praying would ever bring him back to life. She'd have gladly followed him to the dark beyond had it not been for the vow she made to him, the vow to do whatever she must to survive. Somehow she had to endure whatever vile act Gideon inflicted upon her! Somehow she had to save his name and his reputation, even though Gray was lost to her forever.

Ameran tossed and turned on the bed, wondering when Gideon would make his next move. She tried not to think of the events of the past several days, but she knew they would be etched in her mind forever. The attack on the French supply ship had been no victory; it had been a bloodbath. The unsuspecting captain had welcomed the ally of his country, and as soon as the *Fair Winds* had anchored alongside the *Belle Chere,* the pirates had boarded and commenced to butcher its crew. Gideon had made certain the captain and a few of his men survived so they could return to tell King Louis of the horrible crimes committed against them by the English sea dogs led by Lord Carlisle, the commander of the British fleet himself. On the morrow, Monquez and his men would be returned to the secluded bay at Red Snapper cay where their ship had been hidden among the mangroves. There, Gideon and Monquez would part company. With a dozen extra cannons mounted onto his ship and an arsenal of weapons and powder, Monquez had gone off in search of his old nemesis, Billy Blitzen. The Spanish cutthroat no longer feared the Welsh buccaneer whose exploits had been written into ballads and sung by schoolboys.

After another week or so, Gideon and the *Fair Winds'* crew of scoundrels and criminals would set a return course for England. Gideon was anxious to get back to Whitehall and destroy Gray's good name, but he had no choice but to let the *Belle Chere* go on ahead so that news of English atrocities committed at the order of Lord Carlisle would reach the Sun King first.

Ameran stared into the darkness. Her nightmares would never end. Only in death would there be refuge from the terror-stricken faces and mangled corpses embedded deep into her memory. She wondered how much longer Gideon would keep her alive. He couldn't permit her to return to England and risk having the truth divulged. He took great delight in reminding her that if it weren't for his mercy, she'd already be dead. At first, she'd been afraid that he would make a gift of her to Monquez. But after the gales and storms pounding the ship for the last few days, she knew Monquez would never have her aboard his ship, for he was convinced she had caused them. Gideon had no choice but to kill her, or at least try to, and she wondered how he would set out to do so. What was one more corpse when he was responsible for so many others? He was keeping her alive, but why? He had been motivated neither by generosity nor the goodness of his heart. He had allowed her life just so he could torment and taunt her a little while longer. He had rehearsed over and over again in her presence the tales he would recount to the King, tales which would make the name Grayson Carlisle a source of universal revulsion.

But that which Gideon wanted most to do, to defile her body and make her his whore, he lacked the power. Many times during the days and nights of her imprisonment, he had come to her with the sole purpose of subjecting her to humiliations and degradations untold. He had stripped and lain naked on top of her, grunting and rooting like an animal, but he didn't possess the manliness to consummate the act.

Suddenly, as if the thought of him had made him appear, Gideon was hovering over her, his sinister silhouette illuminated by the light of the lantern he placed on the desk.

She hadn't heard the key turn the lock.

"Good evening, my love." His greeting reeked of rum.

Ameran looked the other way. She refused to cast her eyes upon Gray's murderer.

Gideon sat down upon the bed.

She scooted as far away from him as she could go, her body pressed tight against the wall.

"Monquez and his men will set sail at dawn." He

ran his hand up her leg, the leg that had no knife strapped around it. "They're all most anxious for your company tonight."

Ameran swallowed hard. Visions of Jewel and Allison and Affra and poor Annie and all the other helpless victims lying naked and tied upon the decks painfully attacked her mind. And all the while the women had looked at her with such contempt, as if silently accusing her of committing worse sins than their captors for not being among them.

Gideon squeezed the inside of her thighs, his fingers bruising the soft tenderness.

Ameran bit her lip to keep from crying out in pain. Her suffering would give him too much pleasure.

He squeezed harder; his cruel fingers probed harder and deeper within.

"However, there is still enough time remaining between now and dawn for you to persuade me to keep you for myself." He leaned over to her, his face but inches from hers.

He was close enough that she could almost claw out his eyes. While the temptation to do so was great, another idea was slowly beginning to take shape inside her head, an idea, which if successful, would not merely maim him . . . but kill him.

"What is it that you would have me do?" she asked, her voice aquiver.

"Ah, she speaks at last, and surely no sweeter words have ever been slipped through her lips."

Ameran gathered her inner control. If her plan were to succeed, there were words to be said and deeds to be done that she would live to regret if it failed.

Gideon held her face between his hands and stared into her eyes. "If you were to show me some gratitude for having saved you from that filthy horde of pigs up top, I might not be so willing to rid myself of you."

"I . . . I'm not without gratitude, Gideon."

She tried to rid her voice of the hatred she felt for him. Just saying his name aloud left her with a disgusting taste in her mouth.

"I know you could have rid yourself of me days ago had you wanted to."

Gideon looked quite pleased with himself. "Indeed. I could have fed you to the sharks or marooned you with the other poor devils or auctioned you off to the highest bidder. We're making progress for you to finally admit that to yourself and to me."

His hold on her relaxed. His fingers no longer probed and prodded the trembling flesh beneath her skirt, but they caressed almost gently.

"You must realize, Ameran, it was not you who I hated. It was Gray who wronged me, not you."

There was a long pause, and she knew that he was waiting for her to come to Gray's defense. It took a mountain of strength to keep from doing so.

Gideon smiled. "I was jealous of Gray, but only because he had what I wanted. You. With Gray dead, perhaps . . ."

She refused to let the tears swelling in her eyes fall. At that moment, she would have willingly given her life just to sink her fingernails into his lying eyes.

Gideon took in a few labored breaths.

"I don't want to die, Gideon. I'll do what I have to do to live."

Her words tore at her heart. If only he would un-chain her, she could finish what she had begun and failed. This time, her knife would *not* miss its mark!

"Ah, has that fine spirit of yours begun to waver?" His hand clasped her breast, and he waited for her to shirk from his touch.

"I don't want to die," she said again, this time even more softly. "What will you have me do to prove this to you?"

He took her chained hand and put it between his legs.

She could feel his manhood begin to harden, and she began to feel a sickening dread start to gnaw at her when she knew she must make no attempt to reclaim possession of her hand.

Gideon moaned. "You are truly the most beauti-ful woman I've ever set eyes upon."

She could hear her heart's pounding echoing throughout the cabin she had shared with Gray.

"I have no desire to take you by force." He let out another long sigh.

"You could have done that already if such were your inclination." She knew what that foul pig wanted, and she prayed he wouldn't realize the words he spoke were the ones she longed to hear.

"I want you to come to me on your own." His voice was soft, but still heavy with hate.

She lifted her arm, as if to reach out for him, but the chain binding it hindered her, just as she knew it would. With a sigh, she dropped her arm back down to the bed. She didn't dare suggest he remove the shackles binding her. She could only hope the idea would be his.

Gideon eyed her closely. "If I were to unchain

330

you, do I have your promise that you won't try to escape?"

"Escape to what? Monquez and his men? I think not." She deliberately permitted a little fire in her voice. If she seemed too submissive he might become suspicious.

Gideon laughed.

Lips pouting, lashes aflutter, she assumed the pose of a seductress.

Gideon laughed again.

Ameran was beginning to understand. Raping the woman Gray loved, the woman who loved him with all her heart and soul, wasn't enough. He wanted to subject her to the worst of all degradations. He wanted to make her a whore, his whore, and he wanted her to beg him to do it.

He lowered his mouth to hers. He didn't kiss her. His tongue merely skimmed her lips.

Ameran lay still. The last time he had gotten so close, she had brought blood.

"You're not going to bite me?" he asked as his mouth grew braver.

He released her hand, but she forced herself to let it remain in place. He felt as though he were about to burst out of his breeches. A woman resigned to her fate, a willing and perhaps even eager victim, aroused him far greater than a woman he had to take by force.

She prayed he wouldn't suspect the murderous thoughts running rampant inside her head.

Her lips trembled. "I'm at your mercy."

"What about Gray?"

She knew her reply was crucial. If she lied, he would surely suspect her.

Ameran chose her words carefully. "I watched him die. I desire only to live." The words tore at her heart.

He tangled her curls around his fingers. "Even as you professed such great hatred for me, you wanted me, did you not?"

If she said yes, he would surely know she was lying.

She was deliberately hesitant. "There were times perhaps . . . times when I did wonder . . . times when I was curious . . . about you."

His silence frightened her. Had he seen through her deception? She couldn't read the look in his eyes. It seemed surprisingly calm.

And then he lowered his mouth to hers again. This time his lips were not as bruising, and when she sighed a sigh of dread, he mistook it for the tiniest show of the passion she had tried to quell.

Gideon moaned softly. "Don't fight me anymore. I'm tired of being your enemy."

She raised up to meet him again, this time making sure her chains rattled.

"I'm hardly in a position to oppose you."

"I want more from you than that," he hissed.

She forced her fingers tighter around his hardness. "I won't deny you that which you desire."

"If you're tricking me . . ."

"I'm no fool, Gideon." Her spirit began to surface again, this time in a well-calculated move. "I may not love you, but I'd prefer your company to that of the sharks or of Monquez, and I'm quite willing to prove that to you."

"You have no choice." His words were cruel once again.

"That's true; however, the pleasure I choose to give or deny is my choice and mine alone." She massaged her chained arm suggestively. "Just as the choice is yours to conquer by force or to woo with kindness."

She could sense he still wasn't convinced of her sincerity. "Kiss me, Gideon. Kiss me and let me show you that I'm capable of giving you pleasures untold in exchange for my life. Permit me to live, and you won't regret it." She began to relax when his fingers began stroking her flesh in a lover's caress. "If I fail to give the joys and satisfaction I've promised, then yours will be the final revenge."

"Yes, it will," he said threateningly.

Ameran met his gaze head on, just as she had done many, many times before, but this time taking extra care not to show her hate.

Her lips parted, and she rubbed her hand suggestively along his groin. "What say ye, Captain Horne? Are you willing to take that which I consent to give?"

If only he would remove the chains binding her!

Laughing, Gideon lay siege to her lips with a savage fierceness that she knew wouldn't cease until he was convinced of the truth in her words.

Ameran offered no resistance. She forced her mouth to share in his hunger, and when he started to pull away from her, she beckoned his lips to hers once again.

"I believe there's a gentle side to your nature, Captain Horne, that you've kept concealed far too long."

There was the faintest hint of a smile on his face, and he kissed her again. She made her own lips soften invitingly. This time, his kiss was far from being brutal. His mouth didn't devour, but instead melted into hers with a mounting ardor.

Ameran knew his suspicions were starting to fade, and he was even closer to falling into her trap. If only he would remove the chains, she could show him how willing she really was.

The chain rattled as she took his hand and laid it upon her breast.

"I know that you couldn't risk taking me back to England with you, and I know that I am in no position to expect more of a reprieve than the one already given me, but . . ."

She moved her knee alluringly along his leg.

"I've heard you have an estate in Ireland. You could keep me there under lock and guard if you desire."

With her unchained hand, she unlaced the ties binding his shirt.

"I'm not at all adverse to being your mistress."

She hoped God could forgive her for what she was about to say and do, for she could never forgive herself.

Gideon was obviously amused. "You're offering yourself to be my whore?"

"If that is what I must do to live beyond this night." Her hand roamed under his shirt, her fingers kneading and caressing his flesh. "Please, I beg you, don't kill me when you have what you want. Let me live, and I'll do whatever you wish."

She reached for him again, knowing the chain would impede her movement, and she could tell her captor was contemplating freeing her.

"I admit you did surprise me when you didn't attempt to throw yourself overboard to meet your fate with Gray," he said, scratching his recently whiskered chin.

"I'm no martyr," she said flatly.

"What are you?"

She could hear the sick eagerness in his query, and she well knew the answer he longed to hear.

"I'm a whore," she said, her eyes not leaving his.

"Again."

She repeated what he wished to hear.

"Whose whore?"

"I'm your whore, Captain Gideon Horne. I'm your whore and no one else's."

He rolled away from her.

Her breath stopped. She watched, afraid he was going to leave her with the echo of her humiliation, but when she saw him take a key from his pocket, she knew it wouldn't be long now.

Gideon stopped just before he placed the key in the lock.

She feared he had guessed the real reason behind her smile and she worried that he would change his mind.

"There's another advantage in your letting me live," she said when he finally unlocked the lock.

He began pulling up her skirt. "I can think of but one," he said lustily.

Laughing, she moved out of his hold. "Hear me out."

"Tell me something worth hearing," he said, not at all amused.

"What if I show you something of a far greater worth than you can even begin to imagine?" Slowly and with a deliberate suggestiveness, she lifted her blouse over her head.

"I've seen plenty of those." Gideon's smile was slow to come. "But none so inviting."

She turned her shoulder to him. "But how many of these have you seen?"

It took him a few moments to comprehend fully the meaning of the lightning bolt confronting him.

"A whore I may be," she said turning to face him again, but making no effort to cover her shame. "But I am a whore of the House of Stuart, and that could prove quite profitable for you if you were to decide to take me to Ireland."

"Your worth rapidly increases." He burrowed his face between her breasts and sucked greedily on the nipples he had squeezed together.

Her eyes begged him as did her words. "Please, let me live beyond this night or the next or the one after. I can prove myself very valuable to you in ways you haven't yet begun to consider."

"Would you stand behind whatever story I choose to tell the King?" He watched her closely.

"Whatever story you choose to tell would be all the more convincing if I acknowledged it as truth," she said without hesitation.

She longed to cover herself, but she dared not.

"You would not embrace the first opportunity to betray me?" he asked as his eyes boldly feasted on the luscious bounty before him.

"No sooner than I would embrace the first opportunity to sign my own death warrant."

She could tell from his sly smile that he found her answers believable.

"I would expect you to spy for me," he said, easing closer. "And I would expect you to pass on to me certain information that may prove crucial to those of us who want the Duke of Monmouth on the throne."

She nodded. "I am certain my close association with the King would make me privy to knowledge you would find most beneficial."

"You'd be willing to betray your father?" His hands lingered across her breasts.

"He betrayed my mother." She smiled. "Surely you don't think I came to England for the sole purpose of renewing family acquaintances?"

Gideon massaged the nape of her neck while his lips danced across her throat. "And our friend Gray was an all too willing pawn in your scheme."

She could feel his eyes watching for some reaction, but she gave only a smile.

"You are indeed worth far more to me alive than dead."

Ameran blew him a kiss. "How can you say that when you have yet to sample my wares?"

She knew he was lying. He had no intention of letting her live. That risk was far too great. He only wanted to see how low she would stoop to save her life, and it was that, not the luscious flesh that gave the appearance of being aroused at his touch, that gave him the most pleasure of all.

But as long as he didn't suspect that she, too, was lying, she would be safe a little longer, and that would be time enough to do what she had to do. And then, when it was all done, she would make her escape to one of the small, long boats tied to the side of the *Fair Winds,* and set herself adrift on a sea that could be no more cruel than her captor.

337

"I have Lord Grayson Carlisle's ship, his command, and soon I will have his lands and his wealth as well," he announced with a mean sneer.

"And don't forget you have his woman."

Gideon's hands were not as rough when they attacked her breasts again. "There's no need to play the grieving lover, my dear."

Knowing she was under close scrutiny, Ameran let out a loud sigh. "What a pity we weren't wed. I'd anticipated great wealth falling into my possession." She eyed him slyly. "Wealth which I would be willing to share with one who spared my life. Of course if you were to say you saw the ceremony performed by a minister on board . . ."

Laughing, Gideon straddled her and began taking off his breeches.

"It appears you and I make a more likely match than I had imagined."

"Perhaps even better than you think."

Somehow, she had to make her move before it was too late. If she were to go for her knife at that very moment, he would surely wrestle it free of her hand, and she wouldn't have another opportunity to do what she had to!

He tore off his shirt and stood naked in front of her except for the bandage around his waist.

A flesh wound! she thought in angry disgust with herself. The point of her knife had barely nicked him. He wouldn't be so lucky again!

Ameran knew him well enough to know he took great delight in tormenting her with his nakedness, but she pretended to be undaunted as he paraded himself in front of her.

"I can see now Gray had good reason to be envious of you." For one half of a moment, she forced her gaze onto the swollen shaft pointed threateningly at her.

She could tell from his smirk that he had found much favor in her remark.

Laughing that evil laugh, he straddled her knees again and began ripping at her skirt.

"No." She pushed his hands away.

His face twisted in rage. "You dare say no to me? Might I remind you that you are in a position to refuse me nothing?"

Her lashes fluttered. "I am well aware of that fact."

"Then what kind of a game are you playing with me?" Hate and suspicion burned in his eyes.

She smiled through her disgust and fear. "A game that you will most assuredly like."

If he stripped her of her skirt, he would surely see the knife, and under no circumstances could she allow that to happen.

Eyes on his, she began easing the skirt slowly and provocatively down her hips. "Turn around, Gideon."

"Why?" There was a trace of mellowness in his tone.

"Turn around." Lips pouting, she stroked one breast, then the other, all the while praying he wouldn't see through her deceit. "Turn around, Gideon. Permit me a moment to ready myself for you."

His smile was slow to come. "You are indeed a woman of many surprises."

After one more long, sweeping glance at that which he would soon lay claim, Gideon slowly turned his back to her.

"And many talents you will soon discover." Nimble fingers moved swiftly to unfasten the sheath from her leg. "It is your intention to let me live. Is it not?"

"But of course, my darling."

Ameran pulled the skirt away from her trembling limbs. "I have your word of honor you will not kill me?"

"I would be doing myself a tremendous disservice if I did not permit you to live."

"What of the Duchess of Morrow?" she asked while making a great show of tossing her skirt in his direction.

His breathing grew still heavier. "Do I detect a bit of jealousy?"

"Have I cause to be jealous?" The dagger lay on the bed beside her, its point nearly penetrating her flesh.

"I'm growing weary of your teasing and your games, madame."

She was prepared when he turned around.

"Permit me one more question, and we shall utter no more words the rest of the night if so be your wish." She kicked the bed covers off to the side. "Was it you or Constance who hired the assassin?"

Gideon sucked in his breath as he beheld the naked beauty so generously offered him. "I found him. She paid him."

She did well to keep her true thoughts to herself. "Had he succeeded in his task, you wouldn't be plagued with me today."

Smiling, he stepped closer. "That would most assuredly have been my greatest misfortune." He began at her toes and kissed his way up her legs. "It was not I who wanted you dead."

"You only wanted to rescue me."

"Precisely."

Her suspicions were confirmed.

Ameran took a deep breath. She prayed she could find the strength to hold on just a few moments longer.

Her arms opened invitingly. With a laugh from hell, Gideon lunged at her. Her smile held as she lifted her knife. The dim light caught the glimmer of its blade. Hatred filled her eyes. A sudden fear and realization lit up his. Gideon saw the pointed blade sticking up at him, but it was too late. He had already fallen onto it.

Ameran heard the tear of his flesh, and she heard him gulp that one last breath. Blood gushed onto her belly. His hands reached out to choke her, but she felt no pain from the tightening of his grip. She twisted the knife deeper and harder into his gut. "I wish I could kill you a hundred times over."

The blade could go no further. She gave it one final twist and waited for him to die. The hands around her neck relaxed their hold, and Gideon's body fell off her and onto the floor. Ameran dressed quickly. There was no time to wash the blood from her skin. She fastened the sheath back around her leg, and without blinking, jerked her knife from its target of human flesh and bones and tucked it inside its leather holder.

Then, she took Gray's pearl-handled dagger from atop the desk where Gideon had laid it. And, finally, in completing her carefully thought-out plan, she took the diamond brooch from her travel bag and pinned it inside the waist of her skirt. She would need money to return to England, and Constance had unwittingly supplied her with a small fortune.

Her most dangerous ordeal was about to begin. Countless menaces lurked ahead . . . Monquez, sharks, angry seas . . . but she was steadfast in her determination to overcome them. She would not die! She would live! And Gray would live through her and through their child.

Chapter Seventeen

Ameran opened her eyes into the thick darkness surrounding her. There was no moon; there were no stars above her, just a black abyss that had no boundaries.

She was still alive, but she felt little satisfaction in that discovery. Death was so slow in coming, so much slower than she had ever imagined. She had fought it until she could fight no longer, but that eternal, dreamless slumber had yet to take its hold on her exhausted body.

It had been three long days and three still longer nights since she had avenged Gray's death. It had been far easier than she had thought to set herself adrift onto the sea. There had been no battles or confrontations, for Gideon's crew had all succumbed to the same drunken slumber that plagued Monquez's men.

That night she had rowed far away from the tiny cay where the *Fair Winds* was anchored, and she had rowed until her arms were too tired to lift the oars, but she kept rowing upon the sea of darkness to a destination uncharted.

The vicious winds of the next day had taken her still farther away, and by late evening her tiny boat was being tossed unmercilessly upon one tumultuous whitecap after another.

Lightning bolted across the skies; thunder clamored all around her, and the rain whipped her face. Somehow, the tiny boat had not capsized, and its hull had not been split in two.

The winds and rain persisted on into the night and into the next day as well. Her body was battered and bruised until it had become void of all feeling. The oars had been lost in the raging turmoil, and she had clung desperately to the sides to keep from being swept overboard. She didn't pray for salvation, for who was there to save her? She would take her chances with the angry tempest. She would rather be at the mercy of the torrents and gales than Gideon or the pirates. The sea, even in its unforgiving wrath, would be far kinder than the cutthroats she had left behind her.

And now, as she lay surrounded by a calmness that was both eerie and comforting, she knew the end would be near. The storm had passed her by, but there would be no escaping the blistering heat that would begin after daybreak. Her lips were already parched from thirst. She had already gulped down the rainwater that had settled in the bottom of the boat. Horror stories Gray had told her about how sailors had drunk seawater and went mad rang inside her head. Before night fell again, she would be dead. It was too dark to see the black fins cutting through the water beside the boat, but she knew they were there, and she knew their patience would not last much longer. More than once she had felt a bump against the boat, a bump that could not be blamed on the waves. If she had any hope left, it was that her death would be gentle, and by the time her body was being mangled and torn to shreds by razor-sharp teeth she would have already succumbed to eternal sleep.

Her lids grew heavy again. She felt her eyes close . . . perhaps forever.

But she did awaken, this time in a blaze of sunlight. She cowered under the merciless shafts of heat, but there was no escaping the sun's cruel rays. There were no clouds to give refuge. The sky was the same azure blue as the sea. There were no waves, only the gentle rocking of the boat on a sea that was as tranquil as a lake. With eyes squinted, she counted the black fins which she had suspected had been escorting her all along. Eighteen of them . . . soon there would be more. Perhaps they were waiting for her to throw herself overboard. She wouldn't give them the satisfaction. They would wait, just as she had to wait.

She lay back down and waited, waited for the inevitable to come. Soon, quite soon, her thoughts would be clouded with images of Gray beckoning her to join him. She would hear him calling out her name over the gentle lull of the waves, and in those thoughts she would find the courage and the strength to go forth into the great beyond of life with dignity. Her life was with Gray, and with him gone, she had no reason to go on living. She had sent Gray's murderer to hell. Gray's death had been avenged and his good name would not be tarnished by Gideon's lies.

She was tired of the struggle to live. She was ready to be reunited with her beloved Gray. If only that time would come soon . . . soon . . .

She could feel herself drifting further and further away from her body.

"It be truly a miracle, laddies," she could hear someone say in the faraway distance through her dazed stupor. "A miracle indeed. Never believed in them, and now we've had us two in less than a week apart."

Ameran's eyes squinted open. All she could see was the sun. Its bright light blinded her. There were voices inside her head, and clouded visions before her. So her end had been gentle after all. She sighed and closed her eyes again as she felt herself being lifted up. She had to rest, for soon she would be in Gray's loving arms again.

The gentle rocking of a ship atop calm waters roused her from her dreamless slumber. The room where she lay was dim with the fading light of day. Ameran sat up slowly. Her flesh burned; her face was inflamed. She wasn't dead! The sound of breathing was her own. Her body ached. The dead had no pains. She was dreaming. If she weren't in the afterlife, she had to be dreaming. But it all looked so real . . . the trunks, the oaken casks, the sabre, the bottle of rum . . .

Ameran swung her legs onto the floor. Her legs were wobbly. Her hand reached for her face. She could feel the blisters festering. She took the knife from its sheath and pricked her finger. Blood trickled onto the torn shreds of her skirt. She wasn't dead! Nor was she dreaming!

Pirates! *Mon Dieu!* She had escaped Gideon only to fall prey to Monquez and his band of cutthroats once more. How cruel the turn of destiny! She had been saved from one death only

346

to face one even greater.

Her hand tightened around the grip of her knife. She would not be enslaved by Monquez and his evil desires. She would kill any man who walked through that door.

Just then, she heard the sound of heavy boots striding down the hall. As they got closer, she could hear the man singing a spirited tune in a language she knew well.

She hid in the shadows behind the doorway, her knife poised for attack. His good humor was about to end.

The door opened.

The man tiptoed in. He wasn't singing, but humming softly.

Her hold on her knife loosened. He wasn't ugly or bald like Monquez. Nor did he bear any resemblance to the other sea devils. He was short and plump and had a face full of gray whiskers. His long, silver hair was tied back from his face with a red ribbon, and he was carrying an orange and black cat. Whoever he was he looked far too comical to be dangerous.

He stopped humming, then turned slowly around and put the cat down.

"Bloody hell, lassie, put that knife away afore somebody gets hurt."

He was English, and he didn't look like any of Gideon's sea bandits.

Her hand started to lower, then stopped.

"Who are you?"

His heels clicked together, and he gave a decorous bow. "Captain Billy Blitzen, mum, at your service."

The knife fell from her hand. She laughed and cried at the same time. Billy Blitzen . . . Monquez's most hated nemesis, Gray's old friend. Safe! She was safe!

"Ye've nothing to fear from me, lassie. I'm not nearly the scoundrel I'm made out to be."

Tears of joy streamed down her cheeks. "I thought I was dead."

His laugh was hearty. "Took me fer an angel, did ye?"

She collapsed into the nearest chair, a straight-backed one with woven reeds for a seat. "When I woke up a few moments ago, I feared fate had delivered me back into Monquez's clutches."

Captain Billy stopped laughing. He balled up his fist. "I wish fate would deliver me to that devil. I've been after him fer months."

The relief that had flooded her weakened body turned to grief. "Gray is dead."

The weathered face mellowed. He took Ameran's hand. "Come with me, lass."

Ameran walked down the candle lit corridor to another cabin. Captain Billy opened the door, then put his finger to his lips and tiptoed inside.

Ameran stopped. "Gray," she cried out softly. "He's alive. *Mon Dieu,* he's alive!"

She could tell by Captain Billy's grim face that Gray was hovering near death. She fell down on her knees beside the bed. His face was ashen, his chest bare save for the bandages wrapped around it holding his arm tight to his side. His breaths were scarcely more than whispers. She kissed his lips, which were winter cold.

348

"You can't die, Gray. Please, don't leave me. I'm here with you now. We're together."

His moan was soft and pained.

Captain Billy put a gentle hand on her shoulder. "Be brave, lassie. He's not long for this world."

"You're wrong," she said with quiet certainty. "He'll live."

Captain Billy knelt down beside her, his old bones creaking. "Your name is Ameran?"

She nodded. "How do you know?"

"He's called out to you many times."

She smoothed the pale strands of hair back from his colorless cheeks. His lips were cool, but his forehead was burning hot. He would live! Fate wouldn't be so cruel as to reunite them, only to part them again.

"Am-er-an," he gasped.

"I'm here, Gray. I'm here."

Gray sighed, but his eyes didn't open.

"He'll live," she told Captain Billy again. "He'll live," she said over and over as if saying so would make it come true.

"What happened, lassie?" inquired Captain Billy, his voice kind and soothing. "When I found him, he was half dead and hanging onto a plank with his last bit of strength."

Ameran took a deep breath and began. Her eyes didn't stray from Gray's ghostly white face. She told Captain Billy of Gideon's betrayal and of his alliance with Monquez.

"I never liked that Gideon Horne, and he never liked me neither. He knew I could see clear through him." Billy smashed his fist against his knee. "I told Gray to watch out fer him. I did, but my warnings went unheeded. Nearly cost us our friendship it did."

Ameran relayed to him the horrors she had witnessed, of the poor colonists marooned on an island somewhere in the vast chain of tiny cays, and of the slaughter of the crews of the *Fair Winds* and the *Belle Chere*. And finally, she warned him of Monquez's newly acquired strength and of his boasts to rid the seas of Billy Blitzen.

Captain Billy's laugh was cold. "I'd like to see him try. If the sea is to be rid of one scoundrel, it will not be Billy Blitzen who goes up in smoke."

Ameran trembled. She couldn't bear the thought of another encounter with Monquez, and yet he was out there somewhere, watching and waiting.

"Ye've nothing to fear, lassie. Monquez will not come in pursuit of me or me lads. He's a cowardly cur. Ye be safe aboard the *Lucky Lady*."

He looked down at Gray. His face was sad. Tears swelled in his eyes. "I promise ye, my good friend. I shall go after that Spanish devil, and when I have finished with him, I shall go after Gideon. I will avenge ye and yer honor. As most holy God is my witness."

Ameran kissed the cold lips, then turned to Billy. "You may have Monquez. The debt with Gideon Horne has already been settled."

"He's dead?"

She glanced at the knife lying beside the trunk. "He's dead."

Captain Billy nodded his approval. "I was fortunate indeed to have escaped your blade."

A hint of a smile graced her lips.

"Ye must be tired, lassie," he told her some time

later as she laid her head down on the bed beside Gray, but her eyes refused to close.

"I won't leave Gray's side."

"Ye won't have to, Lassie. I'll have a cot brung in here fer ye. Ye hungry?"

Her nod was weak.

"I'll fetch ye some supper and some clean clothes."

Ameran looked down at the shreds covering her. They still bore the stain of Gideon's blood.

"I have a lovely yellow dress that will look grand on ye." He winked. "I wouldn't part with it for anyone else."

Ameran looked up at him inquiringly.

"Sailors dressed as women can lure our enemies right into our hands far better than the fire of cannons," he explained with a hearty chuckle and another wink.

Captain Billy got up slowly, holding on to his legs. "I'll leave ye alone with your Lord Carlisle fer a wee spell. It be a miracle we found him. It be a miracle we came upon you. Mayhaps another won't be too far fetched. They say three's the charm."

Ameran took Gray's cold hand in hers. "I won't let you die. I won't."

Captain Billy left the room quietly.

"I won't let you die, Gray. You're mine, and death has no claim on you," she whispered onto his lips. "Death will not have you."

For three days, she didn't move from his side. She was not waiting for him to die. She was waiting for him to live. Captain Billy seldom left her side. She knew he was eager to go in pursuit of Monquez, but he didn't dare risk the life of his friend. As long as the waters were calm, Gray didn't cry out in pain, but at the ship's slightest movement, he turned and twisted in agony.

Among Captain Billy's crew was a black man from a faraway land, and this man, whose name was Iza, made poultices from a hot, black salve and tied them onto the deep, bloody gashes in Gray's shoulder.

Time passed at an excruciatingly slow pace, but Ameran found much comfort in the knowledge that each minute Gray lived he was growing stronger and healthier.

Early the morning of the fourth day, she felt an arm reach out to her.

She moved from her bed to his. "I'm here, Gray. I'm here," she said as she had said many times during every hour.

She wet a rag in the pail of fresh water beside the bed and tenderly sprinkled the water onto his parched, white lips. "I'm here, Gray. I'm here."

His lips moved, but the words would not come.

"Shhh, don't try to speak." She sponged cooling water onto his furrowed brow. "We're safe. We're aboard the ship of your friend, Captain Billy Blitzen."

Gray struggled to speak. "How . . . did . . . how did we . . ." He was too weak to go on.

Ameran tried to keep her face cheerful. "Fortunately, the *Lucky Lady* crossed both our paths." Lovingly, she cradled his head in her arms. "Captain Billy found you holding onto a piece of planking, and he found me adrift in a long boat."

"Gi-de-on." Gray spit out the name of the one who had betrayed him. "I shall . . . kill . . ."

"Shhh, sleep. you must sleep." She closed his eyes with little kisses. "You must renew your strength."

"The *Fair Winds?*" His voice was barely above a whisper. "My ship . . . where . . ."

Ameran held him close until his heavy breaths steadied, then she lay down his head back upon the pillows. "Sleep, my darling. Sleep."

She smoothed his hair from his face. How pale he was! It was truly a miracle he had survived. He had lost so much blood. According to Captain Billy, had the salt water not drained the poisoned blood from his wound, he would have lost his arm and perhaps his life even though he had been rescued.

Ameran brushed her lips across his forehead. The worst was over. He had survived against tremendous odds. He hadn't endured the worst only to die now in safety.

Several days later, Gray was sitting up in bed and smiling as Iza wrapped another hot salve poultice around his shoulder.

Ameran sat beside him holding tight to Gray's hand while Captain Billy looked on grinning and stroking one of the many cats that roamed the decks of the *Lucky Lady*.

Iza flashed a big, ivory toothed grin when he had finished. His black skin was slick with sweat. "Iza's medicine works good. Arm all better."

Gray reached out for the big, black arm in gratitude. "My arm is better, and I'm most grateful to you."

Iza bowed and left the room. He was a giant of a man, yet he moved with such nimbleness that not even the boards creaked beneath his weight.

Gray gave a big stretch. "Now listen, you two, and heed my words. I want no more nonsense about rest and sleep." His words were strong and determined. "I've rested until my body has grown weary from sleep. I've eaten so hearty a meal my belly will hold no more food."

Ameran and Captain Billy exchanged troubled looks.

Captain Bill scratched his whiskers. "Gray, my lad, 'tis a beautiful morn. Why don't we go topside for a stroll and some sunshine and salty air?"

"Fine, but first I have a great many questions for which I'm certain you and Ameran can provide answers."

Gray folded his arms over his chest and made it perfectly clear that he didn't intend to budge from that spot until his questions were answered.

Ameran looked at the *Lucky Lady*'s captain, frowned, and gave a half nod.

Captain Billy let out a sigh, pulled a chair up to the bed, and settled down onto it with his favorite cat, Portia, curled up onto his lap.

Gray looked from one to the other, awaiting explanations. "I believe there's much you're keeping from me, and I'd like to know everything. I insist that I be told all at this time."

Captain Billy met Ameran's confused gaze. "Perhaps it's time to tell him all, lassie."

Her eyes met Gray's. He was waiting, but she didn't know where to begin. She looked to Captain Billy for the courage to proceed on.

He gave her a nod. "Go on, lassie. Ye have to tell him sooner or later."

Ameran took a deep breath. "The women . . . they were . . . they were tied up, and they . . . they were forced to . . . the pirates all . . ."

Gray reached for her hand and held tight to it. "It's not necessary for you to continue. I can imagine only too vividly the vile horrors inflicted upon them."

Her eyes swelled with tears upon remembering that which she would never forget. "When they'd had their fill of them, those loathsome monsters marooned the settlers on a little island with no hope of food or water. The children . . . the little boys and girls . . . poor baby Mary . . ." Her heart convulsed inside her chest. Her lips quivered with her words. "Martin and John and the others got down on their hands and knees and begged for food and water, not for themselves, but for their wives and the children. . . . And Monquez and his men laughed . . . they laughed."

Ameran closed her eyes. Those evil laughs would haunt the rest of her nights.

"Monquez and his demons would show no mercy to their own mothers," said Captain Billy in disgust.

"What island?" Gray sounded hopeful.

Ameran shook her head. "I don't know. Gideon forced me to watch as they were loaded off the ships like cattle, but no mention was made of the name of the place or the location. There were no trees for shade, just low, barren land. Monquez joked about the island sinking into the sea at high tide."

"There are so many islands in the Bahama chain," said Captain Billy quietly. "I would have gone looking for them myself as I learned of their fate, but I didn't know where to begin, and it's been nearly two weeks. They could not have lived beyond the few days, even less if it was indeed underwater at high tide."

Gray let out a troubled sigh. "You could have combed every cay and still not have found them."

Ameran said nothing; no one did, but she knew what the two men were thinking, for such thoughts stirred inside her head as well. The colonists were all dead, victims of an agonizingly slow death from which there could have been no escape. Even had the tide not overtaken them, they could have lived a few days without food, but they could not survive without water. The children . . . those poor babes . . .

Her hands rested protectively upon her stomach.

"It's over for them now," Gray said quietly. "They've found their peace."

"Amen," mumbled Captain Billy.

Ameran wiped the tears from her eyes, took another deep breath and began again. "The French ship . . . Gideon and Monquez . . ."

"They attacked it?" Gray asked.

Ameran nodded.

Gray's jaw locked. "Gideon told me of his intentions just before he tossed me overboard."

"He made certain the captain and a few of his crew would survive," she told him. "Just so they could . . ."

Gray didn't give her a chance to complete her sentence.

"Just so they could sail back to France with news of the dastardly deeds of Captain Grayson

Carlisle," he said grimly.

Ameran eyed Gray closely. His resemblance to Gideon Horne was indeed astounding. If asked to describe in detail the appearance of the treacherous captain of the *Fair Winds,* the French could make no distinction between the two men, for both Gray and Gideon were of the same size and build, and possessed the same pale hair and eyes the blue of an angry sea.

"Gideon will have achieved two purposes by doing as you described." Gray's look was painfully pensive. "Not only will he have created justification for having killed me and taken my command, but he will most certainly guarantee the likelihood of France declaring war on England. Gideon is shrewd. I'll allow him that. He's far more clever than I ever expected."

"Gideon won't fulfill the wicked mission he embarked upon," said Ameran. "There'll be no war, and your great name and reputation won't be defamed."

Gray's smile was weak. "You don't know him as I know him. He won't stop until he's executed even the most minute specification of his heinous scheme."

"Gideon is dead," she told him quietly.

"And in hell where he belongs," added Captain Billy.

"By whose hand? Monquez?" Gray asked.

"By my hand," she said. She didn't boast. She only stated it as fact.

Ameran said nothing else. She remembered every word spoken, each move made, and she prayed she wouldn't have to recount them. She wasn't proud of the methods she had employed, but the end had been achieved.

"I should have done it myself." Gray tightened his hold on her arm. "I regret never having listened to your words of caution."

Ameran began to breathe a little easier. He hadn't asked how, and for that she was greatly relieved. How could she admit to renouncing her love for him and of lying naked and seducing the man she thought his killer so she could lure him to his death? She had no regrets about killing Gideon, but for the rest of her life she would bear the scars of the shame and guilt of her humiliation.

"What became of Monquez and his Spanish mongrels?" Gray wanted to know next.

"Gideon gave Monquez the guns and cannons from the *Fair Winds* and whatever cargo the French ship was carrying," Ameran answered. "Monquez swore he was coming after Captain Billy."

The Welshman let out a hearty laugh. "I'd bloody hell like to see him try it. Ye can be sure if he did run across the *Lucky Lady*, he'd be beating a hasty retreat t'other way."

Ameran smiled, but she didn't share in their laughter.

"I wish he'd come after me," Captain Billy said with a huff. "I'd show him who'd be blowing who out of the water."

Ameran felt herself tremble. She didn't doubt his words, or his ability to do just as he said, but she couldn't bear the thought of another encounter with that Spanish cutthroat.

Gray gathered her close. "It's indeed remarkable

you managed to escape their clutches."

"Aye," agreed Captain Billy as Portia snuggled under his chin. "And even more remarkable she survived at sea what with the winds and the rains and the gales being what they were." He laughed his hearty laugh. "Tried to plunge that dagger of hers into me, she did. Thought I was one of them bloody demons."

Gray shook his head. "All your misfortunes were my doing. You were nearly killed because of me. Can you ever forgive me?"

Her fingers traced the outline of his scar. "There's nothing to forgive, for there's nothing you did for which you should bear shame."

"Ah, but there is, and I do. I do." His eyes were sad and pleading. "How can I ask you to forgive me when I can't forgive myself?"

Captain Bill stretched to reach for the bottle of port atop his desk. He pulled out the cork with his teeth, then handed the bottle to Gray. "Put some of that blood ye lost back in ye."

Gray all but smiled. He took a long gulp. "Lucky for us you happened along when you did, Billy. I still can't believe two such miracles are possible."

Captain Billy took another long gulp. "Lucky for me, too. Been a spell since I've seen ye, and methinks the *Lucky Lady* has never been graced with such a beauty as our lassie here."

His kind words brought a smile to her face.

Gray squeezed Ameran's hand. "Last I heard about Billy Blitzen, he was down in Panama looting and plundering from those wealthy señors."

Captain Billy smacked his lips. "Cursed Spanish.

Can't steal enough from them." that had no knife

"A privateer more loyal to his King and country can't be found anywhere," Gray remarked with so hard of a laugh that he had to reach for his shoulder. "One half of whatever booty he takes is always turned over to the King."

Captain Billy's plump cheeks turned as red as the bow tying back his silver gray strands. "A buccaneer I may be, but I'm devoted to my King and my country."

"How long has it been? Two years since our paths last crossed?" Gray asked him.

Captain Billy thought for a while. "Best I remember, ye were fixing to set sail for France. Old Louis wanted to prance and parade ye about in honor for your bravery against the Dutch. Ye were the only hero he had. Couldn't find a single one in his own country."

Gray turned to Ameran. Their eyes locked in a loving embrace upon remembering the first night they had lain in each other's arms.

"What I want to know, lad, is how ye kept from being eaten alive by those man killers of the deep," Captain Billy remarked as he passed the bottle back to Gray.

"That will be a mystery until the day I die," came his solemn reply. "The water was red from the blood of the dead and wounded. There must have been two dozen sharks encircling me. They maimed and mangled the others in what can only be described as a feeding frenzy, but they let me be." His eyes were troubled with the recollection. "I don't understand why my prayers were answered and those of the others who were still alive went

360

unheeded. Why? Why was I permitted to live while so many others perished?"

"Sometimes, lad, 'tis best not to question what we can't understand," Captain Billy said gently with a sad smile. "And just be grateful the good Lord saw fit to spare us for whatever reason there might be."

Gray gave a solemn nod. "As soon as Monquez told Gideon that you'd been sighted several days before, I knew if I could only hold on to that plank that had been carelessly tossed over the side Billy Blitzen would come to my rescue if he were anywhere close by."

"When we pulled ye out, ye had half the sea in yer gut, and yer arm was barely hanging on to the rest of ye," Captain Billy told him jovially as he made his own arm go limp and lifeless. "I gave ye up fer dead, but ye kept holding on."

"I couldn't die. I had to find some way to get back to Ameran." He adoringly stroked her cheek. "I should have known she would come after me first before I had a chance to go fetch her."

She kissed his fingers. "I've told you before, Lord Carlisle. There's no escaping me, ever."

They all laughed.

It was Captain Billy whose good humor was the first to fade. "Now that ye have recovered, laddie, what will ye have me do? The captain and crew of the *Lucky Lady* are at yer service." He gave him a salute.

Gray thought long and hard. The wrinkles furrowing his forehead didn't fade. "There's much I want, my old friend. I just don't know where to begin," he finally said after much deliberation.

"First and foremost, I want back my ship, but by now even without Gideon at the helm, the *Fair Winds* is en route to a destination unknown."

"With Gideon dead and a crew of criminals and rogues on board, I should think England would be the last place they chart their course for," said Captain Billy with a scratch of his whiskers.

Ameran well remembered Tommy Tremble and the delight he seemed to take in carrying out Gideon's cruelties. She told Gray and Captain Billy of him and of his criminal past. "If anyone would take command of the *Fair Winds,* it would be he, and he would most definitely not return to England and face certain death for his horrendous acts of terror and violence."

"There are many places a murderer might seek refuge, places on the sea where he would never be found." Captain Billy's look was grim. "I don't mean to discourage ye, lad, but ye may as well face fact. The *Fair Winds* could be anywhere by now."

"And be involved in the same deeds and services she was commissioned to prevent," said Gray sadly.

"Don't fret, my darling. You'll have back your ship," Ameran gently assured him.

Gray fought to smile. "I have back my life and your life, and that's what matters most." He then told Captain Billy of his assignment for the King in Charles Town. "I'd like to go there, if you please, and do for our King what I set out to do." His words grew heavy. "There are friends and families awaiting the arrival of their own as well as that of much-needed weapons. I must tell them face to face the reason why their wait will be in vain."

"The lass here had already told me about your

mission, and I figured that 'twould be the place ye'd want to go first. I be needing to take on some more provisions, and that be as good a place as any." He gave a hopeful wink. "I wouldn't be at all surprised if we didn't find yer ship there, and if the luck of this Welshman holds, we'll find that slick-headed bastard there as well!" he said confidently.

Ameran shivered in spite of Gray's comforting arms around her shoulders.

"Don't ye go to worrying, lassie. Monquez will never touch one hair on yer pretty little head so long as Billy Blitzen be around."

Ameran braved a smile, more for Gray's sake than her own. "What have I to fear when I have as my protectors the commander of the royal fleet, and the finest buccaneer who ever sailed the seas?"

Captain Billy nodded to Gray. "As if the lass has need of a protector!"

She laughed along with them, but inside, her heart was burdened with new worries. She could find no joy in another encounter with Monquez or Tommy Tremble. She had seen enough death and destruction. But worst of all, she knew in her heart that their troubles weren't over yet.

Gray kissed her cheek. He knew the burdens heavy on her heart; she could tell from the way his lips tenderly caressed her flesh.

Her sigh was one of quiet resignation. She would go to the ends of the earth with him. She had proven that once, and she wouldn't hesitate doing it again. His joys and his sorrows would be theirs to share. Above all else, they must remain together; she was certain that he knew that as well as she. Together, they would make a life for each other and for their child.

Several nights later as they lay together in the bed where Gray had very nearly succumbed to eternal sleep, Gray gathered her close in a lovers' embrace.

Ameran was reluctant to return his kisses with the same hunger, just as she had been reluctant three nights before to leave the cot Captain Billy had set up in the tiny cabin. Gray had laughed at her and told her she was being overly cautious of his injuries, and while she would rather endure pain herself than cause the smallest hurt to him, his health had nothing to do with her wanting to remain in the cot.

"I've mended, Ameran. I feel no pain, only desire," he teased as his head dove between her breasts.

She could feel herself stiffen in his arms and she could sense that Gray had felt it, too.

"Have I done something which angered or offended you?" His eyes sought hers through the still darkness. "If I have, I beg your forgiveness and will make immediate restitution."

She put her finger to his lips. "You could never do anything to anger or offend me."

"You do love me, don't you? Though I must confess I could not blame you if you despised me for what I've put you through."

"I love you with all my heart," she answered him.

"Then what is it? Why did you just stiffen?" he implored.

"Oh, Gray, it's because I love you that I turn from you." Loving fingers drifted over his brow.

How could she put into words the reason why she hesitated when once she had been so eager. "I don't want to cause you any pain."

Gray laughed. "But I'm well! I'll say it again. I'm well. I don't ache. I don't agonize. Iza's potion worked its miracles, and thanks to you and Captain Billy, I have my strength back. I'm the same man I always was." His tongue played along her neck. "Though I must confess perhaps a more desperate one. It's been a considerable while since I've lain in the arms of the woman I love."

"I'm not that same woman." She very nearly choked on her words. If she could cry, she would, but there were no more sobs left inside her. How could she tell him she felt as cheap and as violated as one of those women who haunted London's infamous Dog and Bitch Lane? She hadn't sold her body for a few shillings, but she felt just as degraded had she done so.

His words were as gentle as the touch of his fingertips brushing the hair from her cheeks. "You've endured a nightmare. You've survived the worst possible hell. That's all that matters."

She pulled away. "Yes, I survived, but it's the manner in which I . . ."

Tender lips upon her mouth prevented her from admitting the horrible truth.

"You did what you had to in order to live," he reminded her with the firm kindness she so dearly loved. "No one will find fault with that. Least of all when 'twas I who made you swear to do just that, and I who am responsible for your being in such a wretched fix."

She was determined to tell Gray the truth no

matter how ugly it was, and no matter how ugly he might think her to be when all was said and done. She had sworn long ago to herself and to him that there would be no more secrets between them that could later come back to haunt them.

"You must feel no shame at having killed Gideon," he told her with gentle patience. "Gideon Horne deserved to die. I only wish it could have been I who dealt the fateful blow."

"The shame I feel is not the shame of having taken a life. It's not for the act I committed, only for the manner in which the act was carried out."

Ameran was surprised at the remarkable calm that had overtaken her.

Gray tried to close his arms around her, but she pulled away and eased out of the bed. She lit the candle on the little table across from the bed. When she revealed the whole truth to him she would be looking into his eyes and he would be looking into hers. Just as he had to hear the truth from her lips, she had to see the truth in his eyes.

Gray sat up and patted the empty spot beside him.

Ameran shook her head. She had to keep her distance until that which needed to be said was said.

"You have to understand, Gray. All I wanted was to avenge your death, and I cared not for the way in which I had to carry out my plan."

"Your devotion and love for me makes me adore you all the more."

She tried not to weaken at his sweet words. "I was Gideon's prisoner," she said after a sigh of determination. "He kept me chained to your bed . . .

366

to the bed you and I had shared . . . and he would come to me each day and try to take that which could belong to no man but you."

She could see the pain etched upon his brow in spite of his determination to keep his face from betraying his feelings. "But he couldn't!"

"Ameran, my darling, I . . ."

She lay her fingers across his lips. She had to tell him everything, regardless of the consequences. She couldn't keep her shame to herself.

"I knew I couldn't do what had to be done as long as I was in chains, so I said the things Gideon wanted to hear, and I . . . I stooped to behavior unbecoming a woman who has the love of so great a man as you."

There was no anger in his eyes, only love and compassion.

"You're a far greater and nobler a woman than I'm a man."

Ameran grabbed hold of his hands. Somehow she had to make him see her acts were far from noble.

"I seduced Gideon. I became the whore he wanted me to be. I disavowed our love. I lay naked before him, and when he tried to take me once more because I'd convinced him I would give myself willingly, I plunged my dagger into his vile body, and I felt no remorse for having done so. I felt no sorrow, no regret. I felt only satisfaction at seeing the blood of your murderer spill onto the bed."

This time, Gray didn't beckon her into his arms. Instead, he rose from the bed, lifted her from her chair and cradling her in his arms as if she were a wee babe, he stood holding her, his head buried between her breasts, his tears falling onto her flesh.

"Would that I could speak the right words that would convince you beyond all doubt that I love you all the more for what you had to do. Had you consummated the act with Gideon for the purpose of achieving your final objection, I could harbor no hate or resentment for you, not when you did it for me . . . and for our wee one."

Ameran smiled. "You know."

"I know not when, and I know not where, but how could you not be with child?" he said, chuckling, "when we've placed no restraints upon ourselves."

"Promise me, Gray, swear to me on all that is dear that you'll never hate me for what I've done," she said, almost fiercely.

"Promise me that you'll believe me when I say that I could never hate you," he told her in reply.

"You won't one day look upon me with revulsion?"

"Never!"

She couldn't respond yet to his kisses as she had in times past.

"Promise me that my shame won't come back later to haunt us."

He forced her to look upon his face and wouldn't let her turn her head from his. "It's no shame what you did. It is a shield of honor, one to be worn with pride, not with disgrace."

She kept his mouth from hers a while longer. "And make me the promise as well that we'll never again speak of the matters which cause me such grief."

Gideon shook his head without a moment's hesitation. "No, that I will not promise, for if I do, I would be party to that which you wrongfully and unjustly accuse yourself. Your actions were not ugly. Nor were they shameful or reproachful or loathsome."

"I can't bear to look back upon that night ever again," she said quietly.

"If we don't speak of it again, then it will be because of those painful memories and not because it is a subject I find offensive." His lips brushed hers gently. "And until you believe in your heart that I will never stand in judgment of you, then we can never find true happiness together again."

Ameran held tight to his neck. "I want us to forever be as happy as we were our first night together," she said with fierce determination.

He held her tight against him. "Do you remember when I made you the promise that I would love you more with each tomorrow?"

She nodded.

"Then I can truthfully swear to you that even though at this moment I love you with all my heart, come dawn I shall love you even more."

"Oh, Gray." She couldn't kiss him fast enough. "Hold me, my darling. Don't ever let me go."

"Never," he replied, eager to do as she demanded.

With strength but gentleness, he laid her down onto the bed and pulled the gown of faded yellow ruffles and lace from her trembling form.

His eyes adored her long before his hands made the first move to fondle and caress her.

"I won't if you don't wish me to," Gray said.

Ameran caressed his face. She didn't see Gideon's face when she looked upon Gray's face, and she felt no hesitation at satisfying yearnings mounting inside her. Perhaps Gray was right. The end she had achieved was of far more consequence than the manner by which she had made her deed happen. It didn't bother her that she had condemned a murderer to hell. She wasn't the whore Gideon had longed her to be; nor was she the one she had professed to be for his sake. She was good and clean and pure. She deserved Gray, and she deserved the happiness they had shared. And if she had it all to do over again, she would have done no differently.

Tears trickled down her cheeks, but they weren't tears of remorse or bitterness, but of joy, for she had made peace at last with herself.

She felt no shame as she lay naked before him, and the candlelight rippled upon her ivory breasts. Once again, she felt the same eagerness as before to give herself to him.

The cries which slipped through her lips were not cries of panic or caution, but of delight. When her lips quivered against his, they trembled in passion. She felt herself being crushed beneath him as she was sent soaring to a shuddering ecstasy. And when they melted together as one, her world was filled with him, and the joy she had come to know in his arms since the day of their first joining flooded through her again.

That next evening as they sat on the deck with Captain Billy, stuffing themselves with grilled fish and lobster tails speared by a few of the mates in an afternoon dive, Gray reached for Ameran's hand.

"Billy, I want you to marry us."

Captain Billy choked on his port. "What ye say, lad?"

Gray calmly repeated his request.

Captain Billy stuttered and stammered. "Don't know, lad. I never . . . ye know I'd do anything fer ye, but marry ye, well, I . . . I . . . I . . ." He took one long gulp after another.

"Please." Ameran took hold of Billy's arm.

"But I don't know the words to say, lass. God might strike me dead if I even attempted it. Why, it'd be like blaspheming his name fer me to . . ."

Ameran kept smiling as she held on to his arm.

Captain Billy let out another long sigh. "You don't know the chance ye be taking." He turned up his bottle again. "I'd be honored to."

Ameran hugged him. "I knew you would say yes."

He blushed beneath his whiskers. "Never could refuse a beautiful lady."

Captain Billy stood up. "Below ye go, lassie. It be bad luck fer a groom to see his bride on their wedding day."

Gray stood and gave her a long, lingering kiss.

Captain Billy poked him in the side with his bottle. "None of that, laddie. Not until I tell ye ye can." Holding onto his knees, Billy shouted to his maties. "Gather round, lads. The *Lucky Lady* is about to have her first wedding." He gave Ameran a playful smack. "Below."

"Aye, sir."

Iza presented her with a bouquet of braided jupe when he finally came below to escort her topside.

Ameran was all smiles as he led her inside the circle of sailors where Gray and Captain Billy were waiting.

Gray reached for her hand.

Billy slapped it away. "Not yet, lad."

The crew laughed.

Captain Billy stood as somber as he could with a tankard of ale in each hand.

Ameran tried hard to keep a serious look. Gray smelled suspiciously of ale, and he had the silliest grin on his face.

"Ye may take the hand of yer lovely lady," Captain Billy told Gray. "But keep an arm's length between you. They be plenty of time fer that nonsense later on."

They locked hands.

Gray winked at her.

"Dearly beloved." Captain Billy cleared his throat with much decorum. He took a swig from each tankard. "We be gathered here to join this man and this . . ."

Billy hiccuped He tried to stifle it with more drink, but he kept hiccuping harder and louder.

Captain Billy started over again.

One of the mates, a short, fat one who had a handkerchief tied around his head, and two gold hoops in each ear, broke into laughter, spewing a tankard of ale onto the groom.

Captain Billy drew himself to his tallest. "Kindly refrain from such disgusting behavior, Mr. Robards, er ye'll be walking the plank."

The mate burped a loud burp in reply.

"Give this occasion the respect it demands, mates," demanded Billy when the laughter roared once again. He gave Gray a wink and then exclaimed in a voice loud enough for all to hear, "Getting anxious, heh, laddie?" Billy took another long gulp, then lifted his eyes helplessly up to the pink and orange haze above. "Give me strength, dear Lord."

Billy began yet another time. "We be gathered here to join Lord Carlisle with the most beautiful lady of all . . . to join them in the . . . in . . . they be wanting to wed, sir."

The men cheered and whistled and stomped their feet.

Captain Billy laughed along with them. "And if there be something I left out, consider it said."

Ameran was about to embrace her husband when all of a sudden Captain Billy picked her up and threw her over his shoulders. The mates had gathered around Gray and held him at bay.

"Blindfold him," ordered Billy. "Cuff him."

Amid Gray's protests, the orders were carried out.

"If ye want yer bride, ye got to come after her."

One of the mates threw Billy the key to the cuffs and he slipped it in his pocket.

Ameran laughingly begged to be reunited with her husband.

Billy took her over to the platform above the bow and deposited her there.

The mates spun Gray round and round.

"I'll have my revenge," Gray called out.

"I'll have me fun first," cried out Billy.

Gray bumped into a keg of ale, sending white foam sloshing over the deck.

"Ah, laddie," called out Billy. "Ye be spending

yer wedding night alone if ye ain't careful."

Ameran laughed so hard her sides ached. Whenever Gray got close to the bow, the mates would drag him back and spin him around.

Finally, Gray kicked and pushed away from the men and charged up to the platform.

She jerked the blindfold from his eyes.

Their kiss was interrupted by their own laughter.

Captain Billy cackled. "Ye can't do much with yer hands cuffed, laddie." He fumbled in his pocket. "Where the bloody hell is the key?"

Ameran held it up, then unlocked the cuffs and threw them out to sea.

The sailors laughed.

Captain Billy laughed the loudest of all. "Ye get yerself a sly one, Gray. Ye've got yer hands full."

Hands free at last, Gray hugged her close. Then he jumped down onto the deck.

Ameran leapt down into his awaiting arms.

Captain Billy and his men blocked their path to the stairs.

"Hold on tight, darling," Gray told her as he swung her around.

Legs swinging, Ameran kicked out at the barricade, sending several of the mates sprawling across the deck on their bellies.

Everyone cheered and hollered when they finally did make it to the stairs, and they were immediately the objects of quick pursuit.

Ameran leapt from Gray's arms and ran down the steps with her husband close on her heels. Gray slammed the door to their quarters and bolted the lock behind them. Laughing and tearing at each other's clothes, they tumbled down onto the bed.

Ameran began laughing in mid kisses. "You smell like a tavern," she said as she playfully pushed him away.

Gray laughed. "I'm not at all surprised, considering my baptism by ale."

He reached for her again, but she ducked out of his arms.

"Just don't make a habit, my lord, of frequenting the taverns before you seek your wife's pleasures," she told him, pouting, hands on her hips.

His look of surprise was playful. "What? You're not going to make me swear not to seek such pleasure from the wenches in the tavern?"

Ameran reached between his legs. "Don't forget, my darling lord, I'm quite skilled in the use of the dagger."

Gray sprinkled kisses down her neck and between her breasts. "Might I remind you, Lady Carlisle, that mine would not be the only pleasure you would be cutting off?"

Her long sighs were but echoes of her happiness. Lady Carlisle . . . she belonged to him, just as he belonged to her. Eager arms beckoned him closer still.

This time it was Gray who shied from her embraces. "If you still find my smell offensive, I could take a quick plunge into the ocean. Perhaps the smell of fish and salt would be more to your liking, but I warn you, I would, of course, insist upon taking you with me."

Her fingers played upon the thick cords of muscles binding his chest while the tip of her tongue outlined his lips. "We must try that some evening when there are not so many eyes upon us."

Gray bared her luscious flesh from its confines and let out a groan. "I can't believe that we're finally as we belong."

Tickling, teasing fingers traipsed up and down the massive expanse of his chest. "Come on, matie, and lay claim to your booty."

Amid more giggles and groans, Gray pounced atop her. It seemed hours passed before they had finally shed the last shred of clothing keeping them apart.

Arms and legs woven tight, they clung to each other in sweet yearning and desperation as their bodies began a slow, gentle rocking that pressed them together even tighter. In unison, they explored and discovered the gentle tempo that would bind their life and their love forever more.

Their laughter turned to sighs and the tender words of love everlasting to moans of fulfillment and delight.

Gray's hands were hot on her legs as he kneaded a path of caresses down her thighs. So great was the passion of that moment that she would feel herself fade in and fade back out as though she were in a dream world.

When she could wait no longer for the bliss she had come to know so well, she guided him to her, and a deep feeling of peace and contentment overwhelmed her. She could imagine no ecstasy more divine than the one they had come to know in each other's loving embrace.

Chapter Eighteen

Ameran stood between Gray and Captain Billy on the bow of the *Lucky Lady* as the old ship sailed up the Ashley River past swamps and trees and creeks.

From a distance, she could have easily been mistaken for a young seaman. Her feet were bare, her hair was tied back from her face, and the clothes upon her body were a sailor's garb of loose-fitting knee breeches and a white shirt with long, flowing sleeves. She found the attire far more comfortable than the yellow satin of Captain Billy's, for it afforded her more freedom when scampering across the decks or exploring the tiny cays where they put in to fish and swim and take refuge from an unmerciful sun underneath swaying palms.

Captain Billy's crew, who were busy performing the various tasks laid out to them, looked every bit as liverish and mean-tempered as Monquez's bunch, with their patches and scars and pegs and hooks for limbs, but they sang and laughed and went about their shipboard chores in a jolly spirit and never once uttered a harsh word against their captain or each other. Their eyes seldom met hers, but when they did, they quickly dropped their stares, and some, she was surprised upon discovering, blushed like shy schoolboys.

The natural beauty greeting them was every bit as magnificent as that which Martin had described to the group of would-be settlers that first night at sea. Fields of thick marsh grass the color of gold did indeed stretch out before them, beckoning them to venture closer. In the hammocks surrounding the marshes, giant oaks draped in moss reached for the sky alongside pines in dark, towering forests, and shrubs, and graceful palmettoes.

Ameran took a tight hold on Gray's arm. "What kind of a creature is that?" she asked, pointing to a long-snouted, long-tailed animal slithering on his belly through the wet grasses.

"They be called gators," answered Captain Billy. "And no meaner beast can be found anywhere. Their tails can knock a man senseless, and those big jaws can crush the life right out of him. These swamps be full of them," he said, pointing to still more snaking through the grasses. "When the weather be hot, they'll crawl out and sun themselves on the riverbank. Woe be to any man that interrupts his snooze. Why, I saw one take off after a man once."

Ameran listened wide eyed. "Did he eat him?"

"Who? The gator or the man?" asked Billy teasingly.

Gray laughed.

Ameran rolled back her eyes. "Did the gator eat the man?"

Captain Billy shook his head. "Nay. The man climbed a tree and didn't come down until the gator got tired of waiting for him and left." He rubbed his plump belly. "There be no finer eating than gator tail roasted over hot coals."

Ameran made a face.

"I be serious, lassie. There be no whiter meat or juicier flesh than the gator's tail." He smacked his lips. "A plate of gator tails will be the first thing I get when we get to the tavern, and I'll wash it down with the biggest bowl of rum punch you ever did see."

Gray said very little. His gaze was fixed straight ahead. The settlement had not yet come into view. Captain Billy had said it was still four knots away, but Gray's eyes, she knew, were ready and alert for that first glimpse of the second love of his life.

Ameran slipped closer to him. He smiled down at her, but she could see beyond his seemingly cheerful countenance. Already he had begun to look ahead to the prospect that the sovereign of the seas would not be anchored there. If it weren't, where would he begin to look for the *Fair Winds* in a sea as vast as the heavens above?

"Don't ye worry, laddie. If yer ship's not there now, I wager she'll be soon," Captain Billy assured him. "Those scavengers will be anxious for some women and some rum, and that be the closest port to find them. I know. Me and me mates have slipped in here often enough ourselves fer those very reasons." He patted the cutlass hanging from his side. "And we'll be ready for those devils."

Ameran held up her hands to shield her eyes from the sun. Captain Billy's straw hat did little to protect her from the glaring rays. Gliding up one of the many little creeks that cut through the marshes and emptied into the river was the strangest-looking long boat she had ever seen. It was long and narrow and nearly all under water. There were two men paddling the boat, but they were men such as the likes she had never seen before. Their chests were sun bronzed, and their hair stuck up like black prickles atop their heads.

"What kind of a boat is that?" she asked. "And what kind of men are those?"

"The boat be called a pirogue, a canoe, and the gentlemen in it are Indians from a tribe called the Edistoes," answered Captain Billy.

"Indians?" She held tighter to Gray's arm. Were they about to be attacked?

"No need to fear, lassie. They be a friendly bunch. 'Tis the cursed Yemassees and Westoes and Seminoles further south that cause the colonists the most grief, and only then because the Spanish get them to do their dirty bidding fer them."

Her hold on Gray's arm loosened.

He looked down and smiled at her.

"You have no cause to worry, not now, not ever again," Gray assured her with soft words of comfort. "For I'm with you now, and I swear no harm will ever befall you again."

Captain Billy nudged her. "Ye got me, too, lassie."

Ameran leaned over and kissed his whiskered, old cheek. "You honor me, sir."

He laughed. "'Tis you who honor me, lassie." He touched the spot she had kissed. "I'll never wash away the print of such sweet lips."

Ameran laughed with him.

Gray smiled.

She could sense enormous sadness behind his smile. She prayed the *Fair Winds* would be at the harbor. Poor Gray wouldn't have a moment's peace until his ship was returned to his command and to the service of his King.

"The Edistoes call this place 'Kayawah,' " Captain Billy told them.

"Kayawah." Ameran repeated the name softly. "It has a lovely sound to it."

"Much lovelier than Oyster Point and Albermarle Point and Charles Town, all of which names it has bore," said Captain Billy.

Portia, the best of the ratters and the Welshman's favorite cat of all, jumped up into his arms, and the old sailor held her close. He pointed out a watchtower in the marshes and explained that it had been built on poles taller than ships' masts so the sentry could maintain a constant watch up the river and alert the colony of approaching vessels.

They waved to the sentry. He waved back down to them. Then with his musket pointed to the sky, he fired. His two shots were followed by others up the river.

"It would be difficult indeed to attack the colony from the sea," said Gray after thoughtful consideration.

"Aye, when she's attacked, it will be by land," said Captain Billy.

More watchtowers were positioned along the banks of the river, as were small forts made of earth and wood and brick. Shells bleached white by the sun rested upon the sandy banks. A high bluff loomed in the near distance ahead of them.

Ameran knew from conversations with Martin that Charles Town had been moved to that high bluff when attack by the Spaniards and Indians seemed imminent.

A little farther up the river was a walled fortress with brick bastions as high as four men tall. Cannons were mounted and pointed at the river. More sentries were patrolling the ramparts.

"The colonists have organized their own into a militia as fine as any king's army," Captain Billy told them. "All the men, be they farmers or shopkeepers or woodcutters, take their turn alongside their neighbors in the protection of their settlement."

Gray didn't share in his friend's enthusiasm. "Farmers and shopkeepers and woodcutters might make good watch guards, but can they shoot and fire cannons and wield swords as well as a trained soldier? I think not."

Captain Billy shrugged his shoulders. "What they're protecting, laddie, they hold far dearer than any man trained for battle, and methinks they would fight even fiercer to protect what they had worked hard to make theirs."

Gray's expression remained downcast. "I should be bringing these good people cannons and guns and powders and men to help them fight, but instead, I come only with bad news and empty hands."

"Not yer fault, lad. Ye did the best ye could."

Gray hung his head.

Ameran could feel his anguish. On his shoulders he bore the blame for any and all misfortune that might befall the colonists. If it were the *Fair Winds* sailing up the river at that moment, the settlers would have the arsenal they so desperately needed. Instead, the cannons which were to be used to fend off attacks were in the possession of pirates and wouldn't be used to protect or defend but rather to defeat and destroy.

"King Charles believed an attack by the combined forces of Spain and the Indians would be soon coming," Gray said, his tone somber. "He had received reports that the Spanish had enlisted the aid of some of the hostile tribes to the South nearer to Florida, and the march had already begun."

"Such an attack as that of which you speak might well be planned, but if it hasn't been waged, it won't be done so during these hot summer days and nights," said Captain Billy confidently. "Saint Augustine is the nearest Spanish settlement, and it is more than a month's march to the south. If those devils were going to march on Charles Town, they'd have done so in the cool of the year. They wouldn't have waited until they had to go through swamps infested with vipers whose fangs possess a poison that kills at once. Nor would they be eager to endure the stings of pesty little beasts that drink blood and bring on fevers." He thought for a few more moments before concluding, "The Spanish and the Indians could never march together, for one would no doubt kill the other long before they ever reached their destination."

"I hope you're right, my wise friend," Gray told him, a frown still upon his brow.

Ameran nodded in quiet agreement. She prayed he was right. If the colonists were attacked in the days to come, Gray would never forgive himself for not having completed his mission.

Captain Billy laughed that hearty laugh. "Mark me word. When it comes to matters of waging war and attacking, this Welshman is hardly ever wrong. The fevers and the agues and the bloody flux will take far more of them than the Spanish or Indians ever dare."

Captain Billy pointed to row upon row of long entrenchments off the port side. "The entire colony is surrounded by these. A lot of careful thought and preparation has been dedicated to the defense of their settlement."

"And a tremendous amount of hard work," Ameran observed. She was starting to feel a little more at ease. Perhaps the rumors of war such as they had heard in England were unfounded.

Captain Billy pointed out the large, gray shells gleaming in the sun along the banks of the river. "Those are oyster shells, and ye've never tasted a finer stew than one made from those." He licked his lips. "My friend, Peter Poinsett, who owns the tavern, can't shuck them fast enough for me." He pointed to other large oyster banks. "That's why they first called the settlement Oyster Point." He chuckled. "Then they named it Albemarle Point in honor of that pompous arse Duke, and when his money ran out, they named it Charles Town for reasons most apparent." The Welshman laughed even heartier. "I love me King most dearly, and I would defend him till me death, but he's not without his faults."

Gray finally spoke. He was nearer to a smile than he had been most of that morning. "The King's faults are many. 'Tis true. Why else would he desire to make a knight out of a no-good pirate from Wales?"

"A pirate, ye say, laddie. A pirate. Who ye be speaking of? Surely not this Welshman, fer he be a privateer in the service of His Royal Majesty the King of England. And the best damned privateer that ever sailed these seas." His chest puffed out in pride. "Sir Billy Blitzen. Me poor dead mother would be proud of her l'il Billy. Sir Billy Blitzen. It does have a dandy sound to it. Does it not?"

Ameran was quick to agree. "It sounds most noble and grand."

"Just like me," Captain Billy chuckled.

Gray nudged Ameran. "Ask him when he intends to return to England so the King can officially do the honors?"

"Well?" she asked.

His weathered face wrinkled even more. "Just as soon as I give Monquez his due so I can have a good haul for the King's treasury. That's the least I can do fer me King, and the least I can do fer me good friend, Lord Carlisle," he added quietly.

A little later, the docks and wharves of the harbor came into view. Ameran stood on her tiptoes and gazed ahead in hopeful anticipation. Gray's face was strained as he, too, tried to make out the shape of the *Fair Winds* amid the tall masts and furled sails.

Portia sat perched atop Captain Billy's shoulder.

385

Captain Billy took out his spyglass and peered into it. Then with a frown, he handed it to Gray. "She's not there, lad."

Gray looked through the glass, then handed it to Ameran, who did the same.

"My heart was filled with such hope, but my head told me such wishfulness wouldn't be fulfilled."

Ameran kept looking and kept hoping against hope the *Fair Winds* would miraculously appear, but it didn't, and her own sighs of disappointment were but echoes of Gray's.

Captain Billy reached around her and clamped his hand tight on Gray's shoulder. "Because she's not here at this moment laddie, is no reason to think she won't be here within the days to come."

Gray's nod was dismal. "Perhaps she's already docked and has already set out to sea again."

"Be that the case, then someone will know where she's bound," Captain Billy reminded him. "We'll get ye yer ship back, lad. We will. I promise ye that."

Gray clasped his hand onto his friend's wrinkled one. "You're a true friend, Billy."

Captain Billy seemed uncomfortable by the show of affection. He pushed Gray's hand away. "I'm not doing a thing fer ye that ye would not do fer me." He quickly pointed to a tiny, fortlike arrangement of shelters off the left bank and explained that the first houses built by the colonists were made from mud and branches.

"The settlement has progressed much in twenty years as ye will soon see," he told them.

The crew of the *Lucky Lady* let out a loud cheer as they neared the port.

As they guided the ship through the narrow canal, using long poles that went down to the bottom of the water to steer and move the ship along, Captain Billy pointed at the various vessels tied up there. There were several fishing ketches and a schooner the size of the *Lucky Lady*. Most of the ones there were fore and aft rigged boats with only one mast a single headsail jib. As Captain Billy explained to them, such sloops were the favorite of Charles Town shipbuilders, for the boats were seaworthy and sturdy and faster than anything else afloat, and that they were used in the frequent trading expeditions made to the West Indies.

On the dock, men were hard at work unloading one such sloop while another crew diligently loaded the one beside it.

"Charles Town sends port, corn, lumber, tar, and pitch, as well as deer skins and wolf and bobcat furs to Barbados. What they don't want there are sent on to England," Captain Billy told them. "From the West Indies, the colonists get rum and sugar and coconuts and pineapples. It is quite obvious which of the two gets the best end of that deal."

Gray watched closely. "I would venture to say it is Barbados and not England who is enjoying the benefits of this profitable trade."

Captain Billy nodded. "I've heard it said many a time that it is the Barbadians who rule this settlement, not the Lord Proprietors, who have the real control of this colony. Charles Town is here for their benefit, and many of them have moved here for that reason."

Ameran took off her straw hat and fanned her face. "Look. Those Indians sitting along the wall . . . their legs are chained together." The sight greatly troubled her. What could they have done to receive such punishment?

Captain Billy shook his head. " 'Tis a sad sight indeed, lassie. They're most likely being taken as slaves to Barbados to work on the farms and in the forests."

"But how can that be when they were the first here?" Gray asked, obviously troubled as well. "This land was theirs long before it was claimed for the Crown."

"These are not Edistoes, lad. Most likely these gents be Yemasses or Westoes caught spying for the Spanish."

"Hey, Captain Billy," went up a loud cry from the dock.

"That be my old wrecking partner, Bull Rollins. Ye'll like him. He's quite a character and a rogue to boot." Captain Billy gave a hearty wave that nearly upset Portia from her perch.

The man he was waving to was tall and thick and had a bare chest full of black drawings.

"Ye've heard me talk of him, Gray. No finer a ship builder there be than Bull Rollins. Nor a finer ship wrecker." He chuckled as he remembered. "Why, when we was young, me and him used to lure French and Spanish ships onto the reefs so we could board them and take their gold." He winked at them. "All for our King and country, mind ye.

Ah, what a devil I was back then. 'Tis a miracle I survived me own meanness."

Ameran exchanged a quiet laugh with Gray. She tucked her arm through Captain Billy's. "I believe that must be what makes you such a charming rogue today." She could have sworn there was yet another blush beneath the gray whiskers.

"Yo, Billy. Hurry along. I have some news fer ye," Bull called out to him. "News you ain't a gonna believe 'tis true."

Iza tossed the ropes up to Bull, who tied them onto the pilings.

"Yer high and mighty friend that Lord something or t'other Carlisle joined forces with Monquez and attacked a Frenchie."

Gray started to speak up.

"Hush, laddie." He shot his eyes to Ameran and warned her to keep Gray quiet. "The two of ye go below, and I'll find out what needs be known." His usually cheerful face looked worried. "Go, now, afore he starts asking questions I haven't thought of answers fer yet."

Gray was reluctant to go. "It's the right of every man to defend himself against charges which aren't true."

Ameran tugged at his arm. "Let's do as Captain Billy says. He can find out information that you can't. Come."

Gray still hesitated.

"He may be able to find out where the *Fair Winds* is," she reminded him.

He then allowed himself to be pulled away, but not without looking back over his shoulder every

389

few steps along the way.

Captain Billy had a quick word with his crew before inviting Bull on board.

Gray paced the floor of the tiny cabin. Ameran sat quietly by watching him. How had Captain Billy's old friend come about such information? There could be but one way. The *Fair Winds* had to have set in to port there ahead of them and just as they had feared had already put back out to sea.

It seemed that hours passed before Captain Billy finally came below deck.

Gray pounced at him the moment the door opened. "What did he say? What's the news of the *Fair Winds?* How did he know about Monquez? What else does he know?"

"Calm down, lad. Calm down."

Ameran knew from Captain Billy's frown and furrows that the news he was about to deliver was far from good.

The Welshman began and started over again several times before finally finding the words he wanted to say. "It seems that . . . Bull told me . . . From all I have heard . . ."

"Get on with it, Billy," urged Gray. "What of the news?"

Captain Billy uncorked the rum bottle and took another long gulp. "Bull was at the dock when the sloop from Barbados . . ."

He let out another long and troubled sigh before reaching for the bottle again. Gray declined when it was offered to him.

"The news is dismal, lad. Ye'd best prepare yerself."

"I feared the worst. I'm ready."

Captain Billy slumped down into a chair. "Yer ship didn't come into port here. She put in to Barbados, and from there set a course for England."

"For England?" asked Ameran in disbelief.

"I'm most surprised the crew would return there, considering their pasts," Gray said, deep in reflection.

Captain Billy looked at Ameran and shook his head. "I don't know how to tell ye, lassie, but . . ."

"Go on. What is it?" She was overcome by a sickening dread. "Gideon isn't dead." She asked no question, but stated it as fact. "I don't understand. My dagger pierced his flesh. I saw the hole. I saw the blood dripping from it. He didn't breathe. He didn't move. His was the face of a corpse." Her sobs choked in her throat. "Twice I have tried, and twice I have failed."

Gray held her tight. "When Gideon dies, it will be by my hand, and my hand alone, for that is the way it was intended to be. Tell us more," he entreated of Billy.

"According to the captain of the sloop, Gideon was near death, but that didn't keep him from telling his tales. It's just as ye said, lass. He does indeed cast the blame for all the evil deeds he committed onto Gray, and he makes himself out to be the hero, and his gut bears the near-fatal wound to prove it."

"And I am made out to be some vile, murdering monster," mused Gray dismally. "And what of my end? Surely Gideon exaggerated a far greater tale of my demise than having fed me to the sharks."

"Aye, he challenged ye to a duel for control of the *Fair Winds*."

"A duel which he no doubt was the victor," said Gray bitterly.

"Aye, lad. He didn't want to kill ye. Ye were closer than a brother, but ye had defiled your King and country so he had no choice but run his blade through yer heart."

Gray slammed his fist down onto the desk. "And now he's nearing England in anxious anticipation of denouncing me as a traitor and murderer of innocents."

Ameran clung tight to Gray. "We knew the news would be dreary at best."

Gray hung his head. "I have no ship. To all who have heard the tales, I'm a dead man. Even if I were to be miraculously resurrected in their eyes, I'm a traitor to my King and country."

"Even if Gideon were to survive the voyage home, and there is that great likelihood he won't," she pointed out. "Be it his wound or another inflicted by one of his criminal rogues that keeps him from reaching England's shore and spreading his tale, King Charles will never believe him," Ameran assured him. "The King isn't blind to Gideon's treachery and deceit. He, himself, had nearly been a victim of his ill deeds in the past."

Gray jumped up. "We must return to England at once."

"We will, laddie. I swear. I'll take ye there meself just as soon as the damage done by the winds and rains is repaired to me *Lady*." Captain Billy rose and clasped Gray's arm. "We'll sail home, lad, and we'll avenge yer honor. We'll set right those lies Gideon has told, and when we've done that, we'll bring an end to his treachery once and for all."

Gray shook his head. "You don't understand, my friend. There are matters far more important than my honor at stake."

Captain Billy was slow to understand, but Ameran knew at once what was foremost in Gray's mind. The safety of his King! If Gideon survived the voyage back, he would return a wounded hero, and who would dare suspect a fallen warrior of conspiring to murder his monarch? Or even of doing the unspeakable himself?

"I can only pray we get there in time," Captain Billy said when he finally realized the reason for Gray's darkest anguish.

"We will," Gray told him after the longest while. "Gideon will be in no hurry to make his move. He'll plot and connive and scheme so that when the deed is finally done, he'll be the one onto whom suspicion is never cast. And he'll want to bask in his own glory and reap the many benefits of his lies."

"I'll speak to Bull about making the repairs and see how long they'll take to be made. No more than a week or two, I would guess."

"And then we'll be bound for England." Gray seemed almost cheerful. He slapped Billy on the back. "I believe I'm ready to have a taste of those gator tails and oyster stew. And I'm most anxious as well to have a look around this settlement. There's much the King has sent me here to learn."

Captain Billy eyed him suspiciously. "Ye won't be

doing anything foolish, will ye, laddie? Like announcing to all of Carolina who ye be?"

"Nay, my good friend. I won't make any such announcement." Gray's smile held, but it showed no glee. "Never before have I had cause to deny the man I am. But I'll cheerfully do that now, for if I admit to being the villain I'm accused of being, these good folk will undoubtedly clamp me in chains, and I'll be helpless to prevent Gideon from committing his foulest deed yet."

"Ye can trust me men to keep yer secret," Captain Billy assured him. "Not one of them will betray ye. They'd sooner poke out their own eyes than go 'gainst me wishes."

"Tell your men they'll be well rewarded."

Captain Billy locked arms with them both. "What greater reward could they possibly hope fer when they already have the honor and distinction of sailing with the two finest commanders these seas have ever known?"

"Who will you have me be?" Gray asked as they hurried along the passageway to the stairs.

Captain Billy chuckled. "I've already got that one figured out. I have. Ye can be one of me mates, and ye, lassie, will be a gal so smitten by love when we was in the Somers Islands last month that ye stowed away just to be near him. Romantic, wouldn't ye say?"

Gray laughed. "Not far from the truth."

Ameran smiled, but her good spirits were shadowed with thoughts of Affra and her handsome sailor, Jason, whose love was doomed before it had a chance to blossom.

"What was the name you chose . . . Lilly?" Gray asked.

"Lilly Warwick."

Gray thought long and hard. "Then I shall be . . ."

"What say ye to Joshua?" suggested Captain Billy, his smile bittersweet.

Gray's face sobered quickly. "Joshua is a fine name, Billy. I'd be honored and proud to borrow it for a little while."

"Me brother would be proud and honored, too." Captain Billy bowed his gray head. His lips mouthed a prayer. "May his soul rest in peace." With a wipe of his hand across his brow, his good humor returned. "Unless ye have some objection, I believe I'll give ye the surname of Blackburn. I knew a Blackburn once, and a finer sailor couldn't be found anywhere."

"Then Joshua Blackburn I shall be."

Captain Billy skipped a step or two as they hurried across the deck. "Joshua Blackburn and Lilly Warwick, allow me to treat ye to the finest meal ye ever sat down to."

Ameran laughed. "That would be delightful. What say you, Joshua?"

"I'm in agreement, Lilly."

She looked down at her manly attire and was about to suggest she change into the yellow dress, but decided against it, for neither men had any objection, and the clothes on her back did make her story all the more convincing.

Chapter Nineteen

Ameran sat at a back table with Gray and Captain Billy in Peter Poinsett's tavern. Set before them were bowls of oyster stew and she-crab soup, and platters of grilled fish, gator tails and roasted corn. Everything was so tasty, she couldn't get her fill. Already she'd finished off two plates of man-size portions, and she'd be quite happy to start on a third.

Gray gave her a wink and a grin.

Her heart fluttered. The reason for her ravenous hunger was their own little secret.

The owner of the tavern, a fat, balding man wearing a blood-splattered apron, brought a pitcher of Madeira wine and another one of rum punch, and placed it in front of them.

"Eat hearty, *mes bon amis.* It eez a long way across that ocean, and you do not get food as fine as this where you go."

Everyone laughed.

Ameran's laugh was not nearly as cheerful as her companions. The past two weeks had been remarkably peaceful, considering Charles Town's reputation for savagery and brutality. Whitehall with all its culture and civilized refinement was far more primitive, for in Charles Town there was no Gideon or Constance waiting to stab them in the back.

As in London Town, the rowdiest and most dangerous places to be were the docks, where sailors from all over the world robbed and brawled and fought, and the taverns, where drinking, gambling and whoring brought many a man to a desperate end. Pirates with reputations as bloody as Monquez's called frequently at the port of Charles Town, and at that very minute there was an entire table of them out front of Peter Poinsett's, boasting about their most frequent marauding escapades. As long as they caused no trouble, Peter Poinsett welcomed them, as did the other merchants and shopkeepers, for the freebooters spent lavishly, and paid in gold and silver coins.

And there were Indians, true, but the Edistoes were friendly and curious. The only ferocious ones she had encountered were those sitting enchained on the dock that first day the *Lucky Lady* sailed into port.

Fears of a Spanish attack from the South had subsided, for as Captain Billy had pointed out, the march alone in the July heat through marshes riddled with fever causing pests and deadly vipers would destroy half the force before it ever reached its destination. The settlers believed they would be safe until autumn, and hopefully by then more colonists and more weapons would have arrived to take the place of those destroyed or taken by the pirates.

For a while, Ameran listened contentedly to Bull Rollins, who had just joined them, reminisce with Captain Billy about their days long ago as wreckers, and how they had taken the booty of many an enemy ship without ever losing a single life.

Gray squeezed her hand under the table, and once

again her thoughts lingered back to the past days they had shared exploring Charles Town and discovering all they could about the colony for the King. Gray had been able to gather far more information as Joshua Blackburn than he ever would have been able to as the Commander of the Royal fleet, and Ameran was certain that while the King might not look with favor upon the Lord Proprietors who took much from the colony and gave little back, he would sympathize with the colonists struggling to make a new and better home for themselves and their families.

The colony's population had already reached one thousand inhabitants. It hadn't been restricted to solely English. French Huguenots of the names Legaré, Gerard, and Laurens, who had suffered religious persecution in their own country, had sought refuge in Charles Town, and had made many contributions to the colony's economy by growing wheat and barley and burning tar for market. Charles Town had taken an overflow of West Indies settlers as well. From Barbados had come sugar planters, merchants, artisans, sailors, servants, and slaves with names such as Allston, Beresford, Gibbese, Logan and Moore.

Ameran could see no evidence, however, of the Lord Proprietors' boasts of the very air in Charles Town giving "a strong appetite and quick digestion" and making men more "lightsome" and women more "fruitsome." The free men, masters, and servants all looked tired and weary, and the women sickly and frail. Few made it past their fortieth year. The children fared far better, however, than the dirty, ragged little urchins who ran wild on London's crowded streets. While there had been no deaths from rats or pestilence caused by overcrowding, epidemics of fevers and bloody flux took an overwhelming toll on the colonists.

All in all, with seemingly unsurmountable problems, the colonists had achieved nearly the impossible and had created for themselves a place of civilization where there had been none before. They strived hard to make for themselves a place as similar to England as they could make it be. There were shops and taverns, a Town House and an artillery ground much like the one at Whitehall for militia training and exercises. Plans for a theater like the King's very own, and a horse-racing field like that of Newgate were awaiting construction. Homes had been built of weather boarding with cypress panels, shutters, blinds, and sashes much like those of the West Indies with huge verandahs opening up onto the outside to let in the cooling breezes. Like the homes of Barbados, these were built to withstand the relentless heat of the summer and the ferocious winds and gales that frequently attacked the Carolina coast. Large, capacious streets made not of cobblestone but of crushed oyster shell had been laid out and given the names of Meeting, Broad, and Water Streets. There was talk of a magnificent church built of black cypress that would soon be begun. Already there were quite a few two story dwellings on town lots. Plantation houses like that of Martin's dream, houses with their own private wharves and drawbridges, had been constructed on the neck of land between the Ashley and Cooper Rivers by the few wealthy settlers who had the money and the servants to till the corn, peas, and wheat and tend the cattle, poultry, sheep, and hogs.

There was one crop, rice, which Gray felt would be of tremendous value for local consumption as well as of enormous export potential back to England. Rice, he was certain, would one day be the wealth of the Carolinas. One planter, Master Benjamin Robinson, had planted along a creek bank a handful of seeds which had been brought from Madagascar by a black slave, and had harvested enough of the white grain to feed the entire colony.

"I'm confident I have answers to the questions the King asked me to research," Gray told Ameran their third night back upon the sea as they sat on the bow in the moonlight watching the stars dance upon the rippleless ocean. "He should be pleased with the news I have for him."

Smiling, Ameran caressed his cheek, her finger tips lingering across the scar that looked most pronounced in the hazy glow shrouding the ship. "He can be no more pleased with you than I."

"If only it were the *Fair Winds* we were sailing back to London Harbor," he said wistfully. "If only I hadn't been such a fool, a blind, stupid fool."

She brushed her finger across his lips. "What's done is done. We can't live in the past."

His jaw tensed. "No, we can't, but I can make certain our future won't be plagued by the likes of that cowardly traitor ever again." His fist struck the *Lucky Lady*'s teak railing. "I only pray that Gideon doesn't die en route to England, for I desperately desire the opportunity to cut off his breath myself."

Ameran held tight to Gray's hand. She hoped Gideon would die. She prayed above all else that he was dead at that very moment as they spoke, for every breath he drew would be gathering strength to lash out at Gray once more upon his discovering that he had failed in dictating the fate of the man he professed to love like a brother. Gideon had almost killed Gray once, and she wasn't eager for him to have a second chance to get the job done. If only she had done the deed herself! Twice she had attempted to silence him forever, and twice she had failed!

"Just as soon as I've sent Gideon to his grave, I intend to have the Duchess of Morrow expelled permanently from court."

"You'll most assuredly break her heart," teased Ameran.

"I would most assuredly prefer to break her neck!" Gray said angrily. "Her presence has been clouded with suspicion since the death of her first husband. Not even the Queen would dare defend her of the charges of attempted murder of the King and treason against her country."

"I can't wait to see her face when I deposit that cursed brooch right at her feet," Ameran said, chuckling at having envisioned such a scene. She patted the waistband of her knee breeches where the brooch had been sewn into a pouch. "It would serve her right if I sold it and gave all the money to the poor." She laughed so hard her sides hurt. "And tell them it was the Duchess of Morrow who was their generous benefactoress."

A hint of a smile was upon his lips. "They wouldn't believe you. It's common knowledge the Duchess knows nothing of kindness, charity and generosity." He held tight to her arm.

Ameran pressed closer to him. "Surely there's never been a woman who's ever loved a man more than I love you," she said as she held on to him with all her might.

"Surely there's never been a man who's ever loved a woman as I love you."

"We must never lose each other again," she said, her words quiet and fierce. "Never."

His sentiments echoed her own. "Never, my darling." Gray's sigh was weary. "I've debated and deliberated much over what I am about to reveal to you, but I can think of no less hateful way to say it. The man who married us on board the *Fair Winds* . . . Tim Starling was his name . . . He wasn't . . ."

"I know, darling. Gideon took great delight in announcing that fact to me."

"There was a minister in Charles Town, but we couldn't have sworn our vows to God and to each other under false names."

Ameran nodded. She had thought of that as well. She lifted her face to his, and kissed his eyes, her hands framing his face. "You're my husband. I don't care what anyone says. We could be no more married had the Archbishop himself heard our declarations of devotion."

"Our souls were wed the first time we kissed." His hand caressed the growing roundness of her belly. "We'll be joined in holy matrimony soon. Above all else, I promise you that."

Tears of joy filled her eyes. Perhaps the time had come at long last for them to know nothing except the happiness they had found together.

His hands found their way beneath her loose-fitting sailor's blouse.

"Impending motherhood agrees with you," he said as he gently massaged her soft flesh.

"I don't know if I should be flattered or offended," she teased.

"I'd rather cut out my tongue than utter one word that would cause you a moment's grief." With his teeth, Gray untied the ties drawing her shirt together, and nuzzled the warm flesh with his chin. "And I can most certainly think of far better uses for my tongue," he laughed as his tongue danced across her nipples. "I'll be most envious of our babe."

"You have months to have your fill of me before I become a mama with a suckling wee one in my arms." Just the thought of holding her babe and comforting him with kisses and hugs filled her with tiny flutters.

"I'll never have my fill of you. You're the woman of every man's dreams—and perhaps a nightmare or two," he added with a laugh and a shower of kisses. "I've never known a woman with your beauty, your spirit, your confounding tenacity."

"And if you're lucky, you'll never meet another one, for if you do, there's no place the two of you can hide where I won't find you . . . and exact my revenge," she added with a swift grab between his legs.

"How many months?" he asked a few moments later.

"What?"

"How much longer before my son is born?" He rubbed the rise of her belly again. "Apparently it'll be sooner than you'd thought."

There was no mistaking the swell of pride in his voice.

"Your wee one might well be a daughter," she couldn't resist adding.

"I hope not. I pray not, for I would have to spend my old days fending off amorous suitors." He took her hands between his. "A daughter would be the sweetest of all gifts to give me, but I beg of you, let us first have four, no five sons, so the job of protecting her honor may be entrusted to them, so I can enjoy my later years with all bodily parts intact."

"Five sons? And I thought Old Rowley was stabled in the Royal Mews," she teased.

"Old Rowley is right here beside you." Gray whinnied like a horse.

His mouth devoured hers with a hunger they both knew would never be satisfied even though they had every intention of spending the rest of their lives attempting to do so. "When, my love, when will I become a father?"

"Why, when I become a mother, of course." She felt herself tremble again. A mother. She had never said the word aloud before in describing herself. What kind of a mother would she be? She prayed desperately against becoming the kind of mother she had known as a child.

Gray gathered her closer still. "You're quivering."

"I'm afraid," she said softly.

"You, afraid? You, who can wield a dagger better than most men?" He stopped smiling. "You're afraid." His arms wrapped tight around her and didn't ease their protection until her tremors subsided. "But what do you fear? Is it the thought of the pain you must endure in bringing our child into the world that makes you shake so? It'll be painful by all accounts, but it will be over soon, and I won't leave your side. I swear."

"I've known pains far worse than that of childbirth could ever be." She didn't know she was crying until a sprinkling of tears fell upon her breasts. "Oh, Gray, I do so want to be a good mother. I want my child to love me, not pity me as I did mine. I feared Mama.

There were times even when I hated her and wished her ill."

"Shhhh." His words were soft caresses into her hair. "You'll be a wonderful mother to our children . . . all twelve of them," he added with a mysterious gleam.

Ameran forced a smile. "Twelve? Am I to be a brood mare?"

"When you are not fighting pirates or waging war on enemies of our King, I should think that would be a most noble avocation."

Ameran placed his hands onto her stomach. "I've come to the conclusion our son was conceived the very night you rescued me from certain death at the hands of the evil Duke." She covered his hands with hers. "Our son is kicking. Can you feel him struggling to get out?"

Gray's face softened. "Surely there must be more than one set of tiny legs, for he possesses the strength of at least two babes, perhaps even three."

Ameran wound her arms around his neck. "I think you should carry me below. I feel quite faint."

Gray's face paled. "What is it? Are you ill, my darling?"

Her smile betrayed her. "I'm not faint from sickness. I'm faint from the want of you. And if you don't take me soon to our quarters, then the men taking watch will have a most entertaining story to tell their mates."

Gray swung her up into his arms, then deposited her feet back onto the deck, and let out a pained moan. "I forget. You've been eating for two. Perhaps you had better carry me."

"Perhaps you'd better sleep with Captain Billy and Portia, Lord Carlisle," she teased. With a haughty toss of her head, she ran away.

When Gray finally caught up with her, he swung her up into his arms and carried her laughing down the corridor. He kicked open the door to their cabin, then bolted the lock behind them.

"Oh, Gray, I love you so."

He lay her down onto the rumpled heap of covers, then ever so gently he eased the blouse from her shoulders and slid the breeches down her legs. His lips savored the sweet flesh bared before him as his eyes feasted on the loveliest sight he had ever beheld.

Gray rested his ear upon her belly, and when she asked what sounds he was listening for, he motioned for quiet. She heard him sigh, then a few moments later, heard him mumble some words she could not understand into her new plumpness.

"What nonsense are you filling our child's head with?" she asked with a soft chuckle.

"Our son," he corrected. "And I'm beginning to believe there's more than one growing in your womb."

Lovingly, she caressed his face. "Just as long as they're all as wonderful as you."

His kiss searched her soul and beyond. She couldn't get enough of his lips, nor could she deny the raging hunger mounting inside her in spite of her impending condition.

Gray wound his hands in her hair, his fingers losing themselves in the dark tangles. He rolled back onto the bed, taking her with him so that she was sitting astride him.

Satiny and swollen breasts fell upon the hardness of his chest. With a soft laugh, she tucked her curves to his manly contours and moved slowly into him, deliberately taunting and teasing him with the slowest of motions in the assurance that the sweet agony would soon be stilled.

"Will you still love me when my hips bear the curse of motherhood?"

"Without question, for it'll be all the more to love and to enjoy."

Strong hands, hot and fiery, slid across every inch of her silken form, exploring, delighting and adoring.

His firm massages sent shivers of yearning through her, and she was aware once again of being consumed by an urgency that could only be calmed by Gray. The blood racing inside her veins surged forth at the knowing intimacy of his touch. Between them flowed a possessiveness that could be shared only between a husband and his wife, a bond of love that could never be broken.

Her body melted deeper into his, their life forces reclaiming the bliss of their union, and the warmth of their loving desire flowed between them once again.

Gray gave a sigh and a moan, and with his arms protectively enfolding her, lay her back down onto the bed.

She felt his eyes close against her breasts, and she, too, gave way to the sweet exhaustion of their love.

"Ship ahoy!" shouted the nimble-footed lad who climbed the riggings every morning, noon and dusk, and called down his report to his captain.

Captain Billy scrambled up the ladder overlooking the ocean from atop the bow, and stared out over the waters through his glass.

Ameran and Gray stood below him, waiting, hoping, praying against all likelihood that the *Lucky*

Lady was in the wake of the great British sovereign of the seas.

"She be flying the black flag of sea rogues," he called back down.

Ameran's hopes were quick to fade, and she could tell from the sigh of disappointment that had escaped his lips that Gray's hopes had been shattered as well.

"The *Fair Winds* must be nearly to England by now," he said with quiet resignation.

Captain Billy let out a joyous yell. "It be that bloody bastard, Monquez." His men clapped and cheered, and a few danced a jig across the deck.

Ameran's heart sank to the pit of her stomach.

Captain Billy climbed down, still laughing. "He ain't gonna get away this time. Right, maties?" His crew cheered louder. "We'll put him on the bottom of the sea where he belongs." Captain Billy held his fist high above his head. "We'll teach him a lesson he'll not likely forget as he's burning in hell."

His men grabbed hold of Captain Billy and swung him around and around.

"Make ready, lads! Master Starwell, run up the French flag. We'll make him think he's got another willing victim."

The crew hurried about their chores.

Captain Billy motioned for Ameran and Gray to follow him below, and he hummed and whistled all the way down the corridor.

Gray's face was flushed with worry as Captain Billy rolled his charts and maps out onto the desk. "You and your crew would indeed make quick work of Monquez. That is for certain," Gray began, choosing his words slowly and carefully. "But have you forgotten, my good friend, that the devil ship possesses an arsenal of cannons and weapons taken from the *Fair Winds*."

"I forget nothing, laddie. Nothing." He said good humoredly as he pored over his maps. "Now to the best of my reckoning, I figure we be right here." He pointed to a spot in the middle of the ocean.

Ameran couldn't keep still. "But it'll surely be a bloodbath if you go after them."

"Aye, lass, but it won't be our blood dumped into the sea." His smile held. "Don't look at me as though I be a poor, deranged soul. Ye neither, laddie. I haven't taken leave of what few senses I possessed, and I haven't been nipping at the rum." His laugh was roaring. "We're not gonna attack the bloody bastard. We're gonna run like hell from him."

Ameran wondered exactly what plan of attack Captain Billy was scheming behind those laughing eyes. She knew the Welsh privateer hadn't achieved his fame by retreating upon confrontation.

She watched as Gray studied the charts, and when his baffled expression changed to a slight grin, she couldn't figure out why.

"We be near this little cay here," he said, pointing to the northernmost island in a long chain of tiny land masses surrounded by water. "And look at what be enclosing it."

"Reefs and coral heads," said Gray with a nod and a smile.

Captain Billy laughed. "Them reefs have torn the hull from many an unsuspecting ship."

Ameran looked at the map, not knowing exactly what it was she was supposed to see. Then, slowly, she began to understand exactly what it was Captain Billy intended to do.

"With all them cannons that demon ship be carrying, she'll run areef and get stuck fer sure," Captain Billy announced with confidence.

"But what about the *Lucky Lady?*" asked Ameran. "Might not that be her fate as well?"

"Not with Captain Billy Blitzen at the helm," Gray assured her.

"I know these reefs so well, lassie, I could pick my way through them on a pitch-black night," the Welshman assured her. "And, she be so light, she could just glide right over them."

Ameran didn't doubt for a moment that he knew what he was talking about, yet the thought of still another confrontation with the bloodthirsty Monquez made her cringe.

"Those of them devils who can swim fast enough and hard enough might just make it to the island." The set of Captain Billy's face was hard. "But their fate will be none better than the poor settlers they marooned there, for there's no food on that hell rock, and the only water comes from the sea." His lips turned up in a cruel smile. "There'll be nothing fer them to do but kill each other or kill themselves."

Ameran felt no pity for the cutthroats. She hoped the spirits of the settlers who had suffered their last days would be there to haunt them and make their end all the more hellish and miserable.

" 'Tis a pity Captain Monquez won't be joining his men," Captain Billy remarked.

"What plans have you for him?" asked Gray.

"Not what I want to do; that be fer certain," Captain Billy answered as he rolled his charts back up. "Nothing would do me old heart better than to cut off his bodily parts one by one and use them as chum for

410

the sharks, but I have far nobler plans of him." His smile was slow to appear. "Captain Monquez will be voyaging to England with us."

Ameran's hand went to her stomach. "He'll be aboard the *Lucky Lady?*"

Captain Billy put his arm around her. "Never fear, lassie. He'll be in cuffs and irons and chained to the mast so we can have him in full view at all times. We must have him with us when we sail into London Harbor."

Ameran was hesitant in her agreement. "Yes, I suppose he must be held accountable for his vile acts, but I'd rest much easier knowing we had distanced ourselves from him once and for all."

"I'd as soon the sharks be his judge and jury, lassie, but if we're to prove Gray's innocence and clear his name of the foul deeds of which Gideon will accuse him, then we have no choice but take him with us, so he can point his black finger at the real butcher."

Gray's face was doubtful. "I can't see Monquez coming to my defense."

Captain Billy laughed. "Monquez would come to your defense if it meant saving his puny neck." He stopped laughing. Hatred glared in his eyes. "And when he has admitted the truth to our King and delivered the blame on the shoulders responsible, I'll take great delight in performing my duty as executioner."

Up until that moment, Ameran had forgotten that the grandfatherly Captain Billy possessed hands which were not without the blood of victims. Yet she didn't fear him. His ferocious devotion to Gray made her love him all the more.

He was quick to smile again when he caught her eye on him. "I ain't no angel, lassie, and I'd be the first to

411

admit to having done things which I'm not very proud. However, I be a far way from sinking to the bowels of hell. An eye fer an eye, and after what Monquez did to those poor men, women and children, he deserves to die the slowest and most painful of deaths." His teeth gleamed white. "But I'm not one to prolong his agony. I'll make it quick. I'll waste no time delivering him to Satan."

"Don't worry, Ameran, Captain Billy knows what he's doing," Gray told her as they followed him back up the stairs.

Ameran lovingly stroked his cheek. "I'm not afraid. If you're confident in his plan, then I accept it without reservation."

They stood on the bow, Captain Billy with his arms locked behind his back, Gray with his own on hips, and Ameran with hers folded in front of her . . . and they waited . . . and waited.

"I'm surprised they haven't spotted us yet," Gray said well into that afternoon.

"The whole lot of them's probably in a rum stupor from last night," Captain Billy said, patient and expectant. "All the better fer us when they finally do spot us and make their move."

The crew of the *Lucky Lady* stayed at their posts awaiting instruction.

Captain Billy called out to his navigator, Mr. Fenwicke, and motioned for him to join them on the bow.

Fenwicke, with muscles straining his bare chest, listened intently as Captain Billy laid out his plan of action. Fenwicke's face lit up like that of a child's when his captain had finished revealing his strategy. "The men will like that, sir. 'Tis yer best plan yet."

412

"It is a shame all those cannons will sink to the bottom of the sea where they will be no good for anyone," mused Ameran aloud. "The settlers may be safe for now, but when the weather cools, it will be as Captain Billy says, and another attack will be launched from the south."

"The demon ship won't sink that fast, lass. We'll have plenty of time to save the cannons."

Gray laughed. "And if I know you, Billy, plenty of time to salvage all else besides."

Captain Billy laughed and picked up one of the cats darting in and out of his legs. "Gideon paid dearly for Monquez's services. Ye can count on that, and I'd just as soon relieve Monquez of his new wealth as not. Besides, where he's heading, he won't have the opportunity to spend it."

He held the cat close to his cheek, and nuzzling into the soft orange-black fur added, "With any luck at all, Monquez may have made another haul or two since parting company from Gideon. I can think of no finer gift to me King than the head of the most infamous of pirates on a silver platter, and a couple of trunkfuls of gold doubloons to boot."

Ameran pointed out to sea. "Look." She squinted into the sun.

Gray nodded and smiled. "You're brilliant, Billy."

"She be turning around," Captain Billy announced cheerfully. "We've got her now, maties. Mr. Fenwicke . . ."

"Aye, sir."

"Mr. Fenwicke, keep our present heading. Proceed on like nothing is wrong." He kept his glass to his eye. "Look, laddie, they've run up the flag of His Majesty's Royal Fleet." His smile held, but his words be-

413

came solemn. "It's like before. He learned his lesson well from Gideon Horne."

Ameran felt a tightening in her throat. As before, the ship flying the flag of France had no cause to flee, for they were about to encounter an ally. The slaughter of the French crew was still vivid in her mind. Their joy and relief had changed immediately to terror when they realized they were about to be butchered by foes disguised as friends.

Ameran grabbed hold of Gray's hand and held it tight. If Captain Billy's plan succeeded, there was no reason to fear Monquez, but if it failed . . .

She closed her eyes tight to keep out the visions.

Captain Billy looked as if he would burst from the excitement and anticipation swelling inside him. His voice remained calm. "Mr. Fenwicke, be prepared to turn her around the instant I give the command."

"We want to stay just outside the cannon firing range," Gray quietly explained to her.

Ameran was aware of the expectation growing on Gray's face minute by minute. She tried to calm her own worries with silent assurances that those heinous deeds committed against all those on board the *Fair Winds* would soon be vindicated. She hoped and she prayed that that would be the outcome to ensue.

"They be gaining speed on us, sir," called out Mr. Starwell.

Ameran's heart skipped another beat.

"So the bloody curs coming atter us, is he? Think we be an easy mark?" laughed Captain Billy. "I expected nothing less from that bastard, and I'm delighted I won't be disappointed."

It seemed hours before Captain Billy finally gave the command to full about.

The turn was wide and smooth and speedy.

"Excellent, Mr. Fenwicke. Excellent. Full rigging, Iza."

"Aye, Captain, sir," boomed the reply from the black healer.

The sails were all hoisted.

Ameran watched, hardly daring to breathe, as the pirate ship began to close the distance between them. Gray watched, too, his countenance patient, showing no fear.

Captain Billy slapped his stomach. "Those devils think they've got us on the run. They do! We'll show them."

"We'll show them indeed!" Gray said, his eyes not straying from Monquez's vessel. "His sails are full. He's approaching rapidly."

"Come on, you bastard," yelled out Captain Billy, his fists balled. "Come and get me. Ye wanted me. Get me."

The wind died down, then rose again a dozen times before the tiny cay was finally in view. By then, the sun had all but settled in the clouds behind them.

Suddenly there was a loud explosion, then another, a third and still more. Mountains of water erupted in the wake of the *Lucky Lady*.

"Do ye think he's got the idea we're not going to greet him with arms opened wide, laddie?" laughed Captain Billy.

"I would say so, commander," Gray agreed, his laugh solemn.

Captain Billy took the helm from Mr. Fenwicke. "Is he still off our stern?" he asked Gray.

"Aye, Captain."

Captain Billy expertly maneuvered the *Lucky Lady* through the reef-filled waters.

Ameran peered over the rail, waiting, listening for the hull to rip.

"Monquez is still coming, sir," Starwell shouted across the deck.

"Yes! Yes!" shouted the *Lucky Lady*'s commander. "Come on, ye bastard. Catch me if ye dare."

Ameran held her breath as Gray held tight to her arm. "I'm surprised Monquez has not yet figured the reason for the course you've chosen."

"Ye flatter the devil, laddie. He's not nearly that clever."

Ameran prayed Monquez wasn't playing an even shrewder game of cat and mouse than they.

"I'd feel more at ease if you'd retire below until all of this has concluded," Gray told her. His words were calm, but his eyes were strained with worry.

"And I would feel more at ease if I remained at your side," she told him with unwavering determination.

Gray gave a resigned nod and said no more.

More cannons exploded around them, showering the deck of the *Lucky Lady* with foaming cascades of sea water.

Ameran held tight to Gray's arm. The black ship was rapidly gaining on them.

By now, Captain Billy had stopped laughing and begun cursing. His face bore even more creases of worry than those already there from the sun and wind. His whiskers were wet with sweat and determination. Calm and steady, his hands held on to the helm as he gently coaxed the ship on a course that would have brought disaster to any commander less

416

skillful than Captain Billy.

His mates held their posts, ready to fight the moment the command was shouted.

The water was so crystal clear that the treacherous reefs of sharp coral heads seemed to break the surface like peaks of mountains extending upward from the ocean's bed. Ameran wondered how much longer Captain Billy would be able to successfully skirt around their jagged precipices. With every wave that broke across the bow, she was certain the *Lucky Lady* had been snagged, and her hull would be ripped in two, but the ship kept gliding gracefully through the water under Captain Billy's masterful guidance.

Her stare stayed fixed on the black ship, the ship of death and doom, and she prayed that theirs would not be the fate of countless others who had found themselves in its path of destruction. Her heart beat faster, and faster still. She could feel the rumblings of dread and anticipation in the pit of her stomach. If Captain Billy's plan failed and Monquez did overtake them . . .

No! She wouldn't allow such thoughts inside her head. Monquez's foul deeds would not be rewarded with yet another victory!

Then she began to breathe a little easier. Were the shadows of the fading sun playing tricks on her vision, or was Monquez's ship actually losing speed and dropping further behind him?

"They hit, Captain Billy. They hit the reef!" Iza called down from his perch among the riggings.

The men cheered and echoed the news among themselves.

Captain Billy lifted his eyes to the sky. "Thank ye, Father."

Ameran felt as though a tremendous burden had been lifted from her shoulders, and she sank onto Gray's firm chest.

"No seaman but you, Billy, could have performed the impossible," Gray told his old friend with a relieved smile and a pat to his back.

"I must confess, I had a little help, laddie." He glanced up at the heavens once more. "Ye wouldn't believe the promises I had to make to keep these old hands steady, but I'll keep every one of them. I will." His tired body began to slump. "The luck of Billy Blitzen held one more time. I must be leading a better life than me thought!"

Gray pointed out behind them.

The stern of the pirates' ship had already begun to sink.

Captain Billy took another firm hold on the helm and veered his ship through a cut in the reefs and back into the water which was free of coral heads. Tacking a wide turn, he maneuvered the *Lucky Lady* just off the black ship's port side, taking caution still to remain outside the range of cannons and muskets.

"Take the wheel, Gray, and keep her steady as she goes."

"With pleasure, Captain."

Captain Billy wearily climbed up onto the platform off the bow, and at the top of his voice exclaimed. "So ye wanted me, did ye, Monquez? I be here. What ere ye going to do 'bout it? Heh?"

His men laughed while Monquez's crew shouted obscenities.

Captain Billy laughed louder and longer as he waved his cutlass over his head. "Come on, ye Spanish heathen. Fight me like a man. I be awaiting fer ye."

418

Ameran kept her eyes on the devil ship. Some of the crew had already jumped ship and were swimming frantically in the direction of the tiny cay.

"Little do they know they're swimming to a surer death than had they stayed and fought or went down with their ship," Gray told her, no hint of remorse in his voice, only hate and bitterness.

Ameran reached for his arm. She knew he would rather have killed them one by one himself to make certain they met their ends, and to avenge the deaths of his loyal crew.

She said a silent prayer of thanks and steadied herself in preparation for that which would come — yet another face-to-face confrontation with Monquez.

"Iza, take five, no six of our best and bring Monquez back to me," Captain Billy ordered.

Iza beamed. "With much pleasure, Captain, sir." Then he pointed out five and called the men by name.

Soon, the mates were in a long boat rowing toward the sinking ship.

The chains and cuffs were ready and waiting for Monquez when they returned.

"Nary a struggle," piped up a mean-looking mate whose face had been scarred more than once by the sharp point of a sword. "His crew done gone and jumped overboard. Abandoned ship they did, and left him counting his coins."

The *Lucky Lady*'s crew booed and hissed when Monquez was led aboard their ship.

Captain Billy gave an exaggerated bow to his arch rival. "I'm most happy to oblige your desire for a meeting."

Monquez said nothing until he saw Gray and Ameran. Then his bronzed face paled, and his words were slow to come. "But you're dead. Both of you."

Gray's smile was cold. "Either you're wrong, or you've come face to face with a pair of ghosts."

Monquez's beady eyes set on Ameran. "I told Gideon you were from hell. I told him to kill you."

Ameran glared at him, her eyes filled with hate.

Gray cursed him and headed toward him. At first Ameran thought he was going to choke him with his bare hands when he reached for his throat.

"I believe you've taken something that's mine." With that, Gray jerked the cross of jewels from around the pirate's neck.

Gray hesitated, and Ameran knew he was debating whether to end Monquez's wretched life there on the spot. Instead, he walked calmly away and returned the necklace to Ameran.

She didn't put it back around her neck. To do that, she would wait a little longer until she had scrubbed Monquez's scent from the chain.

Her hand closed tight around it. Never again would she be without it, or without Gray!

Captain Billy eyed him through squinted eyes. "So ye were gonna blow me outta the water, were ye? Ye were gonna come after me and give me me due, were ye, ye slick-headed devil?" Captain Billy paced back and forth in front of him. "Looks like yer days as scourge of the sea have come to an abrupt halt, hey matie?"

Monquez said nothing. He just stood staring at Captain Billy, his eyes glaring hate.

"Ye've slipped through me hands before, ye Spanish devil, but there's no escaping me now!"

"If you're going to kill me, do it now. I have no desire to listen to you," Monquez told him, his words

420

calm and indifferent.

Captain Billy grabbed him by his shoulders. "I'll kill ye when I be good and ready, and not before, and certainly not when ye give me permission to do it."

Monquez shrugged his shoulders. "Why didn't you maroon me with my men?"

"Because I have far grander plans fer ye," Captain Billy said with a wink. "Clamp the irons, maties."

Monquez's struggle was in vain as the irons were shackled to his arms and limbs, then cuffed to the mast and locked.

"Mr. Fenwicke, take us up alongside the ship," Captain Billy called out. "We don't want all that booty ending up on the bottom of the sea. Not after Señor Monquez here worked so hard to collect it fer us."

Monquez glared at Captain Billy. "It is possible, you know, that I can prove more valuable to you alive than dead."

Captain Billy shrugged his shoulders. "Looks like that's the closest I'm gonna get to ye begging fer yer life."

"I won't beg," came his hard reply.

"Nay, matie, I didn't think ye would. But if ye had, I would have shown ye no more mercy than ye did those poor men women and children ye butchered."

Monquez laughed. "I've earned my reputation."

"So have I, and ye'd do well to remember that, ye devil." Captain Billy forced himself to stay calm.

Ameran could tell from the way his hand kept reaching for his cutlass that he, too, would be quite happy to execute Monquez before another minute passed.

Captain Billy stood before his prisoner, his hands

421

clasped behind his back. After a long, deliberate pause, he told him. "Ye may in fact be worth more to me alive than dead."

Monquez's cruel mouth turned up into a smile. "My King would pay a handsome ransom for my return to Spain."

Captain Billy thought for a while. "More than me own King would pay fer delivering yer head to him on a silver platter?"

"Decidedly more. I've brought Spain much wealth."

Captain Billy nodded. "First, before I collect the ransom, there's something I want ye to do fer me."

"I'm in no position to refuse," Monquez said smugly.

"Exactly."

Monquez listened as Captain Billy told him exactly what it was he expected him to do in return.

Monquez agreed without hesitation. "Gideon Horne is no friend of mine. He'd have stabbed me in the back had I given him the chance." He gave a sly glance in Gray's direction. "After I've done what you request, and the ransom for my life has been met, I will be free to return to Spain?"

"Ye don't think I'd want ye to stay in England," Captain Billy asked.

The two pirates laughed.

"Aren't you just a little saddened at having captured me, Captain Blitzen?"

Billy returned his humor. "Why should your capture sadden me when I went to great risks to achieve it?"

Monquez sat down on the deck. "You deserve a worthy opponent, and with me off the seas, you'll have none."

Captain Billy eyed him closely. "Oh, I don't suspect ye'll be off the seas long, mate."

Monquez smiled.

Captain Billy turned around and gave all who were watching a wink.

Ameran was certain that beneath his seemingly good humor, and talks of ransoms and rewards, Billy would let Monquez live only long enough to incriminate Gideon, then he, Captain Billy Blitzen, would exact his revenge, and that of all the men, women, and children whose suffering had given Monquez such great pleasure. There had been a peculiar look in Billy's eyes as he had bantered back and forth with Monquez, and that look read of death, of the cold-blooded, cold-hearted death which he would personally deliver to his old nemesis.

And she was most anxious for him to do the deed and erase Monquez from her nightmares once and for all.

Chapter Twenty

Nell stood in the doorway of her PallMall home and stared out at her visitor in startled disbelief. She didn't move. Her eyes were wide open in spite of the late hour, and her chin had dropped to the wisps of green lace fanning her neck. Her cheeks had lost their rosy hue, and she looked as though she had been visited upon by the walking dead.

"It can't be," Nell whispered laughing and crying and hands covering her mouth. "It can't be," she said over and over.

Ameran stepped out of the shadows. "It can be, and it is." She took off her red woolen cap and shook her hair free. "Beneath these breeches and sailor's shirt, it is I, your old friend."

Ameran gave a cautious look behind her. There was nothing there except the carriage that had brought her to PallMall. The driver, Captain Billy's own Mr. Fenwicke, had been instructed to wait until her visit had concluded.

Nell grabbed her hand and pulled her inside. "I take it ye don't want to be seen."

Ameran gave one last look behind her before the door was closed. The square was deserted. Still, she had an uneasy feeling that someone other than Mr. Fenwicke was watching her. No sooner had she departed the *Lucky Lady,* which was at dock in London Harbor a few slips down from the *Fair Winds,* than she had brushed shoulder to shoulder with a ghost that had appeared from her past to haunt her with his stalking eyes and crimson mask of pox scars. He had said nothing. He hadn't even given her so much as a raised brow. Still, she couldn't help but wonder if Tommy Tremble had recognized her, as she had him.

Nell gave her a long, tearful hug.

"What of the servants?" whispered Ameran just inside the hallway where a marble fountain spouted water down into a pond filled with tiny goldfish.

Nell bolted the door. "All scattered . . . here and there for the evening. I'm alone. Both Jamie and Charlie are at Windsor with Mistress Turner and the riding master." Her sigh was heavy, and she made a dour face. "I'd hoped to entertain this evening, but those plans went awry when that sow from Germany insisted me Charlie pay her a visit tonight."

Nell threw her arms around her and gave her another tight squeeze. "Now, I'm delighted she did." She touched her hand, her arm, her cheeks, her hair as if to make sure it was really her. "I thought ye were dead. They told me ye had drowned."

Ameran's smile was grim. "There are those who would like to believe that and did their best to make it so."

Nell had countless questions. "How . . . when . . . how long have you . . . why didn't you come here before . . ."

Ameran did her best to keep her calm. "I just stepped off the ship not more than an hour ago."

"What ship? The *Fair Winds* has been here for . . ." Nell fanned herself frantically. "Come, sit . . . before I'm the one who faints." She all but pushed her down onto the settee, then collapsed atop the bright red cushions only to leap to her feet again. "Wait, rest, ye must be starving. I'll prepare a plate. They's plenty what with the King dining elsewhere this evening."

Ameran didn't try to stop her. She knew it wouldn't do any good even to attempt to do so. Instead, she waited for her to return with her great silver platter filled with food and drink.

After she had put the tray on the long, rosewood table in front of them, sat down herself and caught her breath, Nell poured them each a silver goblet of port.

Ameran hungrily attacked the wine and the roasted joint while Nell looked on quite amused.

"Yer appetite has most assuredly improved," Nell remarked as she poured more wine. She eyed her with good natured suspicion. "It is then true what is said about the sea air improving one's appetite?"

Ameran nodded. "And making women more fruitful."

Nell let out a squeal of delight. Her expression sobered suddenly, and she drew Ameran to her bosom once again, nearly upsetting the tray. "Ye poor darling. Ye poor, poor darling. 'Tis a pity Lord Carlisle will never know the joy his love fer ye beget." She held tight to her hand. "Ye can take great comfort in knowing that ye'll always have a little part of him with ye in the babe even though he has gone to the world beyond."

Ameran couldn't keep from laughing. "It's not as you think. Gray is as alive as you or I."

Nell fanned herself harder between gulps of port. "Ye mean he's not dead, either? I've never had so much wonderful news! Don't know if me heart can take it." She fluttered her hand over her breast. "Ye must tell me all. Leave out nothing. Spare me not one single detail."

Ameran took a deep breath and began her tale.

The big silver clock atop the mantel ticked away the first hour, then the second, and she was still recounting her adventure for her old friend.

Except for an occasional gasp or groan, Nell said very little as the story was told. From time to time, she would reach for her throat or pat her heart or roll back her eyes with each horrible detail revealed. Her face bore many frowns and twisted grimaces, but at long last the furrows and creases relaxed into a relieved smile.

When Ameran's story had concluded, there were more tears streaming harder and faster down Nell's pert little face. Nell couldn't keep her arms from around Ameran's neck. "It's a miracle indeed . . . a miracle ye still be alive!"

Ameran's nod was solemn. She had indeed endured trials few could live to tell about.

"The King's been so distraught these past several weeks. He feels he was responsible fer what happened. He bears tremendous guilt." Nell's hand closed tight over hers. "After all, ye were his own daughter, and Gray was closer to him than any of his sons." She poured them more port. "The King wasn't at all surprised when I told him what ye'd been up to. Said he had suspected as much himself when he learned ye had disappeared from Court."

Nell's smile disappeared. Her hold on Ameran's arm became firmer. "That damnable Gideon Horne! I can't wait to see the look on that traitorous bastard's face when he comes face to face with the man he thought he'd seen the last of."

Ameran nodded, but said nothing. Such a meeting was inevitable, if Gray was to clear his name. But that didn't make her await such a time with any greater eagerness.

"No one believes Gideon's lies, least of all the King," Nell told Ameran as she downed her third goblet.

"Gray will be most relieved to hear that."

"Surely he didn't think these good people would desecrate the memory of one whose life has been dedicated to the service of his King and country?" Nell quietly observed.

"Gideon can be a most convincing liar," Ameran reminded her.

Nell's nod was reluctant. "I suppose there may have been a few who listened to his tales of pirate attacks and mutinies in defense of the King's honor, but only a few, and an even smaller number still who believed a word of it as true." She gave a knowing wink. "It takes more than a hole in his belly to get him a hero's memorial."

A hole in his belly! If only she had dealt that fatal blow as she had intended! Why had fate not decreed it so? Why did Gideon deserve to go on tormenting them?

"So Gideon hasn't had his moment of glory yet?" She remembered well his boasts about the King bestowing honors and titles and wealth upon one who had risked his life to defend England's cause.

"Quite the contrary. Me Charlie all but ignores him."

Ameran contemplated the situation with a frown as Nell went on. Be that the case, Gideon would be most anxious to get on with the business at hand. If he couldn't bask in one way, he would do so in another.

"He's been in attendance at a few gatherings, but only at the Queen's insistence and invitation, and ye know as well as meself who pulls her strings," Nell said with a laugh.

"Constance, Duchess of Morrow." Just saying the name out loud left a foul taste in her mouth. "I did unintentionally omit one slight detail. Do you remember the note you sent me that afternoon at the Custom House?"

"Indeed I do, and they still haven't found that cursed

brooch," Nell told her as she pulled off a piece of the joint.

"I'm not at all surprised." Ameran took the diamond and pearl brooch from her pocket and dropped it in Nell's lap. "I found it sewn inside my travel bag."

Nell examined it carefully. "If she couldn't be rid of ye one way, she'd settle on another. What ere ye going to do with it? Ye don't want her to catch ye with it on ye."

"I intend to deliver it to her personally. The sooner the better, but there are other, more important matters which must be dealt with first."

Nell kept turning it over and over in her hand. "A pity yer so honest. That little bauble is worth a tiny fortune. I'd sell it if I was ye."

"That thought has crossed my mind, I must admit, but then I wouldn't have the great pleasure and satisfaction of seeing the look on her face when I return it, and I'm confident that one look alone will prove as priceless as the brooch," Ameran announced confidently and with the slyest of smiles.

"When will Gray confront Gideon and denounce him to all of England for the liar and murderer he is?" Nell asked anxiously. "Tomorrow?"

She, herself, had asked that same question of Gray only a few hours before. "At present, there are matters far more urgent at hand."

Nell didn't understand. "But what could be more urgent than setting right so wretched a wrong?"

"By preventing an even more tragic one."

Nell's face suddenly went ashen. Her fingers tightened around her throat. "Dear God . . . when . . . how . . . ?"

Ameran shook her head. "Gray doesn't know, but he's certain it'll be soon. Since Gideon hasn't been given the hero's reception he'd hoped for, it may even be sooner than we thought."

Nell grabbed a desperate hold on Ameran's arm. "We've got to stop him. We've got to stop Gideon before it's too late."

Ameran did her best to calm her fears. "Gray will stop him. I swear. He'll stop him."

Or he would die trying. That went unsaid, but it tore at Ameran's heart all the same. The sacrifice he was willing to make to save his monarch made her love him all the more fiercely.

"If only we knew when he was going to strike," Ameran mused aloud.

Nell sat there as well, shaking her head in bafflement and despair.

These questions were crucial, but they could determine no answers.

Ameran rose slowly a little later. It was late. She was fatigued near the point of exhaustion. The day would begin again much too early.

"Why don't you stay here? Please," begged Nell when Ameran persisted in leaving. "I could pass ye off as me niece. The servants would be no wiser. Seems like I've got a niece or a auntie showing up at me door every couple of days or so."

Ameran declined with much heartfelt appreciation.

Nell reached out and rubbed her belly. "A lady in yer condition shouldn't be sleeping on a hard cot aboard a rickety old ship that's full of rats."

"I can't sleep unless Gray's arms are around me."

Nell's sigh was wistful. "I know that feeling meself all too well."

They hugged again.

"When ere ye going to tell the King the two of ye be as

430

alive as him and me? He has greatly grieved . . . on both yer accounts," Nell told her.

Ameran frowned. "I'd like nothing better than to go to him at this very minute, but I can't. I don't dare. His peace of mind must be sacrificed for his health and welfare."

Nell agreed.

Ameran took hold of Nell's hand. "I'll come again in the morning."

"I'll make certain the servants have been sent on errands."

Ameran nodded. "Perhaps together we can figure out the most opportune time for Gideon to make his move," she said hopefully.

Nell's brows were quick to knot together. "Wait, I won't be here in the morning. The yacht races begin at ten, and you know how the King fancies them. Perhaps we could meet . . ."

Nell's face froze. "Ye don't think . . . Oh, God, ye do!"

Ameran shook her head. "I don't know, Nell. I don't know, but it would in all likelihood be the most opportune time for Gideon to strike . . . all those people, so many suspects, unlimited routes of escape."

"We have to warn the King!"

Ameran held firm to Nell's hand. "We can't, for if Gideon has indeed planned to commit his foul deed on the morrow, and rumors begin to spread of the attempt, he'll delay his action to another day and place, and we might not discover those details in time to prevent it."

Nell's voice was hardly above a whisper. "But I can't allow me Charlie to walk to his own execution without warning."

"Nell, Gideon won't rest until the King is dead and Monmouth is on the throne," Ameran warned her. Her words were harsh, but she meant them to be so. "His attempts to assassinate King Charles won't cease until he's been apprehended . . . or he's succeeded and fled to safety." She took Nell by her quivering shoulders and forced her gaze. "Please, I beg of you, allow Gray to handle this matter as he sees fit."

Nell's nod was reluctant. "Gideon will be sitting in the royal box. The King didn't want it so, but the Queen insisted."

"And Constance?"

"There as well." Nell's dimples began to dance once more. "As will the royal consorts."

Ameran's smile came quickly. "And perhaps the niece of the most royal of consorts as well."

Nell giggled. "That could be easily arranged. Charlie be always teasing me about all me relatives that seem to pop out of the trees." She thought for a moment. "With a hat over yer head and scarves protecting yer face from the sun, it would be no trouble at all keeping yer identity concealed."

"That way, we could both keep an eye out for anything unusual." Ameran sat down on the edge of the fountain. "Gideon doesn't dare be so bold as to do the deed himself. He's too much of a coward. He isn't, however, at all adverse to getting someone else to do his evil deeds for him."

"But who?"

Ameran shook her head. "I don't know, but rest assured, he won't succeed. Gray hasn't been resurrected from near-death only to fail at this the most important mission of his life." She stood quickly, kissed Nell's cheek, then gave her a tight hug. "Our King won't die by an assassin's hand tomorrow or any day thereafter."

"Ye will come in the morning and let me know of yer

plans?" Nell asked with quiet desperation in her voice.

"I'll be here even before the cock crows," Ameran assured.

"I won't be able to sleep one wink tonight."

"None of us can close our eyes until Gideon is consumed by the eternal flames of hell."

"Right where he belongs," agreed Nell.

When Ameran returned to the *Lucky Lady* with her news of the disaster which she was certain would present itself the following day, Captain Billy and Gray were quick in agreement for all the reasons she had already discussed with Nell.

"If Gideon is fool enough to make his move, then we'll have him!" Gray exclaimed as they sat around Captain Billy's desk by candlelight, mapping out their plans. "And if he doesn't, then we'll proceed on with what we've already discussed."

Captain Billy nodded. "I'll request an audience with the King fer the purpose of discussing me knighthood, and I'll take Monquez along with me, as well as one or two of me best mates to make fer certain he does not escape and deny me a final pleasure at his expense," he said with a hearty wink.

Ameran nodded. It had already been determined that one of those mates would be Gray, and Iza would accompany them.

"Even if we can't lay the blame for yet another plot to assassinate the King on Gideon's cowardly shoulders, we can undoubtedly prove beyond question the charges of treason and treachery," Gray said.

Captain Billy's eyes lit up. "Ye can count on Monquez to be a fine witness on yer behalf. He's most anxious to get back home to Spain." Captain Billy's eyes narrowed.

"Not that I have any intention of letting his foul deeds go unpunished."

Gray's words were quiet but filled with rancor. "I hope Gideon enjoys this night, for it'll be the last he'll ever spend on earth."

Captain Billy laughed. "Lucifer's already stoking the fire." He reached for his rum bottle, then a moment later, put the cork back in without taking a gulp, and returned the bottle to its place. "Better not dull me senses fer the greatest day of reckoning yet," he said with a sly smile.

Gray paced from one end of the captain's quarters to the other, his hands locked behind him and his thoughts long and hard. Finally he stopped his strides, and with a confident smile upon his lips, he announced, "I have a plan."

And he sat back down at the desk and proceeded to tell the others what it was.

Afterwards, when Captain Billy had left to gather his men together to tell them of the role they would play in saving the King, Ameran and Gray returned to their own quarters and fell upon the bed in exhaustion with their clothes still on. Greeting so important a morrow with a clear head was imperative if the course of history were to remain unaltered. Yet sleep would not come to either of them.

"If I fail tomorrow . . ."

"You won't fail," Ameran was quick to assure him. "Your plan is brilliant. Destiny won't let it fail. With you and Captain Billy and the crew of the *Lucky Lady* protecting him, the King couldn't be any safer."

"Don't ask me how I know, but my heart tells me that tomorrow is the day Gideon has chosen. I wouldn't be at all surprised if Monmouth is on a boat at this very moment awaiting news of his father's death," Gray said grimly.

Ameran reached out in the darkness to comfort him. "This time tomorrow, it'll all be over. The King will be safe, and Gideon will have the reward due him."

She was confident of her words, but didn't reveal to Gray the reason why. Her mama had once decreed the King's birthday would likewise be the day of his death, and he would, therefore, be safe from harm's way for still another nine months . . . and hopefully for many more birthdays to come.

Her arms closed tight around Gray. She feared for his well-being, yet she knew he wouldn't forsake that which he had sworn to do, and nothing, not even the *bébé* whose kicks she felt at that very moment could make her ask him to abandon that which he felt driven to do, not out of a hunger for glory, but out of love and devotion to his regent.

Their kisses were at first soft and sweet and spoke of promises made of a life together, but as their bodies pressed closer, and their limbs became more entangled, their kisses were overtaken by an urgency that refused to be stilled. And they gave way still another time to their desires.

Afterward when their lips had come together one final time in the kiss of night, and Gray had bundled her close to him just as he always did before his body gave way to its fatigue, Ameran closed her eyes, but she still couldn't sleep. She wished she could be as certain of Gray's future as she was of the King's. Gray had eluded death so many times before. Would he be able to cheat it yet once more? She prayed it be so!

Ameran rode beside Nell in one of the gold-spoked

435

carriages bearing the insignia of the House of Stuart. She was attired in one of Nell's finest, a silk gown of the palest of pink. Nell had proven quite skillful with the needle as she hemmed and tucked to make the dress look as though it had been fitted to Ameran. Long gauntlet gloves, beautifully embroidered with tiny rosebuds, hid the blush of the sun atop her arms. Around her neck was not the jewel cross which would be sure to give away her identity, but a simple strand of pearls. Her long, dark curls were atop her head, and lowered onto the pile of ringlets a broad-brimmed hat with a veil and streamers of ribbons and bows. Pink satin slippers adorned her feet, but her toes were cramped and pinched, having grown accustomed to wearing no shoes at all.

It took much convincing to persuade Nell to wear what she had intended, a cherry-colored gown with the bodice cut far lower than fashion allowed. Nell had chosen instead a drab green muslin she insisted was more in liking with her dreary mood. Nell refused to change her attire until Ameran pointed out that if she showed up looking like a dull matron then they would be found out for sure!

There was hardly any of the usual chatter as the carriage took its turn through Saint James Park, for they both sat quietly contemplating the outcome of the day's events yet to happen. Attempts were made at casual conversation . . . the weather, the people, the races . . . anything except the matter foremost in their hearts and minds.

They could think of nothing except the events which would soon unfold around them, so they sat quietly, holding hands tightly, each lost in her own reverie.

Captain Billy and his mates, with Gray disguised as one among them, had already gone on ahead to their secret posts around the royal box.

The streets were even more crowded than was usual with carriages and coaches and sedan chairs and people milling about in anticipation of the royal coach soon to pass by. Windows were flung open, and people hanging from them. Roofs and balconies were jammed with other onlookers anxious to catch a glimpse of the King.

"We could get out and walk and get there faster," remarked Nell impatiently as their carriage slowed to little more than a standstill. "Oh, I do hope me Charlie's all right."

Ameran squeezed her hand.

The carriage stopped and started, then stopped and started again and proceeded at a still slower pace than before.

Ameran looked out the window. There were people everywhere, and they didn't look particularly friendly. In fact, some of them looked quite furious. They seemed to be yelling and making gestures in anger, not in jest.

Suddenly, some men jumped into the carriage and began rocking it on its wheels. "Catholic whore!"

It took Ameran a moment to realize she wasn't the subject of their cruel remarks.

Nell laughed, then stuck her head out the window. "Ye fools. Take a good look! It be the Protestant whore!" she yelled for all the world to hear. "'Tis I, Nell Gwyn!"

The men jumped off the carriage and made their quick apologies.

Nell absolved them with waves and kisses, then sat back down. Her laughter ceased, and the smile faded from her face.

"Hurry, please hurry," she told the driver quietly.

The highway outside the city was lined by the Thames on one side, and on the other, little villages where fairs had been set up along the way for the entertainment of the King and the royal party traveling with him. But nothing, not the jugglers or the acrobats or marionette shows or men swallowing fire or wrestling bears, could distract Ameran and Nell from the long hours ahead.

Soldiers marched alongside the caravan of carriages as far as the eye could see. Regiment upon regiment of guards with their breast plates and iron head pieces, musketeers with bayonets fixed to their guns, bandoliers with their weapons slung over their shoulders and grenadiers in their yellow and red uniforms with hoods over their faces stood ready to defend the King.

Barges adorned with flowers and banners and streamers, and fitted with musicians playing harps, cornets, trumpets, and drums glided down the river alongside them, leading the procession of carved and gilded yachts that would soon compete for the King's pleasure and favor.

The grassy river bank was already filled with anxious onlookers. Sitting upon the red velvet benches inside the royal box were lords and ladies of varying degrees of nobility, most of whom Ameran didn't recognize and was confident they wouldn't recognize her. Hortense and her friend the Prince of Monaco were sitting head to head, and Louise, the Catholic whore the people so despised, was sitting in the midst of her own throng of French supporters.

Ameran spotted Gray immediately, but she was certain she was the only one who could possibly pick him out of a crowd, for in his tattered breeches and shirt, and with his face smudged with dirt, he looked anything but the grand commander of the Royal Fleet. She caught his eye and gave him a discreet nod, which he acknowledged with one just as slight.

"Me heart feels as though it's about to burst right out

of me chest," Nell said as they took their places three rows behind where the King's royal chair had been set.

Ameran did her best to calm her. It seemed that everywhere she looked she saw one of Captain Billy's men, and when she made mention of this to Nell, she began to breathe a little easier.

The King arrived just as the sailing yachts were lining up to give their salute to him. Beside him was the Queen wearing a gown of dreary olive green.

Ameran gave Nell a nudge that brought a smile to both their faces. Constance walked behind the Queen in a flowing white gown of wisps and lace that made her pale skin look even more delicate. Gideon in a scarlet coat with gold laces and white sashes stayed a few steps back. His shoulders slumped, and he leaned on a silver walking cane as he proceeded along, but he managed to cheerfully wave and bow to the crowd's applause.

Ameran felt no pity for him, only hate, and she regretted that she had not completed the job she had set out to do.

The King walked along the long rows greeting his guests, and when he came to Nell, he clasped her hands in his and kissed both her cheeks.

"You're lovely as always, my dear Nell." Into her ear, he whispered, "Tonight."

Nell blushed. "You're most kind, sire."

Ameran drew the scarf closer to her veiled face.

"Might this be another of your lovely nieces, Mistress Gwyn?" The King asked, his voice considerably louder.

"Yes, sire. This be . . . Lilly."

The King took Ameran's hand. "Most charmed." He peered through her veil.

Ameran could feel herself blush under his close scrutiny.

The King stared at her a moment longer. A strange look flickered in his eye. "I look forward to speaking with you later."

"Yes, sire," she said quietly.

Had she imagined it, or had there been the slightest tremor in the King's words?

"He knows," whispered Nell. "We can't fool him."

Ameran nodded, but she didn't worry, for she knew her secret would be safe with him.

Barges towed the yachts further upstream to the designated point where the races would begin.

Another hour passed before brightly colored sails could be seen billowing in the distance.

Nell's eyes didn't veer from her King.

Ameran kept looking from the King to Gray to Gideon and back to the King again. She studied the crowd. There seemed to be no happenings out of the ordinary, no one there who seemed not to belong.

Occasionally, the King would glance her way. Their eyes would meet in recognition of the secret they shared. His look was one of relief, hers of concern.

Ameran and Nell stood at their places with the others and directed their gazes up the river in anticipation of the first yacht to sail past the marker. The King walked down to the river bank, and along with the two guards flanking him, boarded the barge from which he would view the race's finish.

Ameran held her breath, for the King hadn't passed more than two arms' lengths from Gray.

From the corner of her eye, she caught a quick glimpse of something red and yellow moving through the crowd.

Ameran turned quickly to face it. One of the grenadiers had stepped out from his ranks. No one seemed to notice him but she, and she watched his every move.

Something was amiss. He was the only one among the soldiers who had broken rank.

The grenadier passed by the royal box. Gideon looked his way. Their eyes locked. Gideon nodded. Then the man in red and yellow turned away, but not before glancing up onto the row where Ameran was standing looking down at him.

Her heart stopped in midbeat. The face was not that of a stranger. There was no mistaking that crimson mask of pox scars or eyes which stalked their next victim. Tommy Tremble was Gideon's hired assassin.

"Say nothing," she cautioned Nell. "Make no moves out of the ordinary."

Nell paled, but asked no questions.

Without further explanation, Ameran made her way to the riverbank where Gray was standing.

Gray saw her coming and she directed her eyes to Tommy Tremble. Gray's eyes followed hers. Both noticed at the same time that Tommy Tremble had something in his hand. He pulled back his arm as if he were going to throw what it was he was holding. At that moment, Ameran realized Gideon's intention was to blow the King away.

Gray realized it, too, and he pushed his way through the crowd not knowing Ameran was following close behind him. He pounced on Tommy Tremble just as he was about to toss the grenade onto the King's barge. Gray wrestled him to the ground. The grenade rolled onto the grass.

Ameran quickly picked it up and threw it as far down the river as her arm would allow.

There was an explosion; then a shower of water poured down onto the onlookers.

Captain Billy held a cutlass to Tommy Tremble's

throat. "Make a move, ye bloody bastard. Nothing would please me more than to slit yer throat from one ear to the other."

The King's barge was returning to shore.

Constance, Gideon and the Queen had gathered on the bank to meet it.

Gray and Ameran walked slowly toward them, one taking off her hat and scarves, the other rubbing the coal soot from his face.

Constance saw them coming and held on to Gideon's arm for support.

Gideon looked up. His face was shrouded in a look Ameran recognized all too well—that of sheer terror.

It took but a moment for Gideon to collect his demeanor.

"That man, that woman, they tried to kill our King!" he shouted.

The crowd was too stunned to move.

Iza, Mister Fenwicke and the others of Captain Billy's men formed a protective circle around them.

"You're wrong, Gideon," Gray told him, his sword drawn. "I've come to end your miserable life once and for all."

Gideon leaned on his cane. "But I'm without a weapon, my old friend, and as you can see, I've already been wounded in battle." His smile was as cold and as cruel as his glare. "And my beautiful Ameran. You played the role of the whore so convincingly. 'Tis a pity you are not as skilled with a dagger."

His words didn't cut through her as they once had. "Yes, it is a pity, isn't it?"

Ameran then took the brooch from inside her glove and threw it at Constance's feet in much the same manner as she would throw a bone to a dog. "I believe that belongs to you."

Constance said nothing, or made no move to bend down and pick it up.

The King came stomping up the bank through the tall reeds ranting and raving. "Od's fish! What was that all about? We'll have to begin the races again tomorrow."

Then, his swarthy face lost its color, and he tugged at his moustache with a sudden realization that yet another attempt had been made on his life.

Then, with a soft smile upon his mouth, he reached for Ameran and drew her to his chest. "It's you."

Ameran gave a little bow. "It is I, sire."

The King's disbelief turned to exaltation. "Gray? Gray? You're alive!"

"Yes, Your Majesty. Surprisingly so."

The King embraced his commander of his fleet. "The Archbishop will be pleased to learn I'm no longer suspicious of miracles, for the two of you have proven they can actually occur."

"He's a traitor, Your Majesty," insisted Gideon. "Don't be fooled by his words. I, myself, was witness to his wretched acts. I, myself, bear the mark of his infamy."

Gideon looked to Constance for support, but she remained silent. He searched the crowd, but no one spoke up in his defense.

The King turned to Gideon quite calmly. The words he delivered were void of feeling. "I would suggest, Mr. Horne, that you make your amends with God and man, for you, sir, are not long for this world." He gave a nod to one of his life guards, and Gideon was taken away.

The King's gaze fell at Constance's feet. "The rest of your days, my lady, will be spent with the rats and spiders in the Tower."

"No!" Her cry was hardly more than a whisper. "I don't deserve such cruelty."

"You deserve much worse," and he motioned for her to be taken away as well.

"But Your Majesty," interceded the Queen. "The good Duchess has done nothing wrong. I, myself, can attest to—"

"Silence, Catherine. I would suggest that you remember who you are before I forget."

The Queen bowed her head, and she said no more.

Captain Billy brought Tommy Tremble to the King, the blade of his cutlass still across his neck. "On yer knees, swine." He knocked his legs out from under him, and Tommy Tremble fell belly-down onto the ground.

Captain Billy stood with one foot on him and gave the King a salute and a smile. "Captain Billy Blitzen, sire, at yer service."

Tommy Tremble mumbled in pain.

Captain Billy dug his heel in even more. "Show some respect, matie, fer the man ye just tried to kill."

The King slapped Captain Billy on the back. "Are you going to stay in port long enough this time for me to knight you?"

"Aye, sire, and there is the small matter of a governorship in the Bahama Islands I'd like to discuss with ye as well."

"You old pirate!" said the King with much affection. "I've missed your company at Court."

"Missed me skill at cards, have ye, sire?" Captain Billy nudged the King. "Ye cannot even begin to imagine what I've brung ye in this load."

Louise, Hortense and Nell finally broke through the crowd and gathered around the King, but it was Nell to whom the King delivered his soft words of assurances that no harm had befallen him.

The Queen remained stoic at her husband's side.

Nell sought comfort in Ameran's arms. "I pray he'll be as lucky the next time."

Ameran hugged her friend close. "Gray will protect him." She didn't try to convince her there would be no more next times, for Nell knew as well as she that as long as the King's enemies wanted him dead, and as long as there were those lusting after the throne, there would always be a next time.

Nell turned to face Gray. Tears streamed down her cheeks. "I'm most grateful, Lord Carlisle."

Gray held out his arms to her. "And I'm most grateful to you, Nell."

Then Gray gathered Ameran close to him. "At long last, my darling. It's over."

Ameran brushed her lips over his. "No, my darling. It's only just beginning." And she placed his hands over her stomach so he could feel their baby kicking.

The King put his arms around them both. "I can't wait to hear the stories you have to tell. I'm certain your adventures would fill an entire book."

"They would fill volumes, Your Majesty," Ameran told him with a quiet sigh. "They would fill volumes."

Chapter Twenty-One

Ameran and Gray lay enfolded in each other's arms.

The day had been long. Captain Billy had been knighted for service and valor for King and country, and the King had insisted his daughter and the commander of his Royal Navy be wed in a ceremony more splendid than Whitehall had ever seen.

"Why are you smiling?" Gray asked.

"I was thinking about our wedding."

Gray, too, smiled. "And what is it you find so humorous in so solemn an occasion?"

She rested her chin on his chest. "It was truly spectacular, and yet . . ."

"Yes?"

"And yet with all its glory and grandeur, when I think of the day we wed, I'll think of the ceremony on board the *Lucky Lady*."

Gray smiled. "As will I."

She nibbled at his flesh.

Gray stroked her hair lovingly. "The Archbishop was truly lacking Billy's spirit for making the occasion truly momentous."

"I'm sure when we're old and telling our children of our wedding day, they'll find our first wedding far more amusing than our second."

Gray gathered her close. "We shall take much delight in telling them over and over of the time when we were wild and adventurous and wed by a pirate."

"It's certainly a far more romantic tale." She caressed his cheek. "Promise me we'll always be as wild and adventurous as we were then."

His lips lingered on hers. "I swear."

Her tongue danced across his mouth. Her smile was deliciously wanton and wicked. "Promise me I'll always be your booty."

"Always," he laughed as he rolled her over and imprisoned her in his arms.

Her sigh was long and satisfied. "Do you think you'll tire of me now that we're wed?"

"I'll begin seeking prospective mistresses tomorrow."

Her hand began a tantalizing journey up his thigh. "Tomorrow?"

"Perhaps the day after."

She clamped her mouth onto his in a kiss.

"Or perhaps I'll wait until the day after."

"I have but one solution to insure your fidelity," she told him.

"And what might that be?"

Her body moved into his, slowly, deliberately, suggestively. "I'll keep you so exhausted from performing your husbandly duties that you'll have neither the strength nor the inclination to bed another."

Gray drew her head to his. His cheeks caressed her cheeks, and his fingers lost themselves in her tangle of curls. "You're the only mistress I'll ever desire."

"You won't tire of me as a wife and mother?" She

lay his hand on the plump rise of her belly.

"Nay, my sweet, I'll love you all the more."

She hugged him with all her might. Never would she let go!